# ABOUT THE AUTHOR

**Vadim Leve..al** studied Russian literature at St Petersburg State University. He is a literary critic, book editor and political commentator. *Masha Regina* is his first novel. He lives in St Petersburg, Russia.

## ABOUT THE TRANSLATOR

**Lisa C. Hayden** translates literature from Russian to English. In 2016 she won the Read Russia Translation Prize for her translation of Eugene Vodolazkin's novel *Laurus* (Oneworld, 2016). She lives in Maine, USA.

### PRAISE FOR *MASHA REGINA*

'The novel works on several levels at once and is replete with references from Pushkin to Gogol, Tom Stoppard to *Star Wars* and even Hegel. It's a cerebral work that urges its readers to consider the limits of ambition, the price of making art... This genre-defying novel takes on the limits of talent and ambition, fate and art in contemporary Europe.'

*Kirkus*

'Brilliant... this is a story about art and the price one has to pay to become an internationally recognised film director.'

Galina Yuzefovich

'A very fun book, one most American readers will readily recognize and relate to, though it will uncomfortably force that same reader outside the tedious "pull yourself up by your bootstraps via New York City" narrative that dominates their own literature.'

*Words Without Borders*

'A new type of Russian fiction.'

Gazeta.ru

'Sketching Masha, Saint Petersburg and the Russian arts scene with lively and impressionistic detail, Levental swirls in fragmentary conversations, bits of internal monologue and more than a few knowing references to the Russian literary canon to create a sophisticated twist on a bildungsroman.'

*Booklist*

'A spectacularly mature, fine and merciless novel.'

*Vechernyi Peterburg*

'Filled with fine, paradoxical and delicious details.'

*St Petersburg Vedomosti*

# MASHA REGINA

*Vadim Levental*

Translated from the Russian by
LISA C. HAYDEN

**ONEWORLD**

**A Oneworld book**

First published in North America, Great Britain and Australia by Oneworld Publications, 2016
This paperback edition published 2017

Originally published in Russian as *Маша Регина* (*Masha Regina*) by Lenizdat/A-team, 2012

This publication was effected under the auspices of the Mikhail Prokhorov Foundation
TRANSCRIPT Programme to Support Translations of Russian Literature.

 transcript

Published with the support of the Institute for Literary Translation, Russia.

ИНСТИТУТ ПЕРЕВОДА

AD VERBUM

ISBN 978-1-78607-032-6
eBook ISBN 978-1-78074-862-7

Typeset by Tetragon, London
Printed and bound in Great Britain by Clays

Oneworld Publications
10 Bloomsbury Street
London WC1B 3SR
England

# CONTENTS

# INVENTION OF A STORYLINE

Despondence, not spring: snow fell at Easter. Old women in villages dig paths around churches and walk past snowbanks in a procession, with icons and the cross. It's strange to look at them, half-dead, their dry mouths droning: *on those in the tombs bestowing life*. Candles go out, thick felt boots slip from feet, and the old women hold on to one other, but they walk. Though who is there to watch them? Nobody except perhaps the nocturnal birds sitting on bare black branches. The birds are quiet and the stars are silent, and they blink, all of them, the darkness alternating with the very existence of the old women.

Some say village churchyards have their own processions at Easter: the dead rise from their graves and walk in a circle along the fence, their empty chests singing, *Trampling down death by death*. This procession, if it actually does take place, must involve far more people than the one around the church. The living old women are but a drop in the ocean compared to the numbers of the deceased.

Earth spins on its imaginary axis and old women walk around villages with the deceased: *Christ is risen from the dead*.

Rivers flow, labored, through the woods, cold water rolls along with the snow, the wind blowing it forward. It would be terrifying for a person to be in darkness like that. But the drunks sleep and the deceased have nothing to fear. And what could the old women fear when the priests proclaim to them: *Chri-i-i-st is risen?*

Masha isn't asleep. Unsettling music plays in her ears. She imagines she has no home, that she's walking alone along a road in the dark. Her body aches from fatigue and she would give anything for quiet and a warm bed. Masha's feet bleed, stars shine indifferently, and clouds race along the sky like ominous birds. She looks despondently at the windows of the houses: curtains are drawn. Nobody is expecting her. She begins to feel sorry for herself as she walks and her heart sinks, but there she is: at home, wearing a nightgown, with a blanket keeping her warm. And then the music stops when her player loses its charge. It goes quiet and she hears her heart thumping. Masha knows how to calm it. She walks to the kitchen in the dark, boards creaking under her tender feet, but creaking quietly—her parents won't wake up. Masha finds the refrigerator by feel and opens it: in the darkness, the pale yellow light accentuates the shadows of the table, cooktop, chairs, and Masha herself, a slender girl in a nightgown, with coppery coils of hair that fall almost to the floor when she leans toward the lighted shelves.

She takes a dish, closes the door, and uses a fork to eat icy-cold, amazingly delicious jellied meat in the dark. Now she doesn't want to sleep: the cold meat is too delicious and life is too sweet to sleep now. She leaves the dish and hesitantly picks up her father's cigarettes. She doesn't smoke, though she's tried it a few times, and now she feels like blowing puffs of gray smoke, the kind that pensively rolls and floats away. Quietly, so as not to break the silence, she puts on shoes in the hallway. It's cold and dark on the front steps of the house but that will make it all the sweeter when she comes back inside. Masha lights a cigarette and releases a thin stream of smoke straight ahead, not inhaling. The smoke rises, gets into her nose, and stings her eyes. Masha plays with the smoke, letting it out in puffs and streams, and that makes her cheerful because it seems like she's not alone: it's as if the smoke itself is smoking with her. She feels like crying or laughing, but from the fullness of life, in order to fill the world with herself. When she's had enough of the cigarette, she puts it out on the ground and stuffs it in a crevice under the steps. Then she runs up to the fence, squats, and runs back to the house, when the gurgle of water hitting the ground has gone quiet. She quietly closes the door, takes off her shoes, and slips off to her room so she can get under the covers as quickly as possible and sit, hugging her legs with her arms, and experience happiness. Masha is happy.

Masha's parents sleep in the next room, sprawled on their bed. They sleep soundly and don't remember that they conceived their daughter on this very night, sixteen years ago. It was like this. Lena and Pasha were out for a walk, hand in hand, and they liked holding hands. Pasha smoked into a clear, gleaming sky and Lena squinted. They kissed, Lena pressed her palms against Pasha's back, and Pasha embraced her neck with one arm, hesitantly caressing Lena with the other, in the direction of her bottom. Lena's parents were out visiting someone and Lena served Pasha tea in the warm kitchen; later, she allowed her sweater to be pulled off. Pasha impetuously put Lena on the rug but she took him by the hand and led him to her room. There, on a made bed, Pasha frantically entered Lena on the fourth attempt and Lena endured the pain, clenching her teeth, with her eyes squeezed shut. They were both happy, each in their own way. Then Pasha left Lena's house because his parents were waiting for him at home, and Lena stayed and went to bed, her heart pounding hard. Now they're asleep together, and their daughter, God only knows why, can't fall asleep. The years have passed easily for her, moving along on their own: it's only adults who have to nudge time to keep it from stopping, heavy and sluggish as it is.

Masha crawls out from under the covers, sits at her desk, and turns on an old desk lamp covered with stickers. The animals and people on the stickers gaze at her with shabby, worn eyes. Musicians and movie heroes smile in half-shadows on the walls. Masha has a lot of things. All of them are completely worthless to the rest of the world, but for her, for Masha, her room is a treasure trove, stuffed to the brim, like the Nibelungs' castle. When she turns on the lamp, these things—pieces of wood, bark, and clay, little icons and prayers on ribbons, as well as zodiac signs, Futhark runes, Chinese characters, plastic dogs, and little fabric mice on chains, threads, and leather strips that hang from corners of shelves, and from nails and pushpins—all step out of the darkness, covered with blurry shadows in the yellow light, and begin their tense existence. And then there are her books: books too big to hold in her hands, with colored pictures and informative captions; and thick old books with page corners thinned from being thumbed through, where heroes and heroines love each other so sweetly and painfully; and disintegrating textbooks, handed down from class to class each year, are held together with tape—drawn on each portrait, in pen, is a blue stubbly beard and disproportionately large genitalia if the person is standing. The books are lying on shelves, in a cabinet, on the desk, mingling with thin and thick notebooks whose margins bloom with blossoms, fish- and bird-eyes flash, and towers rise in cities; in addition to the notebooks, there are lonely torn-out pages with uneven edges, spiral-bound notepads, pens that have run out of ink, and gnawed pencils. Toys, dolls, and animals covered with dust sit under the ceiling, where darkness thickens. Some of them have glass eyes that reflect the yellow lamplight. Even more things are hiding in desk drawers, behind the closed doors of cabinets, in the underbelly of the couch, and in little bead cases and wooden jewelry boxes. After glancing around her depository, Masha opens the bottom desk drawer and takes out a sketchbook and a large box of colored pencils.

The essence of a river is the fish that live there. But people don't see fish when they look at a river. Meaning the only way to represent a river is to draw it in cross section, with fish swimming in it.

Anything else would be superficial. Ancient Egyptians understood this; children understand this. Masha also grasped this long ago and hasn't ever forgotten. There's no point in drawing what a person sees. In her album, then, a bird has four wings and a person's head grows out of his back.

Masha was six years old when Aunt Valya came to visit from the next town, softened up after beet-and-herring salad and vodka, and let out a piercing, emotional yelp: *You really need to sign your little girl up for a children's art circle!* Masha, who was playing on the floor with pencils and paper, looked out from under her brow at Aunt Valya with suspicion, then shifted her glance to her mother, as if asking for protection. But her mother was already a poor protectress: she'd also drunk some vodka and chased it down with herring. *Oh come on*, she said, waving off Aunt Valya. *But why not? She can*, Masha's father said dreamily.

A week later, Masha's mother explained that the art circle wasn't scary at all, that Masha would draw there with other children and a nice lady would explain what to do. This didn't ease Masha's suspicions: Masha already knew how to draw and didn't need the nice lady's explanations. To be nice to her mother, though, she allowed herself to be taken by the hand and brought to the children's art circle.

The children's art circle turned out not to be a circle at all but a square, a big rectangular room with cracking paint on the walls. Large windows that covered nearly a whole wall had each been fitted with heavy double frames divided into nine sections, as if for a game of tic-tac-toe. The white paint on them was peeling, too. That didn't trouble Masha, though, because something else was far more interesting: there were easels in the room. Masha had never seen an easel before. Easels, cases and boxes with paints, glasses full of pencils, and jars of brushes reconciled Masha to the art circle.

The little girls—only little girls went to the art circle—peeked at Masha over their shoulders, contorting their little faces. They pulled Masha over to their easels and showed her their little houses, little rivers, smoke coming out of chimneys, and little doggies with doghouses. Masha saw that their little houses looked like little houses and their little doggies looked like little doggies but she didn't want to draw that way. When the nice lady tried to find out why (*Mashenka, come now, how many legs does a doggie have? Are there really birdies without beaks?*), Masha tensely kept quiet, though one time she burst into tears. The nice lady left her alone because she was kind and didn't really care anyway. Beyond that, when they put a marble in front of Masha and asked her to make a photolike drawing of it, Masha's face turned tragically tired (like when a person who can crack his knuckles is asked—*Come on, please, please*—to do so) and then she drew the marble so precisely that if there were some sullen guard who fed marbles to a cat, the cat would have immediately pounced on the paper.

Masha's hands fill with warmth and grow hot, like the eggs her mother boils to press against her nose, then they grow heavy like a fishing lure disappearing under water. She tears a sheet out of her album and draws with a pencil. Wind circles Earth in her drawing, catching the tops of trees and roofs of houses. Men and women sleep in high, soft beds, and old men smoke toxic cigarettes, leaning halfway out of doors. The smoke from their cigarettes mixes with a warm, damp snow that rushes from house to house. Old women grumble under stifling blankets, fumbling at the empty, warm place beside them. Dogs sleep uneasily, twitching their ears. The streets in Masha's city are empty and dark.

The city where Masha lives is always empty. The wind fills the emptiness with snow in winter, with sand and dust in summer, and with dead leaves and cold water in autumn. When the wind dies down, the emptiness begins to ring with insects, hum with smoke-stacks, and whisper with little melt-water brooks. Emptiness here isn't like the emptiness of a bottle from which everything has been drunk: here it's the emptiness inside the old yellow guitar Masha's father takes off the wall when despondence poisons his heart. The guitar's emptiness sings along with him. The city answers God's despondency with its emptiness.

The men here are sluggish and the women are quarrelsome, jealous, and stingy. The people who live here are covered with the scab-like days they've lived, and toward old age they grow deformed, like death itself. There are more dogs than people here, and their howling crosses the city from end to end like a wave.

Masha's hands suddenly become light, as if she's asleep. She feels frozen, lifts her head, and looks out the window: dawn is pouring into the street like water diluting milk. Looking at her drawing, Masha is surprised it turned out so gloomy when she was so happy. Surprised, she wraps herself up in a blanket and, when she's warm and stops shivering, falls asleep: her breathing steadies.

Shadows gather around the sleeping Masha, thickening in the corners, flowing down walls, creaking the floorboards, seating themselves in chairs, folding hands on dry knees, and old women appear, out of the darkness, in the doorway and on the edge of the bed: they rub their hook noses with hook fingers, shake prickly chins, barely move the craters of their mouths. Their dim, dark eyes have sunk into the depths of their heads.

Women are immortal. Only men are mortal. Masha's grandmother and Masha's mother's grandmother and Masha's grandmother's grandmother all live in Masha, around Masha, and mumble her name with toothless mouths. The rustle of those voices breaks into Masha's sleep, disturbing it, but she doesn't wake up. She sleeps.

The old women can't scare off her sleep; Masha's cheeks are rosy under the blanket and her nostrils quiver evenly. The old women look at her, sighing and winking at one another from under their gray brows. There is tenderness and condemnation in their eyes. Tenderness because Masha's fresh life is worthy of tenderness. Condemnation and fear because the old women's flaccid skin and cold, lazy hearts know: Masha isn't like them, Masha is different. There is a lot of the masculine in Masha and she wants to steal immortality from them, the old women, without even knowing it herself. To knead it with young, blood-filled hands and soften it like clay in the warmth of her fingers, shaping it into her own destiny.

The old women despondently shake their heads, finger the fabric of their skirts with hands swollen from the darkness, and say something to one other: they are lamenting.

When morning comes and the stars grow pale in the sky outside, the fears melt away because the dead cannot be among the living.

Masha goes to school—first crossing the street (an archipelago of bumpy asphalt in a puddly sea); then through an empty lot where dandelions bloom in summer, ferret tracks appear in winter, and in April frozen frogs shriek from streams that have begun flowing; and then between rows of gray, frightening garages with rusty doors—as if she's headed to war. Masha knows (she's been told this many times) she's "not like the rest." The force with which her desk-mate moves away from her (she rolls her eyes so everybody sees); and the force with which the teacher, fifty years old with a dyed roof of hair on her head, presses her fingers ("lady finger" tomatoes, that's what they're like) as she carefully traces a middling grade in the book; and the force with which her classmates push her when they run between classes (*Regina, move your ass…*) all combine to form the force of the hatred Masha experiences toward school. The only thing Masha thinks about at school in recent months, ever since she heard from a freckled girl in another class who was bragging that her brother… right, that this girl's brother had gone to Petersburg and been accepted to a school and was living in a dormitory, and so that's what Masha thinks about during classes, between classes, and after classes, walking down the hallway, stepping so her feet land only on the chessboard linoleum's green squares, not the gray ones.

But then, when Masha comes home (garages, empty lot, the road), she's by herself: her mother and father are at work. She kicks off her shoes (one sole is coming off a little but Masha doesn't notice), takes off her jacket, tosses her backpack in the corner, and unwinds her scarf in a spiral; her grimace of contempt for the world, which is essentially an item of clothing, too, dissolves.

Masha eats her soup as if she's in a race (it's impossible to explain to her mother that eating is boring), composes a sandwich out of cheese and a roll, and chews it, all yellow and orange, as she goes into her parents' room. Videocassettes sleep a sacred slumber, one on top of another, in that room: take the heavy ficus off the stool, climb up on the stool, open the cabinet door (the hinge groans), and there you have it. Cassettes and a videocassette player are something of a luxury here, though they turned up in Masha's house by chance: the cassettes and player were given to her father by Uncle Misha (who wasn't actually her father's brother, but Masha couldn't figure out how people were related, and she didn't care) to pay back a debt after a videosalon set up on the Moscow model went bust in six months. This was a few years ago, back when Masha couldn't turn on the machine herself; Uncle Misha'd hit the bottle pretty hard since that time and was now, as a former history teacher, often to be found at the market with his drinking buddies, explaining current events to them by drawing historical parallels.

On the cassette boxes, narrow-eyed men with headbands wave their flying feet, men in hats wield pistols, and half-naked women voluptuously squirm (this is why a ficus guards the cassettes). Not many of them have translations (the Moscow vendor forgot to warn Uncle Misha about this) but that doesn't matter to Masha: after feeding a cassette into the dusty black maw, she herself thinks up stories for what the small, bulging screen shows her. The stories are always about her. She annihilates villains, saves gorgeous women, and withdraws from the world (walks away, drives away, sails away) all by herself, hiding a smile: that's the final frame that Masha hardly ever gets a chance to watch because shoes tromp outside on the front steps and then her mother's home from work. There's a series of efficient motions and only the ficus, its leaves quivering, wails about the profaned resting place.

As she washes fingers blackened by other people's money, Masha's mother questions her—grades, soup, what she ate—then nods and squints: sandwiches again? First she washes the filth out of the wrinkles, cracks, and folds on her fingers with lye soap then she lathers her palms with the good soap (the kind she uses sparingly) and dries with a thick towel—each finger individually—and finally, casually, she asks Masha to go to her grandmother's. Her voice quivers with the slightest bit of alarm (*go on, go on, bring her some bread, talk with her, your grandmother's by herself for days at a time, you know that yourself…*). Masha doesn't know it, but her mother has listened to the dull, even sound of the phone ringing all day, pressing the receiver to her shoulder with her ear as she shouted out a little window—*All that's left are places by the lavatory, will you take those?*—but Masha's grandmother didn't answer.

Masha walks to her grandmother's, the city tosses shadows from building to building, dogs howl to one another, and bean soup splashes against the sides of the glass jar in her bag. Masha's grandmother loves bean soup. When she eats it, she brings the spoon to her mouth and pulls out the piping hot beans with her lips, as if they were hands instead of lips. Masha's grandmother loves food.

Masha's grandmother loves talking about her hungry childhood. When she does, Masha feels like her grandmother is reproaching her. That's just how it seems to Masha, though. In reality, when they're talking, the horror of starvation that has penetrated her grandmother's life blends with the pleasure of remembering her youth.

She was five the first time she went hungry, during the Civil War; the last time was after World War Two, when she was already just this close to becoming a grandmother. There's always been bread ever since, but Masha's grandmother feels a platonic passion for food—for the idea of food—just like how it was during Collectivization and the war. Her grandmother loves borscht when they bring her borscht and she loves cabbage soup when they bring her cabbage soup. Today Masha is bringing her bean soup. It won't be needed today, though.

The door is open. Masha pushes the door and goes into the room: her grandmother is lying on the high bed (how many yellowed mattresses are there? two? three?) under a blanket and looking attentively at Masha. *Hello, hello, sit down*, she says and points to a chair next to the bed.

Masha puts the bag with the jar and bread on the table by the window and tensely sits down. Her grandmother catches Masha's hand with a chubby, dry palm and strokes it every now and then. Masha notices that her grandmother is lying in her robe under a blanket. There is a slipper on one foot; the other slipper is lying on the floor. Masha is at a loss over whether to take the other slipper off the floor and put it on the second foot or vice versa. Her grandmother has other questions that Masha knows by heart, and they're awkward to answer: what grade is she in, how are her marks, and does she have a beau. Ninth, fine, no.

Her grandmother nods with pleasure at Masha's responses then sits up a little and nudges her pillow with an elbow. She's now half-sitting in bed and the corner of the blanket has slid to the floor. Masha springs to straighten it but her grandmother catches her hand, presses it between her two palms, and lists a set of instructions: obey your mother; be a good student; obey your mother; love your parents, they love you; be a good student. The next instant, her grandmother dies.

It appears to Masha that her grandmother's eyes are wide open and that she's grasped everything and seen everything from some external point: her life (piglets, cow, drunkard husband, collective farm, bonus pay, one television for the whole village, a son dead of methylated spirits, breadcrumbs in a drawer, china service from Leningrad, Stalin's death, a lover who married one of her friends), the life of all people, the horrible fate of an unlucky country, the heavy din as the cart of that world rolls over the precipice, the whistle of the wind on the streets of a dying city, the pounding of a thousand discos, and the blows of hammers driving piles into Earth's tender body... and then, an instant later, the dead body of a hairless, yellow old woman with a matte, waxen shine to her skin is lying in front of Masha.

Masha sits for a while, vacantly gazing into her grandmother's still eyes. Then she suddenly notices she's still holding her grandmother's hand; it's heavy and Masha places it on the blanket. She shakes her grandmother by the shoulder. Looking around, everything is as it had been—the round white alarm clock with the little copper feet ticks, the shadow of a pear tree moves on the lace curtain, a scratched yellow wardrobe darkens and smells of old things—and Masha turns her attention to the bag she brought. It's standing on the table, holding the jar of bean soup, still slightly warm. Masha's thoughts are so commandingly occupied by the question of whether or not to take the jar home that she forgets about the telephone that stands in the entry hall under a snow-white doily: she ought to make a call. Masha pulls the bread out of the bag, breaks off a piece of a heel baked to black, chews it, and looks out the window.

After she's done chewing, she pulls the jar out of the bag, takes off the tight-fitting plastic lid and carefully—so as not to spill—carries it out to the yard. She slowly pours the bean soup around the pear tree. Masha comes back inside, rinses the empty jar under a stream of cold water that smells of iron, puts the lid back on the jar, and takes it with her. That's everything.

On her way back home, Masha places her feet randomly, either into a wet snowy crème or into dark tufts of last year's grass, and feels a strange power within, as if her grandmother's death has given her some sort of gift: confidence or a lucky opportunity right now to do what she envisioned and planned out long ago. After stopping at a fork in her route—to the left is a paved road with streetlights, straight ahead is a dark path through bushes—Masha chokes for a minute on the clear understanding that this will happen after all.

And it will be like this: Masha will leave this city after overcoming her mother's resistance and surviving a multiday hysteria. Her mother will urge, cry, implore, coax, sob, curse, and forbid, using her parental will. Her mother's despair will be tangible: Masha will see it in eyes red from tears, in the wet wrinkles on her face, and in tenacious fingers closing in to grab Masha by the hair, like when she was a child, to pound some sense into her. And in her mother's pleading humiliation, too, as she sits with one buttock on the sofa, *But what are we going to do without you, have you thought about that?* No. Masha will have an ally in this bacchanalia of female despondence: her father, who will initially bug his eyes out and start laughing for effect—*What?!*—and of course he'll say no, *go do your homework, don't scare your mother.* But then, somehow recklessly inspired, he'll burst into tears and talk with Masha the whole night, after driving her mother out of the kitchen and, toward morning, after keeping quiet for about a half-hour, take out the metal buckwheat canister where there's money hidden away for a rainy day, exactly enough for a ticket to Leningrad (they still call it Leningrad here). A week later, after closing her ticket window for lunch, Masha's mother, who's just aged an entire life, will spill tears on the sickly train-station computer but still manage to pound out a ticket for her daughter.

Masha sees all this not as a sequence of events but in the unity of a complete storyline, in the fullness of a life taking shape. Her clenched fists hurt and—Masha feels this—will spurt warm blood any minute. Masha crosses the pitted road covered with slushy snow and walks away, along the dark, narrow path: it's the short way home.

Masha doesn't know it—and will never know, since the only person who knew this has already died (that being her grandmother)—but this place, the intersection of the narrow path and the road leading to the city, was important in her grandmother's life. Many years ago, Masha's grandfather, who'd gone to the largest city in the region to take courses, was coming home on this road. In the pocket of his new jacket were a graduation certificate from the courses—he's now a machinist's assistant—and a passport smelling of fresh ink. Masha's grandmother is sitting alongside him, squeezing his forearm with both hands. She'd fallen in love with this strong and already mustachioed little man and one morning—her parents, thrown for a loop by new Soviet ways, just tossed up their hands—the cheerful tobacco-scented director of the newly painted civil registry office smilingly pounded their passports with a rubber stamp: *Congratulations to you, comrades!* Masha's grandmother, who is pressing against Masha's grandfather, holding a bundle of clothing with her feet as she bounces around in a truck overrun with straw and cow shit, gazes at a road overflowing with sun, and feels an inevitable, unjustified happiness for what might be the only time in her life. This is the same grandmother whose redundant body is now growing cold in a stinking bed.

Back at home, after her mother's hysterics, screaming, tears, smelling salts, a call for the ambulance, and tears, tears, tears, Masha locks herself in her room and writes *Maria Regina, Maria Regina* in all kinds of ways in her sketchbook, between unfinished profiles and tall buildings in foggy cities.

# MATERNITY SURGERY

Men are totally mortal because their bodies are as light as the handle of a hammer. The weight of their will is the moving cause of their life.

As they age, people tend to live backwards, very rapidly, like a spring that's finally been released. Masha's mother's click that struck the computer keyboard and banged out Masha's ticket to Leningrad was the click of a fingernail that had slipped out from under the spiral of that spring. Her mother had begun aging, and her eyes were the first to age. Newborn leaves were turning green, dandelions were popping out of the grass, the sand on Masha's grandmother's grave had turned wet and densely compressed, and Masha's mother was spinning like a top through stores, preparing Masha for the road—socks, panties, blouse, sweater, hat (*Why, Mama? It's summer!*), pillowcase, notebooks, pens, pencils (*Will you take a little piece of salted pork?*)—but the engine of her life was already rolling from inertia.

As Masha's mother was seeing her off at the train station, she glanced into the carriage (who will she be riding with?) and explained to Masha (*yes, I know, I know*) that there are two lavatories in the carriage and you have to go to that one and not the other one, counted her bags yet again (*looks like that's everything*) and looked with genuine horror at a slightly drunk conductor who smelled of tobacco: *get off the train, ma'am!* After looking under the wheels of the train (she'd heard about this superstition somewhere), she lowered a hand whose fingers wiggled in the air, and began sobbing heavily and desperately, so much so that Masha's father had a lump in his throat. Her mother cried the whole way home and didn't even calm down when they arrived home, either, though what happened to her later scared Masha's father even more. She still cooked, went to work, dusted, and swept the floors just like before, but her hands became covered with a dry crust, her hair slipped out of her barrettes and hung on her temples, and her eyeballs lost their warmth and went still. What had happened wouldn't let Masha's mother go, meaning that after several days of silence, the first question she directed at Masha's father was: *why did you let her go?*

From that moment until his very death—in all the subsequent years—Masha's father never learned how to answer that question. Masha's mother asked it ever more often and persistently. It wasn't so much that he couldn't formulate an answer or stubbornly didn't want to answer. What he could have said—but was afraid to say because he knew this answer was no better than the others—was that, truly, he had simply forgotten why.

And it was like this. Masha's father came home from work and went to the kitchen to wash his hands. Things were not peaceable in the kitchen: Masha's mother, her face red and blotchy, was yelling at Masha. Masha was sitting on a chair, her hands under her thighs, and silent, her head stubbornly bent. A pot of soup presided over a table that was set with dishes.

Masha's father had already almost begun to grow accustomed to the arguments: it had been war in the house for two weeks. Masha had told her mother about a boarding school and her mother didn't believe there was such a school so tried talking her out of it, yelled, and cried. Her father wanted to eat and wanted everything to be as it had been; it was horrible to look at Masha's crying mother. Masha's father told Masha: *stop being a brat*, and hoped she would stop.

When her father went to the sink, he thought Masha and her mother hadn't noticed him. Then he started washing his hands and there was an explosion as he was spinning the bar of soap in his hands: a chair crashed on the floorboards and Masha jumped up like a rocket. She shouted at her mother, who'd stopped crying, and her father, who'd turned toward her with a start: *I don't want to spend my life like you!* Masha ran out of the kitchen, her fists clenched.

Something had shifted in the world, and Masha's father could no longer hear anything as he continued soaping his hands, his gaze following his daughter as she ran out. He heard only the sound of running water. With his eyes glazed over, fixed on the soapsuds on his fingers, Masha's father remembered what he'd dreamt of as a child.

And here's what he dreamt of. He used to escape from his house—from his drunk, clumsy father and his exhausted, enraged mother—by running off into the woods with a neighbor boy. Pasha and Vitya had dragged dry branches and leaves into a trench left after the war. They had a base there and in the base they had a storage area: they collected bullet shells, fragments of helmets, and even a moss-covered grenade they once found. When Pasha went to the hut alone he'd sort through the rusty metal and imagine his ideal life. It looked like this: he lived in a hot American forest, in a cave behind a waterfall. A thin veil of water sparkling in the sun separated him from the world. From the outside, it was a stream crashing down from dizzying heights, churning at the blue lake below. From the inside, it was a cozy and convenient home where the walls were hung with war-trophy weapons and the floors were covered with tiger and bear skins.

Now Pasha saw himself in his ideal home again, as he had two-thirds of his life ago: the American sun was burning hot and the jungle was looking at him through a thin veil of cold water.

And a question forced its way to him for the first time, as if it had pierced through that veil: just how had he lived his life? The water thundered in Masha's father's ears and his brain turned into a pounding heart.

One time, Vitya, the boy Masha's father had set up the base with, went there without him and wanted to clean the moss off the grenade they'd found. The explosion tore away Vitya's hands and took off half his head. Now Masha's father feels like it had been him instead of Vitya: the soap had turned into a grenade in his hands and the heat of the liberated genie was hitting his temples. Masha's father suddenly realized he was alive, that he was a live bundle of will and he had the power of the exploding grenade in his hands. The knowledge of a live life—of life as a mover of the will—abandoned her father right away, but the quiet reverberation of that knowledge forced him, after he'd finished his soup, to tell Masha's mother to *call her in*, then he banished her from the kitchen when she came back with Masha.

Masha's father didn't know what he wanted to tell his daughter. He'd forgotten what he should tell her as soon as he shut off the water. So when he sat Masha down at the table, he asked her, simply, as if he wanted to know, how she wanted to live. Masha couldn't answer her father's question and started talking instead about how she didn't want to live. In answering the question *how is that?* she began describing her mother's life.

Two people can't hear each other when they're just exchanging sentences: Masha's father didn't understand her boredom and his own despondence grabbed at his throat like a pincer. He took his daughter's words as an indictment of his own life and began justifying himself. The news broadcast, which he never missed, had finished long ago, while he was telling Masha how he lived; that was like tearing a bandage from a wound. As he unwrapped, in his daughter's presence, the bloody and crusted bandage that was his life, Masha's father was bewildered to discover that the only thing he could say to justify himself was that he hadn't had a choice. Could he really have not gone to school? Could he really have not taken those courses after he finished school—for drivers or at least mechanics or metal workers—no matter what? Could he really have not married her mother, whom he loved and who one day said to him, blushing and choking, *Pasha, I, it seems like...* And what could he do but get a job with the fleet and turn a steering wheel from nine until six every blessed day, be happy about bonuses, hide part of his salary from his wife, escape for Friday boozing sessions with his friends, help Masha's mother with the kitchen garden, and dream about a new TV?

Masha's father had intended to justify himself, but he burst into tears as he told her more and more, and realized he was reciting the charges against himself out loud. That's when Masha realized she was the victor and—feeling the victory like fresh air in her lungs—said she did have a choice. That she could leave for Petersburg and go to a good school she'd heard about from a girl in another class whose brother had been accepted there, that she'd be accepted there and study hard so she could be accepted to a university later and live completely, completely differently, but the thing was—and this was the only thing—she didn't have money for a ticket.

Masha's mother demanded many times that Masha's father retell that conversation, but he kept quiet. He couldn't, after all, say that at 3:30 there were shadows falling in the pale morning—across kitchen drawers and shelves, a fabric lamp shade, and garlands of onion and garlic hanging on the wall—and they settled so that when he'd looked at Masha, he'd seen not his daughter's sweet face but a flabby old woman's dreadful face, disfigured by deep wrinkles and, beyond that, a dusty mouth forming an unholy smirk. That he'd been scared and wanted to destroy the illusion, so jumped up to turn on the light, and then the proper continuation of that gesture was to take the yellow polka-dotted metal canister labeled "buckwheat groats" out of the cabinet.

Masha's father could never tell her mother all this, her mother was offended and cried, and her father drank and, when he got drunk, he reached for his guitar.

Youth is retribution, a ruthless form of retribution. Masha forgot about her parents as soon as her mother and father had disappeared from the scratched-up train window. The third-class train car—a key Russian chronotope—was filled with people. People were traveling from far away and had already managed to fill the expanse of the carriage, which was split into sleeping berths, with the smells of eggs, chicken, beer, socks, and unfresh breath, as well as chatter (*and that's, like, what I'm telling her*). It was frightening and fun for Masha.

The train carriage received Masha indifferently. The conductor collected her ticket, a guy in an undershirt tore himself away from his card game to help her toss her bags overhead, and a huge woman offered Masha an egg (*thank you, I'm fine, I could feed half the carriage myself*). Masha didn't have a book, not that she could have read: she watched out the window as the train sped across the path of the setting sun; fields, rivers, lakes, forests, and villages rushed by and each new river was more scarlet-colored than the one before.

Tiny villages and small cities flew past Masha and all of them, every last one, looked like where she'd spent her life. Half-dozing—Masha was tired but wouldn't admit it to herself—it seemed like she hadn't left her city, even that she simply couldn't have, because here it all was again: the redbrick water tower with the broken-off triangular roof, and here's the station store where there were queues at night for small and half-liter bottles, and here's the road toward downtown and, in the distance, a flag with who the hell knows what colors over the main building on a city square, and Masha doesn't have to see the building to know there are four columns by the entrance, a peeling Soviet emblem over the portico, and a statue of a bald Lenin. The city wasn't letting her go: it clung to the train's wheels, grimacing. It continued to exist in sagging posts, dead streetlights, crumpled road signs, ghosts of abandoned factories, and memorials honoring war heroes, and in railway marker-posts that seemed to clutch at Masha's breast like fangs. Horror paralyzed Masha—she suddenly realized there was nowhere to get away from it—and she closed her eyes, sensing in the even clattering of the wheels the unavoidability of the sentence that had been handed down: the city would be with her no matter where she went, it had permeated her like radiation, like salt permeates her mother's cucumbers, and all you could do about that was cast away your very life, just as a tumor is cut out along with a breast.

Masha opened her eyes, which required such effort it was like coming out from under a heavy, muddy wave. Sitting across from her, attentively watching her through the dimness of the carriage, was a boy unlike any she'd ever seen: he was a boy with the face of a crown prince, as handsome as the sun shining through a brand-new leaf.

He'd been lying there and reading, far away, on his upper berth, but now it had gotten too dark to read so he'd come down and seen Masha, that she wasn't sleeping, and he'd thought—he was embarrassed—well, he'd thought maybe they could chat a while since they were alone in the carriage and weren't sleeping anyway.

Masha couldn't explain very clearly where she was going. She'd heard there was a school in Petersburg—she knew its name—and that it wasn't just Petersburg kids, there was a dorm there, they'd be holding entrance exams now, at the end of May, so she was going to take them and then study at the school. The boy's eyes lit up even brighter as Masha was talking about it, and when she said she didn't even know the address, *but I can find it out in any phone book, I have the name of the school*, the boy even excitedly slapped the table with his hand.

He'd already graduated from high school, *well, almost*, he just had final exams left and he'd gone… well, he'd had to go, his uncle died, it was a funeral. Upset? No, he hadn't known this uncle very well, but there was nobody else to go and, by the way, if Masha smoked, then maybe they should go to the vestibule, there probably wasn't anybody there so they could chat a while.

The smoke from their lit cigarettes instantly filled the narrow, cupboard-like vestibule and seemed to bring the spirit of that very special location to life: it reeked mercilessly. *I don't really smoke, well, I didn't start very long ago.* The boy looked at Masha's crinkled nose and opened the door between the carriages with a regal gesture.

It was cold and noisy but fun and fresh on the shifting metal floor plates between the carriages. The wind unexpectedly flew into its trap and thrashed from wall to wall, confused, popping out through the black cracks with a whistle. It carried away the smoke.

They didn't talk about anything in particular, Masha and the boy with the face of a crown prince. Masha talked about taking tests (*I don't know what they usually take, math, Russian*), the boy talked about where he was going to college. *Where, where? –Film and television. –Acting school? –They don't teach acting there, I'm going to shoot films. –So a director. –Masha! A director is the person who yells at the actors, it's the cameraman who shoots the films.* Masha smiled like someone who'd been let in on a secret.

The wind of time blows in two directions. It's the rare person who feels its current parallel to his ongoing life. It's a special skill to catch time wafting, from the future, on your cheeks. In the emptiness between the train carriages, Masha felt—her fingers went icy from the certainty of that sensation—as though those ten minutes on the jolting train carriages, with her on one side and the boy on the other, would become a sort of tuning fork for her happiness. From here, within the chanting connector between two train cars, she saw her future self—her adult self—and how she looked back (the past tense fits here) at herself as her girl-self, not even a tenth-grader yet, awkwardly landing a cigarette in her mouth and her gaze sweeping the boy with the face of a crown prince, and she wasn't yet in love but almost, almost. *So what's your name? –Roma*, the boy said, his eyes squinting at the door handle.

That's how Roma ended up carrying Masha's bags out to the platform, then bringing them to the train station (*you don't have to, I can do it myself, really, it's not heavy*), then helping her figure out how to phone the school (*well, okay, see you later... hold on, do you happen to have change?*), and then shrugging off his parents waiting for him at home and going to see Masha off at the school (*you wouldn't find it yourself anyway*).

Masha is in a subway for the first time and the hulking equipment awes her. Of course she wouldn't have found the school herself: the boy maneuvers through people and jumps from train to train as if he'd been born in the subway. On the train, he looks aloofly at the floor as he holds bags between his knees, uninterested in the wires and lamps rushing by outside the windows or the adverts on the walls or the doors that slide open or the transparent life in the next train car or the people sitting opposite: the large, painted middle-aged woman with the soft cube of a book in her hand and the drunken hoodlum trying to rest his head on her shoulder (she looks at him haughtily). Masha tries to pretend she doesn't give a goddamn about any of this, either, but she's not very good at that—the outside observer, had there been one, would have understood everything about her: first time in the subway, *what city did you say you're from, little girl?* Masha glances furtively at Roma and he would have likely been scared if he'd caught that glance: it contained too much knowledge of, and fascination with, the future.

From train to train and then another, they leave the subway and are soon near the school. A hundred paces from the gate, the boy places her bags on the ground (on the asphalt, Masha notices): *you can go the rest of the way yourself. Want a cigarette?*

Masha swallows and nods, which gives her a coughing fit.

The sun is dissolving in the sky, a drill screeches from an open window, and it seems like the smoke is staying with them rather than floating away somewhere. Roma glances attentively at a flowerbed and keeps silent. As Masha thinks about whether to ask for his phone number (she's blushing and putting the cigarette to her lips more often than she has to), the tobacco manages to turn to ash, the boy stamps out the cigarette butt, picks up his backpack and, *well, okay*, he says, *good luck*.

Masha nods and tries not to look at the boy (he hasn't, by the way, gone yet: his unruly curls, big hazel eyes, gentle-sloped nose and narrow chin, and slightly rounded teeth) and only when he's walking away does she yell after him: *thank you!*

The boy waves his hand and smiles, turning as he walks.

Masha went inside the school and a withered woman with her glasses on top of her head told Masha the exam had just started. Masha didn't even have a chance to be surprised: she'd already ended up in a classroom where, desperately ashamed of the smell of sliced-sausage sandwiches that was coming out of her bag, she sketched out formula after formula, then arranged commas and wrote something about how someone or other is portrayed in literature.

Surprise caught up with Masha at the bulletin board with the results (the boy to her right nodded his big head with restraint, the girl by her left arm cried)—out of all the lists, it was three bad grades that stabbed at Masha—and she wasn't surprised about failing but at the thought of what would happen now, because she couldn't go to the train station and buy a return ticket: they wouldn't sell her that ticket, it simply didn't exist at the counter because the wheel had already turned and the cogs had already engaged, meaning there had to be something new now that had never existed before and, besides, it just doesn't happen that a rock that's fallen off a precipice suddenly stops and crawls back up.

The train, the scarlet rivers, the boy with the face of a crown prince (the wave of a hand), formulas, orthography, question marks, bad grade once, bad grade twice, bad grade thrice, the whistle of a drill, the bright sunlight (a huge window the size of a wall, on the first floor of the school): that whole expanse floated in front of Masha but something had established itself within the structure of the world and, armed with that sensation, Masha simply walked away from the bulletin board and sat on the bench where her bags stood, where she'd waited several hours for a stooped man in a crooked jacket to bring papers with columns of figures (*just wait, would you, you'll see it all in a second*) and thumbtack them to the bulletin board.

Parents quietly led away their children and some huge and ungainly mommy ingratiatingly pumped anyone and everyone for information about when they could appeal the test results. In the end, she left, too, and Masha was all alone, staring out the window (she liked that huge window and the sunny parallelepiped on the floor), then she stuck her hand into a bag and fished out her last, almost crumbled, sandwich: the meat on it had wilted but smelled as strong as ever.

As she chewed the sandwich, Masha caught herself thinking it tasted very good: she should have cried but she had sausage, sun, and a gentle breeze outside the window. Masha froze as she licked a greasy drop off her palm: something hung in her chest, like what happens on a swing when you've swung up so high that all you see in front of you is an endless blue sky.

Then there was a melody that suddenly began running from wall to wall and made the window glass resound (the glass resounded quietly but Masha's senses were so keen at that instant that she felt it), whistling, and a rhythmic slapping along the banisters: a man had come down the stairs and walked into the empty hall, and the magical effect of a suit and tie was such that he seemed advanced in years to Masha. He was embarrassed and stopped whistling when he saw her.

*Were you accepted? –Yes… well, no.* The man started laughing: *so were you accepted or not? –No.* Masha hid the hand she'd just been licking. The man stood for a second, looking at Masha, then briefly

looked out the window and sat next to her. *So what were your
marks? –Bad. –What, all three? –All three. –So why aren't you leaving?*
Masha stretched her hand toward her bag and shrugged. *No, no,
that's not what I meant. Everyone that tried but wasn't accepted left but
you. Why? Appeals are in two days.* Masha laced her fingers though
the straps of her bags. *I don't know. I don't need an appeal, I came here
for an education.*

The man looked out the window again. Dust motes were swimming, visibly, in a sunny bath, soaring up and falling. He started
asking Masha questions in such detail that she finally took her hand
away from her bags and answered, sometimes glancing at him.
Adolescents are terse but, slowly, he drew out of Masha where
she lived, where she'd gone to school, how she'd found out about
this school, how her parents let her go, even how she'd found the
address in an unfamiliar city, patiently waiting as Masha searched
for the right words. Finally, after pausing, he unclasped his fingers
and said: *of course your work was awful, your knowledge is on the sev-
enth-grade level, that's best-case, and I don't even know about your math
but it's probably the same.*

But since Masha hadn't left, she'd attend school here anyway. In
the summer program. Live in the dormitory. Study. And everything
was in her hands. If she could catch up to the other kids in three
months (difficult but possible), then she could pass the exam at
the end of August during supplementary enrollment and attend
the school. In tenth grade, with everyone else. Was that clear? By
the way, his name was A.A. *Yes*, Masha quietly said, *thank you*, and
lowered her head. *Go on, cry, cry. It's good for you.*

Masha held on a little longer but then burst into loud tears,
sobbing and wailing, and her crying bounced from wall to wall
through the entire hall and higher, along the stairs, to the dormitory
where A.A. brought Masha after she'd calmed down, leaving her
in the hands of a large oily woman: *give the girl a room. I'll add her
to the lists tomorrow.*

Masha realized in her first classes that what A.A. had said was "difficult but possible" was actually utterly impossible. There were other girls in her class who, like Masha, hadn't been accepted but planned to try again in August. All these girls had done poorly on their exams but each of them knew more than Masha. Masha didn't know anything: equations were like uncharted territory for her, commas were a lottery, and she didn't understand analysis of literary representation and characterizations. Of all the girls who weren't admitted (and were shy about it), she was the one who was genuinely stupid.

She realized that when she was going to bed after her second day of classes. She'd already gotten under the blanket, lights were out, the night sky lit up the whole window, her roommates were sleeping like little pupas, and the shadows were motionless: the horror caught up to Masha, making her lie stock-still. She heard the clatter of her own heart in the quiet and she could discern, unmistakably, the clatter of wheels in her heartbeat. The light in the sky faded, the shadows deepened and grew heavy, and slippers rustled past in the depths of the corridor: the oily woman had completed her rounds and was going to bed. For the first time in these several days, Masha grasped that she was alone, a thousand kilometers from home, in a huge city where only a few people knew she existed, and they couldn't care less about her, just like how you couldn't care less about the person sitting next to you on the subway. The whole world around her was absolute emptiness, there was nothing to grasp on to here, nowhere to gain a foothold, there was only Masha: nothing and nobody other than her, like on Mars, and what she had to do was absolutely impossible, not unlike moving a planet or turning yourself inside out. Masha winds her hair around her hand and painfully, very painfully, tugs on it, pulling her skin from her skull. Terror heaps on Masha (like the fear of someone sentenced to the shooting squad when ten gun barrels rise and then freeze at chest level?), smothering her, and she'll shout if it gets the slightest bit worse. Oh, to turn on the light, but the girls are sleeping—and best to let them sleep. Masha's burning-hot hands throw off the blanket and she puts her feet on the floor (don't let the linoleum melt), gropes in the dark for her stack of books and notebooks, and slowly makes her way toward the door as if she's wading through clumps of kelp.

After going down one floor, Masha steps into the first lecture hall she runs across, turns on the light, sits at a table, and opens her textbooks. Only when her hands are cold and the shivering in her body won't let up for a minute (the building across the way is already red and the windows are gleaming) does she go back to bed. Glancing at the clock, Masha knows breakfast will be in twenty minutes.

For the next three months, Masha sleeps three hours a day, six days a week. She leaves the room when the girls fall asleep and returns toward morning; the other girls don't notice anything. Only one person (later, much later) will know and when he asks if it was difficult for her, she'll answer: *stretch your arm toward the ceiling. Like this. Now don't let it down for three months.* Masha drinks coffee so she won't fall asleep—first one spoonful of instant per cup, then two, three, and without sugar—and when she gets to five spoonfuls (almost all the money her mother gave her went toward coffee), Masha starts brewing strong, opaque tea. Then she drinks tea with pepper: with black pepper, with red pepper. In the bathroom, she fills a bottle with icy tap water and rubs it on her face. When all that stops helping, she reads standing up. One time, after she'd been leaning against the wall and woke up on the floor an hour later, Masha realized she can't just stand, so she walks in circles around the classroom, reading. The blood pounds in her temples: it's still those same wheels knocking on the rails.

A.A. teaches Masha's literature and Russian classes but he makes not one single gesture that separates her from everyone else; he's strict and remote. Only at the very end of July does he nod to Masha in passing as he quickly strides down the corridor, approvingly tossing her a *good*. Indeed, one time, as she's rewriting equations from her textbook, Masha discovers what's on the paper in front of her isn't inky bits of straw but a collection of figures she needs to command to dance something akin to a polonaise. Something similar happens with commas and unstressed vowels, too: the rules she'd interpreted before as if they were a prison routine are becoming rules of the road for her, a condition for clarity within a text.

It's surprising: Masha doesn't feel fatigue during the days, in classes. Sleepless nights are sleepless nights but she's a different person in the classroom, attentive and focused. Only once, as she's going to the blackboard, does she suddenly collapse in a faint, creating turmoil. A.A.'s scared, the nurse is on vacation, and they drag Masha to a chair. After she's come to, she collects herself instantly, looks squarely at A.A. (his face acquires materiality after sliding down out of a colorful blur: it's close, maybe even too close), apologizes, and asks that the lesson be continued. A.A. tries to send her upstairs but quickly understands it's useless, the girl is staying.

At the end of August, Masha takes exams along with everyone else. The questions are no more complicated than in the spring, perhaps even simpler, but even so, the majority of the girls can't handle them. Three are enrolled in the tenth grade, Masha among them. There aren't any bulletin boards this time: they gather the girls in a classroom (they sit, silent, looking at the scratched-up desks, drumming their fingers, and wiping their foreheads: it's hot), and then the school director, mathematics teacher, and A.A. enter. A.A.'s eyes find Masha from the doorway and he winks at her, barely perceptibly. Masha understands everything but she sinks inside when the director lifts his glasses and peers at the sheet (*based on the results of the examinations, those enrolled in class 10b are…*), sternly looking at the public, and calls out Masha's surname. What's happened feels like a void: it's as if those three months had been yanked out

of her and she's become a new Masha, but nothing's managed to
settle in her soul yet.

The girls who flunked cry and go to pack up their things. The
ones who got in behave timidly, as if they're in cold water. They
peer intently at one other, though they'd been seeing each other
every day during these three months. Masha scrutinizes them, too:
one's a diligent girl with plump fingers, her hair in a ponytail, and
a face as open as a saucepan; the other is a restless babe with eye
makeup. Masha notices, surprised, that she remembers the second
one's name: Dasha.

Masha races upstairs to the dorm (the windows and stairs flash
by) murmuring *I've arrived* under her breath. She puts on her
street shoes, goes outside, and makes her way to the embankment
through little back streets. *I've arrived*, she whispers as she kicks
cigarette butts, pebbles, and beer cans. The embankment's empty
and the sun is warming the smooth (there's no breeze) water. After
standing so her knees touch the granite parapet, Masha casts a
fierce glance at spires and cupolas, squints at the sun shimmering
in the sky, looks around (there's nobody), and says, at the top of
her lungs, *I've arrived*.

Then she wanders the embankments, streets, and avenues for
the whole day: for three months, she's been living like she's on a
ship and hasn't left the school. She whispers *hi* to angels and caryatids, winks at lions and stern commanders. By evening, her legs
are pulsing like two turbines. When she's made it back to her bed
in the dorm, she collapses on the sheet and falls asleep right away.
In the last moment, she has time to formulate what's happened:
she was born today.

When she wakes up, Masha finds a book on her desk. It's the
second volume of a popular three-volume set of Pushkin, and on the
title page A.A.'s hand has painstakingly traced out: "Gentle Masha.
Bid farewell to your native doorway, inexplicable delight awaits you,"
and at that moment it never occurs to her to read that inscription as

anything other than an invitation to wild Walsinghamian joy about defeating what is, by definition, undefeatable.

Masha goes off to the telegraph office the next day and calls home after climbing into a booth all scratched up by keys and pens. She tells her mother she's been accepted, meaning that if she visits home now, it'll only be for vacations, and even then not for all of them. Her mother cries into the phone and asks if she needs anything and, by the way, the dog died and her classmates got into technical school. A package will come for her on the Tuesday train, the conductor of the seventh carriage will have it, and there'll be chocolate and a little money in the chocolate. Masha says *thank you* and goodbye, and hangs up. She's preoccupied with the first day of school, September first, which is the day after tomorrow.

After stepping away from the phone, Masha's mother sits down to drink tea (Masha's father is at work), and with her nose nestled into the steam rising from a mug, she remembers how Masha was born.

And it was like this. Fish were hiding in their underwater lairs so they wouldn't hear the booms of the ice on the river as it ruptured and heaved. Empty January air stretched over the world like a veil. People's lips cracked from the cold and cattle bleated in sheds. People twisted their faces and pressed their palms to their ears when they came inside from the cold. In the forests, mighty fir boughs snapped under the weight of the snow and collapsed below with a muffled thud. An agonized echo bounced from river to river, and trees called out to one another from their shores. Animals shook their frostbitten paws; people wiped their noses until they looked like red potatoes.

As Masha's mother waited for her father at home, she lugged firewood into the house to feed the stove's rustling mouth. The contractions began in the afternoon; Masha's mother got frightened and whimpered by the stove. The contractions didn't stop so her mother went to the woman next door, who called for an ambulance, and Masha's mother was taken to the hospital. Seven women in labor lay on cots in the ward. Some were screaming, the others, tormented, shot glances all around.

When Masha's father came home from work that evening, the woman next door, who'd been watching for him, said: *go, go, they won't let you in but you should go anyway*. Her father walked around the hospital corridor for two hours, going outside every fifteen minutes and desperately smoking.

Shortly after eleven, it was all over. They removed the purplish Masha from her mother, her father heard her unhuman shriek, and when he went outside to go home, the tears on his eyelashes iced up instantly.

# LOVE'S TEMPTATION

Whenever a novel threatens to turn into hagiography, a tried and true method for dropping the needle on the right track is to proclaim, immediately, the miracles a character has accomplished (during a lifetime, at the very least) and appeal, without delay, to what works as the engine for any novel: a love story.

Masha's first miracle was heavily tied to Petersburg, a city that, contrary to the canon, she saw for the first time not in early summer—when a mysterious light fills the streets, rivers, and canals at night, forcing everything, from empty beer bottles to church cupolas, to shine like dull silver; when warm water sullenly smacks at granite steps and bunches of drunk, happy graduates dart from store to store, forcing elderly tourists aside; and when the city effervesces like a restless crowd in the vicinity of the Palace Bridge and, in the distance, spreads along Griboedov Canal like the damp stillness that drives Dostoevsky's admirers mad—no, no, this wasn't summer, it was late autumn.

September was just a continuation of that insane summer; Masha couldn't calm down at all. She slept more, about six hours a day, but spent all her free time studying. She was starting from scratch again in her tenth-grade class: everything her classmates always seemed to know already came to Masha though harsh nighttime penance. She read Pushkin, Gogol, Karamzin, and Radishchev; studied theorems; analyzed tangled rules of Russian orthography that resembled a Chinese spiritual practice; and studied pointless Russian reforms—all this was from the eighth and ninth grades, material she realized she'd never truly studied. Only later, in the second half of October, did she finally put on a jacket and shoes, wind a scarf around her neck, and go outside the school. This might not have happened until even later, but that was the day A.A. suddenly digressed from Gogol's "Nevsky Prospect" during a literature lesson, nearly shouting at the quietened class: *my God, young men and women, do you even understand how lucky you are? Millions of people all over the world read all this and understand only every other word, they drink these texts as if they were skim milk. You live in the city where European culture found meaning!* A.A. later admitted to Masha that this was, of course, too categorical, but what orator doesn't wave his arms around? *Take a walk around this city! Not just along a street on your way somewhere: delve into it. Ask the rocks and roadways questions, they'll tell you a lot. Petersburg is the best thing that can happen to you! You'll never hear Gogol whispering to you until you've frozen under the rain somewhere on Karpovka, completely alone and without a kopeck in your pocket. Podporozhny, tell me: where does the main character find his beloved? –In a bordello, A.A. –I do hope, Podporozhny, that's not the only thing your virtuous reader's gaze caught upon?*

All laughter aside, rain poured down an hour after Masha went out. The city she saw was the very same Petersburg that would become the main character in her first film: dark, cold, and submerged in a rain that all its buildings and churches swam in. A city where things reel on the very brink of materiality and the water in the canals reminds one of death. Masha was soaked through and her eyes turned inside out, receiving everything she saw outside her.

After making her way into a bright, smoky café, Masha pulled a pencil and a folder with paper out of her backpack. Coffee cooled in her cup, young waitresses in aprons scowled at her, aimless people made a racket, and music, chitchat, and cigarette smoke swirled around Masha, entering her ears and eyes. But everything she felt now was concentrated in her fingertips, which gripped the pencil so hard her knuckles turned white. The sheet of paper was covered with fog, and shadows began creeping out of the fog: a huge unseeing house floated past along an embankment; people stepped on the tails of reeking wet little imps hiding in gateways; freakish silent fish confused the rain with the river and surfaced; monstrous toothed birds flapped their wings in tree-crowns with half their leaves gone; and then, unexpectedly even for Masha, a person emerged by a granite barrier after having suddenly seen all of this for what it was. His eyes widened from horror and delight, and his hands caught on the barrier so he wouldn't be thrown below by water that had abruptly turned furious, but he stood, despite his buckling legs, and his gaze fixed on a horrifying vision he didn't want to abandon, though that would have been very simple: turn the sheet over, rip the pencil from her fingers, bum a cigarette, and swallow the cold, sweet coffee while exchanging glances with the cute boy sitting all alone by the window. Once clouds had gathered over the seer's head and the shaggy black birds had noticed him, Masha's hands flew up, over the paper—the drawing was finished.

That drawing, like the majority of Masha's drawings, was not preserved. A.A. was the last—and most likely the only—person to see it. When he looked at it, he heavily gathered cigarette smoke in his mouth, remaining silent until he finally began speaking. What he told Masha became the second point of the tension (the drawing was the first) from which her *Pursuit* would come into being several years later.

*Minus One* and *Save* and *Amber* had already been released by the time the general public became aware of *Pursuit*. It didn't (and really couldn't) prove to be a hit, although European cineastes recognized each other based on their possession of the disc of that film, which appeared suddenly, out of inexistence. A student found the file and uploaded it to the Web when he was rummaging around in the HFF archives: when yet another disc went into the drive and "*Pursuit*. Produced and Directed by Masha Regina" flashed on the screen, the student checked the German notation on the envelope, just in case, and let out a shout. The whole Web brimmed with rumors a few days later.

The film was said to be student work, opaque conceptualist handiwork so unlike Regina's clear and absolutely open style that it most likely belonged not to her but to some hoaxer who wasn't exactly lacking in the talent department; and though of course it held a certain interest from a technical point of view, it should certainly not be considered a masterpiece, and so on and so forth. Masha had to tear herself away from filming *Hunger* to fly off to Berlin and admit during a press conference at Kino Arsenal that she truly did make *Pursuit*.

*I made that film in Petersburg about ten years ago and am glad it's finally been discovered. It's a good picture, though now, of course, I wouldn't make something like that.*

After that, all the fervor subsided and the film entered the category of pictures released with an "Art Films" label. It is, of course, black and white (*like any brilliant film*, Roma would jokingly say) or, more accurately, it changes to black and white. As the credits run, the main character is telling a bulky female porter about his unfaithful love. Then, after he's gone up to his office, he falls asleep and the color scheme changes, unnoticed, from dark browns to grays. It helps the transition pass unnoticed that all this happens at night: the unspeaking female porter has only to shut off the muddy-yellow lamp in the frame for it to turn pitch black. A lookalike, a double, then appears and therein begins the actual action, something nine out of ten viewers would likely say is lacking. Masha sends her characters outside and their entire battle takes place amid the scenery of a frightening, inconceivable Petersburg. The hero pursues his double through small streets, courtyards, gateways, attics, and roofs, as the double hides from him behind garbage bins and brick chimneys, amid railway cars parked between stations (and there it is, the primary trump card in the hands of those who'd maintained Masha's authorship even before the Berlin press conference: this scene is similar to the famous pursuit scene in *Minus One*), then the main character runs away from the double along endless flights of stairs and, finally, is cornered on one of the embankment's approaches down to the river, where a heavy leaden wave licks at his boots. The outline of a gnarled paw flashes in the water, as if it's stretching to grab the character. Otherworldly imagery emerges constantly from black shadows and white shimmers in the frame: tails, fangs, and eyeballs the viewer doesn't notice right away or for certain, meaning they might well not be noticed at all or might be regarded as just imperfections or chance combinations of light and shadow. Suddenly, the double can change shapes as if he were a demon and dribble his festering eyes from behind the railings of the Summer Garden; suddenly a giant rat-tail twitches in the broad crown of a tree; and fish scales flash in a dusty window—all this happens by chance and indistinctly, as glimpses, making it possible not to pay attention, if that's your wish.

The rapture that was most often expressed about *Pursuit* was related to the picture itself, the technical skill and perfection of the shots, and even the captivating acting of the two 20-year-old actors, but almost never the film's script, its essentiality or, well, put another way, its message. That's no surprise. During the press conference at Kino Arsenal, Masha said: *honestly, it's hard now for me to recall or understand what I made. There were some pictures in my head that I wanted to set free. I don't know, I'm not really sure there's anything that can be read into that film.*

The double chases the hero though labyrinths of courtyards and streets, demanding something from him, he yells, and the hero mutters, justifies himself, goes on the offensive, rushes at the double, punching him, and everything culminates, as well it should, in a pistol duel, though, strictly speaking, the source of their conflict is unclear.

Nobody that discussed the film knew (and even Masha herself only vaguely remembered sixteen years later) that A.A. explained the essence of that conflict to her in the small kitchen of his smoke-filled apartment. He looked at Masha's drawing for a long time and smoked, missing the saucer with his ashes, then he told her about Gogol, about Bely, and about artists for whom Petersburg had became an elevator to the otherworldly. Bitov's *Pushkin House*, said A.A., looks strange in these ranks (Masha opened the ventilation window to free the smoke, tottered on the windowsill, then reached for the ciga-rettes) because there's nothing mystical in it at first glance and many who've read it are devoutly certain they've read a realistic novel about a young scholar's mixed-up relationships with his women. *What are you laughing at? Well, yes, it's about me.* But there aren't actually any women in that text, only men, and they're not real, either. A demon tempts a saint, that's the whole story. Odoevtsev lives in a toylike world, in theater scenery, and suddenly crashes through into the real world where everything falls into place: a demon is a demon, and the soul stands facing the problem of good and evil. *Ashtray? The saucer, take it.* Mitishatyev tries to force Odoevtsev out of the real world and all its strains, by tempting him, offering an ignorance of what is real and the peaceful repose of closed eyes. And when the temptation has been overcome (a mask comes off, too, that's very important), agon is unavoidable and there's a confrontation between the soul and evil. Evil loses simply because a soul with seriously open eyes is always stronger than evil. This only ends up being a problem for the novel's main character, who must die so he and the novel die together. In the true sense, though, what happens is that the soul is freed from the scenery of this world. *I apologize for not explaining very clearly but we're not in class now, are we?*

Further explanations are pointless, especially since Masha jumped off the windowsill, embraced the pensive A.A., and began kissing him. She spent nearly the entire summer after her first year at the Academy in his little apartment on Pestel Street. When it still stayed light out all night, they would walk to the Fontanka River to drink wine. They'd buy a bottle from the broad-smiling Armenian in the underground shop, wander over to the approach down to the opaque, stern water, a cork would pop, and there'd be an audible splash of wine pouring into glasses. In all likelihood, it was only during that summer that Masha could have seriously said she loved A.A. if he'd asked her. A.A. didn't ask, though. Masha drew things, he read, they took walks together, ate, and made love. A summer like that—when there's good weather every evening and doing nothing isn't oppressive—is granted to a person only once, A.A. said, and he laughed at Masha, who couldn't recognize the quote.

Their tranquil pleasure was disturbed only twice during the whole summer, when A.A.'s wife called. He had a quote for everything and joked that there's no such thing as a Russian ex-wife. After the calls—the purpose of which was some kind of day-to-day formality (*I apologize, I wouldn't think of troubling you, tearing you away... but...* and then the conversation concerned a set of keys or some documents that had gone missing, who the hell knew where)—A.A. got gloomy and smoked angrily. Masha raged, spluttered through her teeth, slammed the front door (torn strips of dark-brown imitation leather shuddered on the door's exterior), went for a walk alone, drank three cups of coffee somewhere, and came back. She didn't understand immediately why she was in a rage. And when she understood, she told him immediately: the sight of a weak man instilled genuine horror in her. A.A. took exception, said he wasn't really so weak, he'd left her, after all, *that wasn't so easy, I'm telling you...* and Masha flung back *damn Gingerbread Man*.

But A.A.'s gaze had a magnetic influence on Masha that summer: she calmed down and began laughing. Even so, when A.A. went to sleep, he moaned as if he had a toothache. Masha held him by the shoulder and told herself she knew about his wife. She'd caught a glimpse of her, back when his wife had come to the school: a slim woman with pained eyes and a striking beauty-mark at the corner of her lip. She loved Bunin, cappuccino with cinnamon, and A.A. In a fit of cynicism, the adult Masha might have called this sort of woman *a laced-up twat* but, in reality, the situation was different.

A.A. met her in the philology department—the girls there were as light as the bubbles from gum, not all of them, of course, and many were just goblins, but there was plenty of room for the imagination to wander—and A.A. managed, between library, lectures, and dive bars, to woo or, as he himself put it (he loved this lacy word) to *court* his smiling, intrepid female classmates and, later, the girls in younger classes (*listen, I heard you have notes from freshman year*, and there were notes, yes, of course there were). He had no "sporting interest": he fell in love, for real, with each maiden (when he told Masha about this—she was lying on her back and he was stroking the tender skin of her breast—she laughed: *each time is like the first time*) and he never cheated on one. Liza was not one in a series (there was not, however, any series in the Stanislavskian sense) even though she almost immediately led him to her bed (her teacher mother and her father, a retired colonel, had gone to Crimea) and A.A. was entranced for a long time, longer than usual, by her pensive gaze, slow fingers, and the beauty mark at the corner of her lip (not even her name seemed plastic to him). They sat all winter in her room, kissing and translating from Russian into Latin. By spring, her dreaminess felt as cold as soup from the refrigerator to A.A., and her fingers were slow from boredom, but it ended up that he decided to postpone a breakup until summer—they had conference papers and a first serious written report—and then his tongue went limp in the summer, like an old man who's had too much to drink.

Liza tenderly stroked his hair and told him she loved him. A.A. hemmed and hawed, and hoped she'd ask: *what about you?* But she, the jerk, didn't ask. All it took for A.A. to feel disgusted was to picture how she'd burst into tears and her eyes would look all cow-like...

and then he'd tell himself he had to do it over the weekend or the next week. He finally forced himself in the autumn, at the zenith of a truly magnificent September. They left the department, the trees were covered with yellow, papery leaves, the Lomonosov statue looked hot to the touch, as if it were emitting its summer warmth, girls squinted at the sun and smiled, and A.A. stopped and told her he had to go, well, somewhere, he had errands so couldn't go to her place, and really, they should think about what to do because a lot had changed in a year and he didn't know what she thought about the matter but for his part he couldn't say he was feeling the same now as a year ago and it would be better not to torture each other and there was nothing so awful in that, they'd be friends, and visit each other, sure, but there was no reason at all anymore to try to… to have close interaction, if it was already an obligation for at least one of them, and there just couldn't be any joy in this for her, so that's it, there's the trolleybus, let's call each other, see you, and he dashed off toward a blinking green traffic light. He ran across the street and made it, but of course he couldn't resist looking back from beside the trolleybus door: Liza was racing toward him. Cars flew by right and left, beeping bloody murder, brakes screeched, tires smoked, papery leaves as bright as streetlights spiraled downward, and Liza pressed her little pocketbook to her chest as she jumped from one life-threatening trauma to another, shouting a heart-rending *I love you*, and A.A. cursed, kicked the trolleybus (which squealed off toward the bridge, its prongs sparking on the overhead wires), and bolted off to save the fool. He waved his arms like a sailor signaling in a drawing, shouted, grabbed her by the elbows, dragged her to dry land, held her by the shoulders, and stroked her back; and when shivering hit her, fear and malice hit him.

Another trolleybus rumbled by after that, and then another and another: A.A. embraced Liza, calming her, and she begged him through her tears not to leave her, asking him what she could do… and he said: *nothing, calm down, for God's sake.* People gawked at them, and A.A. turned Liza so she faced the Neva and he pretended they were just standing there, hugging, what, is that not allowed or something? Horrendously mortifying. He brought her home, they made love, and then she nestled up to him, kissed his chest, and whispered: *you do love me, it's just that now you're…* The lack of a real question in those words bugged A.A. but he couldn't tell her *no*; he wanted to sleep.

*It's impossible to leave a woman who won't let you go, understand? Why? Well, because she's kind of weak and you're kind of strong and it ends up you're the one hurting her and she's not hurting you. No, there's nothing worse than feeling like a dickhead.*

A.A. proposed to Liza a half-year later (there were several more repulsive scenes and every last one of them ended exactly the same), and even before she stopped sobbing she'd started thinking of who'd sew her dress. Her colonel father shook A.A.'s hand, her teacher mother kissed him, and two months later, A.A. and Liza put heavy gold rings on each other's fingers.

Masha, who was already training herself to watch for cinematic quotes, decided this was the story from *Fanny and Alexander*: the heroine marries a monster, thinking she'll have some sort of proper, true life with him, but she finds herself in hell and it even turns out that the silly game of mental leapfrog in her parents' family actually was a life, a true life, and her farting uncle was a fool but not a prick, and the husband was a prick and dangerous besides. *Oh come on, it's not like that at all*, A.A. said, making a face.

All that was five years before the moment A.A. would see Masha in the school lobby after the entrance exams and lead her up the stairs to the dorm. A year later, A.A. would grasp, with deafening clarity, that love is a pounding heart, tenderness rippling on the palms, and a shimmering expanse in the eyes: and what could be more stupid for a teacher than to fall in love, utterly seriously, with a high-school girl, dream of holding her hand and kissing the corners of her lips, cry at night, moan because a spasm makes your body twist, exactingly examine your teeth in the mirror and not allow your imagination to let go of her, the red-haired girl with the hard gaze and confident motions who, beyond everything else (he didn't know, he found that out later), is losing her mind from loving a guy who doesn't give a shit about her.

It's not strange that it was only frantic passion for his student that forced A.A. to leave a wife whose eyes were round with terror, and that it was only two years later, rather than immediately: Point B is always more important than Point A.

When she was yelling, the slender, pensive beauty Liza smeared her wet eyes all over her face and looked scarier than nuclear war. All A.A. had to do was tell her what he'd decided and her face would immediately fall: A.A. had seen this many times and his heart sank nevertheless, as if he were expecting a blow: the main thing now, in order to retain that feeling, was for him to hold on to the sensation of firmness in his fingers that had come to him after he'd looked at Masha. Liza complained, accused, quietly whimpered in the kitchen, made calls, said she'd reserved a table at a restaurant, assured him she couldn't live, offered to start all over again, pumped him about *who is she*, and then, finally, when A.A. came home a week later, he opened the door to the bathroom and found her in a bubble bath, aiming a razor at her wrist, and understood it was all over because if she was lying there and waiting for him so she could take a swipe at her wrist, she would never actually do it. He silently left the bathroom and turned off the light; she couldn't end her life in the dark. Her wet feet slapped out of the bathroom into the hallway, water ran on to the rug, and a soapy caviar hung behind her ears: this was frightening and disgusting for A.A., as if he were seeing some sluglike Hollywood monster in real life. And it is true that obsession is nonsexual. This wet scene was their last: it was the same day A.A. received keys for the apartment on Pestel Street. He was simply lucky (as always happens for the one who gets up and goes) that a classmate had gone to France and handed over his *nest under a roof* in exchange for watering the plants and a token sum, "so it wouldn't be empty."

Now, in that one-room nest, where a piece of the cupola of the Cathedral of the Transfiguration was visible outside the window, A.A. was pressing Masha's hand and moaning slightly through his teeth as he dropped off to sleep. Masha bit her lips. She didn't allow herself to moan.

At the very beginning of summer, when Masha was taking her second-semester exams, A.A. proposed they live together. She agreed, not just because she actually liked the idea but also because she was certain: A.A. couldn't leave his wife, thus his proposal would remain only a small feature of an evening encounter, a tender stroll from Kazan Cathedral to St Nicholas Naval Cathedral and back. After getting the final signature in her grade book, Masha got on the train and went home. She sent A.A. a text: "Went out of town, back whenever."

Masha's mother's love enveloped her as warmly and clammily as a chubby palm envelops a fly. The very first lunch (*you've just been on the road, you're hungry, eat*) dragged Masha off into a dream where her dead grandmother was holding and kneading her hand: this was unpleasant for Masha and she wanted to free her hand (her grandmother was dead, after all) but that was awkward (this was her grandmother) and so, weak of will, she allowed her hand to be used. Masha woke up in a sweat late that evening: her mother had covered her with a quilt, not caring that it was June. The next day, Sunday, Masha's mother brought her to the market. Masha flitted behind her mother from row to row amongst jackets, dresses, fishing hooks and lures, eggs, fish, underwear and socks, discs, chains, motors, gravestones, rugs, armchairs, pants, and boots, and her mother was right at home in this Sodom, knew everybody, and grabbed Masha by the elbow at every booth: *do you need t-shirts?* The horrifying shopping trip wrung Masha out until there was nothing left inside. She consented to trying on shoes, a top, and a skirt, and helped her mother with lunch at home, overate (*eat, eat, you've gotten so thin*), and collapsed on the couch, her arms lying separate from her, like rags. She looked at them with hatred then raised her eyes to her mother and tried to tell her she couldn't spend the summer like this, that she had to work (she said *study*, so there wouldn't be questions) and for that she needed a clear head, coldness, and a hungry stomach. She didn't manage to say everything since her mother (*of course, of course, you'll get started tomorrow*) started telling her how the neighbor'd kicked his wife out and was drinking vodka every blessed day, that Masha's classmate had gotten married, that Volkov (*come on, you remember, your classmate*) had killed—stabbed—a girl he was friends with (apparently she was going out with someone else) and there was a trial and he was put in prison, that Aunt Valya was sick, that the math teacher had finally been fired after they'd found him drunk in the school garden for the fifth time, that granny Shura, that Alexei Semyonovich, that Petya, *come on, the traffic policeman who's so fat…*

Masha was descending into a goopy pudding of news, and her native city came to her as she was verging on sleep, which was already brushing at her fingers: an underwater kingdom that was ancient, ancienter than the rocks and rivers, where hands move slower and the sounds of human speech are muffled and meaningless. Everything here was arranged so the frantic sleep after lunch grabbed you quickly and often, essentially for ever. The people here valued immobility, changes of season, and what was fatty. Lying on the sofa, Masha felt like a squash in a raised vegetable bed, ripening with the earth's juices. The sleep that had filled her body was agonizing and ferocious.

She still attempted to work. After getting up early the next morning—even before her father had gone to the depot and her mother to the train station—she laid out paper for herself, sharpened a pencil, and began setting down line after line, but her pencil strokes cut across the surface of the paper, her hands lacked the strength

to overcome the opposition of the two-dimensional in order to
draw depth, and, beyond all that, she already knew, as well as felt,
that if the drawing was to work, even her very first motion should
remove the moldy skin of what exists by biting into something
substantive. The seaweed homes she wanted to draw came out
looking inauthentic, the spectral fishes and octopi were lifeless, and
she found no blood when she bit her fingers in a rage; when her
mother shyly opened the door a little (*you're not sleeping anymore?
Let's go have some breakfast*), Masha tossed her pencil, balled up the
feeble sheet of paper, and went to the kitchen.

She tried working at home, in the yard, and on the railroad bed,
and even talked her father into firing up the rusty old Lada and driving her far, far away—to a field, and to the shore of a lake blazing in
the sunshine—but in each place she crumpled sheet after sheet of
paper, broke her pencils, and at some point thought that most likely
the special gravity in her hands that came to her whenever she was
truly drawing... that maybe that gravity would never come to her
ever again, that it was a gift delivered to her by mistake, like some
minor contraband that a strict customs officer, shaking his peaked
cap and head, pulls out of some piece of baggage and will never
return, and that maybe that gravity had never existed at all, it had
only seemed to, meaning it was for the best that it was difficult for
her even to remember how such a misapprehension could happen.

After dinner, Masha's mother sent her father to watch the news
and grilled Masha about boys, had she met anyone in Leningrad,
and then took her by the hand, hinting she'd be so glad, so glad.
Masha felt drunk with horror. Her heart thumped madly when
she got a text from A.A. a week later—"When? Ever?"—and she
abruptly typed out, with strengthened fingers, that she'd be back
the next day. At lunch, she made up something about a summer
internship starting the next day, that she'd thought she wouldn't
get it but had after all, they'd written to her just now. Her mother
dropped a skillet with sizzling potatoes and burst into tears. She

begged Masha to stay a few days longer, asked what she didn't like, hunched in a chair, and babbled that she understood everything, Masha was bored here with nowhere to go and no friends, but what about them, her parents, they loved her so much, had expected her for the whole summer, and now she was suddenly leaving, it was unfair, take pity on us, you can go swimming, too, there'll be mushrooms and berries soon, and she'd gotten so thin, she should eat and sleep as much as she could. Masha poked at her food. Her father scrutinized the tablecloth and asked for the vodka.

There weren't any tickets: Masha's mother announced that quietly but joyfully. But Masha wouldn't be held back, so that evening she threw her clothes into a backpack, went to the train station, and made an agreement with a sneaky conductor who had a face like a dry cucumber. He took her into his own compartment for one and a half times the price of a ticket. Masha shoved the bills into his wide-open palm and got off the train to say goodbye to her mother and father. Her father was already drunk and slurring his words when he wished Masha happiness, and her mother, weary from crying, was pallid and taciturn. The conductor winked meanly from the door and Masha's mother said: *you've hurt us, daughter.* Masha jerked her head after deciding against kissing her mother, said (rasped) *forgive me,* and darted off for the train.

The conductor drank vodka and offered some to Masha, Masha refused, hit him on the hand that predatorily clawed at her knee, kept quiet, and tried not to listen to his reeking conductor yarns, but the horrors didn't end there: in the middle of the night, the conductor's (*you can just call me Lyokha*) phone started ringing and the awful word "inspection" began thundering. Lyokha led Masha off to the vestibule by his compartment, opened a hatch in the ceiling and hoisted her up, where she lay in the darkness for two hours under the roof of the carriage, with a tank of drinking water splashing next to her, something pressing into her side, and her bent legs aching. Masha choked up with tears in that narrow, coffinlike expanse, and *hurt, you've hurt us, hurt* swung in her head like a bell. Early in the morning, the conductor, already mean and sober, pulled Masha out of the hatch, sat her on the lower bunk in his own compartment, climbed on the top bunk, and began snoring deafeningly, disgorging a monstrous stench from his hung-over maw. Masha sobbed at the top of her lungs and gnawed at the skin of her fingers.

When A.A. met Masha in the morning at the Chernyshevskaya subway station, he'd nearly gone out of his mind with love for this girl who looked like an infuriated hedgehog that had gone through the wash. They wandered back to Pestel Street, Masha sputtered around in the bathroom for half an hour, then A.A. fed her fried eggs and put her to bed. Masha fell asleep instantly and A.A. sat next to her for a long time, peering at her breathing, the movement of the bottom of her nostrils, and how her fingers occasionally quivered. When her sleep had calmed, A.A. got a book and read in the kitchen until evening. A spring season that had aged for two years, like cognac, was blossoming in his head: he and Masha were strolling around the Summer Garden and he was carefully touching her hand for the first time. Summer began when Masha woke up, tiptoed out of the room, placed a hand on his shoulder, and asked: *did I sleep long?* He set his book aside, they drank tea, then he kissed her fingers, eyes, cheeks, and lips, and she smiled, kissing him back, then he freed her from her nightie and pressed his whole body against her, so his breathing grew irregular and became hot.

A.A. fell asleep and Masha carefully removed his hand that was holding her hand—she didn't feel like sleeping after having a good rest in the afternoon—took a sheet of paper from her backpack, and began drawing. After ten minutes of licking the pencil, a hot sun rages on the paper, languidly pressing down on the head of a shepherd who pulls a worn cap down over his forehead and slowly taps a cigarette against his uneven thumbnail. Cows raise their questioning eyes, chewing with great effort so they won't fall asleep. Hot grass sweats, the lush leaves of trees and shrubs glisten, spots flash on a lake like hot pudding, sated fish sleep in underwater grass, an old man sleeps in a creaky boat, his fishing line having fallen out of his hands, and the old man dreams of a little boy who slaps his heels through the water so he can splash as much as possible. Off in the distance, slanting roofs hang down toward earth like tree branches, exhausted, wanting to fall asleep as soon as possible. Dogs sleep, and old women, too, babies sleep, pressing at a nipple with their lips, and their mothers sleep, their heads leaning against a wall. A train's engine driver fights sleep and leads the carriages along slowly, as if the heat has tightened the air or the melted rails have guttered under the sun. But there is more sky than anything else in the drawing, and Masha has managed to heat up its pale blue enamel so much that, in the morning, A.A. was afraid to touch the paper, lest he burn himself.

Masha draws all summer, piling paper after paper in her portfolio case, distracted only by food, slightly drunken evening strolls, A.A.'s touching tenderness, and sleep. Much of what she will draw appears later, in her films: infernal Petersburg, strange faces that make it easy to guess their owners' entire fate, buildings, animals, human figures, trains, landscapes, soaked trees, fighting children, flights of stairs, drunken student camaraderie in courtyards, a girl in a café crumpling an empty cigarette pack, a bent old woman on a crosswalk with a supermarket trolley. As she draws, Masha gradually begins to understand what kind of films she wants to make.

She feels calm with A.A. His love is light and not burdensome. Sometimes Masha presses her palms to her temples and doesn't understand why she can't love him as firmly and certainly, as simply and confidently. But contrary to what seems obvious, all she has to do is close her eyes for the boy with the face of a crown prince to appear inside her eyelids. He smiles crookedly but Masha's heart sinks. When she imagines his hand on her belly, her whole body turns into tenderly relaxed lips. A.A. sees that, knows he has nothing to do with it, and is enveloped by despondence.

The time Masha went for a walk around the city after the class about Gogol's Petersburg stories and saw another side of the roadways and rivers was not really her first. She'd gone outside the school earlier, too, once in September.

And it was like this. Masha made her way into the teachers' room and pulled a telephone directory out from behind the glass door of a cabinet. The corners of the translucent pages were worn thin, well on their way to becoming spit-stained nothingness, and the book's edge was marked up with ink of various colors, but addresses are longer-lived than phone numbers: it was through that compassionate directory that Masha found the Institute of Cinema and Television, as promised, when she arrived on Pravda Street. The list of enrolled students still hadn't been taken off the wall, and there was only one Roma on it. Masha first found the schedule for freshmen, then the classroom for film history, and sat to wait by the door. The echo of one strong heartbeat subsequently carries through an entire life: it hadn't even occurred to Masha that perhaps this was a different Roma, that Roma might not have been admitted or had been admitted at some other place, so when the door opened and bunch after bunch of students started flowing out and his face flashed in one of the bunches, Masha was happy not because it was actually him but because he hadn't skipped this lecture, and there he was, chatting with friends, winking at them, pushing one's back and then the three of them sail right over to a few girls fiddling with their mobiles and compacts. Masha leaps off the bench and it ends up she's butting in on a conversation that's just gotten underway (*what're your plans, girls?*). He doesn't recognize her right away and waves, irritated, to his buddy (*two minutes, be right back*) and leads Masha off to the side.

*Hi, what're you doing here?* he says to Masha, shooting glances at the girls and his friends. His friends are shooting glances at Masha, the girls are aiming their compacts at her. *I… well*, Masha doesn't know how to answer foolish questions. *Did you pass your exams?*

*Oh, good for you, congratulations. You living in the dorm? Oh, not so bad, either. How is it all?*

Then he tells her he has to run now, tells her to study hard, well, he wishes her the best, see you later. Masha sees he's trying to show the friends who are waiting for him that there's nothing special here, it's all some sort of nonsense, not worth talking about, he waves his hand and strides over to them, *so, what, you decide anything?*

The hurt devastated Masha. She hides her eyes from pedestrians on Pravda Street, rage is gradually awakening in her, and Masha learns for the first time in her life that despondence about love can become fuel for the machinery of the imagination. Masha sits down on a bench and lays a sheet of paper on her knees. Without pondering much, she draws the homeless man sleeping on the bench across from her: he lies there for a long time, so long that snow covers his legs, fills up the pockets of his reeking coat, melts on the purplish pear of his face, and gets stuck in the labyrinth of his beard. She sits down alongside him on the corner of the bench—in profile, her elbows on her knees—and feeds her own heart right out of her hands to a huge brazen dog with matted fur, and his tongue winds around Masha's hands. The dog smiles unnaturally and caresses Masha with his eyes.

"Her own heart" is over the top, of course, but the main character in *Minus One* will feed a dog pastries the same way, sitting on a bench alongside a sleeping homeless man. The dog, which an assistant caught somewhere at the dump (the dog was specially kept without food for a whole day, too), will scarf up pies smelling of meat and Roma will be indignant, wondering why they're tearing him away from the camera, making him up, and forcing him to lie motionless, like a homeless man, on a bench for three takes in a row: *use an extra! why should the cameraman play at being homeless?* Masha explained it to him: *forgive me but it was you I needed in this scene.*

# SEX AS YOUTH

It's horribly cold in the dorm that winter. Whether that's the fault of the shifty building manager or the lazy matron, who were, taken together, like a Russian government in miniature—they could always point at each other: he hadn't bought tape to seal the windows and she'd forgotten about it—meaning that one way or another, it's so drafty around the windows in the rooms that water on the windowsill turns to ice overnight, the girls go to bed in t-shirts, sweatpants, and socks, taking cover under two blankets that they bundle themselves up in like future butterflies inside cocoons, leaving only their noses outside so they can breathe. Masha's sleep is unsettled: she has an unsettling dream. In the dream, she's running her hand along her head but there's just smooth skin, not one strand of hair remains. This dream needs no interpretation because as soon as Masha wakes up, she extends her hand to the back of her head, is convinced she has no hair, and remembers: she couldn't have hair and there's nowhere it could have come from because yesterday she'd convinced Dasha that she'd made the irrevocable decision—and yes, she'd thought it out—to shave her head, so she thrust a razor in Dasha's hand, dampened her hair, and made Dasha remove lock after lock from her head. Initially, Dasha was hesitant, but then she went crazy, conscientiously shaved, sticking her tongue out, and

joking when she finished that now, well, Masha was totally ready
for the nuthouse. Masha laughed along with Dasha.

In reality, though, things were like this. Masha has been waiting
for Roma at the institute, by the exit. The snow was sticking, settling
on hats, gently touching hands, and getting in eyes. Students were
going wild by the door: girls squealed, boys laughed loudly, and
passersby dodged snowballs that disintegrated with a resounding
splat. Masha smiled, uncertain, because she didn't know why she
was there. Essentially, Roma had already sent her packing and it
was unclear what else she could tell him. But Masha couldn't wrap
her head around a world that worked like this: it was as if an entire
machine refused to run properly because one bearing didn't quite
fit in place. Right now, more than anything, she felt like throwing
snowballs and squealing and yelling with that fired-up mob, so now
there's snow in her hands, she presses it, smoothes it, and the snowball gets smaller and denser, and in her reverie she forgets it, her
wool mitten gets wetter, and each time the heavy front door groans,
she gets ready, peers over, and abruptly turns: it's not him. The boy
in the ski jacket who smiles in her direction is Roma's classmate,
he's recognized her, she flashes a glance over him, pretending he's
made a mistake, it's not her. The more people pour out the doors
and the greater the chance the next one will be him, the harder she
presses the icy snowball and the more she's afraid. She figures he
might say something unpleasant to her and get mad, so the best
thing would be to leave right now and not wait, because there's
only a point in waiting when you don't know what will happen,
but there's no point when it's like this, it's all just stupid, stupid,
stupid. When he comes out, he simply doesn't see Masha because
he immediately turns to hold the door for the girl walking behind
him and let her go ahead, then he bends and shoves a snowy spray
of snow down her jacket: Masha can't help but see how this little
joke is something akin to a declaration of love; or how a kiss, all
wrapped up in snow like a holiday package, is flying toward the

girl's neck, which is damp from snow that melted on warm skin, but then a sweet, red lipsticky smile accepts the kiss on the fly.

Roma and the girl join in with the wailing mass of students: faces and hands flash, scarves unwind, buttons fly to the ground, it's everybody against everybody, happy and fast, and Roma bends down—hands cupped—and whoever's there first will get it in the back, on the hat, in the face (*hey, no fair!*), but when he dodges someone else's snowball yet again, scoops damp, white snow off the roof of a parked car, and takes aim for Masha standing a meter and a half away, he lowers his hand after he's seen her, grimaces, and those seconds of bewildered slowness are enough for him to catch it in the back twice, and he flings out *the little bitch*, turns, and keeps playing. Masha isn't offended at that moment (just as she won't be later) because Roma swore at her (in anger) or even that he didn't say hello, she's offended that he dropped his hand, didn't throw the snowball, and didn't draw her into the game (as if that happy student rumpus was by invitation only), and she reacts, without taking time to think, by blasting her own snowball, which had frozen into a piece of ice, at his back (and she hit, right between the shoulder blades), and that was just a reaction to the offense, from which another (he doesn't love me) popped up later, as she trudged back to the dorm, crossing half the city and kicking snow. Roma bends, bellows from the pain, and turns—but only for a second—and then dives into a mob already beginning to tire, grabs the lipsticked girl by the hand, and presses her to himself.

On her way to the dorm, Masha takes the decision to shave her head and it's obvious this gesture symbolically signifies renouncing her own sexuality, which she doesn't need as long as the person her sexuality was meant for is in a snowball fight with another girl. She has no doubt that she no longer has any use for her sexuality: she'd seen Roma four times from September through February and he gave her the brush-off all four times. Eight years later, he would passionately but not overly convincingly justify himself: *Regina, I was a bastard, I was ashamed of myself, do you even remember how you and I sat in the Rotunda?* That was their second meeting; the third, if you count the train. Masha had come to the institute a half-hour before the end of classes but she'd found Roma in the internal courtyard, already fairly drunk; he nodded to his friends and led Masha away to take a walk. Roma drank beer along the way and could barely stand by the time they got to the Rotunda (*I'll show you the sights, want me to? –Yes. –Okay, then, I'm the main sight in this city*), which was dirty, though the entrance still preserved traces of grandeur. As he tilted the bottle into his mouth, spilling beer on his jacket, he looked least of all like the cinematic Napoleon he wanted to be. Swaying from side to side, he told Masha she was awfully lucky to have met him because very soon he would become the greatest cameraman of all time, that his name would thunder throughout the continents, he would totally change the cinematic world, the history of which would subsequently be told as *before* Yevgenyev and *after* Yevgenyev, and that his name would compel viewers to go to the movies—they'd go for the cinematographer and not the director, all of whom only knew how to yell at actors. For the sober Masha, it was funny but not disgusting to listen to all this stupidity: a drunk boy could talk big. She wasn't even disgusted when he came on to her, trying to kiss her and thrust a hand wet with beer under her jacket at the same time; most likely she pushed him away automatically because she wanted him sober and was ready to sit him out drunk, but she was disgusted by his loutishness when he grabbed hold of a peeling wooden banister, lurched up, distinctly said *I didn't really feel like it anyway*, and left, tripping as he walked down the steps, though she forgave him right then and there because you could forgive certain things from a drunk man. And so Roma used that meeting to explain what happened later: *I told you so many barefaced lies, Regina, that I wanted to wail the next morning, how could I look you in the eye?* He didn't remember how he'd come on to her with the kiss; he shook his head and said it didn't happen. It did, it did.

And there was this too. The day Masha comes down to school without hair, the teachers sigh—*good Lord, Masha, what did you do to yourself!*—and the girls understand everything—*radical!*—and the boys tease her out of habit—*hey, that's not contagious is it?*—and Masha feels like the center of attention and can't help but see that as a form of betrayal. The gesture intended to deprive her of gender and make her fly under the radar did the exact opposite. Masha had suddenly gone from being the-girl-from-the-tenth-grade-b-class to *the bald girl*, the girl everybody was talking about, the one everybody was looking at, and the one Kolya from the other tenth-grade class stops in the corridor as she's walking from the second lesson to lunch, to tell her it looks good and she's really pretty, well, she'd been really pretty before, too—Masha is going berserk—and that nothing could ruin her looks, but that's not what I meant to say, and Masha walks around him: *leave me alone, would you?!*

Kolya will gnash his teeth and shake his head every time that awkward conversation resurfaces in his memory. Only a month or two later will Masha understand what happened, just as Dasha will discover for herself on that same day that *God is love!* and will try, with the wide eyes of every discoverer, to convince Masha of that, but Masha will snort in response: *well yes, love's ways are inscrutable*.

Kolya's long glances at Masha when she walks through the dorm corridors or eats in the cafeteria do nothing more than tickle her spine. Masha catches herself sensing that it isn't really so unpleasant to happen upon sheets of paper in her notebooks and pockets, all folded into quarters with rapturous, moving poems (it's not difficult to understand who composed them and rewrote them on the sheet in a maximally distinct hand—there was no reason for him to be nervous and gaze longer than usual, wondering if she'd figured it out). Only one thing disturbs Masha. Thus far she's succeeded at keeping Dasha around each time Kolya's stopped by their room. But she can see in Dasha's eyes that Dasha's ready to duck out at any moment. Dasha doesn't understand the problem: *Mashka, come*

*on! he's an amazing guy, and it's love!* There's no argument there:
Kolya writes poetry and plays the guitar, he's the life of the party
and a leader in his class, and the only reason girls don't hang on
him is that there aren't any girls in a romantic mood—*what can you
do with him, anyway? Eat ice cream or something?*—and they always
wish these types on someone else. Sooner or later, Masha will have
to say something to him and she really, really doesn't want to hurt
him. He should, in the end, figure it out himself. He doesn't figure
it out. When he says goodbye, he catches Masha's hand and kisses
it, and there's tenderness in those eyes half the size of his face, his
fingers tremble and blaze, and half his poems are getting despondent.

Toward New Year's, not long before vacation, the girls gather
in Masha and Dasha's room. After quietly drinking up two bottles
of wine and smoking by a little open window, the girls start loudly
discussing an issue: Should a girl that a young man has been pursuing
for a fairly long time (let's say he's given her flowers and gifts, and
paid for her at restaurants and clubs) settle her debts accordingly
or is this a situation where, as a holder of the opposing view put
things, *it's like a lottery for a man: you win, you're happy; you lose, well,
sorry, this isn't a store*. Masha is queasy from cheap plonk and her
classmates' cynicism, and she suddenly winces from the realization
that this exact same question is breaking into her life, too, with the
implacability of an annihilator (*it would be ridiculous not to yield*, A.A.
would have said, but Masha hasn't read Brodsky). It's not that she
doesn't like Kolya, that's not the issue at hand. But she feels like this
isn't her kind of storyline. She just can't imagine how she would,
hmm, have some fun with him. She firmly decides at that moment
that she'll tell Kolya tomorrow that he's very nice. But.

The next day (the last day before vacation), Masha remembers
her promise to herself and tensely searches for an excuse to break
it. She might have found one in the end, but toward evening (while
Dasha's still taking some test or other), a noticeably nervous Kolya
comes to their room and tells her, *I love you*. Masha holds back her

breath so she can tell him when she exhales, but her tongue gets stuck in her mouth: she understands that no matter what she might say now, everything will be, essentially, the same as what she's already heard from Roma, whom she just can't get out of her head. Masha's fingers catch in the bristly stubble of her hair and she is silent, completely silent. Kolya waits, then quietly says *excuse me*, and leaves. Masha feels like crying; in her memory, she's bringing back the state she was in when Dasha lathered her head here, in this room, and she feels like none of this would have happened if it hadn't been for that.

From that moment on—when Dasha was taking slimy red locks of hair from Masha's head and flinging them into a pail (gobs of thick foam plop on the floor), and Masha was observing Dasha (and herself) in a small oval mirror leaning against a table lamp, feeling cheery and despondent—there stretches, like in some cheesy comedy movie when you have to show the characters' travel on a map, a dotted line to wintry Köln, gleaming with Christmas lights, where Masha'd brought her newly edited *Huguenots* to a European youth film festival and where Roma caught her at the opening reception, and where they then, between screenings and workshops, stumbled for almost a week from *kneipe* to *kneipe* (in one of which she induced a stream of apologetic babble from Roma with a jibe: *Yevgenyev, you ought to be ashamed of yourself, pawing at me like this after everything that's…*) and then, finally, on the fifth day, Masha led him back to her room, where a string of red and green lights blinked in the window and it was obvious that what should have happened eight years ago was about to happen: after setting aside a glass of mineral water, he pulls her toward himself, kisses her, and pulls off her t-shirt. The moment lasts, Roma moves in her direction, and grasps the glass again; Masha, silent, squeezes her arms around her knees (she's sitting with her feet in the chair) and a spark of understanding slinks around in her head: it's not that he's shy of her but that he's afraid. Even if she were to tell him directly, he wouldn't believe that all she needs is his body—the hands, shoulders, and lips are the main thing—and that she didn't need Roma himself, his time, or his freedom. All she wanted was for him to embrace and undress her, and for her to undress him: all the rest—what he'd told her about in an empty smoking room when she'd come to his institute the third time, the next-to-last time, when he said he doesn't want to mislead her and say he loves her because he doesn't love her, and he doesn't want her to have any regrets later, *you're very beautiful, you'll find yourself another guy who'll love you so, so much and you'll thank me for it* (the falsity in his voice still makes Masha shiver now, and that concerns Roma: *are you cold? –Yes, I guess I'm frozen*)—all that is silly nonsense that floated into her life from some other completely different story (*it's like singing a different tune*, Masha jokes to herself, holding back a smile because Roma is already stretching his hand with the glass toward the little table).

And so, when what filled her nights with anxiety eight years ago (and seven years ago, and six years ago) is coming true in real life—Roma's attentive eyes approach and cross the border that separates what's someone else's from one's own, what's another person from myself—Masha catches his hand and presses it to her cheek, responding to his cautious kiss and then, before she focuses on the warmth of a body now common to them, a frightful abyss filled with despondence cracks open in front of her for a second and from that abyss there gleams a revelation that manages to jell before it fades into a formula devoid of meaning: *sex is for the young.*

Sex is a problem that has to be addressed. The girls surrounding Masha at school are up to their ears in sex, electrified by it. They talk, more often than not, about sex and these conversations are endless and, for all intents and purposes, innocent, though Masha has blushed more than once from the stupid details, and when she's had to shake her head in answer to the question *Masha, you still haven't?...*, the girls look patronizingly at Masha, offer advice, and then switch back to reports about clubs, dates, and phone calls;

classmates, students, cadets, teachers, any boy who's entered the field of vision becomes a topic for conversation and appraisal and, beyond that, the girls all close their eyes dreamily when discussion turns to A.A. (in the spring this also gives them an opportunity to whisper behind Masha's back that, you know, *still waters*). As she listens to these conversations, though, Masha's surprised to realize that the discussion isn't about actual sex, about sex in and of itself. This problem engrosses her and the sense that comes to her (and is resolved many years later, in a thought) is this: when scrutinizing sex in and of itself, if you maintain your honesty and set aside the temptation to explain sex as some thing that's manifested only through sex—pleasure, producing children, vanity, power, or business—then you have to admit that sex, in its essence, is youth.

(A culture where the primary sexual fantasy is a skinny, experienced adolescent girl and the main boogeyman is a pedophile is a neurotic culture and it is, like any neurotic, prone to sudden fits of aggression, so one needs to immediately protect oneself from accusations, both of using a readymade cultural model and producing child porno, thus: Masha is not a Lolita, since she was already seventeen at the point that same spring when A.A. dared undo the first button on her shirt in an empty parental apartment; he was only twenty-six himself; and beyond that, even more importantly, Masha's not Lolita because when she helped him undo the belt on her jeans, she was, after all, still a virgin.)

Masha watches the girls, listens to what they say, and is entranced by their youth. The reason she hunches over her desk by yellow lamplight in the evenings and draws women disfigured by old age (she goes to a nearby pharmacy and food store to snoop on them) isn't that she's susceptible to a flaw of early maturity, no, not at all, this is about something else: over a sheet of paper, with a pencil in her hands, she understands that youth can only be embraced mentally, as something that's already passed. It's then clear that sex is despondence over what hasn't and could not have come true:

touching bellies as the only possible way to share despondence with a neighbor.

Masha's eyes glaze over from despondence every now and then when she's with the chattery girls in her dorm room or in a classroom between lessons—and that despondence is joined firmly with a horror of unknown (so far) origin, a horror that flows like a cold rivulet along her back at night, when Dasha's already sleeping: it drags Masha out from under the blanket to her desk, where she attempts to deal with the shivering by drawing her female classmates. She gives lumpy, dark old-woman hands to greedy-eyed beauties, since she already has a knack for capturing their real appearance with her pencil, though she's still dissatisfied because something remains unsaid until finally one night (the wind is whistling through the gaps in the window frame and the window across from her reflects the lamplight) an old woman appears on the paper, chewing ice cream at a table in a café (Masha didn't lie: she's seen this woman and she was actually chewing with her empty gums), a spoon is in her mouth, and her lips are embracing it, but her eyes, which have rolled up toward the ceiling, are those of a schoolgirl. Dasha convulses with repugnance when she sees that drawing in the morning but Masha's heart skips a beat: everything's correct, she's managed to capture the horror.

Essentially, *Huguenots*, which Masha will bring to Köln for the festival so she can run into Roma, will be about that same thing—the impossible existence of youth—and the troupe she assembles for the picture, twenty-five boys and girls about to graduate from high school, was assembled not to prove that grand opera can be performed in a perky and contemporary way (that's just the inertia of the genre) but to bring youth itself into the picture and problematize it.

The decision to assemble nonprofessional actors—and adolescents at that—came about by chance, and it's generally acknowledged to be what made *Huguenots* not just a film adaptation but also a distinctive filmmaking phenomenon. Lelouch allegedly invented the light reflector only because he had a desperately small budget to shoot an advertisement that instead turned into the great *A Man and a Woman*. Initially, Masha had thought the most complicated aspect was to win a competition: La Société Parisienne des Amis de l'Opéra had suddenly grown concerned that "our pride and joy," Meyerbeer's supreme composition, had still never been adapted for screen and so they searched throughout Europe for a director, and, at the time, the fact that it was Masha who was chosen from hundreds of reviewed candidates had seemed like a miracle. Only many years later did people begin talking about how the choice had been obvious and how the spark of genius was already evident in the student work she'd filmed in Munich. If one steps back from fate's stern logic, in reality there were two reasons. In the first place, the budget didn't allow inviting a famous or even experienced director to make the picture, so they searched among beginners and even recent film-school graduates. And in the second place, one of the members of the society, an elderly film critic with a thin cigarette in his lips who wore a dark blue jacket that went almost to the knees, had taught a course in Munich that Masha attended, and he was simply in love with her. Masha didn't suspect a thing because she sincerely thought the critic was a homosexual, so when he suddenly called her during her final spring of school, and, after asking some moving questions (*what are you working on, do you have any housing problems,* and *what are you going to do after graduation*), said she should send him some new work as soon as she finished it (*are you sure it won't be longer than a month?*) and explained why, well, Masha hung up the phone, pounded her fist against the wall (startling her *Mitbewohnerin*, a quiet girl from Slovakia, so she jumped and spilled coffee on the blanket), and had no doubt that *the pansy believes in me, do you understand?*

Meanwhile, one thing didn't preclude another: not only did Monsieur Skinny Cigarette sincerely have faith in Masha as a director, but he seriously intended to lure her to his bed. The thought of having sex with that scholarly parrot staggered Masha so much that when he brought her to some café on Rue Monge (she had, literally, just been approved after all) and said very directly, after a bit of a preamble, that her gratitude could be expressed through some mutually enjoyable time-wasting at his place, which was, luckily, only a five-minute walk away, Masha was so surprised that she blurted out: *what the hell, I thought you...* but then checked herself and went on *that you knew I don't sleep with men.* A childish trick that would sound like a hurtful excuse in any other situation worked 100 percent here, apparently thanks to the energy of her natural surprise that monsieur turned out to be straight: the critic was fuming but "it's okay to be gay" turned out to be a stronger force and, as he mechanically buttoned up his jacket, he began babbling that he'd never imagined, that he respects her choice, and blah blah blah. It worked out that all Masha paid for the opportunity to make *Huguenots* was a persistent rumor that quickly appeared and accompanied her all her life: Maria Regina is a lesbian. The rumor didn't annoy her that much, although one time she happened to give an interview to the London magazine *Diva*, and explained, in answering a question on the topic, that in her opinion, homosexuality represented nothing so much as being in love with one's own sexual organs and that had always been alien to her, like any other form of fetishism. Understandably, the interview wasn't published, though it found its way to the Web nevertheless and the howl that the rainbow community raised in Europe got on Masha's nerves.

But that was all later. Back then, in September, after graduating, Masha discovered that winning the competition was only half the battle. It was impossible to film a historical staging on the 200,000 the Society had managed to hammer out of the ministry. When the producer explained to her about the limited budget, he simultaneously offered a way out of the situation: dress the characters in jackets, and, yes, overall minimalism, with a couple chairs in a studio, and then the savings on costumes, props, and location shooting would be huge. Masha promised to think it over and announced her decision two days later: she wouldn't save on costumes, she'd save on actors instead, by assembling schoolchildren, each of whom would set her back a hundred, rather than having to pay professionals a thousand each, perhaps more, per filming day. Pushing that idea through turned out to be nearly as complicated as winning the competition. Masha had to go for broke and threaten she wouldn't even work if they didn't allow her to film kids. The producer gave in, fearing the filming would be delayed again; a report on expenditures needed to be submitted by the end of the year.

*Huguenots* begins with a quotation: the kids pile out of a small school bus to the do-ti-la-la-ti-do overture—their long crooked bangs and groomed unisex faces distinguish them from Jewison's troupe—but their agile motions and the ardor in their eyes remain a privilege of youth, regardless of changes in hairstyle fashions. (Incidentally, it cost Masha great effort to gather a troupe of totally European faces in Paris and when one journalist reproached her after the premiere that there was not one single black person among the kids, that a blunder like that was unforgivable for a young director who'd come from another country and ought, first and foremost, to adopt European values, Masha had to dryly brush it off, making a wry face: *I made a film about France in the sixteenth century and, as far as I know, there weren't any black people here then.*)

After bursting into the theater, they sort through the costumes, the girls try on fake jewels, the boys grab swords and playfully poke each other with them, and the main character makes faces at his sweetheart; later, when the action itself begins, there is even a sense, too, that these were just school kids run wild and messing around after having suddenly made their way into a whole storehouse of prop treasures. Soon, that all changes drastically, though: Masha managed to make it so there truly was a gradual change in the kids' eyes, from playful to passionate, and the glued-on mustaches and beards seem to take root on their faces, their motions grow solemn, an authentic rage blazes in the main character's eyes when he's jealous, and at some point the viewer understands that he's watching a completely different movie, about vicious, bloody French history, and not some school kids who've broken loose. Toward the end, when the action's moving out of the theater spaces into a seething night street, it seems supremely natural that this is no longer a street in contemporary Paris, with buses and advertising banners, but an authentic street flooded with authentic blood during the St. Bartholomew's Day Massacre. In the last shot—of Saint-Bris, holding his daughter's corpse in his arms, with horror in his eyes—it's a completely adult person looking from the screen into the auditorium and he's already grasped that he's engrossed in a game where death turns out to be the one and only possible finale.

People don't mature, they just get old: that's exactly what the film is about, contrary to the critics who spotted in *Huguenots* a warning against religious conflict. It's simply that, at a certain moment, a person understands that the adult mask he's put on is rooted to his face for ever. There are things that are stronger than the person: that's the logic of how events develop. The hero couldn't not think that the heroine was someone else's lover, and that's exactly why a story that begins with a happy little feast can't help but end with a bloodbath. Becoming an adult should involve stopping and closing one's eyes, but that's practically impossible.

The success of *Huguenots* was fairly localized. Only after *Minus One* did Regina become the most important young European director. *Huguenots* was limited to professional circles when it came out. Masha won first prize in Köln, gave a few interviews—in *Filmfare*, *Premiere*, and *Empire*—read ecstatic notices about the film in those same magazines, and three or four producers jotted down her telephone number. Cinematic showings went poorly and Masha felt like something else was going on, even though her Munich teachers and classmates consoled her, saying an opera film couldn't possibly enjoy serious success because opera just isn't something the majority of people are capable of listening to for their own pleasure.

Masha flew to Petersburg four months after the Köln premiere. The reason for her trip wasn't just that she'd already been out of Russia for more than two years and not just that she'd flown out after Roma—a few words will need to be said about that, by the way—but also that she wanted to see A.A. She had a vague feeling she needed him as a sort of tuning fork, to check the current Masha—who had the film profession on the brain, with all its studios, producers, cameras, and festivals—against the Masha who, despite not having loved A.A. very seriously, had somehow actually experienced a few moments in her life with him that had, as she put it, *special meanings*: she was convinced that "verity" was a word that should never be pronounced aloud.

She arrived in a Petersburg that was dizzy with spring: short-skirted girls on Nevsky Prospect were nearly jumping out of their panties; slivers of leftover ice were floating in the Fontanka River as if it were a forgotten glass of whiskey; nails were being removed from the wooden winter coffins for the statues in the Summer Garden; drunken students on Mokhovaya Street were singing a tongue-twister about how *by the burbling river bank we bumblingly bagged a burbot*; and the cats in the courtyard on Pestel Street followed Masha with a squinting gaze.

A.A. didn't live on Pestel Street anymore, though. A young woman with a child in her arms opened the door for Masha, and the child instantly pouted when he saw the unfamiliar lady: *Ilyusha, come on, she's a nice lady*. The young woman didn't know who A.A. was. His mobile wasn't answering and the only option left for Masha was to call the number at the apartment where he'd lived before their unlikely summer. When Masha got back to the hotel, she lounged around on the made bed for a long time, smoked, and flipped the TV channels; at first she didn't completely understand why it was so tricky for her to dial that number, though she grasped it—well, more likely, honestly admitted it to herself—when she finally pulled the phone toward her pillow, dialed it, and heard *yes* pronounced in a voice she'd heard only once in her life. Masha didn't think much about A.A.'s wife but it was impossible not to think about her at all, if only because those same girls who'd been smoking on the sly by the little windows in their dorm rooms, enjoying bragging to each other about their boys, were the very same girls who talked later with the very same enjoyment at annual class reunions: some one of them would always retell the story to Masha, about how Masha had *stolen* A.A.'s wife and that it was *unseemly*. Who the hell knew why—either Masha's voice faltered in some particular way or Elizaveta (what was her patronymic, anyway?) had been awaiting this call for a long time and now guessed flawlessly—but she knew who was calling and Masha heard that confirmed in how she said, *hold on, I'll take a look*, how carefully she set the receiver on the table, jabbed at the buttons on her mobile and whispered *oh, that little bitch* through her teeth, and then dictated ten digits, clearly articulating. Her upbringing wouldn't allow her to just say "No," but as she dictated, it was audible in her voice (this was obviously calculated) how intensely she hated this girl who—and perhaps Masha had now discovered this herself for the first time—had destroyed her family.

The moment Masha sets down the phone, mechanically stretches for yet another cigarette, understands she doesn't really want to smoke at all, and dully gazes at the figures she's scribbled on the hotel napkin, all as she turns the cigarette in her fingers (fine crumbs of tobacco sprinkle on the nightstand)… this still isn't a realization of the hidden principle of how the guilt-mechanism works but, more likely, a presaging of that realization. Masha's conversation with an unknown woman who's neither kith nor kin leads her into a slow, cautious pensiveness and she's even afraid to move abruptly—it's like how a fisherman sits motionless over a bobber even though the fish, down in the cold water, doesn't care one way or another.

A.A. lives in his parents' apartment now: they died a year ago, one right after the other (his engineer father, his proofreader mother, he from cancer, she from life's emptiness). At the time, A.A. didn't want to think at all that this happened with a great degree of "apropos" but that's how it was, for all intents and purposes, because his friend and owner of the apartment on Pestel Street came back from France for a couple months, expressly to sell the apartment, and A.A. had nowhere to go: he crashed with friends for a while and even rented some tiny little room on the Petrograd Side, but after his mother's death, he felt a relief he tried not to admit, even to himself, when he moved to 3-ya Linia Street, into their now empty two-room apartment full of things—a German china service received in a trade from a major they didn't know well, a radio set with a wooden panel and huge plastic buttons, a dirty-brown floor lamp, a small bust of Tchaikovsky, and a full set of Maxim Gorky's writings in yellow dust jackets—that had served mostly as anchors holding his too-old parents in the era of their youth but now, after the command post had already been completely handed over, the items had begun to resemble the debris of an existential shipwreck that had been thrown into immediate being (this particular shipwreck, after all, struck not only the Soviet Union itself but also the identity of its crew).

A.A. tossed everything in the trash, not because the things were old but for the exact opposite reason. He actually felt a tenderness for old things but was now trying to remove all tenderness from within himself, this after Masha had begun distancing herself from him in the autumn, in her second year of college, throwing herself headfirst into her work—she didn't even always come back to Pestel Street to spend the night now—and the rare penetrating looks, the ones he was still catching on himself during the summer, had disappeared completely; she hadn't broken up with him, no, she'd just inconspicuously disappeared, evaporated, just as water spilled on the floor evaporates (a few of Masha's t-shirts and the Pushkin he'd given her remained), so another year later, after she'd managed to pound the fateful grant out of them and was getting ready for the Munich HFF, she set a date with him in some foolish café on Liteiny Prospect just before her departure and told him there, uncertainly and obviously out of a sense of duty, that she'd miss him (and she herself winced from the obvious unsustainability of that formulation), A.A. couldn't be surprised about that and he had no right to anything except to say, just as falsely, stupidly stretching his lips, *well, do write, or something*, and so then the pain he felt after that (he sensed it like a vacuum in his chest—it couldn't be filled with either cigarette smoke or vodka, and relief set in only when he wept, sitting on the edge of the old enameled bathtub, his face buried in a towel) was a pain that he considered the otherness of the tenderness he'd felt toward Masha, and since it was pretty impossible to amputate only that from his soul, he decided to fight tenderness in general (tenderness for old things was a special case), since A.A. considered it, not without a certain basis, the First Cause of all his problems. His campaign was thoroughly quixotic but to throw oneself on the windmills of fate, while dressed in an armor of words that dully knock against one other, is just as natural for a person as abusing metaphors is for a writer.

Truth be told, the A.A. Masha saw on the threshold of the apartment on 3-ya Linia (she'd insisted on coming right to his house, she didn't feel like slipping, again, into the false tone that's obligatory in public eating places) looked like his reflection in a dusty mirror. His eyes, which had once driven girls crazy because they made it obvious that this person managed to strike a spark of joy from the world in every moment of his life… well, even though those eyes were tired and distrustful, and Masha discerned, through a right that belonged to her alone, that *everything's the same*, as if he'd figured in advance that nothing good would come of Masha's visit but his fatal weakness wouldn't let him tell her where to go.

No, no, A.A. didn't look like some unhappy Pierrot: he had healthy facial color, his shirt fit him with the same old offhand pride, and the apartment on 3-ya Linia was ready at any moment to host any female student enraptured by his lectures (after defending his dissertation, he'd been teaching only at the university). They showed up here often: they drank wine, smoked, admired photographs on the wall, twirled CDs in their hands, examined book spines on the shelf with tilted heads and then enigmatically smiled when A.A. touched their arched necks with his lips, while they peered with one eye at the cabinet's glass door for a reflection. His desk was piled to half its height with books and magazines, and a little light blinked on a snoozing laptop; A.A.'s authority was based not only on his ability to speak and wear a shirt but also on the insane volume of work he did. As he brewed tea in the kitchen, Masha looked through papers heaped up on the windowsill and discovered his surname in the indexes of several academic anthologies and glossy journals: *I'm broadening my genre range*, said A.A., when he noticed she was holding one of the publications. Masha was glad when she saw her disappearance hadn't wrecked his life. Even so, when she caught his glance on her, she guessed it betrayed hurt camouflaged as benevolent indifference.

The meaning of that hurt would remain unverbalized between them forever, but they didn't need it anyway. As Masha peers at how neatly A.A. pours the tea and listens to his unnecessary explanations about the apartment and about his dissertation, and then as she answers his questions (she bragged about *Huguenots*—nobody had heard about it yet in Russia), she suddenly understands distinctly, as some kind of cold feeling arches her spine: after her disappearance, A.A. had needed to admit to himself that all she'd done that summer was plug up a hole in her own heart with his help. She wanted more than anything to hide that fact from him—both then and now—because he had never really been just a man for her, like, for example, the Munich boy who'd smilingly told her when he found out she was leaving, *okay, we never promised each other anything*. It's true she hadn't loved A.A., but it was also true that if some celestial

computer had laid out cards for her with pictures of the men she'd
met at some time or other and then asked whom she'd choose
to love, Masha would've clicked on his icon without stopping to
reflect. Although she listened with her mouth agape when A.A.
spoke, enraptured by his intelligence and surprising ability to live
so that anything foul remained external, even so, she never felt a
special warmth in her palms when he took her hand and her head
didn't spin when he kissed her.

They drink tea late into the night then go to the store for wine,
chain-smoke, and tell each other rumors about Masha's former
classmates. A.A. decides to forget about the article he should be
finishing for tomorrow and Masha decides to forget about the hotel;
the awkwardness that was tangible at the first moment has already
dissolved in their empty chatter. Toward morning, A.A. makes a
bed for Masha on the living-room sofa and goes to bed himself in
the bedroom, and that's not a formality: Masha wouldn't have pretended to be sleeping if he'd come to her, complaining *I just can't
get to sleep*, in the light of the sun beginning to blaze over the Neva,
but he didn't come, whether he really did want to sleep or simply
didn't want to appear impolite.

Squinting (she'd long since grown unaccustomed to going to
sleep with the sun shining), Masha smiles, barely perceptibly, pressing
her knees to her chest: it's doubtful A.A. remembers, but it was on
this very day, the fourth of May, eight years ago, that she lost her
virginity here, in this apartment.

And it was like this. In the spring, it somehow naturally became
established that Masha walked out of the school at the same time as
A.A. But one time she ran into him by the Smolenka River; she was
taking a walk after classes and he was walking to Maly Prospect to
catch a bus. This was only a chance meeting that first time: every
day after that she went there specially, where the old linden's gnarled
trunk hung over the path, and if he knew her classes weren't over,
he'd find something to do to keep him at school. A week later, he

took her hand and didn't let go after he helped her jump over a puddle. They walked along, holding hands, Masha saw a fir tree in the distance, and for some reason it popped into her head that he'd stop and kiss her by that tree. And truly, the closer they came to the tree she'd made the wish on, the slower their stride, but right by the tree, when it was already clear exactly what was about to happen, Masha and A.A. heard a cheerful-sounding commotion and a group of boys came around the bend (A.A. pulled his hand away nervously): out of all the boys (*Hello, Alexei Alexeyevich*), only Kolya noticed anything, and his glance was both reproachful and surprised.

A.A. found no grounds to take her hand again. Masha was surprised at his timidity, and he scolded himself later even as he sat on the bus, squinting at the dusty glass: *like a little boy, like a schoolboy, like it's kindergarten*, but when he was with Masha he felt something that was stronger than himself, the world plunged into some sort of mirage, and he couldn't do anything in that mirage but follow events as they developed.

The next day, Masha stopped at the exact same puddle, which, very conveniently, hadn't dried up yet, and herself offered him her hand. They burst out laughing and this time when they neared the fir tree, A.A. stopped, turned Masha toward himself, looked into her eyes for a long time, stroked her check, and kissed her. Essentially, it's not at all important if he said he loved her because if he did say it, *I love you, Masha*, it must have sounded very funny and official because the teachers and students at the school used the formal "you" when addressing each other; if he didn't say it, well, Masha heard it anyway and stretched toward him with another kiss when she heard it, so she wouldn't have to answer, but also because kissing was good.

All of April went by: their outings grew longer, they were already walking in the other direction on Smolenka, toward the Gulf of Finland, birds were singing and leaves were hatching on the trees, a breeze from the gulf blew through Masha's slightly grown-out hair; they walked slowly, often stopping, A.A. embraced Masha and pressed her light body to himself, looking at her attentively as if he wanted to assure himself she really was in his arms; they sat on the stone steps by the Pribaltiskaya Hotel (children roller-skated on the square, stretching their heads to the sky), and when it rained they hid in building archways or in a café on Sredny Prospect, drinking coffee without unclasping their hands; A.A. might amuse Masha with lore from his profession (*all people are brined-hearted*) or suddenly begin speaking in complete earnestness about Blok, and Masha would look into his eyes; at moments like those, A.A. thought everything around him was rolling off somewhere sideways; and that's how all of April passed until one day they ended up at 3-ya Linia after walking around nearly the entire island and A.A. said, incidentally, that his parents lived here, though they weren't home now, they'd gone to the dacha. Jumbling his words, he immediately started talking about something else, and Masha squeezed his arm and pointed at the front door with her free hand: *here? Do you have the keys?* (And, yes, of course they were already speaking to each other using the informal "you.")

As he was unlacing his shoes in the apartment, A.A. said he'd make some tea now and that his mother had probably stashed away some cookies or wafer cake somewhere, he just had to take a look, but he'd barely stood up straight before Masha, who'd already thrown off her sneakers, pulled him toward herself. He kissed her behind the ear, stroked her shoulders, touched her breasts through the fabric of her shirt and then twisted the button by her neck; Masha flung his jacket, and they went in the living room, where A.A. struggled with her belt, which she finally undid herself, and then, lying alongside her on the sofa, A.A. kept himself from weeping by drawing his fingers down from her closed eyes, along her shoulders, breasts, and belly, and the hairs on her groin were just as long as the ones on her head. Masha lay with her eyes closed, focused on a pain that abated, throbbing.

# THE PHENOMENOLOGY OF GUILT

Even so, it couldn't have not happened, simply because it can't not happen when two people who find each other attractive are left alone in an empty apartment. After waking up, A.A. went out for fresh baguettes, came back, made coffee, and woke up Masha. He clattered cups around in the kitchen while Masha was in the shower, got a terry-cloth robe out of the closet for her (*it doesn't exactly look like it's gathering dust. –Is that supposed to be a compliment? –Whatever you prefer*), poured her coffee, made a sandwich, and straightened the flap of the robe on Masha's knee when she sat on a stool and crossed her legs. Masha was free to interpret that gesture—as either friendly caretaking or a low-key advance—and touched his hand after thinking for a minute: *pass the sugar, please*. This game—which was all the more endearing because both participants already knew their way around the rules so well—ended in the living room on the sofa, where A.A. hadn't yet had a chance to gather up the sheet, blanket, and pillow. Masha lay on A.A.'s chest, he stroked her back, gazed at her profile, and cursed himself for not having kept himself in check.

The male consciousness is susceptible to attributing motivations to the female consciousness that are, in fact, typically male. Masha had decided on that reciprocal gesture not at all because she'd felt like demonstrating something or convincing herself of something. The lazy, sunny morning had to end that exact way, and she simply saw no grounds for depriving herself of that storyline. It's doubtful she herself could have intelligibly answered the question about why she needed this sex. At least not before the moment she was riding the train home, bumping her nose against a window that was darkening, not just with each hour but with each kilometer, and rewinding in her head the four days she'd spent in Petersburg.

Her neighbors are sleeping on their bunks, a spoon is jingling in a glass, and Masha regrets she's never learned to drink on trains. She winds some hair around her finger, winces, and shakes her head: nothing has worked out. In Munich she'd thought all she'd have to do to return to her feeling of a completely seamless world filled with meaning was to return to Petersburg, see A.A., and take a stroll around Kolomna. To that end, she'd gathered up her things at the hotel and prevailed on A.A. to cancel his classes at the university on Monday so they could live a few days the way things had been seven years ago: go for walks, drink wine, and make love. That's why it was important to kiss him again and feel his weight on her thighs: this was a crucial element of the mosaic of the past. Though the spell didn't work, despite performing all the rituals and uttering all the formulas. Everything was the same—the water splashing and the crimson sun—but it remained a mystery how the former Masha had managed to hear music in that world. Sunday was ebbing when she and A.A. were sitting on the steps of the Manege and he was holding her hand, smoking, and peering at the embankment by St. Isaac's Cathedral, twinkling with the sparks of camera flashes, when Masha pressed up against him and said, so that it sounded like a thought inadvertently pronounced and not requiring an answer: *how is it that I was so happy back then?*

A.A. didn't answer right away. He finished smoking, put out the cigarette, found her other hand with his freed-up hand, and said, as if to ask his own question rather than answer hers: *what do you need happiness for? So it's something like a bank account where there's always money. There's no such thing as happiness, that's all just stupidity. Happiness happens, and that's that. You could sit here and wait for it but it'll be over there* (A.A. waved his hand in the direction of the Senate). *And then it's just a flash, all it leaves is a sharp pain in your eyes. Maybe you'll stay a little longer?* Masha shook her head. *Well that's the right thing to do, it won't get any better.* A.A. got up and began pulling Masha further into the silvery darkness of the lines of the streets.

Masha is already almost sleeping, her head slips from her hand when the train goes over seams in the rails, and the last several days fade in her consciousness like the trace of her breath on the glass, outside which, in the harsh darkness of the Pskov forest, there are pictures developing of the Petersburg where she lived with A.A. seven years ago, but it's a Petersburg that will always remain that way for Masha, only that way.

For Masha, Petersburg—a quiet and dark city that you can make the rounds of on foot, if you don't count the outskirts where people went home to sleep, which inspire horror and degrade human dignity—became a genuine proving ground for happiness, a city where something could happen at any second so the world's cogs suddenly start turning harmoniously, strings stretch, and the world resounds with delicate music. Beyond that, it turns out to be totally unimportant what, exactly, you do at that moment: you can peep through the open doors of front entrances at dust swirling in wide staircases; you can sniff the scents of dill at Sennaya Square and hemp at Malaya Sadovaya; you can makes guesses about the remains of houses destroyed during the blockade, read inscriptions on the padlocks hitched to the fence on the bridge by the Institute of Applied Astronomy (*Kitty+Cholera*), peer at the setting sun shining through the gallery of the palace in Pavlovsk, kiss on the overpass at the abandoned taxi lot, step over daddy-long-legs walking along the night streets, examine maple leaves rotting in clayey puddles, nod off at the edge of the pond on Yelagin Island, kick big acorns the size of quail eggs, feed bread rolls out of your hand to swans that look like white ocean-liners, open champagne at five in the morning on Nevsky, get soaked to the skin in warm rain as you make your way along Palace Bridge to Vasilyevsky Island, walk around pricing smelts, squint at the sun setting on Gorokhovaya Street by the river, be blinded by the gold and water at Peterhof, eavesdrop on drunks' conversations under the blue spruces by the Dobrolyubov monument (*I'm a monument not made by human hands, my path will not be overgrown*), look askance at fragments of aluminum clouds barreling right overhead, breathe in an October breeze from the Neva, crunch grass sugared with frost on November 1, use your foot to stir up the delicate skin on top of a puddle that preserves the amber-colored roughness of larch, fling dry and gleaming snow at the sun, stuff yourself with fried dough on Zhelyabova Street, get drunk on the smell of bread that floats over the nocturnal Petrograd Side of the city, knead snow-white sorbet under your feet, and suddenly hear the triumphant chirping of hundreds of birds that aren't even visible.

As she's falling asleep, Masha runs through these possibilities as nothing more than possibilities from her memory. What was once the visible side of verity has now become just a picture, like when a person looking at a photographed sunset wonders how he could have discerned God in a pile of orange clouds.

A guilty feeling is the last jab of reality before Masha is completely blanketed by a cloudy stream of sleep that's clattering its wheels along the rails: Masha's been in Russia for five days already but Roma's sure she's still in Munich. This small deception (particularly small because they haven't yet managed to tie each other down with promises) is the first link in a chain they'll tirelessly forge over many years to come. Masha wouldn't have been able to explain to Roma, who was breathing hotly into the phone and saying *forget about those Herr German guys, come here right away*, why she'd needed those several days in Petersburg without him. On the contrary, she could have told him she was going to see her parents—what's surprising about that?—but, in the first place, she'd only definitively made up her mind about this trip when she was spending her last day with A.A. and, in the second place, she didn't want anybody at all to know she was going home.

Masha didn't tell even her parents she was on the way. That she'd forgotten their telephone number or hadn't had time in all the confusion—they were, of course, just excuses. The main reason was that Masha was simply afraid to call. Masha had dialed her home phone number only a few times during the four years she'd spent in Germany. At the end of each conversation, she'd promised her mother she'd call more often, and for several months before the next call, she'd be tortured by remorse and only pick up the phone again when the torture became unbearable. Her mother tried to tell her each time about how she and Masha's father were doing. And though Masha always managed to lead the conversation toward a non-committal, general tone, it was clear even without details that her mother and father were not doing well at all. They were aging rapidly, her father had hit the bottle, her mother was losing her mind. Meanwhile, Masha didn't want to know anything about it: she had a vague feeling that if she focused seriously on this story, she'd have to admit, in the first place, her own guilt in it, and, in the second place, the impossibility of correcting anything. A call with the words "I'm on my way, the nine o'clock, second carriage" would have been, on some level, a promise that Masha couldn't make, as if she were prepared to take part in the horror blanketing her parents' life.

In the morning, a woman conductor pushes at Masha's shoulder (at that moment in her interrupted dream, Masha's shoulder is knocking against the side of a ship as she surfaces from cold saltwater: it truly is horribly cold in the train carriage), then Masha smokes for ten minutes in the empty, frozen vestibule until she feels nauseous. She gazes out the window and recognizes everything—the brook where she used to swim and fell through the ice one time in the winter; the pine trees by the railroad bed that are *one-two-three-four*, exactly four, nothing at all has changed; the beaten-up railroad crossing; houses where she knows who lives in every other one—and the sweetness of returning to her childhood blends with her feeling of loathing for everything she recognizes. The platform isn't long enough for the whole train, so Masha jumps right to the ground from the third step; fog is settling on the grass and trees around her. A frenzied bird-shriek descends on Masha after the wagons' loud shuddering quietens.

Then Masha boards an empty bus permeated with the smell of gasoline. It's not completely empty: the bus has a driver, a vaguely familiar male face plowed with wrinkles, and the smell of the cigarette dancing in the corner of his mouth makes Masha's head spin. Eyes squinting from the rising sun outside the windshield get distracted from the road and look in the mirror at Masha: *Pashka's daughter, right?* Masha nods. *Wouldn't recognize you!* Masha sits in a closer seat: *what? –Wouldn't recognize you, I said, you've changed!* The driver smiles, knocking ash out the window, and Masha smiles back, understanding that what he said means "you haven't changed a bit" because how would he have recognized her otherwise?

Uncle Tolya (she remembered the driver's name) also asks what people ask kids who've left *for the city*—graduated? working? married?—and enjoys shouting over the roaring engine on the hills to tell her about *my daughter*: distance learning, renting a room, working in a barbershop (there haven't been barbershops *in the city* for a long time but they're still here), go see her, she'll cut your hair. When there's just one stop left before her house, Masha decides to ask how her father's doing. Uncle Tolya holds the wheel with his elbows, pokes yet another cigarette into his mouth and lights it, swears at a pothole, grabs the wheel with fingers that broaden toward the nails, and spits out a shred of tobacco. *He's okay, what else can he do?* and snaps a wide fingernail against his neck under his chin to clarify that, yes, indeed, he means drinking.

Masha holds out money for Uncle Tolya and he waves her away (*next time*) and explains to Masha in parting, before she jumps down on the concrete slab covered with sand that is the bus stop, where the barbershop is.

Everything remembered from childhood is big. The bulging optics of memory have always concerned Masha and she's wanted, several times, to write a screenplay for a film about her childhood into which she could transfer: a fence gate that has to be slightly pulled out of the ground so it can be closed with a rusty hook, hops clinging to gazebo posts, the sun winking through foliage, a kitchen garden stretching to the very horizon, and a huge shed where there's a mysterious scent of wormwood, and sand instead of a floor, but Masha gets stuck every time she thinks about how the heroine, who's returning to the very same time-worn things, opens the door into the house, and sees... what? Masha imagines some sort of corpse in that storyline: a heroine with an indistinct face should have seen a body swinging under the ceiling, maybe her mother, maybe her father. In the end, though, it became obvious that this is crummy generalization because the only thing that could become a true generalization—a real, serious storyline—is what Masha has actually seen, and as Masha was entering the yard through the open gate in the fence, she saw her father lying in a dank morning shadow on the front steps, with his back to the door.

From the hands placed under the head, from the knees pulled up to the belly, and from the main thing—the suffocating sour smell around him—Masha knows her father is sleeping. She sits down on the bottom stair and lights a cigarette. A minute later her father's nostrils twitch from the smell of the tobacco, he wakes up, and looks at Masha (*hi, Papa*, she says to ease his search for words). He then sits up, reeling, hides his face in his hands (there are hematomas on three of his knuckles), drawls out *Masha, how...*, gets confused, and fidgets. Masha has to stand up and follow him back to the gate even though he turns his back to her, mutters something in a whisper

about her mother, that something's bugging her, and waves his
hand to say, let's go, let's go.

He speaks louder and more distinctly on the street, about twenty
paces from the house, and he's already thought something up: he
came back late, Masha's mother had already gone to bed, and he
didn't want to wake her up, she doesn't really sleep very well these
days, and her health's not so good, and he repeats several times that
she's a saintly woman. They walk further and the more her father
gets confused in what he says about health, sleep, and the saintly
woman, the more often his speech is interrupted by referencing the
store, and then, when they finally get to the corner, he's preoccupied
only with the time: what time it is. Masha suddenly understands this
is a question, gets out her telephone, and tells him. *Ah, it's already
open*. Her father takes a drawn-out look in the direction of a plastic
door with the large red figures "9:00–22:00" and shuffles off further,
still hiding his face the same way.

Masha has already figured out everything but she can't imagine
how she's going to say it: "Papa, maybe you need a drink?" or "Papa,
maybe you should get treatment" or something else. She feels a
woozy, dull weakness, stops, plunges a heavy hand that's instantly
grown old into her pocket, and simply (*Pa-pa*) gets out her wallet.
Her father looks at her sideways and from the way he takes the
hundred rubles she's pulled out of her wallet, it's becoming obvious
she's arrived on time, too: if she'd showed up in another year or
two (contrary to a promise she hasn't yet made), he wouldn't have
been so timid about the money anymore, and his whole body would
have shrunken when he'd have said, ingratiatingly and intentionally
loudly, "Give your daddy something for a little drink, sweetheart."

After they've settled on a huge slab of pine in the liquidy shadow
of a birch tree that looks pale-green against the sky, her father swallows the vodka a little at a time and tells Masha the news. Masha
sits down beside him to listen. The news is what she'll have to listen
to all day. Later, her mother will tell her again, in detail, the same

things her father will tell her—this will be after her father's turned a little rosy and suddenly remembered (*what, you mean she really doesn't know?*), dragged Masha home by the hand, and pushed her forward a little in the doorway: *Mother, greet your daughter!*—and her mother, who's withered and bent beyond her years, will be overjoyed to the point of tears, though the joy won't keep her from raising her voice at Masha's father, making Masha's face convulse: *you could at least be ashamed around your daughter* (Masha's father smiles stupidly).

All morning, Masha's mother will fix a celebratory lunch—beet-and-herring salad, crab-stick salad (*if you'd warned me, I'd've made jellied meat*), roast chicken, and potatoes—and during that time, Masha will learn that the neighbor girl went for a walk on the railroad ties and lost her legs, that the nondrinking son of some woman or other suddenly drank some vodka he'd bought on the corner one night and died, that some girl was pushed under a car by her boyfriend (*they say she was pregnant*), and Masha's back starts sweating from it all so she lies down on the sofa and closes her eyes—*you take a nap, take a nap*—and in her doze, her mother's muttering blends with sounds of the boiling of water, the sizzling of a skillet, the knocking of a knife on a board. Within the combination of these sounds, Masha hears a rhythm that commands the fate of people living here—*Volkov, your classmate, remember him? He got*—from the knives, motorcycles, and cut off legs—*married in the winter, to Tanya, from house number 7, she's fifteen years older*—to the small bottle of vodka at 9:00.

Masha's father is cleaned up and combed at lunch, he even looks younger in his ironed shirt with the big pink lilies (Masha remembers it's for special occasions), and he's allowed to have a drink; Masha's mother puts the bottle away in the refrigerator after pouring him a shot because otherwise he'll reach for the next one himself. Even so, Masha's mother has to bring her father to the bedroom in the middle of lunch, undress him there, and cover him with a blanket. When she comes back, Masha's mother puts her elbows on the table along the sides of the plate with the cooled chicken, hides her face in her hands, and starts crying. The little gray ponytail she's started pulling her hair into shakes lightly.

Out of everything her mother could have told Masha, there's nothing she wouldn't already know—that her father drinks, that he's driving her mother crazy, that she just doesn't know what to do, it's impossible, and she's embarrassed around the neighbors—and then, after talking about Masha's father, she imperceptibly skips to her own childhood, to her grandmother, to her brother, but when Masha asks herself why her mother's telling her things she must already know (and of course her mother knows this), Masha suddenly understands that, for the most part, she doesn't have a mother.

Masha's mother fixes her gaze on a cold, bitten-into chicken leg as she pages through her memory in search of the moment when her life's engine suddenly got stuck in dirty snow on the side of the road and an unfathomable force dragged her to the exact place she didn't want to land for anything in the world (she has to keep pushing away—further and further—the moment after which, as is now already clear, everything could have been only that way, and no other way). This search has become the primary content of her everyday life in recent years, so her speech is unemotional, like an actor's "dry run."

It would have been impossible to imagine that the little girl wandering to the bus stop to ride to school (the very same city, and the very same schedule for the bus, 7:30 in the morning), that she, this little girl in rubber boots (there's a change of shoes in her bag) and a coat mended under the arm, who takes a piece of bread out of her pocket to give to a dog that's waiting for her and ruffles the dog on the ears with her free hand, that she, this little girl, will end her life as an old lady thrown off course and with an old man drinking himself to death. In that little girl's eyes (the dog's rough and hot tongue tickles her hands and she says, in a low voice, *eat, eat, Matilda* and squints with one eye, on the side where a dry sunny warmth is pushing through the cold air) and in the gleam of her full, licked lips and the motion of her narrow hand there's a careless happiness that her mother, if she could have seen this scene, would have recognized as her own happiness.

The structure of happiness is as simple as round *bliny* and as insoluble as squaring a circle. After Masha's grandfather's death, the woman who'd come here at one time with her barely familiar husband and birthed first a boy and then Masha's mother would lie at night on cold sheets trying to grope around in her own internal organs for the death that had settled there, remembering as she did how happy she'd been then, though she could never really remember anything more substantial than the jostling truck and the light of the sun. Everything that had happened to her since was—if happiness isn't dumbed down to "simple human happiness"—a dull ache. And that was what the old woman squinting her eyes was attempting to banish—now, right in front of her daughter's eyes—from an imagination exhausted by insomnia because that same little girl who in the mornings hid a piece of bread in her pocket for Matilda and went to school spent her evenings tossing and turning in bed, pressing her ears so she wouldn't hear her mother's howling and her father's long silences and then, finally, his explosion into a cursing shout, a chair clattering across a floor, and her mother screeching; and only when things quieted down would she toss off the blanket and tiptoe her way toward her parents' room, where she would see her mother through the crack in the door, sitting like a sack on the floor under the icons.

The gold on the icons shone with crimson, and the Virgin Mary and Christ, with pursed lips and a blue sphere on his palm, were silent: later, her brother would die under those same icons after burning up most of his stomach because he'd incautiously poured methylated spirits instead of potable alcohol into himself at work. Two years of inhuman pain, malice, and envy killed the 30-year-old guy and withered his mother to the bone; the surfaces of the icons managed to go black with soot during that time. Masha's mother always hid her eyes when she approached her brother's bed, and when he caught her hand—*tell me about school*—she'd mumble about grades and homework but, of course, that wasn't at all what he wanted to hear, there wasn't a word about the boy in the tenth grade who had such a voice that when she sat next to him on a bench the vibration of the boards reverberated in her belly or a word about her girlfriend who was teaching her to kiss: she said each time that she had a ton of homework and as soon as her brother finally let go of her hand, she'd go back to her room to flip through her girlfriend's notebooks that contained secrets whose contents cannot be told.

It's only one step from the princess in the ball gown that the girl toils over in her notebook (*draw your favorite drawing*) and from the yearning in her breast that she mistakenly ascribes to inspiration and causes her to write, line after line, iambs about fallen leaves and birds that fly away: from all that, it's merely one step until the night when Pasha presses his hand to her back and, when all is said and done, until the day when her mother will frantically adjust the gathers on a wedding dress bought from the neighbors and then aunts and uncles, cheeks flushed, will extend their puckered lips toward her: *you're so beautiful today!* Those same aunts and uncles will later fill the house with old things—crib, swaddling cloths, undershirts, toys, a little bathtub—and fix them up with jobs, and then they'll have to lie to the relatives later that *everything's good with us, look, we bought wallpaper*. At some point, it becomes clear that there'd never been a single chance that anything could have happened differently and so, after telling her daughter about her father who drank, but only occasionally, and hardly ever disappeared at night (*I should have already been a little stricter then but I thought he was sowing his wild oats*), Masha's mother is doing all this because she would actually like to talk about Matilda and the feeling of the dog's hot breath on her palm and about how her brother squeezed her hand after the doctor left (*what did he say, did you hear?*) and about her mother who'd whacked her on the cheeks the third day after her son's death, picking on her over the candy she'd eaten… though she lacks the words for all that.

Behind the standard formulas that help archive an entire life into a half-hour story (*and then we needed money when you started school*), Masha hears a thousand knifes knocking on a thousand boards, where tons of boiled potatoes are finely diced each time someone has to be buried, born, or given away in marriage. That steady knocking entrances Masha: as she gazes at her mother, who's already suggesting that Masha eat the rest of the chicken because she doesn't want more (*I'll heat it up, huh?*), she discovers a zone of total loneliness where a person's horror in the presence of life cannot be shared with anyone, where it's impossible to help anyone, despite all willingness, where kinship's bonds lose their binding power, and the words "mother" and "father" become only designations for one's origin. Her mother, who's now pouring tea and muttering *oh, what am I doing here, forgive me*, will—Masha understands (though she answers *what do you mean, everything's fine*)—finish out her life with the very same two or three pictures in her head and with the very same perplexity about "how did this all happen?" and there isn't a single person in the whole world who could have forgiven the poor little girl. And so when Masha's father will come home the next day and lean his shoulder against the coat rack, the coat rack will fall along with her father, her mother will shout at him, Masha will stand in the hallway, attempting to at least unstiffen her legs so she can go into the room, her father will crawl forward on all fours (*I'm sorry, I'll fix it*) and then plop his forehead on to the floor under Masha's feet (*Mashenka, forgive me! Will you forgive me?*) but she won't be able to say anything to him. And when her mother will start putting Masha's father to bed, his listless rehashing, *Mashenka, c'mon, tell me!* will carry from under the door, and Masha will suddenly begin to feel a horrifying, inhuman hatred both for her father and for a mechanism she'll discover that will become the point of departure for beginning her work on *Minus One*.

Masha breaks away and leaves for Petersburg the next day, giving her father an excuse to get loaded again legitimately and her mother the opportunity to grip Masha's hands and beg her in a breaking voice to visit more often (*you're back now, right? From Germany, I mean?*). But it's already clear even without her mother's hints that it's Masha's fault that her life has twisted like a Möbius strip: an ant striding along an endless field of opportunities ends up in the same place it began its journey whether it wants to or not (mathematicians call the four-dimensional version of this model the Klein bottle, and yes, the bottle sounds like an especially illustrative metaphor in Russian). And the occasion for that guilt is not in Masha getting on a train for Leningrad after enduring her mother's tears but in the serial number that was assigned to a nameless little purplish blob screaming out of fear, so as not to confuse, just in case, whose baby is where. That guilt can't be atoned for by returning, if only because moving in any direction is possible only in three dimensions (yes, the speed of memory is, in that sense, close to the speed of light). And this isn't the sort of bill that can be paid in cash, either, though millions of children do just that and Masha will, of course, send her mother money, too. That this guilt is inescapable is a structural peculiarity of the world in which man happens to live. And if the fastenings that hold the world together—guilty feelings and hurt, which are the exact same bolts, just with opposite threads—were to weaken suddenly, then a cold, powerful wave of chaos would surge over all of human society just like the waters of the Yenisei River turned the Sayano–Shushenskaya Hydroelectric Plant's multi-ton turbines into scrap metal.

At the same moment Masha's legs went numb from the premonition of that coldness (she just couldn't move; her mother led her to the kitchen after putting her father to bed), she suddenly realized why she'd come home. It obviously wasn't to return a daughterly debt (returning a debt that concerns parents, the deceased, former wives, or friends, always means only acknowledging it) and not, of course, for confirmation that her parents' life was nosediving. The agitation that had gripped her back in Köln (she hadn't been able to formulate its essence) had come about because she hadn't heard what she was used to hearing—the hum of the meaning of events—as she carefully listened to the fizzing of champagne that waiters were pouring into glasses in the foyer at the Museum Ludwig, or to Roma's shouts when he was trying to outshout the hubbub of a crowd in the beer hall, or to his ever more even breathing when she was burying her nose in his warm neck, or to brisk questions from girls with microphones (*tell me, why are the actors in your film teenagers?* the main thing then was to thin out the goopy spittle in her mouth).

It would have been simplest of all to do the logical thing: fly out right after Roma, who'd invited her to come with him, or sign some sort of contract so as not to be without work if she didn't have her own script she could try to scare up money for, but she'd flown out to A.A. first and then gone home, all so she could stop that slide, hear the rhythmic knocking inside her chest, and involve her whole body in the workings of her mind… in short, in order to write her own screenplay for a new film, a screenplay that would make her legs start shaking when she hurried off to the set and that would make her want to rip out someone's throat just to let her film it.

That sort of script could only be written in blood, and Masha sensed that blood rush to her hands—in a fever of horrifying, inhuman hatred—as she stood in the hallway over her drunk father, and that's also when she clearly saw she was moving along that very same strip twisted into an eight, on to the very same side, and just as inexorably. That she would always live with guilt, both about her father drinking himself to death and her mother being unhappy. That she would never be able to forgive Roma his *the little bitch*, while at the same time A.A. would always gaze at her reproachfully out of hardened layers of memory. And that the longer she'd live, the more cogs would begin catching each other: her mother and father would die, A.A. would hit the bottle, she would have a daughter, a drunken Roma would tell her to fuck off—and there would be new cogs she could only have hunches of and hadn't been able to foresee—and with each twist, they'll all push her harder toward the very end, where there's already a recognizable, solitary, and confused old lady: she places a photo with a black ribbon aslant on a shelf and her lips tremble as she repeats the phrases that were pronounced at the beginning of time. As Masha thinks about this, she tries groping for her own guilt feeling—wondering if she can give it up—and she understands she cannot, it's impossible, it's its own form of moral hemophilia, and the soul's inner juices do not clot. Even though the mechanism of original sin ensures the existence of mankind as a whole, in the specific case of your own fate, there's always the temptation of attempting to loosen the bolts and use the freed-up energy to jump off the conveyor belt that produces corpses.

After she's ended up in her own room (*sleep, Masha*, but of course she won't sleep), Masha sits down at her desk, smoothes a sheet of paper on the scratched, dusty surface, and begins drawing, cautiously, as if she's afraid she'll suddenly pierce the paper with the pencil point. Outside the window it's as dark as in a deep well; drizzle lies on the glass in fine dotted lines; drops reflect a yellow semi-circle of light from the lampshade; a shrub stirs in the darkness like a blurry spot; and a motor revs somewhere, barely audible. It's cold and empty in her room. The things that filled the life of Masha the little girl have been packed into cardboard boxes and now rest on the wardrobe. None of the treasures, whose precious secrets have dried up—badges, netsuke figures, markers, little notebooks, pieces of bark and clay, dolls, and wild animals—could have helped Masha any longer. A calendar with a velvety kitten is tacked to the darkened wallpaper, desk drawers are broken, and books stand flush with the front of their shelves. Lamplight shines through a sticker:

a boy is confessing his love to a girl, the little hearts flying out of his chest have faded to yellow, and they're a strange pair, like dead watchmen at a cemetery that's been dug up and moved. It smells like a damp basement in her room. But the fire igniting Masha's hands eats away at the half-darkness in the room. Square shadows are graying on the ceiling and some sort of current is visible in the triangles where they intersect—the hungry, groggy ghosts of teddy bears, in whose plastic eyes an electric zigzag of fire plays under a layer of dust, look at Masha over a bent shoulder. Masha is drawing a train station.

The train station resembles Piranesi's dungeons—a white sun shines through glass planes, dappling metal pipes and floors polished to ice. The bubble of quiet bursts and sounds explode: thousands of feet shuffle, multilingual speech babbles, loud-speakers thunder, brakes screech, advertising shouts from screens, sliding doors hiss, wheels on bags and suitcases clatter, and coffee grinders wail. The crowd flows along on escalators and in elevators, blending together in the transparent halls, swirling past columns that get lost in the sky; the boiling slows by the ticket windows, then calms by the mouths of the platforms; and trains get underway and gather speed. The smells of coffee, hotdogs, the homeless, leather, glass-cleaners, toothpaste, minty gums, newspapers, and advertising leaflets rupture the nostrils, stupefying overwhelmed mucous membranes, the head spins, and the heart won't stop pounding: the train station is life's territory in all its seriousness. Then a person appears on Masha's drawing: a backlit man stands with a crowd flowing around him as if he were a column, his chin in the air and his unshaven neck visible. He's grasping at his disheveled hair with his fingers, his mouth is contorted, his eyes are squinting, and the flaps of his unbuttoned jacket are angular at his sides; as she's drawing this man, giving him features from her father the way she remembers him in his youth and distorting those features with her own doubts and insights, Masha doesn't yet guess (and she only guesses this when the drawing suddenly implodes, leaving her in a cold, damp room, one-on-one with a dusty lamp and a dark window that's water-glazed on the outside) that the person she's drawn barely resembles her father and is some unfamiliar, bulky, independent person, and that this person will be the main character of her upcoming film.

Masha entrusts the hero of *Minus One*—whose ludicrous scurrying around will make the whole world laugh until their stomachs ache—with her own passion for escaping from the magnetized realm of causes and effects within human society. The story itself, which came together for her in broad strokes right after she made a final motion with a pencil, will be a classic situation-comedy. Max—Masha gave her main character that name not only so he'd have the first two letters of her own name but also because she needed a typical European name—intends to leave his job and his family, so he comes to the train station to go to the airport and, from there, to Cuba (he's already looking at Gauguin's bare-breasted native women during the credits, he's just chosen a different island, and yes, that's also because Cuba's the Island of Freedom). He sits down on a bench to wait for the train and when the man sitting next to him stands, takes his suitcase, and goes, Max is left with a suitcase that looks exactly like his own but is chock-full of explosives. (The choice had been between a bomb, money, and drugs, but wherever there's a train station, there's also a bomb.) Max has to run from Islamists, the police, his wife, and his boss, and that's all Masha knows about her hero thus far. She does sense that she can tell what she needs to tell only by using *Shakespearomeric* laughter because cinema has no right to make the direct pronouncements that, perhaps, literature uses all too boldly.

When Masha leaves her room the next day, she understands she can't write the script at home: she's cautiously trying to retain in her head everything she thought of before going to sleep, and then, suddenly, for no reason at all, she snaps at her mother, who's querying her about whether she wants eggs or farmer's cheese pancakes for breakfast (*Mama, really, it doesn't matter to me*, but that doesn't work, so her mother crashes and loops back to the beginning; Masha has simply already managed to forget this is how things go). And then, on the spot, right at the table, Masha invents yet another ludicrous phone call that forces her to break away immediately for the sake of some unclear but urgent work, and she's aware this is, of course, a betrayal once again. This time when her mother looks at Masha, who no longer even has the strength to lie (though, in terms of logic, there was no lie in what she said), her mother gently sits down on the worn, sagging sofa, puts her old face in her formless hands, and quietly cries but doesn't hide it because what is there to hide if Masha doesn't hide that she's lying?

It's perfectly obvious to Masha's mother that Masha is leaving because this new father of hers is disgusting, because she and her mother have grown so far apart and it's disgusting to listen to her babble, too, and because, finally, it's hard for the young to be with the old for long: it's just like being in church, you have to behave. Despite all her wishes, Masha would not be able to explain to her mother that, though all that is pretty much true, she'd still be able to tolerate things, maybe even for a long time, but she has a realm that's all her own, something she can't share, or rather, knows she shouldn't share.

As Masha pokes at her dish with her spoon, all that remains is to observe the lie cooling like volcanic lava and then pour on new portions when her mother starts begging *just another couple days*: whether it's lies or money, it's characteristic of their family that there's never enough of either, and so the father of lies and the prince (caesar) of this world are one and the same (on the ancient coin). For Masha, this also means that when she gets off the train the next morning, wanders on foot to the Five Corners, makes her way into a café, orders breakfast, gets out her phone, and dials Roma's number, she has to tell him she's *just flown in. I didn't call. Surprise*.

Masha's call finds Roma in bed and though he had one too many the night before and has only managed a couple hours of sleep, he jumps out of bed, hurriedly brings himself back to life, and rushes off to Five Corners (*don't go anywhere, wait for me there*). In his grogginess, it seems like if he doesn't pin Masha down in a certain space, there's a risk she'll go off the radar again: for the entire last week, he's heard a polite woman's voice on the phone instead of Masha's, explaining something to him in German, though all he pulled out of the stream of what she said was *auf*, a prefix that escaped to the end of a sentence, and then he spitefully pressed at the buttons on the phone, impolitely grumbling something with *off* under his breath in time with it; he didn't know German.

Masha could only guess—and most likely she couldn't have done even that at the time—that for Roma what happened in Köln wasn't making up for lost time (as if he'd been regretting all those years that he hadn't screwed, out of stupidity, that girl who was walking into his arms... though of course he did regret it) but rather something new and special he'd been waiting for but hadn't awaited. Never mind the wordplay, though: Roma had fallen in love with Masha, not with some sweet recollection, and not because then she was a schoolgirl from another city and now she was a prizewinner. No, it's simply that when he put his glass of water on the little table in her room and took it back, he caught himself thinking that it wasn't that he wanted to end up between her legs so much as to look into her eyes oh-so-closely at that moment.

The Roma who'd blown off Masha by the doors of the institute (with the ulterior motive that it would score him more points) was a boy for whom the miracle of human closeness was just as taken-for-granted as a permanent erection. The Roma who'd graduated from the institute, the Roma who worked like a horse, the Roma who poured beer into himself going from bar to bar on Fridays (*you guys, there's no normal chicks in this place!*), the Roma who undressed newly familiar girls (*take it off yourself, I can't seem to unhook it*)... that

Roma had discovered that the best thing that could happen between a young man and a young woman was the careful touching of a cheek with a hand and the bat of eyelashes in response, and that he'd somehow fucked up that best thing.

Here's how it was. Roma fell in love with the girl who'd been evading his snowballs and catching his kisses, and a few months later she'd become his girlfriend and he looked into her eyes each time he was at her house and his hand crawled in under her shirt, asking (not in words, of course) if he could go further, and then she'd kiss him, sinking her fingers into his hair. They kissed until their lips swelled, and his groin ached desperately after those evenings, so much that he had trouble wandering his way home, and all that time and later, when the girl decided what was enough (she asked him seriously if he had any rubbers), and then again later, when they started pulling off each other's clothes, after barely closing the door, and he tossed her on the floor right in the hallway, there was no time for rubbers; and when her parents would clear out of town, they'd spend entire days without getting dressed, and all that went on for more than a year, and each time Roma drew his fingers along her chin, neck, breasts, belly, and thighs, he'd feel something like an electrical charge running along his spine. Then they started arguing and making up, then screwing less and less until it got to the point that they stopped altogether and then they were relieved to break up toward the middle of their second year of school, ultimately because you can't not break up when there's nothing left to sex but pelvic motions and you're still only nineteen.

There were two other times when girls charmed Roma enough that he felt like kissing, kissing, kissing (it was over in a month the first time, the second time he was kicked aside and then toasted love for a half-year when he was out drinking with his friends), but they were usually girls it was most interesting to undress and see what they had between their legs. Roma zealously jumped into the fray, making funnier jokes each time and ever more seriously answering questions asked when cigarette smoke was being exhaled (*what do you think, can there be friendship between a man and a woman?*); you couldn't say he didn't like it. On the third try, he managed to lure a half-drunk girl to his place (by that time, Mama and Papa had rented a one-room apartment for him, with the condition that he pay for the electricity and phone himself) and then he took out his camera with gusto: *how about I snap you. –Snap my head off? –Do you have some other places? Show me!*

When he started looking a lot at social-network pictures of a gorgeous classmate who had a grown-up boyfriend, the girl who'd turned away from the snowballs, and, really, all the girls he'd been in love with, he caught himself missing glances, long walks, and holding hands. Then he started scrutinizing his girls (thirty-two frames to get to the panties, yes, he was shooting on film) and realized he wasn't interested in looking them in the eyes. And though he was still getting pleasure both from the sex and the process of role-playing, a guarded anticipation had settled in him: maybe one of them would suddenly turn into a creature who would evoke a tenderness that shot right through him.

You couldn't say he didn't think back at all to the girl he'd spent such a strange night with on the train and escorted to the school, and who'd then come to Pravda Street three times to see him; he did think about her. He didn't remember her face very well but it seemed like he remembered the sensation of her gaze. And that was the very same sensation he just couldn't manage to synthesize now: it was as if a gentle quivering was being smuggled across the boundaries of his body. He didn't think about Masha as a person he could see again sometime: he'd failed in his attempts to find her on social media by searching sites for her school and graduation year (even if he hadn't, it's pretty obvious that nothing drives people apart like daily status-updates), they had no common acquaintances, and he didn't know where she'd gone to college. And so that chance meeting in Köln—he didn't recall her immediately when he glimpsed her in the crowd at the festival opening—wasn't the sudden attainment of an imagined romance (that might have worked with others he'd thought about more often and more distinctly) but just a surprise (*whoa, what a small world!*) and, of course, gladness because in the end, no matter how harshly we tell the people who love us where to go, we're still glad they love us instead of someone else.

Of course as he asked Masha if she wanted to drink beer, Roma wanted to convince himself that everything still applied and even—you never know what the hell might happen, though he wasn't really thinking about this at all—that he was going to correct a mistake from his youth after all (and how: it wasn't just that Masha had transformed from a frightened and plain provincial girl in a threadbare coat to a gorgeous woman; the primary change wasn't in her clothes or her skin tone but in her gestures and gaze, which now obviously belonged to a strong, confident woman who easily commanded a huge production team, no problem) but both those things remained deep down in his perception, with something else on the surface: the simple wish to have a drink with a person he hadn't seen *In. For. Ever*. And even when he started coming on to her in the second bar after the second drink (they were just warming up in the first bar but then ordered a yard for the two of them in the second), he was most likely doing that out of habit, and the mechanism he'd long honed in Petersburg cafés had switched on. Only when he gathered, from Masha's eyes, that he was incriminating himself did he get confused and try to get loaded faster.

Roma watched a matinee of *Huguenots* the next day. He didn't like the film (*where's the cinema and where's the opera, Regina?*) but even so he couldn't help but see that what was in front of him was a genuinely professional work that one even had to find fault in because it was genuine filmmaking. And so it worked out that they drank a lot less beer that evening, though when Masha began saying goodbye to him (*that's it, Yevgenyev, I'm falling over, I could*

*barely get up this morning*), he suddenly noticed they'd spent three
hours talking about cameras, film stocks, and editing.

None of that explains how it happened that Masha went from
being an old acquaintance, and now a colleague, too, one it would
have been interesting to know about, to find out if she was seeing
anybody, into the woman for whose sake Roma stayed behind for
another two days when his group headed to Petersburg after the
festival, despite his free ticket (for some reason they'd given him
a ten-day visa), and whom he would later call every twelve hours
from Petersburg to ask and tell about any moronic little thing, but
in essence to say *I love you* over and over again. When he focused
on that issue—not right away but significantly later, when it had
become obvious that their boat of love had sprung a leak (of all
the poets, he knew only Mayakovsky and he liked thinking he
resembled that rabble-rouser)—Roma couldn't understand what
the hell had happened.

The third evening was warmer than the previous evenings and
they went from the *kneipe* to the bank of the Rhine, where they
started walking down the steps toward the water: Roma offered
his hand to Masha (a reflexive courtesy, that's all it was) but when
her palm ended up in his hand, when he touched her warm and
soft skin, and, then, when he was standing a tiny bit below her
and saw her face lit by streetlights hovering up high, well, that's
how it happened, as if some sort of switch had been thrown, as
if a picture had turned from black-and-white to color. He was
only a little surprised then, not attaching any significance to it
right away, and it wasn't until he rewound the film later that he
understood the importance of that snap: if it would ever occur
to Masha one day to give in to her womanish vitriol and ask, *so
what is this, Yevgenyev, you didn't love me, you just didn't love me and
now all of a sudden*, then he could have said, remaining maximally
honest, only that *I don't know, Regina, I suddenly caught a glimpse
of you.*

Masha never asked that question, but that doesn't mean it didn't spin around in her head. She puts the phone down, promising she'll wait for him and won't go anywhere, she'll have some breakfast in the meantime, and she really does order—and then she catches herself wondering what his face would look like if he came in here and didn't see her. This sweet thought tickles under Masha's skin, she taps at the table with her lighter, and spins her phone: of course she understands she's not going anywhere, if only because that sort of petty revenge is ridiculous, but just at the moment she catches herself wanting to grab her bag and leave for a walk (and later say she'd tired of waiting, couldn't stand it, decided to wander around a bit, and didn't hear the phone…) she starts feeling disgusted. She understands that the pain Roma once caused has become a part of her and she can't ever renounce it, and that pain (though the pain itself is no longer there) will always be the reason for his guilt feelings and it's completely unimportant if he'll feel the same thing; this isn't about him, it's about Masha. Masha's gripped by the most odious of sensations: that everything is already obvious, obvious, obvious. That what she really, truly, should have done was call A.A., go see him, and never take Roma's calls again; the only thing keeping Masha at Five Corners is the sudden flash of the realization that everything's the same there, too.

If a two-dimensional creature could grasp that it's tedious to move only plus-minus ahead and plus-minus to the right, it would try jumping. Rather than doing that, Masha reaches for her bag, gets out her laptop, and concentrates on her screenplay. In some odd way, the energy of pushing away from thinking about Roma and A.A. allows her to return quickly to Max, who happens to be leaving a store with a trunk he's just bought and holds the door for two gloomy-looking bearded men who've come to the store for two of the exact same trunks.

When Roma dashes into the café (the cabdriver from the Caucasus had him all figured out: *you hurry, guy?* and wangled an extra bill out of him: *got no change*), he sees Masha bent over the screen; the cooled croissants beside her have shriveled. Roma attributes Masha's absentmindedness to being tired after her flight.

*Forget about those rolls, they heat them up in the microwave here. Let's go home, that'll be better, we'll buy a bunch of food and fix breakfast fit for a queen. Is this your bag? Wait, hold on, a kiss first*, then they flag down a car to his place and buy cheese, ham, a baguette, oranges, tomatoes, eggs, and coffee, which has apparently run out.

Some time later, when he's running these first (and, for the most part, the last, too) of their several weeks together through his head—he'd quietly crawl out of bed each morning, go for a breakfast fit for a queen, wake her up with a kiss and the smell of coffee, come home from shooting with pizza and a bottle of wine, and tell her about something, though what he said wasn't getting through to Masha, who asked him several times to let her work a little more, and then he'd sit for hours in the kitchen, flipping through magazines and ultimately falling asleep—Roma reinterprets Masha's absentmindedness as evidence that she'd come back to him for role-reversal, to convince herself that the boy who'd told her where to go at one time was now totally hers. Roma attributes to Masha what he himself would already be dreaming of by that point. By hurling accusations at Masha that she'd *returned to seek revenge* back then, Roma is going nuts because he can no longer seek revenge. It isn't just that Roma wasn't inclined toward reflection— he'd also never, particularly not in hindsight, been able to believe in the necessity of working round-the-clock until you're frazzled, so he took Masha's *hold on, I'll finish this scene* as *I don't really love you that much*—so anyway, Roma really did decide she hadn't come back to him because of love.

Of course by that point he will have forgotten the main thing: the irrefutable evidence that Masha's feelings for him truly hadn't dimmed in the slightest, either since the point they'd parted in Köln or even since the time of her trips to Pravda Street. In the evenings, after the wine bottle had rolled into the corner, she'd take his hands, press them to her cheeks, and look at him. That look, which had disconcerted him at one time—as if he hadn't been born, in the words of a medieval misanthrope, between feces and urine—was now a piercing happiness for him.

He carefully took his hands away, drew them along her shoulders, pressed them to her back, cautiously kissed her, smoothed her hair, undid one shirt button at a time, and then—after freeing her of her jeans—kissed her knees, pressed her to the bed, rolled up her panties, slipped his fingers between her thighs to sense, within her burning depths, how her heart was beating, and then he raised himself so their eyes were on the same level and, catching on to her fast breathing with his belly, entered her fully, holding his right thumb close to the corner of her eye, as if that motion compensated for the impossibility of his gaze literally touching her—and then he fell asleep, holding the warm oyster of her breast in his hand.

# THE DIALECTICS OF FREEDOM

Half of all Masha's interviews began with a question about how she happened to start making films. Masha tried to think up something new each time, to strike back at the boredom that popped her in the jaw when she heard that question (don't yawn!): *Frau Regina, how did you become a director? –I had no choice. My father applied to film school along with Mikhalkov, he's one of our Russian directors, but my father flunked the entrance exams. The upshot is, Mikhalkov became a director and my father became a bus driver. When my father was dying, he left it to me to become a director and make such great films that it would be obvious to everybody the kind of shit Mikhalkov makes. The problem is that when I grew up, I discovered that sometimes Mikhalkov doesn't make such horrible shit, so I think I'm going to have to find myself a new profession,* but with time, her answers began repeating, she lacked the energy to make up something new, and one time (after Masha realized the journalist didn't care about her answer, only about her initials in front of every other paragraph) she even answered the question honestly, saying it had happened by chance.

And it was like this. In the spring, at the end of eleventh grade, when the kids were passing around thick, soft books whose transparent pages were crowded with the ghosts of all St. P.'s post-secondary institutions, jabbing their fingers first at one line, then another, and

sensing the long-awaited freedom they'd found, Dasha informed
Masha in confidence that she was going to apply to the theater institute (*what do you think, do I have a chance? –You? Of course you do!*).
Of course Masha didn't know if Dasha had a chance of becoming
an actress or not, she didn't even know how to apply to the theater
institute; ribonucleic acids were what occupied Masha's thoughts:
biology was the crowning exam for the psychology department
where she was planning to apply because of some stray fantasy.
Despite the preciousness of time—life on Earth has been in existence for three and a half million years but Masha had to figure out
everything about it within three months—Masha agreed to go to
the theater institute auditions with Dasha so they wouldn't be so
scary for Dasha.

It was sunny, fun, and noisy on Mokhovaya Street at the beginning of June. Girls in long skirts rolled their eyes and droned lines
from Brodsky, guys stood with their feet wide apart and flapped
their arms like birds in a fable (*Once a Crow Came Upon…*), and, in
the hallways, applicants who'd been through this before shared their
trade secrets with the neophytes (*X's group sings, there's no point in
seeing him if you don't have a voice, and Y likes girls to undress, well,
you know what I mean*, is uttered with a sneer). Even so, you were
supposed to apply to all of them: after a first round with X, you
could still make it to see Y.

Masha and Dasha failed in the first round with both X and Y,
but saw their names on the second-round lists with N (Dasha was
let right in but they asked Masha: *is that natural color? I'm asking, is
your hair color natural?*). Dasha's mouth twisted—the program for
directors was the *lamest*—and she was afraid: old-timer kids who'd
already been riding this merry-go-round for five or six years rushed
to N. Those kids looked down on the mashas and dashas because
they were all already acting after work in semiprofessional little
theaters with abbreviated names that their scornful lips benevolently
decoded, *"RAINS"? What's that stand for?* They weren't applying to

N because they wanted to be directors but because they were too old to apply to anyone else.

They all seemed like celestial beings to Dasha: they walked confidently to the center of the semicircle, looked N right in the eye, and articulated, slowly and distinctly, first their names and then what they would recite. Dasha wanted to give up on the whole thing but Masha felt awkward looking at Dasha's sour face: *come on, let's go, you'll blow them all away, he noticed you. —Just look, he didn't even ask anything.*

It would be dishonest not to mention that Masha liked the fun ruckus on Mokhovaya, with jokes in the hallways and songs on the street. It wasn't that she seriously counted on getting in (during the breaks between rounds, she continued flipping through the hefty *Biology*) but she wanted to keep the celebration going a little longer. Even so, after the second round (where Masha even specially answered the question *and you, what do you want to be* with *a director* so as not to compete with her friend)… and then, again, after the second round, when N's assistant came into the hallway and loudly called out *Regina!*, Dasha ended up never hearing her own name, and Masha had to lower her eyes and promise Dasha on the way back to the school that she wouldn't go to the third round (*what are you talking about, go, go, it's fate, I didn't want the director program anyway*).

Yes, Masha went to the third round, brought a few drawings with her (N had fingered the collar of his turtleneck, pulling it to the right and to the left when he was telling those who'd made it through the second round to bring *everything that you do, guys, whoever sculpts, draws, builds things, whoever writes poetry or music, bring it all, show yourself in all your colors*), staged a small scene with the other *guys* in fifteen minutes (this was totally wild: a man and a woman who've just met in a train vestibule…), and was accepted. For a long time, Masha was genuinely certain that N had liked her drawings, at least until one of her former classmates told her (she was already in Germany by this time) about the master instructor's chance revelation. His group's graduation performance was supposed to be *Anna Karenina. The Beginning.*, which was N's own stage version, but two artistic directors he knew had already rejected it (*Fomenko, you know...*). It had been hammered into the Petersburg Fomenko's head that the English governess most certainly had to be a natural redhead, and there were no other redheads among the applicants.

No matter how much Masha attempted later to imagine how her life might have turned out if it hadn't been for this seemingly unremarkable idea that the woman because of whom "the Oblonsky home was all confusion" had to be a redhead... Masha just couldn't do it. A few years later, making films and thinking about film had become so natural for her that the drawing showing "Masha attentively listens to people and gives them advice" had faded completely in her fantasies; beyond that, she shuddered from the mere thought that she might have managed to be a psychologist.

The phrase "be a director," by the way, had the exact same effect on Masha. After her first year, which was spent primarily in lecture halls on Mokhovaya from morning to night, Masha made the discovery that, in fact, she couldn't stand theater. Masha couldn't come to terms with it being enough for an actor to imagine the bank of the Volga really well (*then the audience will see it, too, do you understand?* No, Masha did not understand), that it's enough to just signify opulent décor (*put three chairs together and a cloth over them*), that you have to speak *so it's audible in the last row—they paid for tickets, too!* but also *so it sounds like real life*, when the main thing was that her work would forever depend on whether an actor's day started on the right foot. Masha ran off to the theater with everybody else several times a week (*we're N's students*) and never once could she escape the strange feeling that there were actors walking around in front of her and—both when they were bad and when they were good—performing a show.

In any case, it's highly improbable that Masha could have articulated these or many other issues with theater for herself, had it not been for A.A., who asked *and what are you going to do there?* when he heard Masha had been accepted at theater school. It's no surprise that when Masha returned to the apartment on Pestel Street every evening after rehearsals, she could argue with A.A. another hour, defending her (future) profession from his attacks. It was a surprise—for A.A., anyway—that future director Masha Regina turned out to be completely uninformed when it came to classic films. Every time A.A. made a reference that came naturally to him, be it to *8½* or *The Godfather*, Masha would proudly shake her head and admit she didn't know what he was talking about.

A.A. had to buy a projector, paint a wall white (*I'll paint the room something light*, he sang out when he came back from the hardware store, and then he had to explain another quote, an Aquarium song this time), and proceed with nocturnal enlightenment. Things got off to a rough start (*I have speech class at nine!*), but it got so you couldn't tear her away (*you sleep, sleep! I'll watch, you already watched it, didn't you?*), and Masha watched everything—completely unsystematically—from *Battleship Potemkin* to *In the Mood for Love*, since the Internet service could handle it. Masha would glance at her phone as she'd turn off the computer (four hours to sleep!), climb into the warmed bed, and, after moving A.A.'s arm from her chest to her thigh so its weight wouldn't constrict her breathing, fall asleep, now imagining films she'd make instead of shows she'd stage.

Adult life begins when you start seeing your acquaintances only once a year. In that sense, Masha-who-goes-to-college-on-Mokhovaya can be considered fully adult. On the street, she runs into boys and girls she went to high school with (Kolya's called a few times but Masha can't get together with him: *classes in the morning, rehearsals in the evening, you understand*). One time when Masha's walking along Mokhovaya in the evening, headed for Pestel Street, she runs into Dasha. Masha begs off—she doesn't have any money—but Dasha drags her into a café anyway (*don't you dare say no*). Masha knows Dasha's parents forced her into the philology department (where else can you send a girl who doesn't know what she wants?) and she prepares herself to listen to how wonderful it is there, but something else happens. After ordering herself a cognac (*how about you? –No, no, I don't need any, I still have things to do*), Dasha quickly gets drunk—only afterwards does Masha understand that Dasha had already been drinking—and begins sobbing loudly. She doesn't know what she's doing in the philology department, she doesn't know what to do with herself, her life isn't coming together, she has to transfer or else just move away, or, *at the very least get married*, Dasha summarizes, her head already hanging toward her shoulder.

There's nothing special in either that meeting or that conversation. But as Masha brings her drunk girlfriend to the subway (she's afraid to let her go, she's staggering, *can you make it home? –Masha, you're so nice!*), she suddenly understands that everybody she's run into like this, on the street, by chance, was complaining about the same thing, in one way or other. Even the people with big smiles who cheerily said that everything's excellent—*school? I like it a lot!*—even they were hiding a secret in the fingers they hid in their colorful mittens: it's not right, it's not right. After this, Masha starts noticing that her college classmates and students in the classes ahead of her (she hears what they say outside and in the hallways) also occasionally let things slip. Jokingly, because naturally everybody's a genius here, but there's joking and then there's joking: in rehearsals, too, Masha can't help but see that lots of people have come to the wrong place. Even when Kolya manages to tell her on the phone that he has a band, it's like he says that for effect, so she won't doubt he's found his destiny. As an experiment, Masha questions A.A.—very cautiously—and, after contemplating, he answers her honestly that sometimes it seems to him that he could have done more with mathematics, if he'd gotten into the mathemechanics department back in the day; he'd dreamt about that until the tenth grade.

It's the rare person who doesn't answer *because it happened that way* when asked why he does what he does. Masha peers into the faces of the watchmen at the Academy, the faces of conductors and waitresses, teachers and salesgirls, guards at antiques stores, doctors who disappear into the doorways of eye clinics in the mornings, women over fifty who trot along the street yelling into mobile phones—*the apartment's very nice! Another couple looked at it today!*—into the faces of balding men who fastidiously carry little fake-leather briefcases in their hands, and aging young women coming out of tanning salons. Masha sees that all these people have been left without a fate.

Masha begins feeling fevered because nothing she's doing seems right. Out of fear, she begins watching more—two or three films a night, going over them again, pressing pause and rewinding to note the border of a frame, and looking at the stopped frames forever—by morning, her head is pounding and her eyes are killing her. During lectures, she doggedly reconstructs the films in her mind, frame by frame. When she wakes up, she catches herself thinking about how in her dreams she'd been watching a Bergman picture he'd never made. The film seems brilliant to her but there's absolutely no way of remembering the whole thing (she did hastily draw what she remembered). When talking with A.A., listening to her teachers' accusations (*you're a future director, you can't be late!*), or standing in the smoking room with kids from the actor groups who're thinking maybe it's worth striking up an acquaintanceship with her even now, Masha sometimes puts the proceedings on pause—*Regina, are you listening?!*—and ponders who or what should be put somewhere else to complete a frame—*right, right, sorry*.

Of course A.A. notices something's going on (at the very least because of these nocturnal cinevigils: he's already starting to repress the annoyance they cause), and writes it all off to the great power of art. And he's right because Masha's watching films like she used to watch them when she'd come home from high school—diving into them as if she were jumping into the water feet first—but there's something else, too, that hadn't been there before: her whole body arches and her hands heat up from seeing perfect geometry in a frame, correct color, and ideal editing. She doesn't know what she'll do with this, but she finally understands she'll never work in theater.

By summer, Masha's perplexity reaches breaking point: she somehow takes her exams, thinks about whether or not to go to Moscow, for the VGIK film school (she's heard a hundred times that they don't take anyone that walks in off the street), or whether to go to the Lenfilm studio, but what would she bring, and for whom? When she drops hints about film to N, he asks who her parents are, and Masha is absolutely sure her life is totally getting its ass kicked, so when Kolya calls and invites her to get together (*there's something I want to talk about*), she agrees right away because she needs to get the sense that at least there's someone who doesn't think she's complete shit (she has no doubt that Kolya still loves her, otherwise he wouldn't have called).

It wasn't because A.A. left town for a conference and won't be back for a few days. Odd though it sounds, A.A. was the last person she could tell, even gently, what the problem was. A.A. was the person closest to her (after all, sleeping with someone in the same bed every night for a year and a half, what could be closer?), he'd understand her all too well, and Masha even knew in advance how he might answer—fate isn't pregnancy, it isn't visible by the belly, you can't tell by looking at somebody if they're happy or not until they're dead, every person with a noble soul carries around a feeling of total existential unsettledness—he'd say something along those lines, but Masha, who might not be fully ready to admit it, wants to hear far stupider things, for people to tell her, for example, that everything will work out for her.

Kolya greets her by the subway with a bouquet of long-stemmed daisies, they go to a café, drink wine, and eat ice cream. Masha talks about how wonderful school is. Kolya talks about himself: the band, which is sort of indie rock, recorded a disc and made a video for the Internet. After they've drunk the wine and eaten the ice cream, they go for a walk. They walk silently. Masha sees that Kolya's torturously turning over options in his head so he can say whatever it takes for this not to end because very, very soon the only logical development to events will be *in the direction of the subway*. Finally (*come on, say something to her!*), Kolya utters the stupidest thing of all: *basically, so, how are things?* Masha tries to hide a smile (*why're you smiling? Oh, sorry*) and catches his awkward pass: *basically, not so great, Kolya.*

*When we were little*, she says, starting to answer him (those two years with A.A. hadn't gone by for nothing), *when we were little, remember how it is?, you think you'll grow up, be an engineer, or well, maybe not an engineer, that's not what's important, it's that you're on a train, and you'll race around in that thing, really, really fast, but what's most important is you can look ahead and not off to the side or, even though this is rare luck, back, at what's already gone by, and you never think about how that engineer comes home after his shift, eats, drinks, argues with somebody, you never think of that, there's just this point in time—and that point is your entire future adulthood—when there's no doubt at all that it will be just like that and so you'll grow up and understand that (oh, I don't know), like I've realized now that life isn't just one point in time but lots of them, you jump around from one to another like a token on a game board, it's like it's all by chance, how the dice fall, but it's like it's not because it's like it's you, yourself, throwing them...* With each word, it's easier for Masha to speak because Kolya's quiet, just looking at her, enamored, so soon it's clear—as if the warmth from her speech has breathed a little hole on iced-up glass—that they can't make do without a bottle of wine, and Kolya says something, too, like, *but when I was little, you'll never guess. –Spy? Submariner? –Geographer. –What!? –Well, yes, maybe I would have been, only I spilled it to my parents and they told my grandmother, and my grandmother was a serious person so she gave me this book, pretty much a college geography textbook, you know? I was probably in about the fifth grade*, so they laugh and talk, interrupting each other and, of course, had passed the subway station long ago. They buy a bottle of wine on Liteiny Prospect and (*we're not going to drink right out of the bottle*) Masha decides to stop at home for some glasses.

At home it becomes obvious that there's no point in going anywhere, they can drink just as well here, so they settle in the kitchen and, out of sensitivity, Kolya doesn't ask, for the moment, who she's living with here, they sit until the subway closes, go for another bottle, come back, and sit until morning. Among other things, Masha finally hears everything she'd wanted to hear: that's she's awfully beautiful, unbelievably talented, and that, yes, everything will work out for her. At four, they decide it's time to sleep (*so I'll head home. –You are such a crack-up*), and since she and A.A. don't have a fold-out bed, Masha puts Kolya to bed on one half of the bed and she lies down on the other: *I don't have a sword but there's a separate blanket. –A board? –A sword! –But why? –To put between us. –Let's make do without that. –What?* As she's rolling up in the blanket, Masha remembers what her high-school girlfriends said: *a drunk chick is not in charge of her twat, I am telling you that for certain!* and thinks, with dull tension, about what she should do now when Kolya's... okay it's pretty obvious what to do.

They exchange drowsy words and Masha wonders what Kolya's wondering, but in the end he turns decisively toward the wall and soon his breathing slows. Masha's heart stops pounding in her ears and the last thing she understands before going to sleep is how much she really feels like kissing him but then the last thing is that Kolya didn't fall asleep because he's so drunk (people sober up by around four) but because he, the jerk, is so polite.

In the morning, everything not said and not done during the night still lingers in the air, and Kolya hides his enamored eyes and hurries to go home: *I need to pack my things, I'm going away tomorrow.* As he's putting on his shoes, Masha remembers something so she doesn't have to stay silent: *you were saying there was something you wanted to talk about? –Never mind, it's silly. –Oh, come on, don't sweat it* and then Kolya says what it is. A camera. The semi-professional camera they used to film the band's video is lying around at his house and it would be dangerous to leave it because... And then he has to say he rents a room in a communal apartment. *I wanted to ask if I might, maybe, leave it with you. For two weeks. I'm going away for two weeks. Or are you going away, too?* Kolya leaves and Masha sits for half an hour in the bathtub with the water running and then rubs her temples for another half-day, while Kolya's getting the camera. She doesn't have a headache, it's something different: she's trying to grasp what to do now so she's not the jerk.

Masha can't make any sort of decision so when Kolya arrives with the camera (it turns out to be three super-heavy bags: *here's the camera, here's the stand, here are the cables, spare batt, diffuser*) and when they're saying goodbye, he stretches to kiss her but she closes her eyes instead of offering him her cheek like usual. She knows deep down that this is betrayal but she says, jokingly, of course, that it's a rental payment—*it's a fee, nothing more, it's a fee, nothing more, it's a fee, nothing more*—so Kolya won't think it's some form of thanks, because then she'd be doubly a jerk. *Meaning?* Kolya asks, burying his nose in her armpit. Masha will use his camera while he's away. *Don't worry, I won't wreck it.*

Human life is a function of events. That function is human will. (And will is always the will to power, according to one of the lords of the world.) The problem, however, is that knowledge of history exists only as a vector to the past, as memory. And though it's thought that history repeats itself—the practical value of the study of history rests on that shaky assumption—it's impossible to know in advance and for certain what will happen when will is applied to an event. From that formal point of view, human freedom is as dubious

as the dubious freedom of the drunk deciding whether or not to
have another. Fortunately, there are sciences more complex than
mathematics (mathematics is essentially a simple science, therein
lies its attraction). But mathematicians, too—good mathematicians,
of course—recognize that the road from "a given" to "QED" isn't
worth much if it doesn't appeal to the sense of the beautiful. The
beautiful is basically the idea of an entity's consistency.

When Masha hears about the camera—it's a Sony PD150 that
isn't even Kolya's, he and *the guys chipped in and bought it used*—it's
as plain as day to her that the supremely correct thing for her to do
now, in these two weeks, is to make a film. She doesn't know how
to use this contraption (the manual alone is at least two hundred
pages long and when Kolya holds out the device for her, stripped of
its case, and shows her where what button is, she tries not to let on
that all these terms are gibberish to her), and she doesn't know what
to film or who to film, but blood is pounding in her ears so when
Kolya finally leaves, after repeating *I love you* for the fifteenth time,
Masha slowly goes to the kitchen, beats her palm on the windowsill, and screams at the top of her lungs: *everybody go fuck yourselves!*

Masha doesn't know where to begin coming up with a film,
so she grasps at what's routine: she spreads her drawings out on
the floor. She vacantly stares at them for a few hours, chain smoking. Petersburg effervesces in her drawings. Buildings, palaces,
old women, bridges, statues of horses, trees, metal grates, street
musicians, obelisks, caryatids, homeless people, shop windows,
stairways, snowplows, figures of poets and commanders, churches,
subway stations, flower kiosks, public squares, trams, courtyards,
manholes, chains, a girl in a white hat, angels, lions, sphinxes,
columns, bottles, underground crosswalks, men in caps, towers
and steeples, the sun, smoke from smokestacks, motorboats—all
that stares at her, eyes goggling, from her sheets of paper, coming
at her, squinting, deceiving, baring teeth, flickering, murmuring,
and droning—and in desperation, Masha allows them to scream,

all together, in chorus, and her ears fill with a cacophony, cawing crows and jingling teaspoons, howling wind and splashing water, screeching tires, beeping traffic lights, predawn quiet, lines from poetry, shouts of *fuck*, the muttering of newspaper vendors, music from a store, *documents please*, the snap of trolleybus wires, clicking heels, slamming doors, the boom-boom of bass from expensive cars, the gentle tapping of snow on glass, the silence of the couple at the next table, the doleful tinge of sirens—and only when everything's run out of fizz and Masha is left in a deep, soft silence does she understand what she has to do.

She gathers drawings off the floor and stuffs them under the sofa. She lays out the remaining seventeen sheets in the order she needs: these are key moments for the film. Masha can now sense she's gotten hungry, so she heads to the store for edibles, but along the way it occurs to her that she couldn't possibly think up a better story for all this than the Bitov novel A.A. was talking her ears off about during the summer.

Two days before A.A. comes back, Masha is working on shaping the characters' dialogue, moving around chunks of text, drawing, timing how many minutes the text will take, shortening the text, redrawing, crumpling paper, drawing arrows, erasing, connecting together everything she's drawn, crossing out, and rewriting—basically, when A.A., still exuding the sun of Pushkin Hills, comes into the apartment and stumbles on the case with the camera stand—*the hell! Hi! What've you got here?*—he immediately sees the script: snaking along the floor are drawings with captions, arrows, numerals, and glued-on bits of paper with text. It's the running time for her future film, twenty-seven minutes.

Fate is a heavy fish to reel in: Masha discovers that making a movie takes more than having a passionate hand in things and the ability to sleep two hours a day. It turns out that if everything's going to work out well, you need to break down the resistance of masses of people: from A.A., who hears her out and of course says she can't do the filming because she doesn't know how, to the policemen in the Summer Garden (*this is museum property, miss, what don't you understand?*) for whom, thank God, all it took was a charming smile, an elaborate lie about a year-end project for school, and six beers. Easiest of all are the actors: Masha rings up two of the slackers from the class ahead of her. One of them is a beanpole with huge mitts and a roughly hewn face (every time she'd run into him in the hallways, he'd fling his arms wide open, booming out *do remember me, O future director Regina! Am I not Othello?*) and he would become the double in her film, so obviously the other one, who's all skin, bones, a dreamy gaze, and thin fingers (*Mashenka, you can't even imagine how beautiful you are! I smile every time I see you in my dreams, seriously!*), would play the main character. Finding a car is the most complicated aspect: for two days, Masha demands that A.A. call around to his friends (*Mashlein, are you out of your mind, who's going to lend their car!* but they're little sweeties about lending them after the fifth call).

Seven years later, when Masha's in Berlin filming *Minus One*, her first film as an adult director, she catches herself thinking that all those difficulties that had seemed so unconquerable at the end of her second year of school—forcing the camera to give the exact right hue, getting lazy-fuck actors to stop emoting and learn their lines, finding the exact same tree she'd drawn, waiting for good light, taking in a jacket so it doesn't drape like it's on a coat-hanger—that none of these and the other difficulties, not a single one of them, is any easier to conquer now. Each assistant she, as the person the consensus considers a genuine director, is entitled to—whether it's the assistant shouting into a megaphone at a crowd scene or the makeup artist, a young thing with an unthinkable number of rings in her ears and nose for whom Masha specially draws large-scale faces—each of them exacts an additional pain in the butt that nobody but Masha would take upon themselves, whether it's the producer with the plastic smile (*Frau Regina, we can't pay the store even one more day, our budget...*) or the insistent studio director that has to be blown off when he really needs the film to include a certain actress in the picture, *one very talented young woman, it's really worth having a look at her.*

She'll be sitting in a fold-up chair on a cordoned-off chunk of the Kurfürstendamm, convincing herself not to get worked up, looking at the sky, waiting for the damned cloud to leave, praying the actors won't run out of steam, and people will walk past, outside the rope, pointing at her and at the set—*schau mal!*—and to calm down she'll go through the sheets with the screenplay over and over, and then suddenly, as if someone's changed a slide, she'll see herself on the embankment of the Fontanka, sitting on a step, her elbows on her knees—a glance at the sky (which way's the wind blowing?) and at her watch—and calming her geniuses. *Regina, let's rehearse it one more time at least, there's nothing else to do anyway. –No, you guys, that would be over-rehearsing. How about you recite some poetry for me instead. What'd you have in your speech classes?*

It's not time's shift to the past that scares her (*coffee, Frau Regina? –Yes, thank you*)—Masha knows déjà vu is just a brain effect—but the sudden realization that this situation will repeat with dismal constancy in the future. There will be other films, other actors, and other taciturn lighting technicians but this pose of hers—with the gazes at the sky, the booming heart, and the cigarettes running out—will all be exactly the same, exactly the same, exactly the same, time after time. Rage clenches her fists and it will take enormous effort for Masha to deny the unexpectedly oppressive desire to leap up and cancel today's shooting in one shout. Roma will come up behind her a moment later (a cup in each hand *–your coffee, Frau Regina!*) and will, of course, be offended when the reply is *why are you screaming bloody murder?* He'll take that—the sharp tone and the hateful look—personally. Masha will calm him, explaining that she's nervous, filming's at a standstill, time marches on, the wind stops, the clouds gather, *and here you* *are shouting right over my ear, I'm just on edge, sorry*, and Roma will pretend he understands everything.

Of course during her work on *Minus One*, Masha will find it pleasant to think about whether she could have imagined, back then, racing along the Fontanka with the guys in a smoke-filled Ford Focus, that seven years later she would be… etcetera. By then, though, Masha has learned to experience suspicion toward any pleasant thoughts. The problem is that only at first glance do those thoughts guarantee a future that can't be contemplated now. In fact, they can't be directly converted into a future. And if something happens now that you couldn't have thought about before, then it happened not *because* of time but *despite* it. In reality, there is, in the nature of time (as in the nature of any of the universe's nonliving objects), an embedded aspiration toward a state of equilibrium: let everything stay as it is. And if anything at all in this world flows or if anything at all changes, that's only thanks to personal exertion. The joke Masha got sick of in renditions from the girls of Mokhovaya suddenly cheers her up once again, but she can't explain to Roma why she's burst out laughing: *everything flows, right out of me! –Regina, has anybody ever told you you're insane?*

Masha didn't know seven years ago that if you're starting from scratch, about all you can film in two weeks is an advert. Work had just started when Kolya came back from his Murmansk trip. He called in the morning when Masha was in the car with A.A.; only Waits growling from the speakers gave her hope that A.A. hadn't heard Kolya's joyful voice say *I love you!* Masha said she'd call back and glanced at A.A.: it would have been easier for her if he'd asked who it was, but he didn't ask. It was impossible to understand if he was, in reality, so intensely caught up in his driving. Masha didn't call back until mid afternoon, when they went with the guys, the four of them, for *bliny* and she slipped off to the bathroom after checking that her phone was in her pocket. And though every boy knows a girl spends a fair bit of time in the bathroom, she was still afraid to catch A.A. looking at her when she came back. A.A., however, was attentively listening to some actor joke or other. As she swallowed her cooled tea, Masha caught herself horrified at a thought: was he listening too attentively?

Yes, Masha told Kolya that she hadn't managed to finish, that she needed another two weeks, and Kolya said no problem. She said she couldn't meet because they were filming from morning to night and Kolya said of course he'd die of impatience but not totally. But when he asked her (as a joke, of course) *can I at least call?* Masha had to keep quiet. Keep quiet long enough that Kolya finally said *got it*. Masha washed her face with cold water for a long time before going back to the dining area smelling of overheated butter.

In the evening, Masha was lying on the floor in front of the camera with the manual in her hand when A.A. shouted from the kitchen, exhaling cigarette smoke: *I've never seen you like this before.* Little boxes from the charts started floating on the manual's pages, blurring. *What? –I'm saying you're a real boss lady with that camera. Commanding, strong-willed, that one there, that one here. Very unusual, really. I love you. –Boss lady? –Request permission to kiss you, comrade director?* A.A. was already standing in the doorway and Masha set aside the manual with the crazed charts.

The reason Masha wanted to hide her infidelity from A.A. at all costs wasn't because she was ashamed (she'd learned to overcome shame with A.A. even before they'd begun sleeping in the same bed: *Regina, admit it, have you read* The Kreutzer Sonata?) but because she didn't want to upset him: she couldn't have explained that what had happened had happened purely by chance. Meaning she knew A.A. would force himself to understand everything and sooner or later, maybe a day later or two days later, he'd come to her and say *you know, Masha…* But Masha knew that the opportunities for reason were not unlimited. Masha imagined very vividly that first blow that A.A. would have taken, if she were to tell him that, well, somehow or other: silence, hidden bewildered eyes, ears turned red. And that blow would remain in the body's memory but Masha—no matter how sleepy she might be, sitting in morning rehearsals—already knew the body's memory is a sort of thingy that's not rewritable. There was a certain something else that made Masha hate herself. As she mentally ran through all those complex chains of mutual concessions and obligations, she was forced to admit to herself that in the final reckoning there was one primary reason she had to leave everything as it was, at least for the time being: she was just plain afraid of scuttling filming.

Until the very beginning of August, Masha set up shots, experimented with filters, and forbade the emoters to act with their eyebrows. She already had no doubt she wouldn't be able to keep her secret from A.A., so whenever Masha's understanding of things caught up to her on the set, she tried to work faster and faster, not so much in order to finish things "before" but to concentrate on something else.

Kolya called exactly two weeks later, in the evening of the same day that Masha had said, not fully believing it herself, *that's it, guys, we made it.*

The guys brought beer while A.A. was putting the camera in the case and loading it in the car but Masha couldn't drink: tiredness after finishing work was familiar, but this was the first time she couldn't sweeten that tiredness with a look at what had come out of it. The guys sang and counted their Oscars, passersby scowled under their brows at the loud young people sitting on the curb, the sun warmed the bottles, and A.A. kept silent and smoked. Horror chilled Masha: she didn't have even the slightest idea of how to begin editing.

When Masha and A.A. were at home that evening, the phone began ringing and Kolya started explaining to Masha that two weeks had gone by and maybe later he could work out more time if she needed it but that he needed the camera right now so he'd stop by in something like an hour if she was open to that. Masha heard that Kolya's words were clogged in goopy spittle and she felt disgusted that he wouldn't just ask what he needed to know: it was as clear as day that he wanted to happen upon an answer. Even so, of course Masha told Kolya to come over, told A.A. that Kolya was coming soon for the camera, and Kolya came.

When Roma will try to find out why she's been so pensive all day, Masha will tell him that she's reminiscing about her first film—*that's the one you sent to HFF? –Yes, fools get lucky*—and later, when they've agreed they just can't sleep, they'll leave the hotel and seek out doner kebabs close to Potsdamer Platz, and Masha will tell him there's something to filming without money, without some studio-schmudio, because that way you don't owe anybody anything, and if it doesn't work out, well then, it doesn't work out, nobody's expecting anything from you. Roma will smile because that's obviously moronic, this was just an unlucky day, everything will have to be reshot tomorrow if the weather's right, and that's why she's out of her mind.

But everyday truth differs from verity because it can vary so much. Beyond all that, Masha will be tortured by the picture of Kolya, who was ready to see anyone at all that night—a young guy, a sugar daddy, or a girlfriend—but went totally limp when A.A. opened the door for him (*well, hello there, Ozerov, haven't seen you in a while*), looked at Masha (*just don't look away*), looked at A.A. (*hullo, Alexei Alexeyevich*); and A.A. turned to Masha then extended his hand to Kolya when he came in, and Kolya just couldn't not extend his own, and there was no doubt at all that A.A. understood everything and that was exactly why he'd insisted Kolya come on in, tell them how things were and all that, and so Masha had to say *of course, Kolya,* too, though she wanted nothing more than to just toss them both out the door.

The three of them went into the kitchen, where they had something to eat and drink, and talked about film. Despite everything, A.A. said, cinema isn't an independent art: like comics, it's just the otherness of literature, of a text, and is, in that sense, secondary (he looks at Masha from time to time, to see if she's going to be offended), but, at the same time, a text has immeasurably broader capabilities because a text is a phenomenon of language and, according to Heidegger, language is the house of being, whereas a picture, particularly a moving picture, is just like theater in that it has no direct relationship to verity, and it only allows language to have its say in a place it could not have been under other circumstances; and this is, in some certain sense, a profanation, just as the first Greek performance freed of the sacral function was a profanation. Kolya got angry, looked at Masha, lit a cigarette, forgetting he'd just put out the previous one, and shook his head that, no, he'll agree, fine if it's secondary, but that doesn't change the fact that film is the future, something that's just absurd to demonstrate, like how atomic energy is secondary with respect to the steam engine, too, and, well, if you stop at any café, people—students, accountants, smart people, stupid ones—they're all talking about movies and nobody's talking about books, they retell plots (*that's exactly it!* A.A. raised his index finger), discuss the actors; fine, it's secondary to both painting and photography, but that's the thing: all the arts joined up and film came out of them and its power is greater than any of its components, its power to affect a person, just you try to force anybody to read *The Iliad* in its entirety… but everybody's seen *Star Wars*, though essentially they're the same thing. *That's the thing, that* and Masha listened and listened, not so much to what they were saying as to the sound of the teakettle, the crackle of tobacco, and the rumble of the refrigerator, trying to imagine how this could end, and then she suddenly realized that nothing in particular would happen: she'd just say she was tired and wanted to sleep, A.A. and Kolya would bring the camera cases downstairs, she'd undress and crawl under the covers, and then A.A. would come back, hug her, and say, as if it were nothing in particular: *I think Ozerov is in love with you.*

And it was exactly this—not how she struggled with Adobe Premiere for two months and made an agreement with a sullen

sound guy, not how it suddenly occurred to her to send a disc
with a packet of drawings to HFF, and not how a message arrived
with a request to send a full packet of documents ("see our site")
(the chapter's false finale is playing: yes, this is exactly how Masha
Regina became a director), and not her childish joy combined with
equal bewilderment: sure, they were inviting her, but why was it
the cinematography department (and by all appearances, A.A. was
right in figuring they needed a female cinematographer for political
correctness, and from Eastern Europe besides; she figured that out
as soon as she was in Munich, when she was trying to get transferred
to another department)—that would stay with her as a set of facts,
though what would truly burn into her memory, what would force
her fingers to clasp so the bones under her skin went white, was a
feeling of what's left unsaid, a lack of finality in a minor and clumsy
little subplot. The hatred she would experience toward that story
was of a purely aesthetic nature: her body twists and her mouth
grimaces in a similar way when she watches a picture where loose
ends aren't tied up, the conflict isn't worth a damn, and the actors
are overacting as if they'll get paid triple.

Later, Kolya called a few more times: he still had trouble believing
that Masha couldn't, that she didn't have time, that she had things
to do, and each time he said he'd call again and he even stopped
saying *I love you*, but during the winter he stopped calling, too. Masha
never did understand if A.A. truly did grasp everything because
of Kolya's eyes or her silence but pretended with his otherworldly
magnanimity that he hadn't noticed or had decided that Masha just
didn't want to offend, even by extension, a pleasant young man who
wasn't at all bad (anyone can fall in love). Stupid, stupid, stupid.
And Masha would laugh loudly at Roma's jokes after drinking too
much beer (because it's impossible to eat such a huge doner kebab
without beer). The jokes weren't very funny but there was lots of
beer and the big thing was that Masha would grasp that this was
all stupidity and all the rest was even more stupid. Kolya challenges

A.A. to a duel. With righteous anger, A.A. shows Masha the door. When Masha greets A.A. as he's tripping on the camera stand, she confesses right then and there that Ozerov gave her the camera, they'd gotten wasted all night, and then acted like the beast with two backs the next day.

*That's it, Yevgenyev, enough bullshitting, we have to work tomorrow.*

# HOW CAPA BECAME A PHOTOGRAPHER

It's this thing from childhood: your parents sent you to bed but they're watching some kind of movie and you're lying there and of course you're not sleeping, there's these muffled sounds on the other side of the wall, maybe some kind of fights, maybe music or street noise or conversations, you can't catch the words, just the intonations, and so you're lying there, almost pressing your ear to the wall and making up what the movie is, just from those sounds. You fall asleep like that, without noticing.

Plus your snoring is an awesome track for the sound. It's the upstairs neighbors, right? The audibility in those buildings is insane. It was back then, two years ago, they were torturing us, well, it was their daughter. The parents would take off for the weekend and she'd have a houseful of people: chicks in hippie headbands, guys with guitars. But no, they're just into historical reenactment: they're peaceable kids, just really sucky singers, wailing away for two nights in a row.

It wasn't till later that I understood you were offended. You thought I'd fly in and we'd lounge around in the sack for days at a time and walk around in the moonlight but I, what an asshole, just say thanks for dinner, now leave me alone. Good Lord, you and I didn't really know each other; really, it was like we'd just met. So what was I supposed to say to you? You know, hon, when I work, it's best not to interfere; here, hold on, I'll finish writing the screenplay and then I'll be all yours, every bit of me. And I... You know, I didn't have a hell of a lot of relationship experience, either, Alyosha was a smart devil so that made me think you'd figure everything out, but you, it turns out, wanted me to look into your eyes, with total devotion. Three times a day, for ten minutes after meals. What, was it really not obvious I was madly in love with you, like the very first time? You sleep, keep sleeping, don't wake up, I'll get myself another beer, I can't stand the stuff but I have to drink something after all this.

And what about later, after I'd finished? We went, like, on vacation, it was a real, true honeymoon and I even thought about maybe hinting to you about getting married. This is where you're supposed to ask why I didn't hint. Well, what for? It's nonsense, it's like, I love you so much I'm not even afraid of a marriage-registration stamp in my passport. You have to get married if there's kids, but this wasn't the time for kids. I had to make movies. And you, too. There was also that universal hurt: I stalled and didn't get in touch with you right away about the film. Do you at least remember what you told me here, when you were holding on to the wall? Yes, as soon as I saw how you work, I knew right away that if there was going to be a movie, you'd film it, I knew right away, there's just that thing: you can't start talking about it while there's still nothing definite. I'm afraid of black cats, too, I wait for somebody else to walk by. You're not just a looker, even if you're a fool, you're as talented as Karlsson, too, you have this absolutely insane feel for the geometry of the frame. This is your chance, I'm not saying anything when you're sober.

Okay, so, Berlin. You know, later I thought *Minus* was actually just a torrent of all kinds of improbable coincidences and good luck, I don't know, and it seems like no good films would be made at all without that, even if you're Eisenstein. First I ran into you, then we up and went to Berlin. I'd hardly ever been to Berlin, I'd only ever gone there one weekend with everybody: people usually drive to Italy from Munich because it's closer and warmer. Anyway, so we came in at the Haupt train station and I immediately realized this was exactly the station I needed, the one I'd drawn. And then we were walking around the city and I was automatically looking at locations, pulling you closer to the railroad, and you got all mad, saying I have to see all the sights, those streets, an island of museums, Tiergarten, beer, and you didn't know yet that they don't drink dark beer in Berlin.

And now you're telling me you were stressed out because we're living it up on my money. Oh, my God, what crap! Well, if you'd said you were stressed out, I would've lent you money, only we'd have partied everything away anyway, everything I had left from *Huguenots*, there wasn't much… No, if this is for real, then I can't live with a guy who's bugged by that kind of bull. It's like some kind of shitty political correctness: you know, we can screw but we'll pay our own way for dinner. If only you could hear what you sound like. And, as a matter of fact, somehow I didn't see you were stressed out. You were like a happy baby: it's my first vacation in a year and a half! we're on vacation! the hell we're going to a pizza place! let's go to a normal bar! And how was all this working out for you, anyway? You were walking around and thinking: oooh, rich little bitch! That's how it works out, isn't it? That is all so, so, so vile. Not only is it vile but I'm sitting here on the floor in front of you, talking all this crap with your fake Holsten.

If only you knew how much I sometimes feel like telling you to fuck the hell off. The first time was about two months after we came back to Petersburg. In the beginning, I thought these were all just little jokes: who are you writing to and calling, who do you have back in Germany… But then when I went to Moscow and you went into that fit of hysteria about me not picking up the phone, and about who I was blowing, fucking whore, well, that was the first time I felt like saying it. I'd never made a film in Russia and could've figured things out but I'd never realized there's so much of that rubbish here, like if a girl's making a film or being filmed, it means she's putting out for somebody. And everybody's so sure of it that even the girls don't question anything. And me, what a fool I was to tell you, all honest to goodness, that, yeah, like people had hinted that, oh, you have such beautiful hair. And then you... You know, the horrible thing is that I saw in your eyes that you believed I was letting somebody have it for money. This isn't about *what* you said to slander me, it's just that when I saw it, I was bursting with hatred, like some ripe pear, and wanted to do something that would be painful for you, like you'd croak, for real, and then I realized, at that moment, that I could easily just leave you.

We made up. You and I always make up and we'll make up in the morning this time, too, what else could we do? It would be stupid to tell you—when you start making those guilty eyes—that no, one thing you can give and still keep is your word. Really, though, that's probably what I should do. Or maybe not, since the result is that everything's worked out like you thought it would anyway. Somebody smarter would say that, like, what you think about is how things will work out. Or that it's like this everywhere, not just in Russia. Karma, flipping hell. You know, it's just these storylines that pop up in your life for some reason and then repeat over and over and you can't do anything about it, the same thing just keeps happening time after time, with other people or in other situations, but it's just the same. Remember when we were filming the scene by the store? It was a sucky day, the sun never did come out, and we had to reshoot again later? Right, and so you started asking why I just didn't seem like myself and I told you I was thinking back to Petersburg and all that stuff. And that's how it really was but something else suddenly hit me then. That everything had worked out exactly the same. When you're actually living through these moments, you don't pick up on how all this already happened: you only understand that later. And it's the same work I was doing in Petersburg, too, really... Well, there wasn't any money at all back then, no producers-puducers, but it was the same rubbish anyway. So, long story short, it worked out it was like I'd put out for this guy, for his camera. It looked that way even if it really wasn't like that at all. He was a good guy. Well, is. He's in this band, sometimes even invites me to gigs. And it's the same thing there. You think I knew in advance that Peter would get money for me and that's why all this happened?

Fuck, it's working out here like I'm justifying myself to you. And I don't want to justify myself. Well, sure, I'm aware that I'm feeling guilty, but I don't know where that's coming from and I know for sure that I'm not at all guilty. Okay, fine, I am justifying myself. You remember it took me a really long time to try to find money for the film. I sent out screenplays to dozens of places and everybody sent me packing, I was always going somewhere to meet someone, and everybody complimented my hair. That went on for a whole year. I even had to find work here, so I made corporate videos. Did you ever once tell me anything like, damn it, Regina, that is not worthy of your talent? Sure, I almost went crazy and I was about ready to just toss up my hands. Everybody was telling me the film I wanted to make was total shit and nobody would give me anything to make it—that went on for a whole year!—so what was I supposed to think? Well, of course I had to believe in myself, and, yes, I did. That's just, you know, hard.

As for Peter... I never did tell you how that all went. Only during arguments, never calmly. Want to have a listen? Whatever you want. Anyway, back then in Munich... I went there like it was a holiday. Change of scenery, at least get away from you for a few days—kidding, kidding!—but also to see people I hadn't seen in a long time. Of course it hurt to hear how they were all working there, for real, but I didn't sweat that too much. Peter randomly turned up there in a *kneipe*, our master instructor had been his master instructor a long time ago. Star, handsome dude, pals around with two of the great German directors, the whole works. Sure, right, everybody was looking at him there like he was a god. Probably me, too. But not because of that. I told you before, it's just that the shape of his head is like my father's and that got under my skin. But that's not the point. I know that *when* he got the screenplay from me to read is a matter of principle for you. Well then, I'm telling you: after. After, do you understand? Of course I told everybody that I was looking for money for a film but it wasn't like he threw himself at me and said, give me the screenplay and let's jump in the sack. He didn't talk with me at all really. Asked where I was staying—a normal social question—and so, sure, I told him and I didn't know he was going to drag himself over there early the next morning with flowers.

Why would I try to put anything past you here? Honestly, yes, those three days were awesome. He treated me like he was really in love. I even fell a little in love with him. It's hard not to fall in love when you're, well, taking walks and talking, but that's not the point. He's just genuine, you know? That's why he's a good actor, because he's genuine in and of himself. People don't actually turn into actors on Mokhovaya Street. If a person's brimming with life, it means he's an actor and you can't get that with any techniques, all you can do is polish it a little. And there are actually so few of those people, you just have to fall in love when you do meet them; I'm not the guilty party here, it's just the way the world is. Well, sure, I remembered about you. But I hadn't planned on this, that we'd go for walks for a day or two, and right then and there I'd put out for him. Really, planning things like that is about like sticking a mop up your own ass and walking around that way. It gets in the way, you know? But the point of life isn't that we'll never be guilty of anything and then croak after we've told ourselves, Oh, I am so cool, there's nothing to accuse myself of.

I understand this sounds stupid in justification mode but it's true: it happened by chance. Well, he thought up some excuse for us to stop by at the Radisson, pick something up there, forgot his credit card. It was obvious he basically wanted to screw. He didn't even hint at that, he said I could wait for him downstairs, in which case I could have waited and then just flown home the next day. And then it would have worked out that I was just messing with the guy for three days, had plenty to eat and drink, then see you later, thanks for the flowers. No, you have to understand, I could have easily done that but I thought why should I deny myself the satisfaction of having sex with a person who, by the way, I liked an awful lot, just because of some silly rubbish? Go on, be like Mayakovsky, tell me I should set my heel at the throat of my own song. Do I owe anybody anything? You? So I told him I'd come up and then I told him we didn't have to go anywhere if he had booze. Luckily, there aren't any rooms at the Radisson without booze.

And it was only later, after we'd already been lounging around with whiskey that night, that he asked about the screenplay. See, I don't know—since I can't answer for him—if he was thinking in advance that, like, if she puts out then I'll get her scribblings and have a read. In theory, I'd be surprised if that's how it was. And of course, for my part, going by the rules, it would have been the right thing to do to make excuses and not give him the screenplay. I might not have given it to him if I'd finished it a week before, but I'd been running around with it for a whole year, so I gave him the screenplay because I realized this was an opportunity, a serious opportunity and maybe the last one, even though I'm handling it like an asshole.

And the story doesn't end there, mind you. Later on, when I was here, and he wrote to me saying this was his role, that he even looked like Max in my drawings, that it's an awesome screenplay, that he's going to show it to this one person and I should think for the time being about if he suits me, and I honestly answered that if, like, there suddenly turns out to be money, then I couldn't hope for a better actor, but I'm going to shoot it with my boyfriend—meaning you, Comrade Snore—and if he got the hint, then maybe it's not worth his bother and that's that. Fuck, what a noble soul! Take a lesson, Yevgenyev! You know what he wrote back? That what had happened was a ridiculous, but lucky, accident! And—take this down!—though he's storing away in his soul the memory of the first days we knew each other as one of the dearest reminiscences of his life, he nevertheless hopes that in the future our relationship will develop into something maximally productive and remain, by the way, within professional boundaries! You got that, Yevgenyev, about how to treat girls? *Fool! Prostitute!*

So, what, you really think I should have told you all this right then and there? You know, Roma, they gave me money here for the film and a wonderful actor turned up; sure, I slept with him but don't sweat it, I won't do it again, promise. Can you even imagine a conversation like that? Beyond that, you have to understand you'd've had to stay in Petersburg then. Or I'd've had to turn down the film but I wouldn't have turned it down for anything. And I actually wanted it to be you that shot it. And then, yes, Peter's a good guy but I didn't want to break up with you, didn't want that at all. I was thinking then in the vein of, okay, so you and I fight sometimes, make up, yell at each other to get the hell out, we argue over idiotic things, then we screw and forget everything... But, anyway, that's fine. Everybody lives like that, right? And all those little lovebirds you visit, oh, sweetie, give our guests some slippers, please put on the teakettle, dear, they look at each other amorously, show you how happy they are together, it's always like that, and we act the same way. In reality, those lovebirds were planning to slice each other up an hour ago. That's how people live. And not because the bastards are so hypocritical but because otherwise it wouldn't be polite. Actually, it really is unavoidable. I lived with Alyosha for two years. He's older than me and smarter—that was especially noticeable back then—and he's as calm as an elephant, but he and I would give each other shit anyway. Not like you and I do, of course, but then we'd go to different parts of the apartment or he'd take a walk somewhere. This isn't some kind of common thing: everything always happens over some kind of nonsense. You know, some kids are taught to put the toilet lid down when they're done, others aren't. And people draw conclusions from that, that they're not compatible. Well, that's not exactly Newton's binomial theorem, everybody knows how relationships work even if they don't say so, and they keep living together anyway. Sorry I'm talking nonsense. I'm saying all this because even back then I no longer had the illusion I'd find the kind of guy I could live with on good terms and not ever give shit to. I thought very seriously about this before *Minus* and decided I loved you and didn't want to dump you.

Was it really so bad? You were the first to shout that hurray, hurray, finally, some serious work, and for decent money, too. I really don't know, but in all seriousness, the only thing I'm truly guilty of is not being capable of leaving you in happy oblivion. In fact, I don't know how you guessed. Did somebody tell you? It's not like anybody could have: nobody knew. Somehow I don't believe Peter told you himself. God, it's lucky this at least came up toward the end, otherwise who the hell knows what would've happened. And not because you'd've left the film; I don't think you'd've gone. It's just that I couldn't have handled you at all then. You'd already decided anyway that I despise you and think you're shit because I didn't like this and didn't like that. But that's normal, Roma! That's normal work for a cinematographer and a director. The cinematographer proposes something, the director says no, I have my vision of things, you have yours: this is, like, a creative quest, that's what filmmaking's about, and the director's the director because the director has the final word. In your imagination, though, this was my way of letting you know I'd pretty much fallen out of love with you. But if I'd fallen out of love with you, I'd've told you then and there, on the spot. And I will tell you, if anything happens. I'm as honest as the Soviet government, damn it.

And you say I could have at least lied. Well, just imagine: you come to me and ask, totally serious, if I slept with Peter or not. And so then I should have been all bright-eyed and bushy-tailed and said, *good Lord, what is with you, Romochka, what are these thoughts inside your head?* Well, that's just lunacy! Do you yourself understand that it's just lunacy? No matter what, I wouldn't have been able to lie so you'd believe it. And not because I'm fuck-all of an actress, I'd have had enough in me for that. It's just that when ideas like these get going, they're like tooth decay, you know, and you yourself wouldn't have been able to believe me, even if you'd really wanted to. If you truly wanted me to deceive you, then you shouldn't have asked the question back then.

Long story short, Roma, I don't get the joke. It seems like it was kind of jinxed from the very start. It's just that everything's been all wrong from the beginning and there's nothing you can do about it. Maybe everything would have been different back then if—and I'm thinking about a very long time ago—you hadn't started showing off but had just slept with me, the smitten little provincial fool; maybe we'd have broken up, I don't know, or maybe we'd have lived happily ever after. I'm not saying that to pin something on you, you know I'm hung up on that. Of course you're not to blame for anything: so you didn't want to sleep with me, well you didn't want to, what do you know? Nobody's to blame, really, it's just the way damned life is, and that's all there is to it. Something was broken right from the very start. Maybe even before we were born. And you see that, try to mend it, and say to yourself: this fucking bullshit will never happen to me. But just as soon as you try to step away, it turns out that all the fucking bullshit is over there. Someone smarter would say that's fate. It's fucking bullshit and not fate, there's no such thing as fate. There's only logic. It's pretty much fuck-all, but it's logic.

Just don't tell me I'm all unhinged here. Okay, I'm all unhinged but it's your own fault because if it weren't for you I wouldn't've gotten so drunk that I'm composing obscene monologues for you here. So what did you do, you noble don? You didn't go and kill Peter, didn't quit your job, didn't leave town, didn't kill me, didn't tell me to go far, far away. That was the right thing to do. It was right, and you know what? I can't say anything. We have a contract, work, and the picture's almost all shot. If you'd suddenly balked, well, then you would've been the idiot. But you're a trooper, you swaggered around a little, got wasted, shouted yourself out, and got to work. Honestly, I even think you were waiting specially until the end of shooting so you wouldn't have to ask the question bluntly: Am I, like, a trembling creature or will I leave right now for Petersburg? Because then you'd've had to leave, but you didn't want that, you couldn't help but see that the picture's basically coming together.

So you see, it works out again like I'm telling you how low and calculating you are. That's not at all what I want to say. I want to say that this is all like little dance steps, and if you've already gotten tangled up in them, well, be ever so kind: two step to the left, three step to the right, just like in that song, there just aren't any other options. It's just nasty, though, how it's not the person that gets all tangled up: I get the feeling it's the dances that tangle some-one up in them instead. You're not living those storylines, they're living you, see? If you think about this seriously, then the question arises: where the hell are you? If you start methodically deducting everything from yourself that isn't you—the storylines foisted on you, the guilt feeling you're being pushed into, the belief you're being inoculated with, like, oh, I don't know, love for the motherland, the books you've absorbed, all of that… well, then it works out in the end to something strange: you don't exist! There's no way to detect you anymore, no matter what you grasp at, everything that's in you settled there from somewhere else. Well, the flesh is yours and the bones, blood, veins, and skin, too, but if you look at it the right way, even all that is only everything you ever ate.

I thought about that when I stayed in Berlin to edit and you flew off. They'd overdone it with the contract and planned in twice the amount of time we needed for editing, either to play things safe or because they really thought I wouldn't know what order the scenes should go in but, anyway, these Germans never have any less dicking around than we do. I never intended to make myself a super-productive Stakhanovite worker, I came to the studio by eight, Marta and I sat there and did something until two, then I left. You know, Berlin in the spring is something totally special. It really does all smell like lilacs, no matter where you go. I also finally escaped the hotel and rented an apartment on Pflügerstrasse in Kreuzberg: say what you will, but East Berlin is nicer than West Berlin. At some point it started to seem like I'd begun a regular new life as a simple Gretchen, and it's an awesome feeling: you get up, go to the bakery, then make your way to the studio, cut something there, put it together no fuss, then there's lunch, go shopping for food, and fix something at home. I even started watching TV.

You probably thought I'd be tormented, suffering from uncertainty, and all that because you went away without definitively explaining anything. But I lapsed into a sort of tranquility, I don't know, and all I needed was to walk around the city a ton, lie on the grass, people-watch, pop into stores, and work a little at a time. There's actually something to that. If you'd come back then, I would have told you to relax, buddy, this is all such rubbish, imagine how you'll look back on this in forty years, when you're seventy: you won't be in the mood for sex, only to have a drink of something warm, and you'll remember all this with a smile. It won't be a smile of aversion but maybe of blessing or something, that you'd been so young and worried so much about who was sleeping with whom, and you know, you'll take a look at the boys and girls who'll be passing you on the street and be happy for them, that they're still playing and still have plenty of time in reserve. Anyway, the upshot is it's like I've abruptly turned into some nice old lady, the only thing is I don't feed the cats and the pigeons.

I even stopped thinking about *Minus* then. Well, no: I mean I was thinking about it—the editing and sound were in my head—but overall it was already clear the picture worked. And that was the main thing, so somehow its future—distribution, festivals, critics—no longer concerned me. The whole stir that came up was, well, maybe not unexpected, but I just didn't immediately understand that the stir was there and that it was because of my picture. And you know, I even remember the exact moment when I figured that out. It was in Venice, two days before the announcement. I was standing by the Palazzo, smoking, and there was a bunch of people waiting by the entrance for some big Hollywood fish, cameras at the ready and actually making a loud stir. And then something clicked and I even started coughing because I'd inhaled too much smoke too fast. Somehow I suddenly realized or saw, I don't know, that I wasn't exactly some nobody dicking around there myself, that I was also there for the competition and, really, why couldn't my picture win: I'd seen the others and seen that mine was no worse. My heart started beating faster right then and didn't stop later. Meaning that's what broke me, not that you and I had made up and started screwing again.

I knew you were swinging your member around every which way while I was gone: reconnaissance reported back, you know. Right, I understand that was probably how you got revenge. Or maybe, what is it they say, go on and screw ten other girls, you shithead pickup artist. Or even forty, that's not the issue. That's just not the issue, see? It's really a strange thought, that you have problems and these problems can somehow be resolved mechanically, by adding in other people. Like in a bad book: for some reason things aren't coming together for the author so more characters are brought in, more and more and more and then everything just keeps unraveling but the book has to end and so, finally, the author has to kill everybody so they're not underfoot, and *that's* the problem, Roma, not that the book's bad.

So, right, I knew. Maybe I should have done the same thing you did? Come back, reveal to you that I know everything and start tearing out my hair? So you'd shit your pants in fear. Like I thought you were this kind of person but you're not this kind of person, so we can't live together, etcetera. Pick up your toys and don't piss in my pot. And all that to finally agree we're quits and let's start new lives, but on top of that you're still more guilty than me so you owe me and don't forget it. I just wanted to live with you, do you understand? And when I flew back and saw you, I knew right away that's what you wanted, too. So then what's with all this debit-credit stuff? And you know, I could do without all the promises and blood oaths that it'll never happen again, and the ostentatious throwing away of condoms shoved in pockets. And without the words, too, because everything's clear anyway. I could have just not come back to you at all and that would have been it, right? But I'm back and if that's how things are, everything's clear.

It seemed then like you'd figured that out. Because, well, you didn't say anything, you just greeted me, hugged me, and kissed me, like nothing had happened... Remember how we froze here? And it turned out you'd decided to just put off settling our accounts for another time. You suffered along for a whole year but didn't forget. Chose the moment that would be the very most awkward and inconvenient. When I was really not in any shape for personal stuff. Nobody was pulling you in a million directions, you weren't doing three interviews a day, dozens of people weren't pestering you to introduce themselves even though you don't know a damn thing about them—maybe it's just some crazy person, but maybe it's some super-duper big shot. And there was nowhere in that reeking little city to escape them without diving into the Grand Canal. And there you were, telling me I don't need you anymore, look how that fag's smiling at me, maybe he'll give me money for the next film, ask if he sleeps with girls. Probably the only reason I didn't kill you then is I didn't have enough strength to lift a knife.

You were saying later you were, like, ashamed, the things you did, the things you did. But why do I need your apologies now? You didn't just ruin my celebration then, you caused me pain when I was at my weakest, which made it twice as painful. I don't know, has anyone ever driven needles under your fingernails? Me either, but I don't think it's much more painful. And after that you say, I'm sorry, like, I don't know what came over me. Oh, you prick, what a prick you are!

Imbibe in bubbly beer. Well, on the other hand, as Fyodor Mikhailovich Dostoevsky said at Sennaya Square, no matter what happens, it's all for the best. When the English get into an awkward position, they pretend they never got there. There's a great homey truth in that. If some sort of rubbish happened and there's nothing you can do to improve the situation, then it's just an illusion. The only way to improve it is to act as if nothing happened. The magical "as if"! But the problem is—and I figured this out back then—mankind's society is built so you're not allowed to act that way. You think you're the only one? Absolutely everything's left on the balance sheets, nothing goes away. The last straw for me was when Peter started coming on to me. He'd apparently decided that since we'd finished our work and I no longer depended on him at all, my womanly pride wouldn't suffer and we could finally get laid after all for our mutual pleasure. No, he didn't say anything, he just smiled, kissed my hands, and looked in my eyes, but I saw it. Long story short, I understand him and there's really nothing bad in that, well, he truly does like me and he knows I don't think he's so hideous, either. He'd probably go the hell away if I just told him no again. But for some reason, I attached significance to it and couldn't hold out…

And then when I came to Petersburg just now, it suddenly dawned on me that what I'd made was fuck-all. That it's all some kind of crummy outline that's too simple and nothing can be that simple, it's an incomplete truth: it's a lie and it turns out I'd wanted to make something about life but made something about my own head instead. And yes, it's this symbolic story. This dude tries to go off the rails but he's not allowed. Not because somebody's against it—who the hell needs him?—but the actual chain of events starts resisting. Sure, there's little gags, funny stuff, but what's the substance? It's a five-kopek thought: that you can't escape the mechanics of life by just moving around. Otherwise all sailors would be Buddhas and the world would have been saved long ago. I already knew all that, I mean about *Minus*, when Alyosha started explaining it to me. And thank God, otherwise I wouldn't have believed him.

And that old-lady philosophy is rubbish, too. Be glad you can still get it up, and don't sweat things, there'll still be time to think about the eternal… but for now, let's dance! All of Europe lives that way, so what? The trick isn't to come to terms with having been caught, that's impossible anyway if a person's still even the slightest bit conscious. The problem is you have to get out of whatever caught you and get out while your head's still functioning. This, by the way, is not at all obvious. You know, I really have noticed that my head's started functioning worse. The speed's not the same, that's what's scary. Even when you're still just thirty, you already sense you can't think as fast as ten years ago. It's not that I've grown stupider, no, it's the opposite, of course, because of books—they've got conversations with smart people, everything's all thought-out and then thought-out again—but it used to be that I couldn't keep up when I was writing down my thoughts, you know, and now it's like I have more memory but the processor's obsolete. There's not much time but you have to manage to become a person.

So there you have it, I'm saying this because if you're going to make a film about these things, then you have to make it seriously, about what truly does happen in life. But I don't know what you need for that. Are you are aware of how Capa became a photographer? Long story short, he shot his first reportage for *Life* at an airfield in England. Twenty-four airplanes, gallant pilots flying out for a mission. And so he photographed them, they flew off, and only seventeen returned—seven people turned to roasted meat while he was drinking tea. They land and he comes up to them with the camera. And one guy, who's being carried away on a stretcher, looks at him and says, like, oh, it's you, photographer, so are you satisfied, you had to have pics like that? So there you go, and then there was the landing at Normandy and Capa became who he became.

Now, that's how you have to work. But I don't know how to film like that, meaning in real life, not theoretically.

So, once again, it's clear that these things don't work out easily: you know, go to Africa over there and lounge around with a camera, under fire. You can go wherever you like, including to kiss my ass, and nothing will change if you yourself don't break yourself down and pull yourself back together. I told Alyosha that, too, we had this really serious conversation but holy crap, we did not screw! Good Lord, do I regret that now, maybe it would have blissed me out and then I wouldn't have had to listen to all your hysterics for nothing. So what can I do so you'll believe me? I haven't slept with him, not once, since you and I have been together, not once! I've known him as long as I've known you and we lived together longer, if you don't count the breaks, so get this straight: we don't need that anymore, he and I are just, well, somehow connected now and that's forever, you can't put an end to things like that. No, of course you don't understand: you think it can only end one way if a girl goes to visit a guy. And basically, everybody walks around and only thinks about how to screw with somebody, especially if they can really do you.

You called at the wrong time, when I couldn't lie to you. Then again, if I hadn't answered, that would have also meant that we were otherwise occupied. But he and I were talking. Basically, he's going through a hard time in his life, he needed something like advice from me, maybe for the first time. I basically came at the right time, he even said it was like I'd sensed it. Well, I can't tell you about it, and why the hell do you need somebody else's problems anyway? You

have your own. Take a look at yourself. You've rammed this idea
into your head that your girl got it on with someone somewhere.
So what did you do? Made a scene, smashed crockery, broke the
door, nearly popped me right away, and for what? You left, spent
two days wasted who the hell knows where. And came back in the
end. To tell me again, almost puking, that I'm a whore. You want
so much to be a real man, but real men don't act like that, can you
understand? That's how chicks act. If you only knew how vile you
are when you get drunk. Pathetic and disgusting. I felt such loathing
the first time I saw my father wasted off his ass, I was already an
adult then. And I just remembered that now, looking at you: the
two of you are exactly the same.

Now, that is exactly what I never ever wanted again. As I go
through life, some things cling to me—situations, voices, storylines,
people, words, clothes, addresses, memories, sensations—like some
kind of crumbs that scatter while you're eating lunch, and brushing
all those crumbs off the table is really hard but if you don't do it,
then, well, you might as well just do yourself in right now. Things
had just started to seem like they were going to work out for me
but, as it turns out, nothing of the kind.

Damn, I can't believe it, could it be that all these things really
don't worry you? You can't not understand that sooner or later
you're going to croak. But before that moment, come hell or high
water, you have to figure out what's going on, otherwise you're no
different from a cockroach. Instead of being horrified about that,
though, you're preoccupied with who's sleeping with whom. Well,
you're asleep yourself! Yoohoo! Hello! Wake up! It's pointless. A
liter down your gullet and I know there's no way in hell to wake
you up before twelve.

So I'm going to bed now, too, the hell with you. Here, last thing,
let me tell you what'll happen in the morning. You'll wake up in
the morning and want to have your way with me something awful.
But you won't be able to do that until we've made up, so you'll tell

me in a big hurry that, like, you had too much yesterday and really, let's forget it, we love each other no matter what happens, you'll say you trust me, that no, I didn't sleep with anybody. It'll still smell disgusting in here, we'll be too lazy to pick up the bottles, you know that sour smell of flat beer. And so then you'll press yourself on me, you'll turn your face away so you don't breathe the alcohol fumes into my nose, you'll push for a long, long time because it's tough with a hangover. And the horror is that it'll be good for me, do you understand? It's beyond me. I love you.

# GAMES PLAY PEOPLE

There was no need for Masha to lie to Roma, particularly since he actually was sleeping as she was choking down warm beer, knocking ashes into the neck of the previous bottle, and composing a monologue for him that occasionally erupted in speech: Masha truly hadn't slept with A.A., not once, since the time it happened all by itself on the living-room sofa two years ago. Beyond that, she was so sure nothing of the sort could happen that when she was on the Berlin vacation, she'd even told Roma who she'd seen while he was screwing his classmates. Masha couldn't have suspected A.A. would become an *idée fixe* for Roma in drunken contexts like *you already had one egghead, so go to him if I'm not right for you*—but if she could have known, maybe she wouldn't have considered telling Roma anything. Roma's attacks on *the egghead* were all the more disgusting because Masha had to defend A.A.; she still felt a tenderness for the two years she'd spent with him. Despite that, it felt impossible to even imagine she could go back to him: that storyline was simply closed and its resuscitation would have been akin to petting with Mnemosyne, and Masha had always experienced a loathing toward unnatural pleasures.

Beyond that—there's no point in turning Roma into an insensitive bonehead—if Roma did see A.A. as a rival, then it was only concerning Masha's head, not what was between her legs. Appeals to return to an ex, after all, never mean exactly what they say, their point is the simple taunting: your ex is an ass and you're a fool for having lived with him. And if one keeps in mind that, by default, we're assuming the wholeness of human identity throughout time, it's all even simpler: *Yevgenyev, the least you could do is give Eric Berne a read. –Masha, you're a fool yourself!*

After Masha received her medal and abruptly escaped Venice without telling anybody anything, Roma sat in the hotel room for another two days, watching TV and drinking. Several times he was forced to explain to unfamiliar men and women that he didn't know where Regina was. He truly didn't know. Maybe she'd moved to another hotel, maybe she'd gone for a spin with someone to Rome, Florence, or Milan; there had to be plenty of places and people to go for spins. It was complicated to admit Masha had flown off to Petersburg: he'd also have to tell himself that it was he who'd driven her to it. It was simpler to convince his unshaven reflection that she'd driven him to something: at most, she'd spent two hours with him the whole week, smiling at everyone right and left, any mangy journalist was more important and necessary than Roma, it was as if she basically had nothing to do with him here, and if there wasn't any producer nearby, then, excuse me, I'm asleep already, I love you but can't do a thing.

In the end, Roma flew to Petersburg simply out of inertia, it wasn't as if he was following Masha, but he wasn't going to feed the pigeons in Venice. When he entered the apartment, he didn't immediately throw himself into looking for traces of Masha's return, and so he discovered them—a cup with unfinished coffee, a smudged ashtray—only after he'd painstakingly torn all the tags off his suitcase, crumpled them into a sticky wad, and begun looking for an empty plastic bag. Roma had been reiterating accusation after accusation to himself the whole time, from the moment he'd returned to a hotel room that was already half-empty until the moment he sat on the unmade bed and started dialing Masha's number. The quantity of volumes in the virtual case of Yevgenyev vs Regina multiplied and multiplied. Touched by emotion, the jury members fingered their handkerchiefs. After craftily taking possession of the claimant's heart, the accused woman had ignored his amorous feelings, flirted with other men, displayed inexcusable inattentiveness, placed professional achievement above family obligations, etcetera, etcetera, etcetera. On the basis of the facts set forth, the prosecutor demanded Regina be found guilty in the cooling of amorous feelings and that punishment be imposed, in the form of correctional tasks, in order to start everything from once again in the beginning—yes, prosecutors are inarticulate.

All joking aside, if a truly impartial observer had happened to sort through this case, Masha's attorney would have had a tough time. And not just because a court opinion is always more willing to lean toward the offended man: equal rights, after all, only exist on paper, which tolerates any heresy. In reality, equal rights means only an equilibrium of love but since, as it happens, the equilibrium of Masha and Roma's love had been irrevocably disturbed, denying that would have meant lying under oath. The equilibrium under discussion here is always an unstable equilibrium because the art of love, in this sense, is akin to the art of the clown who holds a big, colored balloon on his own nose to delight children. To the outsider, if the balloon falls, that represents one indivisible event, but the clown knows the final fall is preceded by a sinking heart and a roaring in the ears. Roma heard that noise whenever they were alone and Masha's gaze would stop for no reason, when she'd grown bored during insignificant chatter where enthusiasm can only be natural between those drunk and in love. He saw that some sort of work was going on inside her, something that had no relation to him. His heart also sank when he joked: *Regina, you swear so much, how are you going to raise kids?* and she answered, just as jokingly: *well, so then you'll raise them, you're not exactly the ideal contemporary yourself.*

The gavel strikes, the judge announces a break, Roma listens to long tones on his phone, he dials over and over, it grows quiet in the courtroom, and there should be enough time for us to tell a little something else while Roma tries placing his call.

Masha most likely knew for sure that she'd call A.A., even as she was madly throwing socks helter-skelter into her suitcase along with her business cards, cramming in t-shirts so cosmetics vials wouldn't knock up against the case holding the medal, calming down a little at the airport (the hassle of changing the ticket and the deferential joy of the customs officials had a therapeutic effect), and, finally, as she was approaching the Petersburg airport in a drowse. She wasn't intending to foist a psychoanalyst role on A.A., no, he was simply the only person she wouldn't be ashamed to brag to about the symbolic gravity of her suitcase. Masha, however, was more muddled in explaining, to herself, her desire to call A.A.: he'd find out *about her* anyway and her call would be a sign that she wasn't considering putting on airs. She'd intended to dial his number as soon as she arrived, but as the taxi was rushing her to Venice Airport Marco Polo, a story about a nameless woman and three men had popped into her head: she's choosing between them, thinking she's choosing her own fate, but, essentially, she has no choice. When Masha was on the plane, screening her notebook with her hand against the curious gazes of an old lady with dyed hair, she suddenly realized this was her new screenplay and it was, in broad strokes, ready.

And so, after she'd flown into Petersburg, Masha stocked up on hotdogs-oranges-coffee-cigarettes (thank God, at least in this country every last store doesn't close at eight in the evening) and sat for two days with paper and a pencil. Only on the third day—after she'd begun to feel like any word written on paper irritated her—did Masha dial A.A.'s number. He answered instantly, as if all he'd been doing for the last two days was staring at the phone.

The apartment on 3-ya Linia had changed terribly. At one time, it had given the impression that a tidy and inconspicuous woman lived here. Now it was the apartment of a solitary and unhappy man. Arrays of bottles stood on the floor by the wall, clumps of matted dust trembling between them, ashtrays were full, the sheets on the bed were gray and obviously hadn't been changed for about a month, and the tables were heaped with piles of empty cigarette packs, books, pieces of paper, receipts, and some sort of computer junk. The air was stale and heavy. Water burbled in the bathroom. A.A. himself was unshaven, his shirt was missing a button, and his restless gaze simultaneously apologized and seemed to say *so what, who cares*. After looking at A.A. in the semi-darkness, Masha suddenly realized this person was nearly forty years old.

Things like this don't happen all at once. When they were in the kitchen and Masha couldn't hold back any longer—*what happened here with your cups*, meaning everything, not just the cups—of course A.A. grasped what she was saying and it was obviously unpleasant for him to think back to how all his crockery had once sparkled with a natural whiteness, but when Masha decided to at least take two cups and wash them, he muttered through the noise of the water that *everything seems to be fine*. Masha didn't hear him and A.A. didn't consider repeating. In the end, it was impossible to up and explain, just like that. It seemed as if this whole time he'd been living each day just like the one before. Reading, writing, preparing lectures, hosting guests. The guests inconspicuously started getting older and there were ever fewer women among them. Preparing lectures grew ever simpler and ever less necessary. In his work, he could switch off his brain ever more frequently and write using outlines he'd come up with years ago. His cigarette brands grew cheaper. Masha refused sweet, sticky port wine and a regretful A.A. took out the tea bags. He said he'd grown old now, that girls used to stop by sometimes before, that he hadn't been expecting her; and Masha listened to how everything was just the same with him, *I scratch something down but only God knows what or why*, but judging from his nervous gaze and jumpy fingers, she saw (at first she wondered if his throat was burning for a drink but then she grasped that no, this was another matter) there was something else A.A. wasn't talking about but was on the verge of saying, *you really did call at just the right time*.

Masha was again forced to feel something akin to guilt: after all, his love for the redheaded schoolgirl had been inordinate. Persistent hurt had drained the sap of joy from his life. As Masha listened to A.A. say he hadn't truly had anyone during all that time, that he'd tried living with someone simply because of a necessity to live with somebody but nothing had worked out because it was too disgusting and people are basically pretty disgusting creatures, only love turns everything upside down (A.A. is joking, joking), she feels like she's plunging into the horror of what's right here in front of her: what's taking place and what already took place is the mystery of the death of what's human within a human, and she's guilty of it, there's just no need to talk like everything's all tra-la-la, he's a big boy after all. In the end, when A.A.'s still joking around because you just can't say these things seriously to someone you haven't seen in years (though yes, this is exactly the person you want to tell it all to), he says that because of all this nonsense, he's started seeing his wife again, his ex, that she hadn't found anyone for herself, either. As a matter of fact, it started by chance, by chance they'd run into each other in line at the store, they couldn't just pretend they didn't know each other so they started asking each other how things were, and then, there you go, everything was like when they were young, they visited, and somehow it worked out that they ended up in bed, no, she didn't do anything on purpose either, and the most foolish thing is it appears she's pregnant, a 35-year-old woman. A.A. lights a cigarette and Masha tells him she can't stand it any longer at his place so why doesn't he wash up and shave and *let's go somewhere and sit, just at least put on something decent*.

A.A. attempts to beg off—he doesn't have any money—but Masha brazenly replies, *on the other hand, I'm doing pretty well for myself now, come on, come on, I'll check my email while I wait,* and so he has to wash up and shave because he does, after all, want to hear what she thinks about this subject, though he also knows it won't change anything at all.

Masha shuts off the sound when she sees Roma's calling, dialing her number over and over: she and A.A. are already sitting in a strange restaurant with Chinese food and karaoke, and she's not up for explaining where she is or with whom. What was impossible in the smoke-filled apartment, with the sound of water running in a malfunctioning toilet in the background, had become possible as evening fell on Bolshoy Prospect: she and A.A. slowly strode down the street, their hands sometimes hitting, just like ten years ago, and the current of a common language suddenly began running between them once again. On a Friday evening, cars barely arrive in time to find parking by shopping centers, Bolshoy Prospect teems with loud groups, the 6-ya and 7-ya Linias smell of beer and tobacco, and shop windows gleam on Sredny Prospect. Sometimes Masha has to shout so A.A. can hear her. *Of course you have to get married,* she shouts, *did you get divorced?* A.A. shakes his head. *Then all the more. A child's a good reason.* She lowers her voice when a sharp-nosed young girl walking in the other direction looks askance at her after those last words. Masha has trouble finding the right words. What she wants to tell A.A. is that in reality there's no difference, whether he goes back to his wife or not. It's not that he's almost forty, that his female grad students have stopped coming by to visit, and that there won't be another chance like this. It's just that it's pointless for him to run away now that he's messed up in this storyline, which will catch up to him anyway, in some form or other. Though maybe it'll be the opposite and he'll manage to fool it, like how people catch a fish by gently letting the line go a touch. The most widely circulated argument against having a family—not wanting to get tied down—is the stupidest of things: our hands and feet are tied from the very beginning. In any case, the way out of this story isn't in the sameness of its events. Whether it's a bachelor who's let himself go or a parent who's getting on in years, these are identically banal little pictures. In attempting to explain all that so it doesn't come out sounding offensive, Masha goes off track, to herself, her own work, and the film.

The film that cinemas all over Europe were roaring with laughter about is something A.A. has, so far, only seen on his computer—a junky bootleg shot in the movie theater—and of course that's not the same thing at all, but he himself is glad to change the topic; he doesn't start talking more about his wife, he's already heard what he needs to hear. He couldn't think Masha would want to come back to him but he needed her to know. They're already talking about something else when they go inside the restaurant.

A.A. is prepared to admit that *Minus* is visually precise and wonderful, that the whole film—from the longhairs in a passageway in the subway who sing from Carlos Puebla's "De Su Presencia Gigante" to dialogues like *what's up with the damn suitcase? –What? What's up what? It's up your twat! –My twat's got what? –That's just my thought!* (that's the Russian translation of what they say but why the hell do Germans really need the rhyme if they haven't even read Pelevin's dialogue?)—is made such that the enormous metaphor of the train station organizes the entire expanse of the picture so the final scene, where Max walks down the street and stops at a newsstand to buy a paper with job ads, imparts a new depth to the whole picture; and as A.A. was saying all this, Masha blushed and pulled at her fingers (so, is there anybody who could hear all this out with a cold nose?) but even so, he couldn't not say something about how (and this was precisely because he wasn't a magazine reviewer)… but Masha already knew herself what that "how" was.

How if you were to remove from *Minus One* all the gags and all the subtle innuendos (even to Tolstoy: there's a guy in one scene who sits in the corner and bangs with a hammer, and he's even asked if anyone's run past, and he answers that he's never once seen anyone walking here because they all run), then all that's left of the film is a bare outline that's entirely and totally something she thought up out of nothing. It's true that an escape like the one the main character of *Minus One* conceives could never work if you don't have your mind on escape of the very largest scale, the kind accomplished by Pushkin, *if we're to believe Yury Lotman,* adds A.A. And that happens (Masha's already conjecturing here) not in view of certain supercircumstances but, to the contrary, simply because of the nature of things.

Masha turns off the volume on her phone at just the right time (it's not that she doesn't want to hear Roma at all, just not now), as A.A.'s relaxed voice is saying that *it is, after all, a first film* and there sounds in his voice the weariness of an almost elderly person who's just about to say that, basically, a 26-year-old girl can't say anything about life because what does she know about it, and of course you have to agree, but Masha's simultaneously glad for the protest growing inside her: he's telling her she's on the right track anyway and the only person who can do anything is the one who can do the impossible.

Roma keeps calling, Masha sees her phone lighting up like a semaphore in the depths of her purse, and A.A. pretends not to notice. Shouting over a drunk, middle-aged woman singing karaoke, Masha replies that she's going to make another film, already has proposals, and just needs to finish the screenplay, she's even started already, written ten pages (she catches herself thinking that she never tells Roma about her work), that it's the kind of story made up of several segments; it's about a girl who's marrying one man, then there's another story about what if she married another man, and then it happens again, and in the end, all three stories, for the most part, lead to the very same thing: a life lived in tedium. Masha herself feels like she's retelling something silly and she wants to explain in more detail about how it's all the same idea—it doesn't matter what you choose in life because you'll end up in the shit either way—A.A. nods, he understands everything (he's reaching in his pocket for his phone), *but it's the outline again, see, you already know everything about your film*, and he barely has a chance to finish saying that because he glances at the number with surprise, answers, says *yes, certainly* into the phone, and hands it to Masha.

A jealous person is about the same as a collections-agency employee: resourceful and stubborn. As Roma's dialing Masha's number for the ninth time (he chose the number nine), he already knows Masha's with him, with A.A. (he knew himself whom he'd be with in that situation, besides, the closer you are to the fourth decade, the fewer options remain). In a rush of somnambular confidence, Roma enters a name into the search field of a social network, filters by year of birth (eight years older than Masha, she'd said so), and, out of three options (game shows with three mystery-prize options come to mind but do not amuse) faultlessly chooses a page with the number that solves his problem. If nothing else, he thinks, I'll be a crank caller, and then, when the phone's picked up on the fifth ring, he calmly says, *may I speak to Masha?*

In the film that Masha does end up making—despite A.A.'s and even her own doubts—there'll be this scene: the heroine's sitting over a thrumming phone and deciding whether to pick it up. Masha's not usually inclined toward explaining things to actors (*I need joy here. –But where's she getting it from? –I'm not your Stanislavsky, just do it like I'm asking, only don't act with your eyebrows*) but this time Masha sits with the actress during a break –*At what moment does she understand it's all over? –Well, when he tells her... –That's rubbish, nothing of the sort, it's when she's sitting over the phone, she's already understanding, it's this vibe—because, really, it doesn't even matter if she picks up the phone or not—that he's even calling her right now, that already means it's over. It's like an orgasm: at some point, it's not there yet but it's unavoidable, no matter what happens... Nothing can be fixed, not at all... We always seem to think we can still fix something until the most horrible thing happens, but suddenly, at that moment—it's like something's cut to the heart of the matter—she understands it's an illusion, and a scary illusion, scary because huge numbers of people contrive to drag that state out for years.* The actress will bat her eyes and nod and then after filming, when Masha's already wrapping herself up in a blanket like a cocoon (it's horribly cold in the Berlin apartment), she'll think there was no reason to unload on the girl, all she accomplished was that the actress started to play *understanding*, when Masha should have just told her to play hidden rage, that's it. Because you live through impending doom as if it's a quiet, powerless rage.

The directorial mistake is unforgivable—the actress will have to be tricked and the scene reshot—but you can understand Masha on a human level: this isn't the same as sharing your innermost secrets with a journalist, and as Masha replays that Petersburg Friday evening over and over in her memory, she discovers that when she was taking the phone out of A.A.'s hands, already knowing whose voice she'd hear, she also knew how everything would end.

Either the blankets shrank or Masha's body can no longer roll itself up into an impenetrable cocoon after stretching and growing in all directions during the years that have passed since childhood, so Masha crawls out of bed and goes to the kitchen, wrapped in a coverlet. The kitchen smells like old smoke, Masha lights a cigarette to cover the smell, climbs up on the windowsill, and opens the window. Outside she sees the roof of an old garage, and a large gray tomcat leaping to the side, out from under a bush that's growing out of the slate. Masha sees the cat's button eyes dully shining up from the ground: *Murzik, Murzik* she calls, but the buttons fade and Masha's left by herself. An October breeze stirs the leaves and drives the smoke out the window. Masha tucks the coverlet under her toes and the cold that cautiously seizes her from below brings her a strange satisfaction. Half a cigarette later, she already wants things to be like this forever: open window, cold, the cat running off, spiral plume from the cigarette, and darkness.

No matter who authored the Book of Genesis, he was just as wrong as the author of *Capital*: labor's not a curse and not a joy, but a gift to the proletariat exiled from a futile paradise (because in the final reckoning, any tools of labor belong to God) and labor's the only option for escaping existential horror. Masha forces her arms and legs to move—slowly, as if she's in a gloppy pudding—brings paper and pencil to the kitchen, turns on the light, and draws a line, her teeth clenched. Each movement of her hand is agonizing and Masha bites the inside of her cheek so the pain can distract her from surges of wanting to curl into a ball and cry. Gradually—in keeping with the progress of the outlines of a face coming through the whiteness of the paper—Masha stops biting her cheek so hard and finally forgets it. Masha's hands fill with blood, she slams the window shut, puts on coffee, and relocates to the table after moving unwashed cups into the corner.

Summer's fattening up on the paper. Leaves juicy with green blood hang from the trees, a curtain sighs in a window, a bench under the sun smells of varnish, an old woman squeezes her knees to hold the flaps of her robe and fishes in her pocket for sunflower seeds, delivering some to her mouth with one hand and using the other to drop seeds on the ground, where babbling pigeons with mean eyes mill around in the dust. Masha erases the old woman's eyes time after time and draws them over again, until she finds the right ones: as empty as glasses with the dregs of last night's tea.

Masha has to be on the set at eight in the morning but she'll crawl her way to bed at five so she can at least calm down a little. The ash-covered sheet of paper with the old woman remains on the kitchen table. Several scenes for her next picture are sketched on the other side.

Before waking up from her assistant's persistent calls (Masha hasn't trusted alarm clocks for a long time), Masha dreams about a new generation of mobile phones where all you have to do is accept a call and the caller will instantly be with you. Roma calls and Masha persistently presses to hang up but either the button's stuck or this phone's design doesn't offer that function, and she realizes Roma will be with her any minute now, there's nothing she can do, and she jerks her arm, powerless.

Of course this dream ought to be interpreted as her repressed fervent desire to get Roma back. It should be noted, though, that in some sense it replicates the situation from a year and a half ago, in the Chinese restaurant with karaoke, when Masha took the phone from A.A.'s hands with the feeling of a pinball player who knows perfectly well that the ball will return to the gates no matter what, if, that is, it doesn't disappear into the place where, in an even more symbolic game—hopscotch—kids write "fire" in the final square and lose their turn if they land there.

And this is how it was. Masha took the phone and said *yes* three times, answering three foolish questions: *are you in Petersburg? With A.A.? Invite me?* Roma arrived in a half-hour. By that time, Masha and A.A. had already managed to move on to empty chatter that had about as much purpose as playing some foolish card game where the jack of funny life-stories gets trumped by the king of brand-new jokes, resulting in a win from the player with the most aces of common memories in his hand. Nobody, however, needs the winnings, either in a foolish game of cards or in a conversation like this: what's important is fingering through all the cards in your hands.

After jouncing through half the city in a reeking little car headed toward Lieutenant Schmidt Bridge, Roma thought he was finally on his way to clearing things up completely. In his fantasy, he was entering the café, where A.A. was embracing Masha, and Roma suggested that A.A. step outside. Or, after drinking a shot of vodka, he wiped his lips with the back of his thumb and then calmly announced to Masha when she could pick up her things. Masha made excuses, he accepted them. Or didn't. But as he entered the restaurant, which smelled of pork, he'd fallen into a completely different tempo and rhythm: Masha and A.A. were as relaxed as snails left to their own devices, smiled at him, and A.A. extended his hand (Roma had to shake it) and poured him a shot.

As Masha glanced at Roma settling in across from her, seeing how he held his menu, how he lit a cigarette, how the cigarette pack awkwardly grazed a shot glass filled to the brim (A.A. reached across the table to put down a napkin), Masha saw that what Roma wanted was a scene in the Dostoevskian spirit, with packets of money flung into a fireplace, stylized dialogues that last a page and a half, troika rides, and epileptic fits; despite all her wishes, though, Masha was in no condition to play along with Roma. That wasn't because she didn't have the strength—quite the contrary, she felt like she could have even filmed the Battle of Borodino right now (a deceptive sensation that soft drugs, alcohol among them, grant to us)—it was because she was feeling too good and wasn't prepared to swap her condition, of absolute correspondence with what was happening, for any other sort of defined advantages.

There was the momentary awkwardness with the spilt vodka, the hesitation in choosing food (*get the pork, we just ate it, it's really pretty good*, Masha poked her finger at the menu), *glad to meet you* with glasses raised, and Roma still searching, agonized, for an excuse to ask what was happening, but A.A. had already remembered how social dialogues go: *I went to an exhibit at the photography museum the other day...*

The waitress brought over the pork, a fat man with the knot of his necktie dangling on his chest nearly upended them as he made his way to karaoke, Roma flung up his hands (*photography is the art of time! Of time, not what someone's thinking, what's in the head!*), A.A. poured another round, and Masha experienced a strange feeling, as if some third person has appeared inside her. She had a body that felt good, then there was Masha herself, who'd made an agreement with her body that they set aside their concerns for later, and now there was this third person who was simply an observer, following the happenings through openings in Masha's head as if from on high, not giving a damn whatsoever about anything.

The Russian boys had already reached the meaning of art (*what we get out of works of art are ideas, whether they're consciously embedded or not, and if there's nothing to get out of it, then what's the need for the work? –But maybe it's just simply beautiful! –There's the thing, though, it can't be!*), the fat man stuck his necktie in his pocket, found what he was searching for in karaoke and looked sideways at the screen after turning toward his table. He was what now interested Masha's third person most of all: he was obviously behind and would have to catch up –...*ove all ages must submit*... He sang as the letters appeared, turning yellow on the screen—*I would not think of hiding it: maaadly I do love Tatyaaaana*—and he opened his mouth wide there, as if he'd lifted a toilet lid. He wailed like a vent pipe, now pressing his left hand to his unbuttoned shirt, now extending it toward Tatyana, who'd hidden her painted laughing mouth in her hand, as someone slapped her on the back and shook a joking fist at the fat man filled with operatic passion.

And at the same time as Masha's vodka-burned tongue pressed at the hot pork, at the same time as Masha herself attempted to remember if the bridges were already being lowered back down over the Neva, the third person inside Masha was, in some strange way, enjoying the unalloyed banality of what was happening. This third person's unnatural enjoyment mixed with Masha's annoyance that the bridges were still up after all.

It wouldn't be much of a stretch to say that this third person was the force that had pushed Masha to run herself ragged at work immediately after her breakup with Roma. When Masha was in Moscow signing a contract for the ten-part series *Bolshaya Yakimanka Street*, she thought least of all about honoraria (and one must assume this is the very reason the honorarium wasn't as stratospheric as the public imagination, which is so preoccupied with such things,

depicted it) and what was important to her was being able to start
filming tomorrow already rather than having to wait for anything,
so after she'd paged through the script and pounded away to get
herself the right to touch it up along the way if need be, she received
an advance, rented an apartment on Nikitsky Boulevard, right
downtown, and lived there for almost half a year, going to sleep
for two or three hours in the morning, filming for whole days at a
time, editing, adding sound, rewriting the script for the next part
in the evenings, and working at night on scene after scene of *Love
for Three Jackasses*; that was the working title of *Save*.

Masha needed work the way an alcoholic who's hit the skids
needs hawthorn tincture in the morning: without it, she would
have had to stop and look with cold attention at the fact that she
was almost thirty, she'd betrayed her parents, crushed two men's
lives, suffered from loneliness herself, and hadn't made anything
yet that she wasn't ashamed of, if a real, true reckoning were to be
totaled up (don't tell Shklovsky's man from Hamburg, who created
the rating system, so there's no need to reminisce about A.A.). They
were still trying to socialize her that summer at the studio (*Maria
Pavlovna, today's Lyuda's, the makeup artist's, birthday… –Okay, we'll
finish up an hour early. –No, that's not what I meant, we're inviting you…*)
but after Masha refused four times in a row, trying to produce a
well-intentioned facial expression, alluding to either exhaustion or
things to do (*maybe I have a personal life, too*), they stopped bugging
her, and tapped a finger to the head to make "crazy" gestures behind
her back (*did you see that smile?!*), albeit respectfully: *now that's talent!*

In Masha's hands, the idiotic story of middle managers, their
love and romance, their drugs, and their office-based despondence
(for some reason, the channel's executives decided middle managers really wanted to see themselves on TV) transformed into ten
installments about people who, like restless flies, got tangled in a
web they took to be adult life. *I've grasped that life only rules until
you're eighteen…* says one of the characters, as if the *ultimate* truth

about that world has been submitted for the people to judge and, yes, this was generally what Masha thought about these Moscow guys and gals who'd decided, in all seriousness, that apparently the gloomy god of commerce would give them the gift of eternal youth on Friday evenings in exchange for ten hours of their lives five days a week.

Later on, when Masha gave an interview to a nice young man from some *cultural site* or other three hours before a flight to Berlin (as the guy was unearthing his Dictaphone from his backpack, he set a copy of *The Power of an Exploding Wave* on the airport café table; A.A. had read Sekatsky at one time so Masha was a bit more candid with the guy than usual, without specially thinking about it) and when he asked her if it was too bad she hadn't been allowed to finish making the series, she answered honestly that no, it wasn't too bad: *I think that in those four parts I said everything I could say about the problems of office life, I don't know what else could have been added: it's really not such a big problem, nothing to go into excruciating detail about.* Masha squirmed out of the direct question about why filming was stopped. She could have talked about how she'd been invited to an office with a view of the Kremlin, where she'd been told they were disappointed with the received product (Masha felt queasy from that one word), and that the series had been conceived as a comedy, *the viewer won't understand us, and we're oriented on the viewer above all*: maybe she would have told him all that if she'd indeed felt offended, but, in reality, she didn't care. She simply kept quiet there, in that office, because literally the night before she'd received a letter from Berlin, so it was only in the café, for the Dictaphone, that she answered the confident guy in the office who'd been constantly glancing at his own watch and out the window, as if he were checking his watch against the clock on the Kremlin tower outside. No, she hadn't thought about the viewer when she was making it. That's generally a faulty idea, orienting yourself on the viewer. You just have to be maximally honest and absolutely serious, and film what you think and feel. People aren't really that different from one another and, in the final reckoning, we're all in the very same shit, whether you're the head of a branch office or a cashier. When they talk about having to be oriented on the viewer, they mean you have to be oriented on human laziness and stupidity. And there's already more than enough laziness and stupidity in all of us that they don't need to be stimulated more. *At least I don't need to, maybe someone else does.*

Those four episodes of *Bolshaya Yakimanka Street* didn't air for another half-year, late at night, but they'd already taken off online and thousands of young people around the country were bandying about phrases: *so what should I wish for you? The most expensive car, the most handsome man by far!* (the girl who played the secretary Elvira with the multi-colored nails was really something, but this scene came off especially well for her), *we were walking along the embankment and saw Abramovich's yacht and took pictures of ourselves* or *kissing a dog, oh, come on, even kissing people is disgusting, after all!*

The third person, whose indifferent curiosity had been torturing Masha, was with her on the set at the Mosfilm studio and in the office with the young man wearing the watch who was oriented on viewers; the third person rarely left her at all now. Only when she'd take her laptop under her arm and go down to Novy Arbat Avenue to hide out in the corner of a plasticky café did she force out a few lines for her screenplay: she didn't manage to make the third person disappear every time, only sometimes, and it must be said that Masha herself and her body, too, disappeared along with him and all that remained was a fuzzy buzz of phrases from which someone-instead-of-Masha tried to grab the juiciest by the tail.

Masha wrote the *Love for Three Jackasses* screenplay—the film that would, in the final reckoning, end up being called *Save* because what did Gozzi and Prokofyev and their three oranges have to do with anything—in three and a half months, and translated it into German in two weeks, but she didn't stop there after sending the file to Berlin. This wasn't so much because of a secret confidence that the screenplay would be accepted (Masha saw all its shortcomings and it was still pretty good) as because she couldn't live without the nightly self-flagellation with insomnia: and so, swigging down coffee, she scribbled out sheet after sheet, drawing the scenes of her future picture.

Masha flew off to Berlin with a huge portfolio case of drawings. When the young journalist guy was glancing at the case leaning against the wall, he finally couldn't hold back: *do you draw? –Yes,* Masha answered without thinking, *to tell the truth, that's my main income, I draw all sorts of balderdash on the canvases of the Old Masters and carry them across the border.*

The Dictaphone was already off, and the guy volunteered to escort Masha to the green customs channel: *playing my flute I passed the green janissaries,* he muttered (erudition's brilliance vanished in vain: Masha didn't recognize the quote) and he still couldn't leave as he was saying goodbye. *Well, go on, I still have about ten minutes.* The guy adjusted the backpack on his shoulder. *You... you're totally fleeing, right?* Masha burst out laughing. She'd already had to discuss the Russian intelligentsia's eternal question of *to flee or not to flee, forever,* once with A.A., when she was leaving to take her exams at HFF. It was then, from A.A., that she first heard the ritual mantras about *the decline of the West* and about Konstantin Leontiev's *secondary simplification,* which, incidentally, took on an additional overtone in A.A.'s rendition: *there's actually a beauty in what they're all advocating* (A.A. waved his hand in the direction of *them all) and you have to see the beauty of that gesture: Archimedes, who doesn't say* noli tangere *but leads the armed barbarians to his own circles so he can deliver the last lecture of his life for them. –Cool, cool...* Masha pretended at the time that she'd understood but only later did she understand: this was A.A.'s way of laughing at her. This time Masha herself laughed as she remembered that conversation and risked offending the guy, but instead of starting to tell him about Archimedes, she simply said, *dude, all you can totally do is croak*, then picked up her portfolio case and walked under the green sign. The interview Masha scrolled through later on the *culture site* was titled just that: "All you can totally do is croak."

After arriving in Berlin the same way she'd once arrived in Köln—during the Christmas rush—Masha experienced the very same cognitive dissonance that her characters from *Bolshaya Yakimanka Street* were so clueless about, albeit with a difference in scale: they couldn't indulge themselves in a Porsche but she had to count her change and refuse Glühwein at the Gendarmenmarkt. She found a Russian attorney, showed him the agreement she'd signed without looking six months ago, and he scolded her for being a fool. The attorney walked around an office as white as a dentist's, an office in a half-empty building with windows looking out on the s-Bahn; his hands were folded into a triangle and he was weighing how to *resolve the issue*. Masha was listening to the building's sounds—water spoke in pipes, doors groaned, heels argued with one another—and even before the attorney had broken his triangle in half as if he were releasing a jinn into the air, Masha understood she didn't really want to *resolve the issue*, she simply wanted money. An office as white as a dentist's was obviously not the place where money could be procured.

Only at first glance do cause-and-effect relationships appear to work in mysterious ways. That Peter appeared in one of the roles in *Save* was the direct effect of the aversion to *issues* that Masha experienced looking at graffiti on the other side of the railroad tracks. As she left the office, she thought a bit, grasped that she had no other way out, and called Peter. When he and Masha met that evening at a Beatlemania café at Zoo, he went out to the bank machine without saying a word and brought her ten 500 euro notes. Obviously, she couldn't not offer him a role after that.

Masha will spend two months waiting for the studio to prepare to sign the agreement (each week she'll have to listen to them say

over the phone that it won't work out this week, though it'll probably be next week, *sei sicher*). She'll sleep until evening, aimlessly
wander the streets, read books halfway through, go to Hollywood
movies, eat curried hotdogs in underground crosswalks, surf the
Internet until her lower back aches, even start going to museums
and drinking beer and coffee with lemon in bars in the evenings,
and when she's drunk, she'll shake her boobs on the dance floor
(at first she'll be surprised and wonder why nobody comes on to
her but then she'll figure it out: no, it's not political correctness, she
just scares everybody), and then she'll come home at seven in the
morning, licking the last drops of flat beer from the neck of the
bottle in sight of her neighbors saddling up their bikes... all that
time, Masha's third person will be observing her and his silence
will become ever more mocking, and it will be as if Masha herself
starts going away somewhere, there'll be less and less of her, and
sometimes she'll think she's now the one peering through the small
crack at what her third person sees, using her eyes.

Peter will call her in early March and ask how things are. Masha
will say she doesn't have any money. Peter will keep silent and say
that's not what he meant: how are things with *her*. Masha will keep
silent. Then Peter will come over. Masha will sit on the windowsill
and smoke, Peter will sit on a chair, shifting his glance to her from
the sink and the floor. Masha will be ashamed to wonder if he
didn't come to collect on his debt and she'll start estimating how
long she'll have to sleep with him for the five thousand. But Peter,
not knowing what to do with his hands, will be silent and only ask
what's happening with the studio. Masha will say they're all holes
in the ass. As he leaves (*I still have to make it to the store*, and Masha
will think, well that's some excuse), Peter will falter at the door
and tell Masha to be patient and that, well, you know, she should
find something to do. Only a week later, when they call Masha and
ask her to come sign the agreement (*you can do it today?*), and after
she's flung the phone on the couch, will she understand why Peter

came over. And three days later, after they've already wired part of her honorarium, she'll ask him: *so tell me, does this mean they can't give me money to make a film until you've interceded?* he won't even begin denying anything, he'll just say, also joking, *well, listen, I just wanted my money back.*

It will be tough to get down to work. After the first day—when Masha will be in the crosshairs of four pairs of attentive eyes, forced to wring out of herself how many days to allot to casting and how many to locations, she'll hear her own voice as if she's under water and follow the twists of her own tongue as if it were a clam that's taken up residence in her mouth—she'll come home, open a can of beer from the refrigerator, and pour it down the sink muttering, in Russian, *fuck it, fuck it.* Instead of lying down to sleep, Masha will take out paper, lay it on the table, and sit over the sheet for several hours: she'll chew at the inside of her cheeks, pound herself on the head, drink coffee, and groan plaintively, but she won't be able to draw anything at all except little squares, arrows, and triangles. But then when she wakes up the next morning, she'll feel like her hands are her own, not someone else's.

Masha tells the crew the next day that she wasn't herself yesterday, that she hadn't planned everything out properly, and is going to adjust the filming schedule so they'll have nearly twice as much work each day. She'll do that specially so she can fall into bed from exhaustion when she returns to Friedrichstraße: lacking the strength to even toss an egg into a frying pan, she'll drink raw eggs (like when she was a child, beating them on a saucer, pouring on salt and pepper), stirring them a little with a fork and swallowing without fully stirring them.

The day Masha will explain to the young actress about the phone call (the girl they'd taken, at her insistence, is nearly a debut actress so there's enough money to pay Peter, though of course Masha couldn't not understand that, if she'd been thoroughly brazen, Peter would have done the picture almost for free) is the very same day the girl's partner won't be able to fly to Berlin because of a restless volcano. Filming will have to be halted and the crew released, and Masha will be left in an empty, half-dark pavilion, not understanding what's happening or what to do. When Peter stops by the pavilion for a forgotten jacket, he'll try to look surprised and tell Masha the one thing she can't snap at—*my God, boss, the last time you ate was half a year ago, let's go stuff ourselves now*—and he'll drive Masha to that same Beatlemania café in his ostentatiously old Mercedes.

That night, after dinner, the shape of Masha's next picture will come together, first in her imagination, later on a sheet of paper. As she attempts to grasp how that worked out, Masha will calm herself because today, for the first time, she finally didn't get dog-tired and because when she explained to the actress girl about the phone, she'd inadvertently resurrected in her memory the agitation of that Petersburg Friday night, and because, later, sitting with Peter in the café, wondering if he really might, indeed, be in love with her, so much that he could even keep it under his hat, she'd also inadvertently grown agitated and basically remembered that sweet stupor and gotten angry (it goes without saying that anger is the best fuel for idle hands)... but something in her memory will be painfully itchy, like some sort of splinter that lets her know not everything's over.

Of course Masha won't remember, but therein lies our advantage over our heroine: we know a little more about her (or, in any event, about her story) than she herself knows. In reality, things were like this. Peter nodded to the waiter as if he were an old acquaintance; ordered something from the menu (the well-done beef steak called "Wait," the "Every Little Thing" seafood, "A Taste of Honey" for dessert, and the like); chatted, gossiping about people he'd briefly seen at the studio; drank beer; only allowed himself to look at Masha for any length of time when she turned toward the plasma panel; then, so as not to fall silent, he started chattering about the establishment's heroes (*that film, the one on the screen now, was shot in London in 1969 and the funniest thing is that none of the Beatles were at the premiere!* and Masha grinned, though she didn't see what was so funny) and didn't stop jabbering until the very end, when they headed toward the exit after paying (*it doesn't matter, but pay for yourself if you want. –Let's just split it*), stumbling on a chair, apologizing to a fat biker with a Maß and a thimble of vodka, and then when Peter was flinging the door open in front of Masha, the sound of "When I find myself in times of trouble…" was carrying from the screen.

Masha had heard the very same keyboards a year and a half ago in Petersburg. All three of them had already drunk themselves into senseless agitation when the fat man, his necktie stuck in his pocket, made his way to karaoke once again and—nearly knocking himself in the mouth with the microphone—began wailing in the direction of his chosen one, not knowing the words and not keeping up as the little line turned yellow: *leht eet be, leht eet be, speeking vords of vizdom, I vas tops in my Engleesh class, leht eet be, leht eet be…*

They left the Chinese restaurant, stifling the karaoke with the entrance (exit) door and found themselves in bright nocturnal stillness three steps later. They silently reached 3-ya Linia, where A.A. started inviting them in, saying he'd put them to bed in the living room, there were no hungry bears in his apartment (*this isn't like your northern Pskov land*, he winked) and it's highly likely it was that wink that made lodging at A.A.'s absolutely impossible. Roma loudly and distinctly said he didn't want to sleep, that he and Masha would walk around and wait for the bridges to come down. Masha looked at A.A., closed her eyes halfway, and he teetered, said goodbye, and disappeared into the front door.

The silence that hung after A.A.'s disappearance was agonizing for Masha. It was easy-peasy for her to see that all Roma needed was any excuse to start having it out. Masha loathed this form of communication but there are things you sign on for when you say *I love you, too*—it's like receiving advertising messages when you register on a website—and so she eased Roma's task by asking how he'd guessed she was with A.A.

They had it out for the next several hours, striding along the roadway of the various Linia streets, taking a seat for a smoke on the peeling black metal fences of garden beds, and stopping at all-night stores for beer. They snaked their way between Bolshoy Prospect and the embankment, walking as far as 16-ya Linia, and returned to the bridge, managing about a dozen times to play the exact same set of moves from *make up your mind already about what matters most to you* to *if that's the way it is, we should break up*.

Roma had had it out to his heart's content by the time they approached the sphinxes with a half-hour left until the bridges would come down; his intoxication had shifted to a stage of full harmony with the world, and they stayed to wait by the sphinxes and opened the last cans of beer. The water was calm.

Roma's voice screeched in the gaping silence and he asked for forgiveness, saying: *tomorrow we'll wake up and we'll have breakfast and everything will pass like nothing ever happened*. Masha was silent, totally silent, thinking—*you and I are walking around in circles, just walking around in circles. You know where people walk around in circles? In prison*. She was swallowing the beer, looking into the water, and sobering up. Roma said: *let's have a baby*.

The sky had already turned a gentle pink tint, cupolas and spires now blazed, Athena was solemnly extending a gleaming laurel wreath, remainders of the pale night caught on the corner of the Rumyantsevsky Garden, first cars murmured, St. Isaac's Cathedral swelled on the other side of the Neva River, the Senate languidly curved, Peter the Great sat motionlessly on his horse, and suddenly Masha sensed with a penetrating clarity that she wasn't the one looking at them but that they—the monuments, buildings, churches, water, steps, bridges, openings in clouds, caryatids and oriel windows on the English Embankment, the barely identifiable figures on the roof of the Winter Palace, the Angel surfacing from behind the Admiralty—that all that motionless stone, cold from the night before, was looking at them: at drunk, muttering Roma and at sober, horribly tired Masha, whose degree of indifference to what was happening might have even been enviable to the sphinxes "from ancient Thebes in Egypt."

Roma stroked her hand that lay on her knee and said *I love you.* Masha, silent, shook the remains of the beer foam into her tipped-back head. *So, so what's wrong, why are you silent, say something.* Masha put the can on the corner of the step and stood: *they'll lower the bridges now, let's get a car.*

Roma began undressing Masha in the apartment, searched for her lips with his hiccupping mouth, kneaded her breasts, and pushed her toward the bed; Masha shoved him aside and went to the kitchen to put on the teakettle. Roma came into the kitchen, leaned his shoulder against the doorjamb, and drew out his words, *I'm asking for your body, as Christians ask: give us this day our daily bread! Maria, give it!* Masha didn't know the quote and answered the question automatically, just as they'd done in kindergarten: *give it went to China for a visit.*

Masha slept a few hours on the little kitchen sofa, tossed everything she wanted to take with her into a suitcase in the morning, put her keys on the table, and left the door ajar. She could still hear Roma's snore receding for two flights as she walked down.

# THE EVENT HORIZON

*Save*, which was filmed, edited, and audio engineered in five and a half months (Masha battled with the actors, had knock-down-drag-outs with the producer, and spilled liters of coffee in the editing suite), is a film about a young woman whose life is saved at a key moment—she's choosing between three men: which one gets the yes?—as if it were a computer game. The storyline tracks her fate until her first collapse (mutual hatred, *you ruined my whole life! –Just look at yourself, look at what you've become!*) and then the "return to last saved" button kicks in. The heroine chooses another man, endures yet another new collapse, and returns again to choose the third man so she can spend her third life coming to yet another collapse. Game over. Cast. Masha, who'd never played computer games, most likely knew they always end with credits, just like the movies.

It was right after the release of *Save* that Masha happened to give the interview to *Diva* and explain herself about homosexuality: certain frenzied biddies had decided the film was about them, about how you don't have to choose between different men, about how men are all jackasses. As Masha answered questions from a 50-year-old woman with expressively desirous masculine eyes and close-cropped purple hair, she was staggered at how wrongheadedly her simple thought could be understood: the lady softly demanded the same answers she'd already decided to hear (...*but yet you didn't depict one single positive male character in the film, why's that?*) and thus, it seems, she also didn't understand that the film she liked so much was about the impossibility, on principle, of a different screenplay, either with females, males, or little green men.

At some point in time (that point is impossible to either fore-see or acknowledge in the present, one can only think back to it, exactly like the moment when human life explodes; the Big Bang of post-natal screams was always already there), and so, at some point in time, human life inevitably begins imploding and it's no longer possible to overcome the gravitation of death: no matter what you do, no matter what buttons you push, the singularity of full and definitive solitude is inevitable and it's possible to guess that moment has already passed, based on the ever-accelerating spiral rotation of all the exact same events, places, tasks, connections, and people (in this, by the way, lies the secret of the "small world" effect of a city, Europe, and the whole planet), and that's exactly why there's nothing surprising about the fact that one day Roma, who's earning extra money on one of the Lenfilm Studio's never-ending series, will hear actresses on the set discussing Regina's *Save* and one of them will say, as she tucks her hair behind her ear in an offhand way: *Regina? I went to school with her*, and all gazes will turn to her but Dasha (surprise!) will look straight at Roma because, actually, she'd taken an immediate liking to the manly cameraman.

Not much time will pass before they'll be lying in bed—he with a cigarette, she with a towel between her legs—and they'll be surprised it's worked out that they're together: he's the one who'd escorted Masha to the school where she'd studied along with Dasha, and she's the one who'd dragged Masha to Mokhovaya Street to apply along with her at the Theater Institute. The main thing, by the way—that this was a mockery, not just some irony of fate—would remain unsaid: Dasha had gotten an ersatz version of her acting dream (perpetual episodes in series she hated, endless gushing with assistants she couldn't stand), and Roma had a substitute for his love, a stepsister instead of Cinderella, or in *Eugene Onegin* terms, Olga instead of Tatyana.

It won't be difficult to lure Roma to bed: his seductive powers had broken down after he'd woken up two years ago in an empty, Masha-less apartment with an aching head that felt like it had been drilled, and though he still dragged home half-sober girls on Friday nights to mess around and take photos, the girls sensed dirty tricks, and if they weren't already totally drunk, they begged off, citing lectures, Mama and Papa, and that time of the month. Roma decided old age was approaching but the problem lay elsewhere: in reality, this had all become horrendously boring for him. His eyes no longer gleamed, the girls, who'd needed a sense of play to justify things (*I don't know myself how it happened*), left with other guys, and Roma bookmarked more and more porn sites: things were always serious there.

And so Dasha—after casting a glance at Roma, who'd gotten distracted from his camera—immediately made a silent decision (and not without the ulterior motive that maybe she could somehow get a normal role this way) and will simply claim him like an ownerless object by walking past once, lingering to straighten her skirt, and taking a glance once, by which time he's already asking her, as he watches an assistant lug rails around: *so are you in touch with Masha these days? –With Masha? –Regina. I've worked with her. –Seriously?*

She'll give him her number, he'll call a week later (she'll have enough time to curse herself ten times that she hadn't just gotten his number) and ask her out to a pizza place (they have a 50 percent discount on the salad bar after 4 p.m., but not on Fridays; there's a boy and girl who look like school kids next to them, and the boy, haughty and surprised, looks at Dasha and Roma: *chill out already, aren't you a little over the hill for this?*) and then, either to raise his own status or immediately dot every "i,", Roma will tell Dasha: *she and I didn't just work together, we lived together, too*.

They'll get together three more times (Dasha will endure the seemly wait the circumstances demand) and the fourth time she'll say she doesn't need to go home today (*you mean to your place? How about mine? –Is that a proposition? –Are you agreeing?*), however sex will not ensue: for some reason Roma will get drunk on vodka (*for some reason*—meaning he won't understand the reason, though from the outside it's obvious he's getting drunk out of spite, as if he's making the decisions here), and he'll get drunk and only be capable of drunken confessions: *you can't imagine how sick I am of this... I can tell you this, we're friends, right?... I'm sick of this, screwing around left and right... it's get the hell out, and we go our separate ways... it shouldn't be like this... fuck it, I'm not twenty... and not even twenty-five, for fuck's sake... I want a family... with a nice girl, so there's none of that fucking shit... I'm sorry...* Dasha will put Roma to bed, wash the dishes, and lie down with him. He'll screw her in the morning and think he's fallen in love.

That same morning he'll manage to vaguely regret he told Dasha about Masha because when she's holding her hand on his belly she'll say *hey, listen, I forgot to ask you what you think of Masha's film anyway?* and it'll already be awkward for him to tell the truth so instead of that he'll reach for a pack of cigarettes so he can turn his contorted face away: *well, it's fine, it's okay.*

It's funny but that very same evening, Dasha will call Roma, to dumbfound him, *have you heard yet? About Masha, I mean?*: the day Dasha will begin commemorating as the first day of their *together* will turn out to be the exact same day *Bild* published SHOCKING PHOTOGRAPHS, though all that's shocking in them is Peter and Masha getting out of a car, Peter and Masha sitting in a restaurant, and Peter's hand on Masha's knee, but this spread through the European news wires and even rolled its way to Moscow sites: Masha Regina's living with her own actor (who also happens to be almost twice her age!) and they're planning to get married.

The tabloids always write the truth, just as myths of people around the world never lie: Masha truly had already been living with Peter for more than a year; however, this was only in a figurative sense since he lived in his own house and she lived in her own rented apartment, and so they went to restaurants together and slept together, either in her rented apartment or his house.

It worked out like this. After the triumphal premiere of *Save* at Potsdamer Platz (the audience demanded Masha come on stage and didn't let her go for twenty-four minutes; the famous Spanish woman heading the jury found Masha once they were in the courtyard under the Sony Center roof and told her something that nobody heard; plus there was a big article in the next day's *Die Welt*: *Who'd dare not give the Bear to Regina?*, which was the awkward translation from the German), Masha was at a loss. Every moment in her life for the past five and a half months had been scheduled down to the minute, there'd been no time to just stand in place. In the noisy crowd, amongst the multicolored lights and loud music, Masha didn't understand what to do next: go left or go right. If someone had asked her body, it would have spoken up for the quickest transport home, but what would it have done if it had ended up there? After thinking for a few minutes (someone shouted something in her ear, shoved a Dictaphone to her lips), Masha suddenly remembered what she had to do right now. She looked around for the producer, made her way to him, and pulled his ear toward herself: *in Russian this is called* abwaschen *but it's not about the washing up, it's about the celebration.*

Waiters lugged beer and vodka, and shrimp and cocktail sausages to tables that had been pushed together; the colors of the roof changed, and Masha's head kept spinning faster; later, Peter invited a small group of people to head to his place, where that small group raided the bar and headed for home in the middle of the night though Masha couldn't: she was lying on the sofa, sleeping, curled up in a ball. Peter brought the dishes to the kitchen, wiped the tables, smoked a cigarette, and sat alongside Masha: *hey, boss, let's go, I'll bring you to the bedroom.* Masha sat up, muttering that she'd go home now, that she couldn't inconvenience him, *we have to call a taxi. —What taxi, Königin, I have three bedrooms, don't sweat it —no, no, I'm sorry, I'll just use the bathroom,* however Masha threw up, even before making it to the bathroom, right under the cover of *A Hard Day's Night* that hung on the wall, Peter washed her face with cold water, wiped remnants of shrimp and sausage off the floor while she was soaking in the shower, brewed some strong tea, wrapped her up in a robe, gave her tea, put her to bed in one of the three bedrooms, covered her with a blanket, and sat next to her for about a half-hour, watching her. He even stroked her red head one time.

The morning was spent on apologies: for yesterday, yes, but also, latently, for today since, according to the rules of the genre, you're supposed to put out after something like this, but she couldn't because her head was splitting, though the main thing was that it would have been disgusting to put out because of guilt feelings. And so, feeling doubly guilty, Masha picked at her breakfast and hinted about taxis. Finally, Peter sat Masha in his Mercedes and took her into the city. Masha crawled out of the car on Friedrichstraße, waved, went in the front door, waited a minute, then came back out and slowly wandered to a little Russian restaurant: breakfast at Peter's had been good, but she always wanted some normal, decent soup for a hangover, ideally sour cabbage soup.

There wasn't any sour cabbage soup in the restaurant but the owner—a man who proudly announced to his clients that Masha Regina stopped in at his place from time to time—didn't tell Masha. Instead, he asked her to wait a while, the chef rushed to defrost some cabbage, and the waitress ran into the office: Masha agreed to wait a while if they'd give her a sheet of paper and a pencil. No, this wasn't showing off: Masha couldn't simply sit and wait, otherwise she'd have to think about what to do after waking up.

For the last three months, after first making the production crew's blood boil (and, later, the editor's and sound director's, too), Masha would come home at one in the morning, collapse on a stool in the kitchen like a sack of potatoes, reach into the refrigerator for the juice (she had no strength to stand), and, clutching her head with her hands, fix her gaze on the ash-strewn sheet of paper where one night she'd drawn an old woman feeding pigeons. She couldn't remember why she'd drawn her. Each time, she'd move the sheet back under the sugar bowl after finishing her juice; she definitely had to manage to get a decent night's sleep.

There, in the Russian restaurant, with the sour cabbage soup on one side and the sheet of paper on the other—it was totally impossible to draw with hands as dry as sticks—Masha began drawing, just to draw. She drew a table with a tablecloth. After eating another two spoonfuls, she added in a sideboard, then a piano with a small bust of Tchaikovsky, pictures on the wall, a windowsill covered with plants, a bookshelf with long rows of identical spines of yellow books crawling from shelf to shelf, and a clock with a pendulum... Masha's bowl was already empty, she felt the pencil falling out of her wooden fingers, and, as a final effort, she began crossing out everything she'd drawn, but right before her consciousness fully imploded, leaving her on just autopilot—to pay, shove the sheet in her pocket, get to her apartment, close the door behind her, and fall, crashing on the bed—she realized she'd just drawn what she'd tried so long to remember about her old woman: her past.

That same evening, Masha called Peter and apologized again: *if you want, you can come and puke in my hallway.* After hanging up, Masha realized she'd just invited Peter over to her place.

Peter came over with a huge *quarto stagioni* and two bottles of prosecco. As they settled in on the living-room floor, he began telling Masha who'd said what today at the theater. The pizza was hot, the champagne was cold (she wondered how he'd managed that), and Masha wanted terribly to hug Peter and make love with him but she didn't know how to accomplish it. Finally, when Peter set to opening the second bottle (*how am I going to puke if I'm sober? I have to get drunk first. —You don't have to puke. —Why? —Because then it'll be disgusting to kiss you. —Are you planning to kiss me? —Yes. —So what are we waiting for? —I don't know, probably the pop of a cork*), she just sat on top of him and stretched herself toward his lips.

Peter set aside the bottle, pressed a palm to Masha's back and then, after they'd kissed a whole lot, drew back to catch her gaze: *you're certain you want this, Königin?* Masha answered *of course* since, under the circumstances, giving a stupid answer to a foolish question was simpler and quicker than explaining why there are questions that should not be asked. A half-hour later, when Masha stretched to open the second bottle—the champagne wasn't as cold anymore but it still seemed cold compared to the heat of his tongue, which still seemed to be caressing her—Peter couldn't hold back a second foolish question: *what was that, anyway?* he asked, running his fingers through her hair. Masha shoved a glass in his hands and said, as the foam subsided: *friendly sex, Peter, you and I are friends*. Peter noisily drank off the foam so Masha could finish filling the glass.

Later, when Masha's gearing up to go to Russia—to make a picture she'd initially just call "the Russian one" to herself, that was the first reason to go, and the second was to break the regularity of her relationship with Peter, since it would have to be cut off sooner or later anyway, no matter what it cost her or, even more important, him—she'd remember these foolish questions of his and think with something like relief about her past, that those questions were relevant. And relief, too, that she'd sent him home immediately after all, the first time.

Because when she went to the kitchen to brew coffee and he went to the bathroom to attend to his business, she still hadn't decided whether or not to send him home. That question flopped around in her head and twitched its tail like a fish under the baking sun, but it didn't seem to demand an immediate decision. It was only when Peter settled in on a chair and pulled the sheet with the crossed-out table, bookshelf, and all the rest toward him—the sheet

Masha had shoved in her jeans pocket as she crawled out of the Russian restaurant and then tossed on the kitchen table with coins and completely forgotten—and so when Peter took that sheet in his hands and asked what it was, so as not to be silent, Masha turned on the coffee machine, the coffee machine started rumbling, *what? What're you talking about?*, Masha then saw what Peter was holding in his hands and remembered everything, and only then did she understand it was time to send her *friend* on his way as soon as possible.

Masha nearly poured coffee into Peter by force (*you can't have champagne now, you're driving*), closed the door, and, with exacting focus—like when you hold a little frog in a squeezing fist so it won't be either crushed or able to jump out—cleared the table, got a new sheet of paper, sharpened her pencil, and washed a cup so she could pour some fresh coffee. Work was now a way for Masha to not think about what she'd just done and why. It was as if Little Masha was telling Big Masha, *see, I'm busy*, and Big Masha went to do something to herself that was spelled with four letters.

Both Mashas disappeared, though, as soon as the pencil made contact with the paper. Wind touches lacy curtains and the slightly dusty flesh of African violets; a clock with four twisty, ropelike brass columns ticks on the sideboard; slightly downcast World War Two trophy dishes glance from the wall; in heavy painted frames there's an armload of lilacs in a large-bellied vase, a birch tree on the side of a muddy, rutted road, and Pushkin with childlike little arms folded on his chest; and on the piano there stands a plaster head of an inspiring Tchaikovsky, lacquer gleams, and a ballerina is frozen in a fouetté. Balls of dust drowsily twitch behind the sofa, tectonic plates of parquet flooring creak inaudibly, and smells flow out of the kitchen like drifting snow. The distant knock of a knife on a cutting board bounces off flowery wallpaper, a thin stream of water running from the tap into the sink echoes with a ring. A starched tablecloth's bulging folds divide the table into six parts, a tower of dishes interlaid with shabby napkins soars, and forks and knives huddle together, wrapped in a towel. On the sideboard, black-and-white people who'd prepared to be photographed gaze at the ceiling from alongside the clock. A fly lands on them but then, frightened by shuffling steps, flies off behind the curtains, toward the African violets, on which sunlight flows, out from behind a cloud.

The glass coffee pot was empty and Masha suddenly and simultaneously realized that she was horribly cold and that now she knows everything about the old lady shuffling around in the kitchen.

Masha sent Peter on his way the following evenings and wrote a new screenplay. A week later, to applause, she was pushed on a stage and took a cold, heavy Bear in her hands as a battery of lenses aimed at her, but not one photograph came out as it should have—with uncontaminated joy and a picket fence of teeth—because Masha came out absent in all of them, biting her lip: she saw the heavy movement of drapes instead of the narrowing pupils of the camera and heard shuffling steps in a kitchen instead of the clicks of shutters. She agreed to give one interview and then slipped past Peter, who'd offered *abwaschen* (counting on waking up together)—*I'm sorry, everybody, I have a headache*—and hailed a taxi in the square to go home.

Two weeks later—two interviews in the morning then lunch then filming for TV plus the hassles of working on getting citizenship, too, something the producer insisted on, *the hell, messing with visas every time, particularly since now they should hand you that passport on a silver platter* and then Peter, *Königin, what's going on with you? Is everything okay? I love you*, and then home with her drawing paper until dawn—and so two weeks later the draft screenplay was ready.

Masha hadn't noticed (and how could she have?) that she'd written a screenplay that was impossible to fund. Ms. Regina, who had a Berlin Bear raising his paws over a Venetian medal on her bedroom windowsill, will be received in a dozen clean, expensive offices and fed coffee and pastries, but everywhere they'll tell her the same thing Peter had told her right away: alas, a film about

Russia, about Russian problems, isn't interesting for anyone, you have to understand that the screenplay needs to be rewritten, it's not that complicated to change the setting, shift the key points, get a European star into the picture (a hinting smile), then even a million, even ten, but otherwise... the understanding smiles and apologetic gestures will stupefy Masha, and she'll shake her head, returning again and again to this thought: she knows how to make this film in Russia, otherwise let someone else make it.

History isn't a text, but it's only accessible to us in text form, and it's not at all surprising that there are things that only become clear toward the end. Only when Masha ends up in Petersburg, after she's sat down in the apartment she'd already rented from Berlin and has a pencil so she can write down the numbers she needs to call, does she discover, to her horror, that there are three reasons for her persistence in wanting to film the future *Amber* in Russia and nowhere else but Russia.

The first is conscious and meaningless: the screenplay is allegedly about Russia. But her film isn't about purely Russian problems: a person who's grown old finally understands that a life lived fits in the palm of a hand that's filled half with meaningless sunflower seeds and half with hollow shells, and what's most torturous of all is that you just can't explain that to whomever is coming next after you in life (simply because there's no avenue at all for someone to convey that revelation) and this problem is just as Russian as it is German or Chinese, and the colonel's Petersburg apartment (hello, A.A.) Masha has snatched up could easily have been replaced by a mansion in London or a house in Rome. The second reason was semiconscious and not completely meaningless: filming in Russia meant filming with Russian actors and that was the only way she could explain to Peter that she wasn't putting him in the picture since she really couldn't just put him in and say goodbye; he hadn't hurt her in any way. But that, too, as it happens, was nonsense.

The real reason Masha had to make the picture in Russia was beyond the limits of Masha's head and related to the gravitational force of life's events, to the storyline she'd once stepped into, like a fly on flypaper, in that space between the carriages of a beat-up, jouncing train: filming in Russia meant filming with Roma and anything else would have been madness since finding another cameraman meant resisting the natural course of things, she truly didn't know a better cameraman, and, finally, she simply wanted terribly to see Roma, though she could not, under any circumstances, allow that thought into the place where she might have laughed at it or argued with it, meaning her own head.

Regina is the trendiest young director in Europe, Regina, whose face in a haystack of red hair graced a cover of *Time* that April, Regina who'd been in the most trying negotiations several dozen times over the last several months and who, finally, gathered her worldly possessions without saying a word to anybody, returned the keys to her apartment on Friedrichstraße to her landlady, didn't call Peter until the airport (*Königin, the hell! You've lost it! You can't just up and fly off!*), and flew off to Russia, where she hadn't been in two years… all so she could spend her money, sweetly smile at all the Moscow dickheads who think too much of themselves, and sleep with anyone she has to if that's the only way, but also so she could use her teeth to extract her share, that being the opportunity to make her own film the way she wants to make it: this same Masha who's in the half-empty, Ikea-furnished apartment on the Fontanka, gnawing on a pencil and drawing little squares in a graph-paper notebook, will realize she's caught again, like a little girl, because she knows what will happen next, just like she knows that two times two is four, meaning she'll get together with Roma, they'll screw like wind-up toys again, and hate each other again.

After realizing that, Masha laid the pencil in the cleavage of her open notebook, went to the kitchen, found a glass, filled it halfway with whiskey from duty free, drank it in three swallows, lit a cigarette, got the phone, and called home, to her mother, pressing at the buttons as slowly as if she were in a milk-like fog.

Nobody really needs a reason to call her mother—Masha called hers every couple months, just because, to ask *how are things?* and say everything's *same as always*—but it worked out differently this time: Masha was operating in a panic, the panic that forces a person to run from a smoke-filled room into the next room, where the ceilings have already collapsed. It was as if this call would help her come to terms with the fact that there wouldn't be any more turns off the main track of her life and no matter how hard she pulled the brake, the train was just speeding on to wherever it wanted to speed and, in some sense, after this conversation it was, indeed, easier to just dial Roma's number (the fire victim springs back to the smoke-filled room after seeing crimson beams falling from above): when Masha's mother picks up the phone, she tells Masha how she and Masha's father are doing, that all's well, everything's the same as before, and *we'd love to see you, come visit, will you come?* but during the whole conversation, never erring once, Masha's mother called her Lyoshenka. Chilled with horror, Masha realized immediately that her mother—her mother who's not, in essence, so very old—is talking with her own unfortunate brother who died at thirty from methylated spirits.

Masha sat down on an Ikea chair, wrapped her arms around her belly, bent, and sat that way until she remembered the whiskey. She drank three more half-glasses before calling Roma: she didn't feel like standing now and had no strength to sit on the chair, so she slid down to the floor and started coughing into the phone as she felt the cold from the painted wall stealing into her back: *hel-lo, Yevgenyev! Need work?*

Masha had counted on a long conversation about *long time, no see, how are things, what're you working on*; on cautious insinuations and inquiries of *who're you with?*; and, who the hell knows, maybe even on *come over right now, want something to eat* but there was nothing of the sort: Roma hurriedly set a time to meet tomorrow and hung up. Of course Masha couldn't have known and Roma didn't tell her that she'd called at the perfect time because Dasha happened to be in the shower, the water was running, and all she heard as she was coming out of the bathroom was Roma saying goodbye to someone: *who is it? –That called? –Uh-huh. –Oh, just a friend from the institute. –Why? –What's the difference? Why do you always have to know everything? What are you, an investigator on someone's payroll?* and Dasha got offended, went into the kitchen, and then, after they'd made up (Roma lied, lied, lied), asked him three times *so who called, anyway?*

There wasn't anything rational in his wish not to tell Dasha who'd called—if he and Masha were going to work together again, there was no way Dasha wouldn't find out about it anyway—so the point lay elsewhere, that he wanted, come what may, to put off a conversation in the *why-won't-you-talk* genre, not just because it would be a horribly unpleasant conversation but (and this was the main thing) to make his moment with Masha last, like before, *just the two of them.*

After hearing Masha's voice on the phone (he was surprised at his own surprise because, after all, he'd been expecting the call), Roma imagined himself as if it were actually happening—there he was asking Dasha's forgiveness, (*you're amazing, but I truly can't live without her, will you forgive me?*), pressing his ears, shouting, and slamming the door—and cringed. In another second, he'd already decided for himself, once and for all—and later, making up with Dasha and smoking in the kitchen, *you go lie down, I'll sit a little longer,* tidily using the corner of the ashtray to take off the ash and raging that he couldn't manage to calm his heart, he would only become more reassured of his decision—that none of that will happen, he'd had enough insanity, that nothing could work out otherwise with Masha, and that now he'd found what he was looking for: quiet confidence and measuredness, a calm, comprehensible, and normal person, what the hell else do you need, and he wouldn't refuse that for the sake of another half-year of everything feeling upside-down. Roma shook his head and devoured an apple cake bite by bite: his feeling of hunger just wouldn't go away.

Roma cuts the cake, Masha swills the whiskey; neither cake nor whiskey lasts forever, so they go to bed.

The reason Masha and Roma's fate never did lie down on the rails of any decent storyline—be it Philemon and Baucis's or Bonnie and Clyde's—is something Roma himself acknowledged without realizing it himself, as he was devouring the apple cake, and something Masha would only grasp when it had already become impossible not to notice it, no matter how much she might wish not to: the reason was the monstrous, mocking discrepancy in their notions of the future, notions of which, after all, are always a wish. It threw Masha into a rage just feeling like she was the main character of some screenplay as foolish as two times two, where everything's clear beforehand. Roma, on the other hand, went crazy every time he didn't understand what to expect the next minute (like how the two of them had messed with his head in the Chinese restaurant, not telling him straight off what was going on, *what did you two decide without me?!*).

None of that means Roma didn't meet with Masha. He'd meet with her the very next day.

After telling Dasha he's going to negotiate a job (*I can't say, come on, otherwise it'll fall through*), Roma will drive to Kamennoostrovsky Prospect, leave his VW stationwagon by the Flowers store (all late-Soviet buildings look like mausoleums, as if the system could feel what awaited it) and go up to the second floor of the Lenfilm studio: Masha will be waiting in the café under an *Amphibian Man* poster and accepting congratulations from an actors' assistant of indeterminate advanced age; these women are always addressed by first name only (informal diminutive forms, no patronymics) and they always know everybody, remembering them from nearly the cradle. After waiting for Lyusya (or is it Stasya?) to give Masha a

scrap of paper with her number (*call me, Mashenka, honey*), Roma
will sit across from her and congratulate her, too, how could he not?

They're unable to converse like normal human beings—people
will approach their little table every three minutes to congratulate
Masha (in those moments, Roma will think that nothing changes,
though they've already been apart for two years), and leave their
business cards, photographs, and scraps of paper with phone numbers, but the main thing will be expressed anyway, meaning Masha
will tell Roma there's a screenplay, that money's needed, question
him about who she needs to see now, who to talk with, who might
know, but the main thing is that she asks him: *so how are you?* Roma
looks her right in the eye to answer: *you went to school with this girl,
Dasha, remember?* And then (otherwise, why would he have started
talking about her): *you living with her? Got it. –It's hilarious. –Love and
romance? –Something like that.*

It's striking, but despite all Masha's hatred for rigid screenplays
and despite Roma's love for them, what awaited them was the exact
opposite of what they'd wanted: for Masha, it was as plain as day
that his *something like that* was nothing more than an attempt to
ignore the inevitable. For Roma, who'd decided, once and for all,
that his relationship with Masha could only be business-based, it
was a surprise that the decision he'd made for himself didn't worry
anybody: the screenplay would remain flexible for him.

Of course the little boy who's set the bar of chocolate in front
of himself because he's decided to train his willpower and thus
can't touch it for any reason, will eat the chocolate... and a TV
viewer won't just laugh because he's switched on a comedy show
for kids (what else do people switch that on for?) but also because
the viewer knows about that little boy in advance: why else would
the screenwriter put the chocolate in front of him?

It would be tempting to think Roma's that same little boy, only
deprived of the flaw of reflection, but that's too simple and, in
reality, this is a more complex matter: by power of his profession,

Roma is obviously used to thinking in pictures (and each frame is, essentially, static), and couldn't suppose that in order to search out meaning in what happens he must not only stand in the position of an observer of what's happening (meaning become one with the lens) but also, out of complete necessity, abstract himself from the camera and take the position of someone who's observing the cameraman.

And Roma will only grasp what happened—just like that little boy who's stuffed himself with the chocolate finally understands why the chocolate was lying there in the first place—when he wakes up alongside Masha (yellow sunlight will stream in the window through fine lace curtains and explode with color as it falls on Masha's hair, fanned out on the pillows; a pine bough will swing in the wind so drops of glistening water fall to the ground; Masha will lie with closed eyes, slightly open lips, and her hand will also be vulnerably open) and stretches for his camera.

Things were like this. Masha found money for the film unexpectedly easily. In a Japanese restaurant, picking pieces of fish off a plate with chopsticks, constantly pressing her phone to her ear, and cooing into it in an affectionate voice: *no, dear, I'll call you back in half an hour, all right?* they'd explained to her, delicately, and with a sweet smile, that they'd give her money, since she didn't need much, but the documents would indicate three times the sum and if she's not against that –*We're all adults here...* Masha felt like grabbing hold of that well-groomed face to explain that as a matter of principle she was against dickheads in second-hand t-shirts and shoes from that most expensive boutique in town, but her revolutionary impulse was crushed by the thought that she doesn't like dickheads in cheap shoes, either, or, on the other end, in expensive jackets, so there was no reason for poses here, and so Masha bowed her head: *okay, got it.* Masha wasn't interested in the committee with the impossible name under whose support her film would be released; to her, the main thing was that nobody interfere with her work, and they promised her that. For the dickhead drinking green tea (*just not with jasmine, for heaven's sake*), the main thing was to *get thoroughly familiar with how this budget works*, that's what he said.

And so Masha and Roma checked out locations. There were three unsuccessful trips—either the location lacked character or the buildings were too brand-new (*we have a wonderful bathhouse. –Thanks, we don't need a bathhouse*)—and then they finally found what they were looking for on the fourth try. After an hour tearing along the Scandinavia Highway, it was immediately obvious as soon as they turned on to a dirt road, then rattled along for about another half-hour and rose up a steep sandy entrance to catch sight of an old building (peeling but solid, like everything our grandfathers built, with a high portico, four columns, pilasters that seemed to rhyme with one another, a palimpsest of a tympanum) surrounded by gleaming pine trees. So as not to frighten off good fortune, they walked silently around the building with distrustful faces, listened to the awkward story of the director lady with the clean, pretty hands she didn't know what to do with (*so, here we have this, it used to be for the medical staff, but then later, when everything changed, now the rooms, too, we have very comfortable rooms, construction recently finished on the bathhouse*), checked that the bathhouse wasn't too close, and asked to be left alone. They got out their cameras to take photos.

To the right of the old building (*we have new ones, want to see them? –Are they close? –No, about a ten-minute walk. –Then there's no need*) was the top of a slope that Masha and Roma slid down a bit on a carpet of dry pine needles: there was the steep diagonal of a hill, the vertical of pine trees, the horizontal of stagnant sunbeams, and the overly blue lake below, *it's the realest Myst*, Roma muttered, clicking the shutter, but Masha wasn't familiar with that gamer classic and only heard a German word: *Mist?! The hell with you, this is just what we need!*

Then they came back, found the director lady, walked with her through the inside of the building in a silence fraught with significance, got a room, asked for food to be brought, and flipped through the photos on the laptop, clicking their tongues while they waited for lunch. *That's it, I'm already itching to do this. –Hold on, let's think this through again. –What's to think about? It's an hour from the city… –Hour and a half. –What's the difference? What, don't you like it? There's oceans of sun, you can film as much as you want.* They ate in silence. Masha had already decided everything, the only question was would they jack up the price? She was thinking about something else, that it was three in the afternoon and rapidly darkening outside: *it's going to rain, we have to shoot something in the rain. –Oh, jeez, then how're we going to get back?* Roma froze with cutlet in his mouth then reflexively jerked his hand for the phone: he hadn't told Dasha he was going this far away because, well, why bother?

Masha was thinking about Dasha, too. She'd seen her a month ago, the day after Roma had come home and declared to Dasha with exaggerated joy: *there'll be work! Real work!* and then declared, with exaggerated offhandedness, that he'd run into Masha at the studio by chance (*she just came back from Germany yesterday, can you believe it?*) and that's how it worked out. *Maybe she'll find a part for you.* When Roma went for a shower, Dasha took his phone, found the number that had called him the night before, carefully copied it on the back of a grocery-store receipt, and hid the receipt in a purse pocket.

They met up two days later. Masha understood why she needed this meeting: the mobile she'd torn from her ear was still warm when she decided she'd just tell Dasha where to go as soon as Dasha gave her the opportunity, and that was precisely the reason she came to Gostiny Dvor (every city has a place where people meet when they don't know where to go) but then she had to change the plan on the fly: *you got in on Monday? And called him right away? And there I was thinking it was strange somehow, he told me he'd randomly run into you at Lenfilm, he's funny* because if he'd lied to Dasha, that meant things were serious, so Masha could easily lose her cameraman with just one false move. Masha resisted when Dasha pulled her into a café: she was trying to stall for time (*listen, I haven't seen Petersburg in forever, let's have a look around*) and they started walking along the Fontanka and then along streets with poets' names on every house.

They walked around for a solid hour exchanging ritual *and he, and she, and that one* before Masha grasped that the loser in their situation—as in any bargaining—would be the one who's the first to name a price and, in their situation, the first to speak. After grasping that, Masha said she was frozen (it was twenty-five warm Celsius degrees outside but Dasha paid no heed) and then walked through the first door they came across. (It's too bad Masha didn't look at the name before entering: the first thing she saw inside were the faces of Lennon and company. It was the Liverpool Bar.) Masha swallowed that dig, sat down, ordered a beer, and just began waiting. Dasha finally broke after exactly half a glass and yet another awkward pause: *Masha, I wanted to have a serious talk with you... –Hmm? –Do you have your eye on him?*

After wording like that, the beer immediately tasted bitterer than it should have, but Masha swallowed that, too: *uh-huh, he's going to shoot my next film. –That's not what I meant, you know what I mean...* and Dasha explained that she and Roma are an ideal fit, that they're so happy together, that when she met him he was barely a human being, he'd let himself go, was weak-willed, drank, and now everything had changed so much—this template she'd prepared at home turned out to be pretty pitiful (she's decided to simultaneously show me what a fab actress she is, flashed through Masha's mind) but Dasha's finale was beyond all praise: *Masha, honey, I know all you have to do is beckon to him with one finger and he'd go, so I just want to ask: do you truly need him?* (Her eyes are filling with tears.) *Tell me if you need him and I'll just leave, no hard feelings.*

People dream up the bizarrest methods of extorting promises from each other, and Masha barely refrained from the temptation of offering to make a pact with Dasha right then and there and have it notarized, too: she was simply being offered, once again, to play a game whose outcome—and even every single move—was known in advance. Of course scarcely had Dasha realized that since *beckon with a finger* is something out of schoolgirl life and that if things like this really do depend on fingers, then it's only on the fingers of the one who's sitting at the control panel, so what she was truly requesting was that Masha experience as many guilt feelings as possible if she and Roma were to end up together again. Of course Masha should have told Dasha to kiss her ass or even tried to explain to her in detail about what was happening, though that would have been really harsh, and since Regina needed a cameraman—and a cameraman who was thinking about the film, not about some ballistic chick—Masha decided to play along: *I'm telling you, I need a cameraman. Yevgenyev's the best, that's all there is to it and I have a German boyfriend, by the way, he'd like it here. –Promise?* Masha gnashed her teeth. *Promise.*

Dasha's eyes dried instantly but she still went again to the *little girls' room* to wipe off her mascara, and she started chirping when she came back (*listen, I'm just so happy for you, who would have thought I wasn't living in a room with just anybody back then…*) and then chirped on to her second main question: *so what's this film you're going to do?* For the sake of propriety, Masha repeated the text she'd memorized for the producers and then said directly (this looks like revenge, she thought, but what can you do): *I could put you in it, but only in the nurse scene, because it's a film about people of a certain age…* (She'd just now thought up the scene; if nothing else we'll shoot it and cut it.) *Too bad*, Dasha drew out her words but kept on chirping anyway. Masha loudly ordered more beer to drown out the thought of what wretched people these actors were.

The beer suddenly went bitter on the western and eastern regions of her tongue and Masha hurried to wash away the bitterness with the sanatorium's compote (made of dried fruits, the flavor of big smudged floor-to-ceiling windows in the school cafeteria): *let's wait out the rain and then head home*, she said coldly, which gladdened Roma: *well, if that's...*

Later, when this whole story had taken on a very suspicious resemblance to a tacky Soviet film, Masha wondered when Roma himself had understood what was happening. Was it when they left their things in the room, asked the lady director for plastic rain coats, and went outside again to shoot the pounding lake below, the dark seething sky, and the solitary note of a pine tree just before the edge of the forest with streams of water flowing from branch to branch? or was it when they came back to the room, feeling like they were horribly frozen, and Roma remembered he had a bottle of cognac (albeit already opened) in the car? or was it when they decided that since they'd already sat up this late it would be a sin not to shoot the setting sun (which had now come out)?... and it occurred to her that Roma hadn't understood anything until the very last minute, when the sun had basically already gone down and she'd slipped right into his arms on the wet carpet of pine needles and their two cameras pressed against each other, hampering their kissing. And even when they'd come back to the room, asked for dinner, and poured some cognac, and Roma left the room (*I'll ask them to make some coffee; want some coffee?* uh-huh, she thought, don't forget your phone) to call Dasha, telling her a pack of lies about his old friend he was getting trashed with (*Masha? Oh, she went back to her hotel!*), though he did that not because he couldn't tell the truth but because he didn't want to upset her for no reason: he still wasn't sure (meaning he just hadn't asked himself) if he and Masha were going to sleep in the same bed or different ones (he didn't, by the way, forget about the coffee).

Later, however, when the work will already be in full swing (they'll start by first shooting scenes on a house set at the studio, and they'll reserve the sanatorium on the hill that looks like an old hippie's head—bald on the top and long-haired on the sides—for late September and early October), Masha herself will no longer be up for reflecting on her own love story, a genre not at the disposal of *Amber* (she thought up the title while they were climbing up the hill in the dark: what could have been simpler than naming the film after the establishment, which should have been named "Amber" since its real name was a mistake), which is more like a detective story without a crime. Roma will never announce to Dasha that she was correct in all her suspicions, Dasha will pretend she believes him, it will seem to Masha that there's nothing more banal than for her to *get a conversation going*—and so, as a result, the story will become more and more banal with every move. Dasha will come to The Pines for two days, Masha will proceed to film her, not noticing Dasha's significant and long gazes (and the equally mocking-and-all-understanding eyes of either Stasya or Lyusya, who's always, by tradition, in the loop) and beyond that, she'll decide she won't cut Dasha out: her little face equipped with a little nose all ready for battle will contrast well with the main character's face, which looks like it was rolled out by hand, though Dasha won't ever understand her good fortune and they won't get away without some whining: *a line, just one line, any line.* And the night Roma will catch Masha in the hallway and incoherently explain to her that, *well, we don't need these rumbles here, really*, Masha will remain alone in her room, unable to sleep, angry, forcibly closing her eyes and then giving in and opening them—there will be matte clouds (a shadowed pearl) floating in the sky she sees in the window, and if you really, really try, you can click your vision again and see a milky-white sky with streams of dark-blue watercolors flowing along it—toward three in the morning, when she can no longer tell if it's hurt feelings that make her want to wail or if it's anger at herself, she who won't have had enough sleep tomorrow, and that's when Masha will grasp that she's caught again because, as always, the best possible thing has already happened: when she woke up three months ago from the sun tickling her eyes, she'd hastily and amusingly stuck her lips together after licking them, and Roma was sitting on the edge of the bed with a camera and already turning a little screen toward her with a just-clicked shot where she—redheaded and sunny, highlighted by the whiteness of the pillow that her arm encircled, and a blanket treacherously breaking away from her chest—was sleeping as if there had never been anything in her life but this morning.

Dasha will leave the next evening and when Roma comes to see Masha, he'll sit next to her, say he specially got drunk yesterday with the guys so nothing would happen, and she'll believe it because of course this is the truth (he's not a heel, he's just a coward, how could she not know him), but there won't be any peace for Masha and that's not because of jealousy (the hell with all that rubbish, she has no patience for it) but because her gut will sense that this vaudeville sketch lacks the counterpoint of genuine misfortune, and when she checks herself the whole next day and then another, she'll grasp that this feeling was not, in reality, a momentary fantasy, and that she has to prepare herself for something, but how do you prepare for who-the-hell-knows-what, and so she won't prepare herself... and so when the phone rings on the third day and the voice inside it, which she heard once and only once, five years ago, but remembered (just like some bullshit that goes around in circles in your head for your whole life—its end always coming back to its beginning, endlessly reversing—gets remembered), announces to her that Alexei Alexeyevich died, heart attack, then Masha, who's sitting at the monitor, will shove the phone into a coffee cup, hoarsely announce a break, contain herself as she makes it to her room, and then, after she's locked the door, she'll finally burst into sobs that make her shoulder joints dance.

# THE ONTOLOGY OF DEATH

Saturday may lurk behind Friday, but our days do jumble, so A.A. will need to be resurrected in order for the story to be told of yet another meeting that has a place here because—as things turn out—it happened not long before his death. This meeting wasn't a fateful one for A.A., but Masha made a decision because of it... No, it's not as if the backbone of events would have been different if she hadn't made it (hardly: what could have been different there?) and, beyond that, she would likely have made this decision anyway because, in the final reckoning, seemingly very little really depends on our decisions in this life, but different circumstances and emotional background can matter, and it's the latter that's what's so very, very important because it could be capable (unlike the manifestations of will nourished by Spengler) of changing every vertebra-like event so much that the storyline's arc turns out to be different.

Things were like this. Masha ended up in Petersburg with nothing to do (meetings and phone negotiations took more nerves than time) and all by herself (Roma was still in a state of certainty that he was master of his own fate; Dasha had pushed to get in touch but Masha wasn't picking up the phone), but the main thing was that it was July, when the city's half-empty and warm, like a big, scratchy rock in the woods that's heated up toward evening, and so Masha went for long walks. The feeling of nostalgia she experienced a few times during the course of a day sometimes became the center of gravity for her day, whether she was walking along Mokhovaya Street (the flash of the ghost of a first-year student hurrying to stage-movement class) or ending up on the Linia streets (a girl in her last year of high school came to life for a moment, screaming herself hoarse with everyone else in a half-drunk, unruly group: *on-one-legggg!*) or going down to the water across from the Summer Garden (it wasn't despondence itself but the remembrance of it, as precise as the latest copies of ancient originals), etcetera, etcetera, etcetera… and, objectively, that feeling was very pleasant and initially gladdened Masha, but then it caused suspicion in her, just as all pleasant things should cause suspicion for a thinking person.

It finally became clear to her that since the buildings, landscape details or geometry of an expanse (the world has no intentions with regard to us, A.A. would have said, waving a cigarette back and forth, and Masha would have again been shy to ask where the quote came from) could not have been the reason for the effect she was getting, what was happening must be happening only within Masha herself: each time her heart convulses sweetly, this is a dead Masha rising from memory's grave (Masha-the-girl-finishing-high-school, Masha-the-girl-starting-college—these weren't graves but streets in the cemetery) and she derives a voluptuous happiness from life, which is fleeting and ephemeral, but life nevertheless. During one of her outings, on Liteiny Prospect, Masha stopped to eat and remembered a café that had been across the street (there were now hotdogs and a food store instead of a coffee shop) and then it was suddenly as if she'd seen with her own eyes that whole bunches of corpses were hanging from her, from Masha, clinging to her blood-filled shoulders, arms, breasts, hips, and neck: each gripped her like pliers and each had one hope, to live longer, if only for a second. Panicked, Masha muttered an order and began dialing Peter (he'd called yesterday and Masha hadn't been in the mood to

talk with him, though that now seemed necessary) but she dialed
A.A. instead of Peter because ghosts acquire a special power over a
person at the exact moment the person squints to catch them in his
field of vision: they're the ones prepared to attack, not the opposite.

A.A. still had lectures but Masha caught him two hours later at
the corner of Pestel and Gagarinskaya Streets. A.A. didn't look like
a person who'd let himself go—contrary to what you might expect
of someone who meets up with an old lover and immediately drags
her off to a dive bar—to the contrary, he ordered two double shots
as if he were reciting well-known verses, his eyes looked weighty
and calm, his wrist lay motionless alongside the ashtray, occasionally
soaring to his mouth, like a swan from the water. They flooded their
initial awkwardness with half the shot so the issue of what to say
and how with a person you turn out to know nothing about (you
don't want to know!) faded. No, the old A.A. was recognizable in
quotations as natural as breathing (in response to Masha's innocent
boasting about the Berlinale and *Save*'s rabid distribution: *as one
Roman emperor would have said, take heed not to be transformed into a
film director*, but okay, fine, it seems Masha figured that out); in his
reluctance to talk small talk (*well, I'm working, telling young people
all sorts of blather, well, there's family, little articles, what could there be
in that; take a look, what an old woman, just like in Dürer*); and in his
inquisitive attention to her, Masha's, stories (even if she understood
this was due to his upbringing, she couldn't bring herself to say it
was "only" due to that), but even so, he was still a substitute and
Masha only grasped the point of that when she was asking A.A. yet
again about *things* and A.A. responded that talking about him *isn't
interesting because, as it happens, everything about me is already clear.*

At the time, only surprise stung Masha because he'd never have
said anything like that before, though later Masha rolled those words
around and around, like a wave polishes a pebble, and it became
clear to her that A.A. didn't die because he was somehow particularly unhappy (though really, for a couple that doesn't have a first

child until forty, there is, speaking purely technically, a mechanism of deferred tragedy) but because the screenplay for his life had been completed, approved, and sent to the printer: this was abominable at best, it's true, but it was plenty nevertheless.

And yes, admittedly Masha's upbringing wasn't as good as A.A.'s: they ordered another double then moved on to all the various numbered Sovetskaya Streets and had more there, but Masha kept on talking about herself (you had to forgive her, though, if only because A.A. certainly didn't have a Dictaphone) but that wasn't the main thing, the main thing was that, in thinking about herself, Masha suddenly discovered that A.A. now existed for her in the very same way as Mokhovaya Street and a repainted front door and the view of the edge of the Summer Garden from the corner across from the Church of St. Panteleimon: in and of himself, A.A. was just a person that nothing tied her to, not even common memories, because they remembered everything differently, meaning that A.A. for her is exactly the same as the corpses she's dragging around with herself, like some kind of invertebrate that's grown an exoskeleton. She sensed that so clearly it was as if a huge A.A. really would have grasped her ankle with his big bony hand; after sensing that, she began asking him about his wife and child, reflexively, just like twitching a foot.

A.A. rubbed his cigarette on the edge of the ashtray for a long time, uncovering a fire that was hiding ever deeper: *I don't know. I don't know why you want to know that but if you do, then fine: yes, sunshine, I remember everything but that doesn't matter a bit. All's well with the girls.* Masha, flustered, started muttering that she *didn't mean that at all* and *I hope everything's all different, all new, for you* but the faster she mumbled, the harder it was for A.A. to part lips that seemed frozen, *okay, listen, what I'm saying is it doesn't matter, calm down,* and then, either responding to the annoyance that's just audible in his last words, or perhaps simply according to the logic of how intonation develops in chunks of speech, Masha almost shouted:

*I'm not nervous! You started it!* And A.A., relieved, agreed: *I really did start it. I was born first.*

After that, they were silent for about five minutes, then they started talking about vodka (because vodka's various brands constitute a conversational topic unmuddied by any emotions), then A.A. alluded to needing to prepare tomorrow's lecture and left to catch a trolleybus on Nevsky. Masha said goodbye to him, already knowing she was saying goodbye forever. That decision seemed natural to her (though if someone were to ask her: if her corpses are the people she carries with her, then why does she have to get rid of other people, then she obviously wouldn't have been able to answer) and, so it seemed, came easily. Nevertheless, when Peter called in the evening, she found an excuse to go off at him after a minute of meaningless conversation, burst out sobbing, and throw the phone against the wall out of hatred. (*Königin,* he'll say to her later, *I just don't understand what there is to get offended about.*)

And so A.A. died twice for Masha. And when it happened the second time, among coppery pine trunks and under a sky as dark blue as if it were on an icon—heart attack: that's what a broken but nevertheless calm voice had told her—Masha first wailed herself out, then she went numb, dried her tears, washed her face, took a long drink of water, raised her face over the sink, looked in the mirror and, with hatred, gave her reflection the middle finger, before going into the fresh air and continuing filming as if nothing had happened. The whole procedure took no more than a half-hour; she decided not to go to any funeral, so as not to lose precious filming time.

The Russian language is no less entertaining than a house of mirrors: by saying "she decided not to go to any funerals," it, the language, doesn't lie, because Masha didn't go to the Smolensk Cemetery (it was there A.A. wished to be buried, not in honor of the poet who didn't keep his word, as some female admirer might have thought, but simply to be alongside his parents, too), though the language did lie after all because Masha would go to a funeral, albeit a different one.

After nearly missing the train and jumping on to a carriage where there was a compartment she'd bought up entirely for herself (the desire to be closer to the people usually passes by age thirty, and a person has an urge for solitude), then opening a bottle of cognac (because there's no other way to fall asleep), Masha will drink half the night, with a face stony from tension, so as not to burst into tears, getting drunk, of course. In her drunken, lonely, delirium, she'll imagine that her father's death, which occurred four days after A.A.'s heart attack, didn't happen on its own but because of some sort of unscrupulous and extrajudicial design, like an impersonal sentence: she'd only just decided to detach one of her corpses when another was grabbing her by the throat, a hundred-fold more demandingly. Of course it's not because *you can't not go to your own father's funeral* (he's a dead-end alcoholic, so what) but because all the endlessly postponed love for her father was, with his death, unavoidably turning into the precipitate of the purest form of inescapable guilt.

Masha sleeps; the nostrils of people walking past her compart-ment inflate; in a jiggling window, shadows of balded shrubs and bristling spruces, one darker than the next, give way to one another as if they're in some crazed filmstrip; and suddenly everything pales and dies down, and blue-gray nocturnal water slowly breathes: Masha sleeps without dreaming, there's a reason she drank the cognac.

In the morning she jumps down into a mucky sludge of fuel oil and rain, icy water instantly catches her feet, and when Masha's jouncing in a cold bus that smells so much her head spins, particu-larly on an empty stomach, she regrets she left the cognac on the train. The further the bus goes from the station, the more it fills with old women flocking to the market—in their hands are pails with apples, enigmatic bags, and the smells of food and death—and they inspect Masha with a slow curiosity that seems to have been satisfied in advance, muttering something to each other and masking the whistling and rasping of their speech behind the natural racket of the motor. When Masha steps on the concrete slab at the bus stop and the bus drives away, it's as if she's ended up in an expanse of absolute soundlessness, and that deafens her.

Masha's gaze is caught by eyes pressed deeply into a head that comes out from behind the fence of the corner house, and though Masha has known the old woman who lives in that house perfectly well since the beginning of time and it was she who'd called The Pines the day before yesterday to report that *your poppa died* and *you have to come right away*, Masha still can't remember her name and the old woman's already creaking the rusty gate and holding her skirt with a meaty hand as she takes tiny steps toward Masha so she can inspect her, nitpicking, and take her by the forearm, *so that, Mashka, is how it happens, the Lord giveth and the Lord taketh away, here, let's go*, and as they're walking to the house, the old woman tries to explain something to Masha, convolutedly and a little roughly because she feels flustered, but Masha doesn't understand what it is that *has to be thought about, to decide what to do* and why *the house is empty now, your mother's not there, she's at old lady Lyusya's*.

The old woman unlocks the door of Masha's native home with a key she's fished out of her skirt pocket, goes inside as if she owns the place, stamps her feet, turns on the light, and softly pushes Masha into the room, taking her by the shoulder: *go on, he's in there*. She indicates the door with her face and goes into the kitchen: *I'll count the dishes*.

Left by herself, Masha notices she's surprised for a second, wondering why the mirror is covered and the air is so horrible—ah, right, right—and pushes the door. It's dusky in the room and Masha's eyes get accustomed to the dusk for about half a minute before she discerns the coffin standing on the chairs and, in it, her father in a suit and tie. Masha doesn't really know what to do; she sits down alongside her father and looks at him, but doesn't want to touch him at all, not his hands, not his face. She turns away.

In the kitchen, dishes clatter, cupboard doors groan, and drawers scrape as they're pulled out: Masha's chilled from fear and powerlessness, her fingernails sink into her palm until they draw blood. Of course the only thing she feels like doing is what she won't do, which is to stealthily slip out of the house and, while the old woman's recounting forks and dishes, run to the station, climb on any train, even if it's for freight, even if it's under the roof of the carriage, to be jostled, frozen, whatever it takes, just so long as each minute brings her another kilometer away, away, away. Masha sits, her palms hidden under her arms, and can barely refrain from starting to rock. It grows quiet and a minute later (during which Masha feels a studying gaze on herself) the old woman is slipping in through the door, which was left open. At first she sits down on the edge of the bed on the other side of Masha's father, sitting there for a few minutes, sighing and either inclining or lifting her head, then, as if she'd noticed something, she straightens a cuff, the necktie, the collar, the hair, and comes back down to his palms, taking them in her hands and stroking them, and the only thing that prevents Masha from pushing the old woman away with a scream—*cut it out, he's dead, he's dead, he's dead*—is that the old woman wouldn't understand what Masha's talking about: there's adoration and satisfaction on her face.

Finally the old woman lets Masha's father's hands go, as if she's regretful; drives a slight, radiant smile from her face; and says to Masha, *well, let's go, let's go, you can sit a little longer later, you and I have to decide some things, funerals, after all it's not like going mushrooming*, she jabbers, and she jabbers as she takes Masha by the shoulder, and she jabbers as she softly pushes Masha toward the door, as if Masha herself wouldn't remember where the door is. In the kitchen, where the old woman (what the hell is her name, anyway?) can already speak at full volume, it becomes clear the questions are about what will be free and what won't and who needs to be given how much: *the priest should get something, he might refuse but he needs something, the men in the churchyard cemetery should get two bottles, that means…* Masha tries to get out her wallet but the old woman stops her and it looks like Masha will have to hear out the mournful list to the end whether she wants to or not, and it's endless, there are jars of peas in a procession behind sticks of sausage, vodka bottles marching behind stools, batteries of oranges rolling out to a forward position side-by-side with potbellied jars full of firm salted cucumbers, and all those lines are under the command of the crafty, experienced—and here the old woman counts on her fingers—*Lyusya, Auntie Pasha, we'll ask Anka, and your mother, too, no doubt she could at least slice some cheese*—then she switches over to the disposition of the feast, stands, and shows, waving her arms, how they'll place the table and how many people to seat on each side, and, distracted, brushes against a stack of dishes (Masha manages to come to her aid but one dish falls down anyway, perishing), *well, twat on paws!* the old woman screams in anger. Masha's head shrinks into her shoulders, as if her father could now begin yelling that they leave him alone.

Later they're walking somewhere and Masha makes an effort to give money to the old woman, who pushes her aside—*hold on, you, waving that around*—and explains again that, *there was money, she said, she's probably not lying, huh?*, there's a sideways glance at Masha, *you probably sent it, didn't you, she should've kept it on the bank book but no, she hid it in some sock, and now she's saying "I don't remember." Mashka!*—it suddenly dawns on the old woman—*she didn't tell you where, did she, huh?* Masha shakes her head, her mother hadn't said anything about it. *And what, she doesn't remember?* Masha hears herself as if from a distance. *Right, I'm telling you, what're you listening with, your mother's in a bad way,* the old woman harps on this, irritated, *you'll see for yourself now.* Masha's legs become wobbly; mumbling something, she lowers herself onto a bench by a gray fence and reaches for a cigarette to impart some legitimacy to the delay. *Go 'head, have a smoke, have a smoke, Mashka, hold on, we're almost there*; the old woman's speech is affectionate and stern.

Before Masha grinds out the dry cigarette and pushes the butt into the cold October earth so she can rise from the bench, staggering slightly, and catch a simultaneously condemnatory and forgiving glance that wasn't intended to be seen but came out from under strands of the old woman's gray hair that have broken loose, stirred by the wind... and before Masha will walk to the corner and five houses to the right (and for some reason that will be especially memorable, so, basically, all that will remain from this whole day, as a memory rather than as a logical construct, will be yellow birch leaves as bright as streetlights, helplessly twitching in the blinding, icy sky) so that—and this has to be done, too, no matter how much you put it off—Masha will find her unfortunate mother inside the house where, when she was a child (as she suddenly remembers), people said they thought a German spy woman lived because, apparently, everything there was always too *orderly*, with flowers in little squares, wooden garden beds, and little triangular drapes... and before Masha does that, it must be noted that this whole sequence, beginning with her meeting with A.A. and ending with her meeting with her mother, is not even a sequence of events (what kind of events are they? There's just shapelessness) but of pure, distilled horror—and, judging from everything, it's this sequence that will push Masha to the thought that (though once again this wasn't even a thought but just the earth's attraction for a cannonball flying—hello to Stoppard—from the Tower of Pisa, and, thus, characterized by a certain external inevitability) she needs to have a baby as soon as possible.

One time, when answering a question about *Save*'s heroine and why she refuses to have a baby (the interviewer was nocturnal, wearing glasses and playing smooth jazz in the background, thus he posed the question broadly, about childlessness in general among European youth), Masha said *it's just that these people live in places where they don't have a chance to meet anybody they could have a child with.* The interviewer nodded his glasses, started talking about the Internet and virtual reality, and Masha, relieved, agreed, though in reality, of course, that's not the direction the conversation should have taken. Masha meant that the birth of a child is a radical form of meeting with an Other, even though all human exertions in Western civilization are expended on evading meeting with an Other, and, in the final reckoning, in avoiding a meeting with an Other every day; nothing frightens a person (and this fear is the object of reflection in numerous horror films) so much as the very possibility of that meeting, or even merely imagining it (and this is why "childfree" is nothing if not "fearful").

But it seems that the point of the artist's everyday work is to carry all the age's sores inside, and it was autonomously that Masha came to experience panicked horror at the thought of a child, of a person you have to come to terms with whether you want to or not, and as she picked at that wound ever more and more, she discovered, deep down, a very simple but fundamental fear: the fear of the impossibility of having a backup. (There it is, the monument to Undo Last Action: a figure with a flaming torch raised high over the head, and a lash in the left hand, stretched behind the back.) And just as you can betray one empire merely by switching it for another, fear can be smoked out with the fire of another fear: everything that happened during the filming of *Amber* made Masha feel like wild game driven into a narrowing corridor; and it was as if pregnancy was what-I-never-could-have-expected, an attempt to deceive the hunting party, to say nothing of the symbolic contrast: a nascent life opposes death that's approaching from all sides. Of course none of that changes the fact that Masha was already a grown woman and this was, really, a long time coming for her.

The pregnant Masha had to give several interviews just ahead of the release of her new film, and each time she had a different answer to the question, which was asked with a particularly serene smile and a glance below her breast. In a moment of irritation, she could say she wasn't sure whose child it was and was curious to have a look. If she liked the journalist for some reason, she could tell a long story, a very long story, about how they hadn't entrusted her with a course at the film school in Moscow and she wanted so much to leave behind a legacy, but you need to have a serious approach to the issue of nurturing a future director, beginning when the child's still in diapers. It was usually too late by the time the journalists started figuring out what was what. Obviously anyone who would have taken it upon himself to seriously enumerate the arguments in favor of a decision to continue the bloodline would have blundered, just like anyone who's decided to finally explain why you have to love your motherland or why you have to say "thank you." Something else is more important: destroying the illusion (unavoidable, evidently, for the structure of a text) that decision-making was an accomplishable act because, in reality, that was an agonizing ongoing effort for Masha.

Right up until the moment the Swiss doctor with the Georgian surname determined that labor had stopped after a grueling two-hour marathon and sternly tilted his head toward his shoulder: *we're going to cut, hon, since you don't want to do this yourself...* right up until the moment they put the mask to Masha's face, when she was breathing hysterically and then finally stopped pushing the baby—right until that very moment, it was difficult for her to make a decision.

After diagnosing a severe case of gestosis with all the symptoms, the charming old German woman threw up her hands: what were you thinking before?! And what was she thinking before? Editing, so Masha had no time for thinking; Masha attributed the horrendous edema in her legs to being tired from work (they edited ten hours a day) and a little later wrote off terrible, inhumanly high blood pressure to the same thing. But she begged off even after it had become difficult to fool the doctors, when it had become obvious even from the outside that something was amiss and people started pestering Masha to go to the hospital for *an evaluation* and had already picked up the phone to call for the medics: she said she was a citizen of another country and it would be better if she flew to Germany tomorrow. Then, of course, the phone was set back down and the nice lady doctor shook her head and said: *then you have to go right away, tomorrow, don't put it off, it's just an evaluation.* (Saying the real reason—that sound and editing had to be finished, no matter what, and that she didn't give a damn what happened after that—was obviously not allowed, not because the nice lady doctor would have insisted (no) but simply because it would have been a loss of time.)

Miraculously—by now in Switzerland, three weeks before giving birth and the day after watching the final cut three times in a row—Masha went to the hospital after all and the doctors managed to hold the toxicosis to a minimum and stave off hypoxia, but they weren't able to explain to Masha where the damned gestosis had come from. (What was unclear to the doctors and, as yet, only vaguely perceptible for Masha herself, might have been clearer from a distance: the child—who was growing in the body of a mother who'd evidently decided to have a baby but wasn't, on the other hand, sure if she hadn't been forced into the decision, just as a voter is forced to endorse the only possible correct decision—well, this child couldn't help but think about getting the hell away from this overly self-reflective mommy. However, yes, one could offer a simple, more natural explanation, which is what Masha's doctors in her motherland offered when they wrote *advanced maternal age* on her records; ultimately, this was true.) Be that as it may, once the xenon had worn off and they brought Masha's daughter to her, placed her to Masha's breast, and a panicked wail gave way to an efficient snuffling, after a second of horror and loathing Masha was gripped by a powerful and rapid tsunami-like wave of love for the purplish little wormling. If not for the fear of tearing her away from her food, Masha's whole body would have shaken but instead—as if in compensation—she burst out sobbing, not at full volume but quietly, with some indecorous bawling that soaked the pillow in three seconds. Masha felt as if everything had been decided and that everything had been decided without her. When the Turkish nurse covered Masha and the purplish little wormling with a sheet shortly thereafter, she was struck by the sleeping woman's facial expression: it was as vacant and used-looking as the expression of an athlete who's been holding a barbell over his head that is then taken away on a whim.

In reality, of all the small efforts that came together every day to form Masha's pregnancy—just as pieces of colored glass form a mosaic—only the very first was accomplished relatively easily and immediately: after deciding to quit smoking on that same return train ride to Petersburg, she left a pack of cigarettes on the little compartment table, placed her lighter down on top of it, and a week later barely even thought about cigarettes. The next task—getting pregnant—turned out to be far more difficult.

Roma met Masha—who hadn't had enough sleep but was sober—at the train station, they had breakfast, and drove north. Masha climbed into the back seat so maybe she could at least nap a little in the car. They rode in silence: Roma was aware of Masha's gloominess; Masha, who was dazed as well as gloomy, wasn't in the mood for Roma's anxiety. Somewhere, about halfway, Roma looked in the tilted mirror: *not sleeping?* Masha grunted. Roma hesitated a little more and finally said *there was some minor bedlam, discord, and instability here because of these three days, basically some people left, some the opposite, well and Dashka, too, anyway, she came along, though, well and... I'm not her boss, you understand, I can't force her...* Masha took so long to answer that Roma decided she was sleeping after all. In fact, Masha was on slow speed after the sleepless night and just couldn't understand what she should say. She'd already started to put together a sentence about how since he's a big boy and Dasha's his woman, even if she's an ex (if, indeed, that's how it was), then he should be dealing with her himself; Masha even opened her mouth, started to say something, and stopped short, but Roma caught the reflection of her swollen eyes in the mirror and this is where it crossed her mind that of course he himself can't not understand all of this but if he understands this and refuses to deal with it himself anyway, then why should she educate him, particularly since that's now the most pointless thing of all? So in answering his question of *huh?*, Masha instantly blurted out (as happens after long, difficult rumination) what had come into her head: *why'd you wait so long to say this? We could've stopped at your place and at least screwed.* Roma was taken aback but he soon started prattling on, relieved about *we'll finish shooting and then... it's just not the place here, in the middle of work...* but now Masha had finally gone to sleep.

She only managed to boot out Dasha on the fourth work-day (Masha wasn't just in a hurry because she found Dasha obnoxious—sprouting up all over the place, bursting out laughing, and letting it be known in her manner of address that she and Regina were on familiar terms—but also because Masha was about to start her period any minute). Toward evening, the director of the picture explained sharply, since Dasha didn't want to take hints, that the accounting office wasn't paying for an unauthorized person to be on the set, and Dasha, all covered in pink blotches, settled herself into Roma's station wagon to trade angry silence for his expressions of long-term commitments the whole way: *sweets, if this were another picture and another director, I'd chuck it all but you know Masha, it's more trouble to tear her away from her work, we'll finish filming and then... want to go away somewhere?* and Dasha kept silent.

Roma was horribly cranky when he came back from the station (they'd had to wait an hour longer for the train than expected), looked at the shots his assistant had made during that time, and rejected everything but couldn't film more because it was now dark and rainy. That night, sitting with Masha, a whiskey in his hand

and a cigarette out the window (*why'd you quit smoking, anyway?*), Roma said, trying to soften his wording, that, *essentially, Dasha's feeling really awkward, you have to recognize that, since the two of you did live in the same room at one time and copied each other's schoolwork, and now you're a director but she's a bit-player.* Then he set down the glass and kissed Masha, and she said, *we can do it today.*

Roma was surprised (he wasn't so drunk that he didn't remember that Masha had always had a far more scrupulous attitude toward this issue) but he should have been even more surprised in the morning when he saw how she ran into the bathroom, grabbing panty liners from her purse: *he should have been* because in reality he'd decided to play things safe and not notice anything, but then five minutes later, he stopped noticing anyway, thanks to a marvelous characteristic of the male psyche. All as Masha sat in the bathroom, ready to cry from fury.

As it happened, Masha's period wasn't late until the next month. She had to stretch out shooting, risking a fallout and feathers flying with the producer, and, in the last days, filming more and more of the location, which was ever more wintry, and then reshooting scenes that had originally been shot long ago, though Masha stayed even when the crew started heading out and made Roma stay another two days, too, until the rest of the props and equipment had been taken away. They slept together for the last time in the empty building, in complete quiet: it was cold and the director brought them two extra blankets but even under those, they had to shiver from the cold for what seemed like a half-hour and muffledly scream when their cold feet touched before they could start thinking about anything else. Roma, who'd already grown accustomed to the entire previous month being "we can do it today," thought a little about how to try counting the days (a few days after she'd come back, but just what date did she come back?…) but he didn't do that because, in the end, Masha would know best. Most likely if she'd asked him if he wanted to become the father of her child, right on the spot, he would have suggested waiting for more favorable circumstances, but she didn't ask him and so he didn't just experience a well-known, incomparable (alas, in comparison with safe sex) pleasure when he was leaving his seed inside her, he also permitted himself (only in a hypothetical sense, of course) to have fantasies, very highly varied fantasies, about Papa Roma: from Papa Roma bringing a brood of children to kindergarten before work to Papa Roma grudgingly admitting that yes, he had children in Germany, too, but couldn't say whose they were.

What Roma experienced as he was rocking away under two blankets that had slid off halfway ought to be called thrill-seeking; and by saying "we can do it today" each time, Masha, too, was specially maintaining the thrill-seeking while also giving Roma the opportunity to seize upon that deception if he wanted. A man means offensively little in matters of child production. Roma simply continued not to notice things later, too, just as he *didn't notice* the first time: the main thing was that Masha became a completely different person, both on the set and in bed. As she pressed against him, adjusting to his rhythm, she focused inward: Roma had become an instrument (truly a dear and beloved one) for her, and she was like the musician who places a tuning fork on an instrument's soundboard but concentrates on her own ear instead of the tuning fork.

The truth lay in the fact that during the several weeks following A.A.'s death, her father's funeral, and seeing her mother, it had seemed like Masha was floating in a milky fog, a milky soup of images that had arisen from some depths or other. She had the feeling that, by using the energy it took to bring that imagery to life, she could pull herself into reality, too, as if she were contraband, and emerge from the fog into the clear, bright light of day, along with some soggy macaroni of images. In her condition, she apparently didn't distinguish very well between the image of her future child and cinematic scenes that had not yet come into being. At any rate, the expression on her face when she kissed Roma and when she sat at her monitor was absolutely the same. For obvious reasons, only Roma knew this and said nothing to anyone.

However, a certain tension was now always palpable on the set since it's the director, after all, who should bring the whole crew into synch with herself, just as an artist should become one with a brush, a marksman with a weapon, and a skier with skis: sudden collective flares of rage or general apathy triggered by the fact that, for example, the makeup artists work two hours nonstop while the gaffers wander around like ghosts, or maybe a sharp, involuntary change of the tempo and rhythm in a scene, or a prop that smashes and bashes for no apparent reason are all things that people are inclined to attribute to either blind chance or the action of otherworldly entities, meaning Masha was above suspicion. Paradoxically, cautious, frightened glances were directed at Masha only when she deserved them least: for example when she resolutely demanded they reshoot a scene that had been shot almost at the very beginning (dialogue of the heroine and her son, only them), set a big piece of cheese and a box of self-tapping screws on a table, and requested the old woman act more stubborn but slightly detached while boring the self-tapping screws into the cheese in the process (but not, under any circumstances, portraying insanity), and if many from the crew hadn't feared catching hell, they'd have grumbled that things like this just don't happen in real life, but even if Masha had sensed someone's hand stretching to tap a finger to a head, how could she have even begun to explain to someone that she knew this did happen in real life and she'd *seen* it?

Things were like this. Masha finished smoking a cigarette, ground the butt into the soil beneath her feet, and the old woman brought her in to her mother (Masha nearly remembered the woman's name, it was on the tip of her tongue, so when they went inside and the voice of the woman who lived there came from the kitchen, *Galya?* it was as if a scab had finally been pulled from a wound: of course, this was *Auntie Galya*). Masha's mother was sitting in the square of a brightening window, backlit, and as Masha's eyes adjusted to the light, silence creaked with the old women's steps in the entryway. When Masha's eyes finally adjusted, she saw her mother's cautious smile. And her mother welcomingly said to her, in a slightly questioning tone: *hello, how do you do?*

Masha sat down on the edge of a made bed and, though she had no idea at all with what tone she should say "Mama, hi, it's me, Masha," those were the words she uttered and they sounded as if she'd cautiously knocked on her parents' bedroom door in the middle of the night. And only when her mother nodded, *oh, hello, hello*, could Masha frantically inhale. This all looked very much as if her mother simply hadn't discerned who she was from the start but had later recognized her. That was believable, even for a fairly long time.

In fact, that could even be believed a couple hours later, at home, after Auntie Galya had positioned her temporary duty-troops of old woman in their battle positions and then, after thinking a bit, sat Masha's mother down in the corner to slice cheese; the women worked like an orchestra, like a football team, like mission control, meaning nobody had been looking in the corner until Masha gasped: Masha saw her mother raptly and stubbornly boring one tapping screw after another into the piece of cheese, pulling the tapping screws out of the drawer where Masha's father had always stored greasy rags, tacks, nuts without bolts, and bolts without nuts. And even when Auntie Galya said *Lena, why the fuck are you wrecking the cheese?*, it was as if Masha's mother surfaced from her state of concentration all at once, frantically thought a bit (it was obvious she truly didn't know *why*) and barely mumbled out *the deceased very much loved,* then raised her questioning, pleading eyes at Auntie Galya; even after that it was possible not to take heed.

A bit later, though, right before leaving for the cemetery, Masha's mother took her by the elbow, led her to the furthest room, Masha's former bedroom, made her open the storage compartment under the sofa, heavily shifted around dusty boxes and bags for a while, then finally pulled out a bag and extended it to Masha, meaning- fully saying: *here, they've been lying here, they'll come in handy for you.* Masha looked inside the bag and realized her mother was taking her for someone else: there were children's toys inside the bag. It was frightening to look at her cautiously smiling mother and terri- fying to see inside the bag, with the hand puppets of her childhood, generously stuffed with cotton, and solidly mended: *they were a tiny bit torn, I mended them up.*

Masha took the bag, hid from her mother, and quickly stuffed the bag between the wardrobe and the cabinets, as if it had burnt her hands. But along the way to the cemetery (they jounced around in the van, knees pressed against the coffin) Masha's heart leaped and began thumping: it suddenly occurred to her that she couldn't have thought up anything better than those silly rabbits and bears for the credits of her future *Amber.* The joy of her luck suffocated Masha inside the vehicle's cold, frosty-walled belly, which was permeated with the smell of gasoline: her head spun from the inappropriateness of the discovery, and it was a little frightening, but this was probably how the Spanish felt, carrying the golden gods from abandoned Mesoamerican cathedrals.

After migrating to film, these toys became a universal metaphor: the cotton-stuffed hand puppets with two paws and the heads of a rabbit, a wolf, an escaped gingerbread man, a mouse, and a fox con- veyed a thousand things all at once but the main thing was that they inspired horror, inspiring it stealthily so at the film's final opening credit—"Directed by Maria Regina"—a hall stuffed with the most cynical of critics and cinephiles went very, very quiet.

Something similar happens at the end, when the heroine runs across a deer in the forest (a close-up: the animal's delicate, wide nostrils, the old woman's delighted eyes, pads of fingers stroking wooly antlers) and this scene, which concludes the picture, doesn't easily lend itself to an unequivocal interpretation, either. (It doesn't follow the example of *Save*'s finale, where the heroine is pounding her fists on a glass door that corresponds to the theater's screen: let me out of this effing movie!) Masha "exported" the deer from her trip home, too: the screenplay initially ended with just the heroine's death but the deer appeared on its own at the funeral, when Masha's mother suddenly picked up a branchy stick and placed it on the coffin, which was already lying on the ropes.

The realization that her mother was not in her right mind had conclusively reached Masha before that point, and now Masha felt as if she were drunk: her head was buzzing and events in the surrounding world seemed to come on in spurts. She was frightened not just because it was frightening to find something like this out about her own mother, but also because, as things turned out, she was making a film about her and, primarily, because a day from now she had to go back to the crew and continue making the film, now knowing who she was making it about.

Because even though the circumstances of her mother's life and the heroine's were not, of course, similar—her mother didn't own a big, ancient apartment, she had no children other than Masha, her children didn't act in cahoots to send her to a government nursing home so they could take turns visiting and fucking with the batty old woman's head—in the main, everything's undoubtedly the exact same story: the story of how a person progresses toward the absolute finale with accelerating speed and in deafening loneliness, and how things become clearer and clearer for the person before the screen conclusively darkens, only for him to run into the tragic impossibility of conveying that experience, in any way at all, to those who remain.

Life is absurd, but it dons the mask of logic when it wants to joke: critics who'd previously been very well-disposed toward Regina principally accused *Amber* of incomprehensibility, because previously Regina had made pictures about something familiar and already comprehensible—religious tolerance, moderate leftist discourse, or feminism—and now she'd disappointed the hopes attached to her and made something foggy about what was probably the Russian soul.

That, plus distribution problems (rights to the film belonged to some TV channel that barely existed on paper and, according to the initial oral agreement, transferring them at some token sum to an enterprise of a friend of Peter's required drafting and redrafting a whole truckload of documents, during which time the festival cycle passed so the film was no longer a new release and the distributors turned up their noses at it), meant it worked out that *Amber* "flopped." That flop, however, should be considered purely technical: a month after the film appeared on the Internet (a high-quality rip appeared right after the official release; journalists would ask Masha more than once if she had anything to do with the file's appearance, and Masha would loudly and distinctly answer "no," winking unambiguously), and so then, just two months later, more than 100,000 people around the world had seen *Amber*.

Of course even before that and long before *Amber* was regularly, as if on schedule, making it to "must-see" lists for the decade, and prior to the new generation of critics who cast blame on their elders for overlooking *Amber*, Masha knew, with the calm knack an artist is granted once or twice in a lifetime, that things were now working out for her. Peter was the first person to tell her. He met her at the Zurich airport, puzzled until the last minute about why suddenly Zurich (she'd said: *you'll understand when you see me*) and he truly did understand when she floated out from behind a bend in the corridor with one light little bag, and even that was being carried by a girl with a yellow scarf around her neck walking alongside Masha, because there are certain privileges for women in the ninth month. After grabbing the bag from the girl, who was silently cursing that she wasn't allowed to take out her phone and snap the celebrity pair, Peter slowly led Masha to a rented Audi Q5 and drove, as slowly as a snail licking the road with its belly, the whole way to the Golden Küste rental house with a view of the lake (these were all Masha's instructions, which he'd blindly fulfilled: you have to do what you have to do) and he kept silent, knowing that anything at all would sound false except the sole question he was afraid to ask: not even *who is he?* but *why the hell isn't he here?*

The screenplays Peter was sketching out in his imagination were all only partly true. The child's father really was in some sense nothing more than an instrument for Masha, but even so, it would have never popped into her head to get preggers with anybody else, and he was, indeed, an asshole, although this wasn't so much that the father didn't want the child as that another woman wanted the father, and, finally, he did actually have things going on, the kind of things that didn't allow him to fly in with Masha, though it never occurred to Peter, who possessed a dark blue passport, what these things might be, and the truth, as often happens, lay in a banality: Roma simply wasn't given a visa.

The problem is that things do not occur of their own accord, the way they ought to occur, because that's the natural way for things to occur, too. Roma and Masha should have gotten married but they couldn't do that, if only because they couldn't bring up the subject.

Masha worked all winter on post-production but it wasn't that there really wasn't a minute to start the conversation—the work was more likely a convenient excuse to brush aside the thought of that sort of conversation every time. The issue also wasn't that Roma didn't start the conversation: women know a thousand and one methods for making a man start any conversation in a way that makes the man certain he'd initiated the conversation. Put bluntly, Masha was ever more suspicious about any kind of things that seemed—to her, above all—to happen as they ought to, of their own accord (because where's the subject in that "of their own accord") and she drew further from clarity each day when faced with the answer to the question "why should we?" It was that question—not "why are you silent?"—that she should have asked Roma at the time, but somehow it just sounded too bizarre.

Strange though it was, Roma wasn't keeping silent because he didn't want to marry Masha: it was actually the opposite and the problem was that in reality he was—sweeping between the *or* of Masha, who was pregnant by him, and the *or* of Dasha who was always waiting for him with a meal—using a fully oneiric logic and would have liked to marry one *and* the other, too. Essentially, he didn't want to upset the unsteady equilibrium of the situation with the question "will you marry me?": he woke up with Masha in the morning, made breakfast for her, and, after sticking his ear to her belly for a minute, brought her to the studio, and then spent the afternoon and much of the evening in his own, now feminine, apartment where Dasha tempted him for sex, something that demanded increasingly fewer twinges from Dasha's conscience.

At the same time, Dasha was the only one aware of what was going on and that time was on her side. Each time she sat on a chair, unfastened his jeans, and said *well, hello there, Romanchik* (at first this designation for what he'd become accustomed to considering just *his* member made him grimace, but the initial conditioning phase passed quickly and the greeting began rousing an erection), Dasha understood she could extract a proposal from him but that then she would lose because the longer he resided in the comforting aura of lack of commitment, the less he understood why he would ever leave Dasha.

There was nothing unnatural in all this passing, rather than bidding a hand (what had caused Sodom and Gomorrah to be destroyed, after all, was not what people often think it is, but simply *regular life*) so initially Roma didn't even grasp why they were looking at him so scornfully at the consulate: *well, yes, not married. What, don't you understand she's giving birth in a month?*

They'd gotten married the day before Masha brought her doubled body to the airplane so she could become the middle piece of a matryoshka—Masha nestled in the plane, the baby nestled in her—that wailed furiously on take-off, then Roma waved to her and went off to the store (because Dasha had asked him to stop by the store, too): for the most part, Masha now couldn't have cared less about Roma's pathetic tone, his apologizing that *it's a formality, stupidity, but there's no way I can do without it* and she was utterly focused on the strange situation where someone dead (in speaking about the deceased, we, as it turns out, always have in mind some sort of particular form of life and, proceeding from there, all that's left is to deem the child the deceased until it's been born) controls the life of the living.

What Peter didn't know was that the airplane delivered not only Masha to him and not only a formed child who was already vigorously reacting to the Brandenburg concertos that were sounding in the car, but also a disc with a new picture. The doctors had insisted Masha needed to be admitted to the hospital upon arrival but Masha had come a day early, so she could, first off, shut herself in the living room and run the final cut of *Amber* twice in a row and then, that night, show it to Peter, who shifted his glance to her as if it were difficult to break free of the power of the picture (though there was no more picture now, only credits) and didn't know what to say (he couldn't say, *Königin, you made a masterpiece* because things like that are read in the eyes) and so, not expecting it himself, he said (meaning the picture): *Königin, you're so frightened.*

And how could she not be frightened? Masha had reason to be frightened.

Things were like this. After they'd come back from the cemetery, the efficient group of old women, commanded by Auntie Galya, dug into the salads, vodka, boiled potato, and roasted chicken legs. Toward night, they crammed the refrigerator to overflowing with leftovers and everybody took home oranges, fistfuls of candy, and jars of salads tied up in plastic bags. Everything floated before Masha's eyes—not from the vodka (she wasn't drinking) but from exhaustion—and she put her mother to bed; her mother even nodded and bowed and said *I do thank you very much*. Then Masha sat alone in a half-dark room—only an old table lamp turned toward the wall was burning—and smoked, staring out a dark, gaping window. A burp returned the flavor of herring-and-beet salad, and Masha chased it back with cognac. Old women were coming out of the shadows in the corners and sitting down all around the room: her mother's mother, her mother, and her grandmothers. It was as if they wanted to say something but then reconsidered: they sighed, shook their heads, looked away, clasped their fingers, and exchanged glances as if they were thinking about something together and had all agreed on something together. Their mustached lips twitch, their creased eyelids rise and fall, stiff fingers grasp at one another; the old women shake their heads, making their chins move as if they're chewing on something. Masha has gone too far away from them, far into the cold and far into the emptiness. And this means it will be all the more painful and frightening for her to return, but how could it be otherwise?—they'd all returned.

# DOUBLING THE WORLD

Masha will never return to Russia.

Emigration is a rewarding topic for reflection but Masha will speak unenthusiastically about this fact of her biography. At the famous Kino Arsenal press conference regarding the discovery of *Pursuit*, she'll answer a related question by saying: *just try replacing all your blood: fully draining your own and pouring someone else's into your body. No matter where I am, I'm in Russia.*

And one of the characters in *Hunger* will say: *My homeland lost the greatest war in the history of mankind and was pillaged and ravaged by the victors. And there's a particular tragic aspect to this because the best, most talented part of the people helped arrange that defeat. That's why it's agonizing for a person with a conscience and intellect to be in Russia.*

Masha will have nearly stopped interacting with journalists before that point, so her public statements regarding emigration are limited to those one and a half instances: in the first two years, it simply never occurred to journalists to ask about anything of the sort since lots of people leave their country for a couple of years, and Masha never mentioned not planning to go back.

She only said it once, and that was to Peter, on the very same day she arrived. It was then that she'd uttered an enigmatic phrase about how, for her, leaving Russia might be a method for doubling the world. That remark went in one ear and out the other for Peter—a woman who's about to give birth any day now might say anything—though you have to pay very close attention to those remarks because they're how Masha spilled one of her innermost thoughts, albeit not fully formulated.

A return to Petersburg is now necessary since it was there, a few months before her departure, that the workings of this mechanism were themselves revealed to Masha. Things were like this. Masha was sitting at the editing desk and replaying, for the hundredth time, the scene where the son and daughter are having it out, in the presence of their unwell old mother, arguing over which of them is less guilty before their mother: their contorted faces and the agonized gaze of the old woman, who's straining to understand why they're shouting, were shot using the 180-degree rule, and, as with all her pictures, Masha knew this scene and each of its frames by heart, in the minutest of detail, but even so she kept pressing "play" again and again so perhaps it might dawn on her what's missing, but then the telephone in Masha's pocket started getting twitchy and she saw an unfamiliar number on the screen.

The voice Masha heard was familiar, though: it was Liza (the word "widow" is foolish, but the longer we live, the more foolish words turn up in our lives) but this was the first time Masha heard her voice as neither annoyed nor haughty. Liza was speaking conciliatorily, as if A.A.'s death meant something for both of them and was not just a catastrophe in and of itself. It turned out that Liza needed to give some thing to Masha, but Liza couldn't fully explain if A.A. had instructed her to give it to Masha or if Liza simply wanted to give it to Masha as a gift; in any case, Masha decided to go and didn't ask questions.

The thing turned out to be Pushkin, the second volume of the yellow three-volume set. Masha had managed to completely forget about that book, so it was as if she was reading for the first time:

"Gentle Masha. Bid farewell to your native doorway, inexplicable delight awaits you," and though only a very recent student could have made an inscription so touching in all its pathos and ambiguity, Masha now caught herself sensing she was receiving that message not from a 25-year-old but from the A.A. who died a few months short of reaching forty. Masha stuffed the book in her bag; Liza served her tea. A little girl with curly black hair was busily playing with dolls in the corner, and Masha felt a little queasy from the smell of tobacco but, so as not to put herself in an idiotic position, she didn't complain since her belly could still be taken as nothing more than the consequences of an excessive love for baked goods and, more than anything, she disliked answering unasked questions. From what Liza said, it was obvious that it had been her own initiative to hand Pushkin over to Masha; she'd found the book on A.A.'s desk: *he probably needed the text for an article or a lecture*, and that sounded questioning, as if Masha could have confirmed that no, that wasn't the point, that until his final days A.A. had been pouring out tears on the thing he'd once given to a girl he'd fallen in love with, and it was as if Liza herself didn't understand that by the very fact of both her call and this meeting (*I thought you should have the book, it's the right thing to do*) she was, to some extent, revealing her own discovery, which had obviously just been made (and which explained the conciliatory and respectful tone of her voice), that A.A. had loved Masha and died without getting over that love.

Liza talked about how *he kept fading in his last years, all of him was fading, a heart attack isn't cancer, you know, you don't expect it, but you unwillingly start believing that these things, that people... well, that they somehow have premonitions*, and it was suddenly clear to Masha that the intent of this whole event was to share at least a little of the responsibility for A.A.'s death—*I didn't bring any joy to his life but it was you, after all, who took it away from him at one time*—and though obviously Liza didn't say that, that's exactly how Masha understood her, and then she started to feel so disgusted that her tongue went still in her mouth and she couldn't play along anymore so just nodded, squinting at the little girl with the almost familiar face: the little girl was putting a doll to bed. The doll didn't want to sleep and the girl was closing the doll's little eyes with her index finger and telling her to go to sleep because *otherwise it'll be bad, go on and sleep*. The girl raised a hand over the doll as if to strike her and remained like that, pensive. It crossed Masha's mind at that moment that the child wasn't simply using her doll to reproduce, like a piggly repeating something wiggly, the way her mother treated her (what else could you expect from a woman who smokes right by her daughter?) but was doing this—doubling her world—as a way of trying hard to understand *why* her mother treated her like that. Liza, who was following Masha's gaze, detected that the girl was betraying her, clasped her fingers as if she were defending herself, and then, drawing out her words, asked her *little bunny* if she wanted to watch a cartoon, which was when Masha immediately grasped two things at once: that the scene she'd watched today until it was worn to pieces lacked the play of the old woman's hands, that was the first thing, and the second was that she'd just stumbled upon the fundamental theme for her next picture.

Doubling the world is the only way to make the world cognizable. Not just because this operation allows you to determine a framework and separate the piece that requires understanding from the pointless meat of impressions, but also because it's a way for a person to provide a third lever for his shaky position in this world: "I and the world" is just a tragic situation but "I, the world, and a second world" is already a structure that allows you to establish yourself and attempt to use your head.

The third day after moving from the little house on Golden Küste to the clinic, Masha will request paper and a pencil, and begin drawing. She'll draw faces that surrounded her in her youth, and it goes without saying that this will be the preliminary stage of her work on *Plague* (there will be fifteen actors in the film and Masha will find each from several thousand photographs: assistants will run their legs off, cursing *diese Geistekranke*, but she truly only needs the ones she'd drawn in advance: in *Plague*, the very rhythm of how the boys' and girls' faces appear in a scene will become something like a load-bearing structure, and there's a reason that, all told, Masha will draw several dozen faces; back on Friedrichstraße, she'll select those fifteen, arranging and rearranging the sheets on the floor of the large room, from which she's removed almost everything for the occasion) and that by simultaneously forcing her memory to work at its breaking point, pulling face after face out of oblivion, Masha will discover that this rapidly growing catalogue is also nothing less than the world of her youth, which has inconspicuously turned into the past, and that by forcing ghost after ghost to materialize from the paper's surface, she's essentially trying to grasp, for the first time, what that world was.

As far as unfinished storylines go, though, Masha will still have occasion to remember the moment when she was watching A.A.'s daughter and thought for the first time about doubling the world. Her own daughter, Anya (Roma chose the name and all Masha could do was cover her eyes when she realized her daughter would have the same name as A.A.'s daughter, but of course Roma couldn't have known that), will be a little older than three when she turns out to be capable of more or less explaining her own drawings. Anya will bring her mother a sheet of paper she's scribbled on with colored pencils and begin telling a story: *that's my house, that's me, that's a crocodile, that's a cow... –And where's Mama?*, and Anya will mull that over, looking off to the side somewhere, and say: *Mama's not there*.

After putting Anya to bed, Masha will pick up the drawing and burst into tears, choking them down so she doesn't scream: the little girl who'd been closing her doll's eyes four years ago was blaming her mother for being undiscriminating in her child-rearing methods; Masha's own daughter will turn out to have a far more serious account to settle with her mother: Masha, who'd been disappearing at the studio, for shooting, day after day, beginning almost immediately after giving birth, is simply depriving Anya of her presence. And that will mean her daughter will supplement the cohort of people before whom Masha is mortally guilty: when Anya grows up, she'll take her seat on the bench in court with the other accusers (since this bench should exist) right alongside her grandfather, alongside the father of another Anya, and alongside her mother's mother.

Masha wipes the tears from the sheet of paper with the edge of her hand; the paper warps, and the colored lines blur. Berlin rejoices: dance clubs roar, beer sputters as it escapes from spigots, hot dogs burst on griddles, the air fills with the smell of hemp, and trains shake underground; Berlin is a city of raging youth, testosterone splashing over its brim. Torn down to its foundation and then built on its own ashes, Berlin denies the very idea of continuity but Masha, sobbing in her little cabin aboard a space ship whose passengers were all born in flight, is doomed to return, in thought, to her mother, who was left on the inhuman icy wide-open spaces of an Eastern European plain.

The day after the funeral, Auntie Galya woke Masha up with the clanging of dishes, and when Masha went out to the kitchen, Auntie Galya served her reheated chicken and a big bowl of salad: *need some vodka? That's right.* It would have been difficult not to guess why Auntie Galya had come to see Masha when the sun was barely up—it wasn't to feed her breakfast—but even so, her question, *what are you thinking about doing with your mother?*, rang with a degree of directness that Masha wasn't ready for. It wasn't that Masha hadn't thought about it at all, but she picked at her chicken with her fork as if she were appealing for help. Auntie Galya sighed and sat down across from her, leaning her elbows into the table: *you're not coming back here? You're not. Can you take her to the city? –I don't… –I hear you, Masha, don't explain. So it works out we'll put your mother in the state home?* Masha laid down her fork. They were silent for a very, very long time. Finally, Auntie Galya stood, dried the washed dishes, hung the towel on a line over the stove, and, businesslike—just like when she was calculating who needed one bottle and who needed two—began listing how much money would be needed per month for food, how much for firewood, how much to pay for electricity and gas, and how much, finally, had to be added for her labor, so she could buy herself a bottle. She named the final sum: *that's per month. Can you manage that?* Masha nodded, still not completely understanding, and looked up at Auntie Galya. *What didn't you understand? I'll take in your mother. It won't break my back but you know, you wouldn't send a dog to that roachy dump, let alone your neighbor. She doesn't wet herself yet and if she does, it's not a problem.* All that was left for Masha was to insist on doubling the sum "for her labor." Auntie Galya shrugged: *I won't refuse it, the main thing is for you to send it on time. And eat your chicken, watch it doesn't get cold.*

A situation where the best possible solution turns out to be hopelessly bad is bad not because the solution is difficult to reach (quite the contrary: nothing could be simpler) but because it will never resolve the problem: a person who's had a tumor removed will die sooner or later of cancer, rather than simply of old age. And this isn't just a matter of the awareness of a debt to her mother, one that's been incorrectly or incompletely fulfilled and never lets go of Masha (and nothing will change that, neither the money she'll wire regularly to Auntie Galya nor the boxes she'll send of some medicines that a Berlin doctor will recommend highly: *early-onset Alzheimer's is a rare thing, no, there's no treatment, this is essentially vitamins*) but also that when this story reaches the public domain, of course in a distorted form, Masha will be reminded of *Amber*, and it's only the rare newspaper rat who won't write about how Regina first abandoned her own mother in a nursing home and then cynically used that storyline for a film, too. Within that context, of course, the dedication prefacing *Plague* will be construed as refined mockery because—as the insiders will crow, all trying to outdo each other—it was intended initially for *Amber* and it was only later that Regina's conscience got to her and she moved it to the next film. According to another version, somebody talked Masha into removing the shameless dedication from *Amber*.

In reality, it's clear that the circumstances presented to the heroine of *Amber* weren't at all comparable to the conditions in which Masha's mother remained, sinking into the abyss of her own unconscious mind. The main thing wasn't even that the old woman in the film is surrounded by people who squabbled and skirmished and tried with all their might to use her, not caring at all about the mysterious sacrament of her slow withdrawal into madness, but that, unlike her, nobody had thrown Masha's mother into the horror of another world that's unfamiliar and hostile. (This is exactly why Masha's mother, according to Auntie Galya's monthly phone reports, will become even more at home in her house and even help with little things in the kitchen garden, whereas the fictitious old woman will be forced to go to additional horrendous efforts in order to escape from that world, too, into a world of indifferent nature, with matte-eyed cats that Masha and Roma so raptly, carefully depicted, bushes slowly waving their leaves, and pine trunks, transparent in the light of a setting sun. The shot that will go into all the textbooks: a little dove corpse, dotted with the green glass of flies.)

And of course Masha knew what she was doing when she put the dedication "To my mother, who left" in the *Plague* credits. Because it was in *Plague* that this dedication clarified an essential point and drew out, at the proper level of generalization, a story about boys and girls whose parents *left*, who went away for two weeks.

Initially, Masha drew faces. Only a little over two weeks was left before the baby was due. Her days were taken up with a strict sched-ule: procedures, tests, walks, and eating (journalists were allowed to see Masha several times: they had identical sets of questions, as if they'd been approved somewhere in Brussels, and Masha told one of them she'd decided to have the baby in Switzerland because, as she'd just noted, she was expecting a girl and in Russia there was a very high tax on newborn girls; the Russian ambassador in Berne was forced to refute this bosh). Even so, Masha drew right after dinner, reclining, spreading a big, rough sheet on a drawing board that lightly pressed on her belly. By the time Roma had arrived (he flew in four days before) there was a portfolio case with a couple dozen sketches standing in the corner of her room: *why are you working so much? Don't you believe in God?* Roma had brought an armful of long-stemmed daisies that would barely fit in the vase, and Masha, answered, off-point, *nope, I'm not afraid.*

Masha was all rather aloof but Roma didn't sweat things, crediting that to the upcoming event: along with Peter (who'd declined a lucrative contract in order to come, though Masha would never find that out), Roma rushed around from store to store and stocked up on things for Anya (a person should already have things when coming into the world, after all), stopped by to see Masha for an hour or two in the afternoon, and was all hyped up and unable to sit in one place, not just because that befitted a young father but also because he was out wandering Zurich in the evenings, enjoying his solitude in an absolutely unfamiliar city. And no, of course he wouldn't have managed without Peter.

Peter, who'd already been married *in a former life* and whose son went to school in Munich, turned out to be the only person who knew precisely what, exactly, had to be done in a house where someone planned to bring home a baby. Roma couldn't have imagined that the list of things would turn out to be so long (he didn't even know the word for bib and later, when Masha asked him to pass her a bib, he asked: *is this that? The bibchen-shitlich?*) and it was as if Masha wasn't present, both before having the baby and the week after: she covered sheet after sheet with drawings, falling asleep from exhaustion (she wanted to sleep all the time). At that point, she didn't fully understand why she needed the drawings: no story had flashed in the gaps between them as yet, but she felt, vaguely,

that she had to draw as much as possible while she had the chance
to work, if only a little, and that sooner or later a film would hatch
from the portfolio case, which bloated more every day.

The portfolio case pupated and displayed no signs of life for a
half-year: only in January, by now in Berlin, when Anya had grown
calmer and more or less slept for at least half the night, and when
Roma had flown off to Petersburg yet again (he'd gone four times
during that half-year, each time for no less than a week, *work, my
sunshine, what can you do*) did an opportunity come up for Masha
to untie the ribbons and attempt to remember, drowsily peering at
the hastily done drawings, what kind of sensation she'd managed
to capture back then in Zurich. During that time, *Amber* had gone
into limited distribution and been subjected to baffled criticism, and
the fact that her best picture had not just met with a cold reception
from professionals (which is unpleasant, no matter how much you
detest critics) but had also never been properly shown, only exacer-
bated her state, which Roma characterized with the simplicity of
a person cultivating the image of a regular guy: *Regina, do you even
understand that you've totally lost it?*

What Roma didn't understand (because if he'd understood it,
he'd've had to think about the *why* behind her habit of always going
back to work: *most people would rather die than think –Regina, speak
Russian, even German makes me sick, but you're speaking English…*) is
that the other very important reason for Masha's withdrawal into
herself was none other than Roma himself. Roma was studying
German (it goes without saying that the cinematographer for *Minus
One* and *Amber* could find himself work anywhere in Europe but
he had to have at least some command of the language) and Peter
got him into the best courses in Zurich, but Roma worked at it as
if were the most pointless of school subjects and he came home
nearly every day totally snockered. Masha had no patience for that:
Anya took up all her time and in the rare moments when she allowed
her mother to do nothing, Masha sat and silently drank tea with

milk, allowing her glance to aimlessly journey over the walls and windows. In his sober moments, Roma attempted to rouse Masha, telling her world news, but when he was drunk, he shouted that she'd changed and she doesn't give a shit about him; either way, Masha had no energy to answer Roma. Each time Roma was heading for Russia, he softened and behaved like a total honey bunny a few days before leaving—he did laundry, ironed, studied his German, and took the baby for strolls—but then he came back a week or so later, as gloomy as a rain cloud, and headed for a *kneipe* the very first evening. Sex is generally considered the highest manifestation of love—and thus its consequence—but in reality, sex is the only reason that can force a person, for a relatively long time, to make peace with the close proximity of another person. Roma and Masha will definitely stop sleeping together toward the end of filming *Plague*.

It would be tough to just go ahead and say how or where the idea for *Plague* originated. As should happen in these sorts of situations, *Plague* was born from unavoidable external circumstances (Anya was still nursing, which meant they could only film on a set), from Masha's thoughts (in this particular case, about how the mechanism of turning the world into an intelligible world works), from chance (the second volume of Pushkin that Masha carried around with her), and from what constituted her everyday life (and this, by the way—the story of a main character who just can't get relationships going with two girls at once—is the only case where Masha directly transferred circumstances from her personal life into a picture; the only person who noticed, however, was Roma but he didn't ask anything, lest he end up being correct). The film's archetypical backdrop—young men and women who are shut away from everyone and indulge in merriment—binds all that together while simultaneously concealing everything individually.

A certain discontinuity in the composition—the film probably most resembles a multitude of photos that appear, at first glance, to have been chaotically mixed up, rather than a monolithic story that develops from an opening hook to a denouement—was also a consequence of circumstances. Masha wrote the *Plague* screenplay in fits and starts, noting down, with her right hand, what came into her head, all while she held a lunching Anya with her left; scratching with a pencil on the first paper she came across; hunching over the stroller; and, finally, hanging over the edge of the bed whenever she couldn't sleep because some line was boiling down in the murky flow of her consciousness. Sometimes Peter would come over (he came once a week and would have come more often if Masha hadn't gently forbidden it) and stay with Anya, freeing Masha to sit in the café across the street for an hour or two; Masha would then write down an entire scene at once or string together lines from a pile of little papers torn from various notebooks on a page, drawing key frames on the reverse.

Peter always called the night before and came over in Roma's absence, though not in secret: to the contrary, when Masha would say Peter was coming over the next day, Roma always cleared out for half the day. Peter didn't just bring Anya gifts (with torn-off price tags, though even without tags it was often obvious he'd spent as much on a toy as others spend on new electronics): he also brought trunkloads of diapers, baby wipes, laundry detergent, tea, ice cream, and cheese; took out the trash; and washed the floor a couple times. When Masha decided it was time, it was Peter who found a nanny for the child and a housewife for the apartment (a radiantly beautiful Moroccan woman, *she's too good for me*), but there was something else, too: for nearly a year, Peter was the only channel connecting Masha with the outside world, with the professional world above all, and so when it came time for negotiations with producers and, later, the pre-shooting phase, and, finally, filming, the fact that Masha was basically in a condition to quickly get into the work and didn't look to an outsider like a mommy who'd sat in the director's chair for who-the-hell-knew-what-reason, well, that was primarily Peter's contribution, too. The same Peter who, when he asked her, jokingly, if she was writing a role for him, Masha answered honestly that the picture was young, so only if he'd agree to a quick part in the very beginning, as a parent behind whom the main character closes a door (all Masha could do when he agreed was raise her eyebrows). The same Peter who, as was obvious without saying a word, would have moved in with Masha on Friedrichstraße if that had been possible. The same Peter about whom Roma asked *so how's the heroic lover? Did he satisfy?* each time he came home in the evening; Roma's rudeness made Masha queasy, but she just silently shut herself in her room with Anya.

It goes without saying that Masha should have sent Roma to the damned dogs: it's easy to reach that conclusion in the format of women's get-togethers with a bottle of red (*oh, girls, if I were her*) and it's easy to take that sort of decision when a story's already almost over (I guess I probably should have stayed with the old man and the old woman, thought the gingerbread man). In the force field of a life currently in progress, though, there was a heap of reasons not to do that. Beginning with the fact that every time Masha and Roma put Anya to bed, went through a standard, diminishing cycle of mutual *oh, forgive me* and *fine, whatever*, and took off their clothes, their sex resembled something worth living for and forgiving each other for. On the other hand, Masha, who held no belief that you could force an adult to change—either with the power of persuasion or the fear of hysterics—continued hoping that an adult can one day ask himself a direct question, answer it honestly, courageously take a decision, and so on. In the end, the point is that the question "Why didn't Masha leave Roma?" really can't elicit a proper answer because a person never leaves *one place* but rather always goes to *another place*, and thus the only question that can be answered without the risk of a big lie, is "Why didn't Masha leave for Peter?" but it's not yet time to answer that question.

A few more unseemly and, essentially, random details, since it appears there's no way to get by without them. Here's Roma, who's

absolutely seriously and calmly trying to convince Masha that her
decision to have a child was a mistake (it's night, they're sitting in
the kitchen drinking tea with ice cream that Peter brought—Roma's
just shoveling it in). Here's Roma, who's brought home a bottle of
vodka and refuses to go drink somewhere outside (*quiet, woman!
So this is what it's come to: a man can't drink in his own home*, Roma's
drunk off his ass and his tone changes from vaudeville to holy fool:
*oh, excuse me, your highness, it's not my home but yours*, and Masha,
who can't take it, slams the door between the rooms and locks it).
Here's Roma in post-coital serenity pensively saying that love is a
sickness that can't last longer than four years, scientists have proven
it (Anya naps during the day and Masha still has to find time to iron
the linen but she suddenly numbs, curls up, and turns toward the
wall, where a ray of sun flickers after pushing its way through the
lilacs). That's enough.

The last day shooting *Plague* became the last day of their *together*
and, simultaneously, the last day of the existence of the Regina–
Yevgenyev creative tandem. They bought two bottles of wine—for
Roma to celebrate and for Masha to use to brighten up some water,
and the squabble pendulum set to work halfway through the second
bottle, gathering amplitude. Roma began by blaming Masha for
despotic behavior on the set (*Yevgenyev, and how, in your opinion,
am I supposed to film? "My dear Roma, please do tell, might you care to
shoot another take?" It's work! We're not husband and wife there, we're
director and cinematographer!*), but that was just a solitary beginning
note. What Roma was driving at was that Masha had enslaved him,
forced him to marry her, tied him down with a child, and made
him move to Germany *because you needed a cameraman! Just look at
yourself, you're a monster, you've devoured everybody around you, you
use everybody for your own work, you even had a child not because you
wanted a child but because some idea came into your head, you're sick,
you're not a human being!* Masha listened to Roma's hysterics and then,
after catching herself with the passionate wish to grab him by the

throat, she jumped up, overturning the table as she did: *you low-life bastard!* and after the bottle had finished rumbling around on the tile, she calmly said, *you're a low-life bastard and I wish you'd croak.*

Another special "female" disclaimer may be called for here: Roma wasn't just guilty of falling out of love (that goes without saying; the pardonable necessity of that guilt, however, should be taken into account) but he also—and this is the main thing—didn't want to admit that guilt. Essentially, Roma needed events to develop in a way that resolved the situation, all the while keeping his white tuxedo unstained, and the illusion that this was possible is the primary thing to blame him for since illusions, unlike mistakes, are unpardonable. In the end, the problem isn't that Roma felt more comfortable with Dasha (of course Roma flew off once a month, to see her for a week, not to work) but that this whole year he'd been striving to get Masha to tell him where to go—or to *Arshloch*, which was one of the first German words he'd learned—so the result wouldn't be that it all looked like he'd abandoned his wife with a small child and that, in striving for that, he just couldn't admit to himself what he was doing. However, in presenting that ruthless accounting to Roma, you can't help but also note that Masha could have (and, in all seriousness, should have) helped Roma. In the end, of course, she did: by overturning the table, she'd already figured out what Roma was expecting from her, though that understanding had come unpardonably late.

In fact, ever since the moment back at her father's funeral when Masha found herself immersed in something resembling a murky, viscous milky fog, she'd continued floating in that fog. From the outside, this looked like indifference: Masha participated indifferently in any conversation, gazed indifferently all around when she was alone, and cared indifferently for Anya when Anya demanded it (this is what gave grounds for the most horrendous of Roma's accusations and it's likely that if Masha hadn't felt this wasn't just baseless bosh, she wouldn't have found the strength within to blow her top). That's how it looked from the outside, but Masha hadn't yet lost her mind and she was aware of what was happening, although the very form of that awareness was a variation on that same indifference… or, put bluntly, it was its source and cause. The third person, who'd taken possession of Masha's consciousness ever more and more, was indifferent: there was the Masha who acted as circumstances demanded, there was the Masha who acknowledged what was happening, gave commands to the first Masha, suffered, and experienced pain and joy, and then, finally, there was the third person, who simply observed all this and, with the very wordlessness of his own observation, confirmed the muddleheadedness of first-Masha's actions and the pointlessness of second-Masha's sufferings. In any case, this was exactly how Masha understood, from inside, everything that happened, and it's perfectly clear that whoever registers, within himself, the effect of that third person's systemic authority cannot help but agree with the probity of the third person.

The only thing that had extracted Masha out from under the power of that systemic authority was work (she'd become even harsher and more precise on the set than before; Peter, who'd last worked with her on *Save*, flung this at her: *Königin, when you were in Russia, what, did you find time to command a regiment or something?*) and if, after the break-up with Roma, which was abhorrent no matter how you looked at it, Masha hadn't gone into her shell completely, that was only because *Plague* had been shot and now she couldn't not edit it.

Fifteen boys and girls acted in *Plague*, though it would be a mistake to regard Masha's film about adolescents as similar to Larry Clark's agitprop. After seeing his parents off for a vacation, the main character establishes something like an ideal government, moreover this utopia, straight out of Hegel, has both social and existential characteristics. *So're your parents happy? Well, content with themselves? Mine aren't, either*, the main character explains to his buddy. *And nobody's are,* he waves an arm at guests unpacking bags of bottles and snacks, *no matter who you ask. But we're all planning to do the same things as them anyway: school, work, have a family, and run off to our lovers. The result's obvious from the start! So what should we do? —What? —Something that's different, on principle, you think? —Drink? —You guys, we have something a little better!* (A pale brunette of almost ideal beauty appears in the shot.) *Come here! —What is it, is there some puffing going on? —Oh, do we have a breeze!* It goes without saying that, within the framework of typical realism, they can't do anything but smoke and drink. A work of art, however, is a work of art because its purpose is to catch reality on an allegorical hook. The utopia the main character establishes is, as with Pinocchio and his friends, nothing more than theater and it goes without saying that any such project is, in some sense, Theater of Cruelty. It's clear that by formally remaining a picture that depicts the typical behavior of adolescents, *Plague* is a generalizing statement about the universal mechanism of how to live a life: in the final reckoning, a person never "takes experience into consideration" but simply mechanically repeats it.

Since Hegel has already come up here, we'll have to wait for him to leave on his own and not send the old man packing: *Feast During the Plague,* which is played out by characters in small roles, is the antithesis of the leading storyline, not just ideologically but also artistically. When answering an interview question about how it occurred to her to use Pushkin's text, Masha said (not answering, of course, but just saying what seemed important to her) that not one of the existing adaptations of the tragedy had found success, precisely because adults had acted out the story, even though the way Pushkin's characters behave is like kindergarten, and only nonadults can behave that way: it's a story about cruel children, which is what the adaptors didn't understand in 1974 or even 1979. Put more simply (since the correspondent's eyes had gone glassy), *that text can only be played in a nonserious way, does that clear things up?*

Of course the half-drunk adolescent wrapped up in a curtain who turns up in the doorway so he can shout, in a screeching voice choking with laughter—*A godless banquet, godless madmen all!*—is, objectively, funny, and auditoriums all over Europe roared with laughter when he appeared, but there's a moment of sincere horror in *Plague*, too, when Walsingham suddenly understands that the ideal government he's established has turned out to be nothing other than the adult world. Yes, the doubled world: it's all the very same choice between Mary and Luisa, *our homes are filled with sorrow*, it's all the same wagon filled with dead bodies, with Pushkin steering. In that sense and, notwithstanding the canon of similar stories, it's extraordinarily important that morning doesn't come in *Plague*: the action finishes after midnight and the feast continues. The final title, offered on a dark screen, reads *Walsingham remains, immersed in deep thought*, and it doesn't just comply with the original, it's the only conclusion that Masha, as a responsible artist, could have made: all that can be done in this life is to remain deep in thought.

What became an abstract construction for shrewd critics was the flesh and blood of Masha's own fate. Because if you take notion after notion right from someone's tongue, as if you were peeling layer after layer from an onion, then you have to admit that—even as Roma was driving the drowsy Masha toward The Pines in his old Volkswagen and explaining in an unapologetic voice (because what was there to apologize for?) about Dasha, who was there, and why should they kick her out or anything now—Masha had already pretty much figured out Roma would stay with Dasha in the end. And, once again, it wasn't exactly a mystery as complex as Newton's binomial theorem that Roma was flying off to Petersburg (by regularly transforming himself for several days before takeoff, Roma literally acknowledged that no suspicions would be ungrounded). And finally, when Masha was hurrying off for shooting and nearly knocked over Dasha, who was in her own little world, with her neck craned up, on the Alexanderplatz (only new arrivals are so out of the loop that they don't know it's best not to walk on Berlin's bike trails), the understanding that Roma had essentially already escaped her could only be set aside. But Masha's damp palms—her palms were sweating, though this was from joy because Dasha hadn't recognized her—were nothing more than a fact from her biography. From a biography that already excludes any fact about Roma taking the same route an hour and a half later with Anya in a little 10-year-old BMW (found, incidentally, by Peter), and possibly coming across Dasha and giving her a ride somewhere.

That was when Masha grasped that the real abyss opens up not where you understand something but where you discover that there's no point whatsoever in your understanding. *I know what will happen but I can't do anything*—Masha couldn't have said how that line surfaced in her head and she didn't have A.A. to explain it with a chuckle. Understanding doesn't rescue you: you can understand everything and see everything but be unable to do anything because you're spinning around like laundry in a washing machine. That, then is the shot—of a washing machine in operation—that will open *Plague* and you can't help but agree with the witty critic who noticed that this image must have been particularly familiar to Masha, the young mother.

As it turns out, sketching a circle with *Plague* in the center was the only possible way to draw near the answer to the question that was posed and, very significantly, abandoned in the middle of this chapter: why Masha didn't leave Roma for Peter. Because, of course, there was nothing else Masha saw as clearly as how all the logic of the storyline's development was forcing her to drift from Roma to Peter. It was the clarity and certitude of that logic, though, that plunged her into a state of paralyzed horror. And this was no longer because her own uniqueness wasn't taken into consideration by the unknown (and, without a doubt, not existing anywhere in reality) compiler of this storyline but also because—*komisch!*—she muttered, armed with scissors in a kitchen illuminated by the light on the ventilation hood—*this is the exact same thing, this already happened, I was already there.*

And here's what happened. Two days after Roma spent an hour and a half collecting his belongings around the apartment (fortunately, there wasn't very much) and departed for points unknown-but-known, Peter called. He asked how things were, about the heir to the throne (*she's already walking, holding the wall, it's insane!*), and he asked if it was true that filming was over, and then invited Masha to celebrate. Masha arranged with the nanny for an extra three hours and Peter came for Masha that evening in his sports-model Audi, which gleamed as if it had just come from a jewelry shop; Masha knew this car only left Peter's garage on special occasions. No, Peter wasn't planning to confess his love to her; he truly had nothing more in mind than holding a modest celebration of the beginning of post-production. But Peter found Masha in a mood that was far from celebratory: she was silent, didn't respond to jokes, barely reacted to questions about her little girl, and shrugged off attempts to start talking about work, *ganz normal.* By the time they'd finished their main course, dinner had already begun to resemble a wake. They were sitting in a corner in the dark, far from a screen that was showing some sort of football match, and of course Masha saw that Peter was suffering from the disparity between the lovely setting, the wonderful dinner (*they have Berlin's best selection from the Loire Valley here*) and the celebratory occasion, and the sepulchral mood of the flow of their meeting: the duty of politeness required that she assure him that he wasn't the problem. And though Masha didn't want to explain what was going on (particularly since what was going on was not, strictly speaking, that Roma had gone) even so, as she took the bottle (Peter didn't even blink an eye, he actually liked her organic negligence of etiquette), she said, overcoming the wine's astringency, that *Roma left, that's why I'm so out-of-it, really.*

It goes without saying that, as always, Peter responded with something foolish: *I knew this would happen, Königin,* but that was only the beginning: after drinking two more glasses and chasing it with strudel plus questions and answers in the spirit of *what, permanently? –Uh-huh, forever and ever and ever*, Peter's face was more and more flushed, he hid his hands under the table, and then, when he took them back out again, he finally said, decisively, that he knows he's *fifteen years older and you're horribly young and all that and forgive me I know what I'm talking about it's all very horribly stupid but really it's true I'm already an old guy and Königin I'm feeling certain, right inside, here, that there will never be anything like this for me ever again I love you I love you so horribly much. Marry me please I'm begging you, you know I'll do everything for you and for Anya you can't even imagine how I'll take care of you and love you both. And you know even if you don't want that just don't send me packing then I'll just be alongside you and take care of you both and never ever say anything like this again if you don't like it.*

Masha's silence while he was talking was not yet a negative answer, nor was the fact that she didn't utter a word even several minutes after he'd gone silent: that entire time passed in absolute quiet, during which all that became audible were the commentator's excited voice, the sports fans' shouts, the candle sputtering, and snow swishing outside the window. Masha, however, remained silent even longer; she'd fallen into a daze and, after shoving her hands into her jeans pockets and rocking ever so slightly on the chair, her gaze explored an inane drawing on the varnished surface of the wooden tabletop. Peter spoke several more times, which assumed a continuation of communication—*Masha? You feel okay? Shall I ask for the check?*—but there was no communication and one might have thought Masha had been teleported somewhere. When Peter stood, she stood with him, climbed into the car, silently stared ahead as he slowly drove her home, and, in parting, lifted her hand as if her body didn't immediately obey commands, then she carefully shut the door behind her. Anya was sleeping, focused, her knees splayed. Only after letting the nanny go did Masha allow herself to burst into tears, moreover she approached that procedure meditatively, as if it were a matter of taking an evening shower.

Masha didn't cry any longer than she would have taken a shower, though: a few minutes later, she was already rinsing her face under the kitchen faucet and proceeding to make coffee. Then—to somehow release the rage seething within her—she took out scissors and began cutting thick sheets of drawing paper into little triangles, whispering something every now and then as she cut, as if some sort of speech was bursting through her lips. The third person was laughing softly and indifferently the whole time—not at Masha but just because this was objectively funny—he, after all, knew that doubling the world is a crappy method of cognizing it because with that method you're inevitably counting yourself in the world, so it works out that the world slips away from you once more and you end up one-on-one with yourself again, and "with yourself" here means "with what was introduced into you." The paper didn't yield easily but when a small mountain of triangles the height of the steaming cup had formed on the table, the rage was buried underneath it and all that hurt were the reddened fingers on Masha's right hand. Finally, Masha burst into laughter, constraining it so she wouldn't wake Anya: she suddenly caught herself thinking that though she was already a thirty-something biddy, she'd been told "I love you" (and even *"ich liebe dich"*) in various situations and asked "marry me?" a couple times, too, but nobody had ever said that to her *the right way*, as it should be, as it's supposed to be said. *Komisch*.

# THE SEEDS OF THINGS

*Plague* was released two and a half years after *Amber* (and four after *Save*) and it returned Masha to newspaper front pages and magazine covers in one stroke. There's no reason not to acknowledge right from the start that this return was, in many ways, caused by a scandalous press conference at Cannes that was cut short—even a photograph with the Golden Palm won't make it to the covers of the most-read (which are also the most pointless) publications without a shabby scandal—but there was, nonetheless, a particular justice in the fact that the film receiving the Golden Palm was, in addition, also the most successful picture of the year in the Old World and it goes without saying that it left *CypherMan Part 17*, *The Nighlight Saga*, and other excuses to stuff yourself with loads of popcorn out of the rankings. Certainly many among the public went to the movies for nudity and belly laughs, but Masha understood like nobody else that there's no art without laughter and lust if only because they're what places a person right in front of the reality of death. Masha attempted to explain something of the sort at a press conference introducing a screening in the Palace: *the problem with comedies is that they're not at all funny; people only laugh at them because you're supposed to laugh at a comedy, but if that weren't required...* but the journalists were exchanging glances and only half-listening: who would ask, and how, about what actually interested everyone?

That same evening, Masha sat on the embankment, lividly Googling "maria regina." As Peter finished off his third glass of whiskey, he urged her to stop that pointless exercise, if only for the beautiful view: *just have a look: yachts, city lights, what a sky. What does it matter what they write about you there?...* But there was a difference to Masha: in the photos accompanying a publication in some little Russian paper ("If You Only Knew What Trash Gives Rise: Maria Regina Stuck Her Own Mother in the Loony Bin"), there are crooked gray little houses and a miry road, and smashed windows of a provincial state home gape sinisterly, but Masha couldn't imagine where these "illustrations" had been shot because all they illustrated was that *they'd been too lazy to even find out where I was actually born and go there, don't you see? –Königin, let it go.* When she slammed the laptop shut and ordered a bottle of champagne, Masha already regretted what had happened a few hours earlier, though it's possible the thought was nothing more than an illusion: that she would have had time to prepare if she'd known in advance about the translation of brazen lies that had appeared a few days earlier and managed to fly through hundreds of blogs; in reality, Oedipus has nary a chance to prove he's not a camel, since that thought had occurred to someone.

Essentially, nobody's interested in Oedipus's fate, but everyone's interested in what he will *say*: Masha grasped that instantly, as soon as the young man representing a popular French publication rose, displaying the impeccable cut of his shirt for everyone, and said that Masha's film is prefaced by a certain dedication, thus everyone would be interested to know why she'd used that particular dedication and what, exactly, Madame Regina had in mind. *I doubt the specifics of my personal life will be of interest to anyone among those present, suffice it to say that my father has already died and my mother is alive—if you keep that in mind and watch the film to the end, you'll certainly understand.* The Furies, however, had already sensed the scent of blood and one of them, a hefty woman with a violet buzz-cut, *wanted to take the liberty of clarifying that, most likely, my colleague had in mind a publication that recently appeared, in which it's alleged that Madame Regina's mother is being kept in… a highly regrettable position and it's as if Madame Regina isn't doing everything her daughterly duty for her mother would demand: there's no doubt that there's not a word of truth in that publication, although since Madame Regina has not yet commented on this information, then…* so, check and mate.

*Königin, come on, who was preventing you from responding that, you know, I haven't read any articles like that yet so I can't make any comment, and now there you go, you're silent again.* Yes, Masha was silent, silent, and silent. At first she was thinking about how to respond and later she shut herself off, after she'd grasped that it didn't matter how she responded: she liked the quiet and her body was absolutely relaxed, the only thing was that her stomach ached terribly and all she needed now was a glass of mineral water. And then Masha stood and left, not even noticing it herself, when Peter took the microphone to say *we gathered here to discuss a picture, therefore…* The press conference ended in uproar and noise, then there was a screening, Masha appeared on the stage for a minute, and then she asked Peter to take her somewhere there was no chance whatsoever of running into anybody from their crowd. The sky's black jaw opened wide, Masha puked bitter foam into the sand, the noise of the surf concealed her moans, and an approaching wave from the south hid the consequences of three bottles of champagne. Peter reeled as he held Masha by the shoulders and urged her to let it go, *you haven't even eaten anything today, let's go have something to eat.*

The theme of hunger requires a prefatory remark: since we've already referred to Masha's travels in search of locations for a new film, it wouldn't be out of place to say that the birth of the last (in order of filming, at any rate) film that Masha would manage to make was tied (in reality, that *trash* from which everything grows has nothing in common with poetry) to the fact that when Masha was editing *Plague* in Berlin she met up with Kolya, that woeful Tristan. Even before something broke down in Masha and she'd stopped giving interviews that hoaxed the public, she spoke out once about the issue of firearms that so occupied Russian dramaturges and screenwriters: *there's something redemptive there, that the imperative quality of that maxim is inseparable from the hazy indeterminateness in the question of who the maxim belongs to.* Masha didn't refer, though, to the fact that, in saying this, she was repeating something she'd once heard from A.A.; that was the right thing to do: the ideas we've thought up are always only ours.

So this is what things were like. Masha was riding along Leipziger Straße and she suddenly stopped at the intersection with Wilhelmstraße, leaning down on her right foot: a poster pasted to a wall notified her about a Russian band's gig and the frontman's face was familiar. Masha didn't notice immediately that the poster was still relevant—the gig was the day after next—but when she noticed, she instantly decided to go. There was nothing sentimental in that decision—except, perhaps, a flash in the very depths of her memory, like the tailed shadow of some, essentially, moving youthful sex, but Masha knew that fish had come off the hook and swum away long ago anyway—and so what forced her to buy a ticket for the dingy club with the self-explanatory name was an almost utilitarian consideration: she was counting on that attribute of memory with which our own feelings come to life when ghosts of the past revive (despite the ghosts not looking anything like themselves) our own feelings with absolute, albeit objectified, precision, and those feelings were exactly what she needed before working on *Plague*. Praise be to the eternal Königsberg male virgin, thanks to whom we know that the sole clever bit of verse that follows attempts to echo Nabokov, inasmuch as it can.

Masha didn't like the band (it always seemed like people play heavy music out of a hopeless inability to compose even the simplest melody), beyond that, she just wasn't used to the club atmosphere anymore and, even taking refuge in a corner by the bar, she felt like she was visiting a museum that was noisy for no apparent reason; what's more, she distinctly saw the long-haired frontman, in a sweaty lather, was perceptibly drunk: she sat to the end anyway so she could hand a message into the besieged dressing room with the haughty text (from annoyance, nothing more) "I thank you again for the camera; do you have a quick sec? let me know, M.R." Masha paid up, ready for the message to stay in a bottle for all time, but a man emerged in front of her two minutes later, extending a business card: *Maria Pavlovna? I'm Andrei, the band's producer,* and, well, of course he was, who else would be wearing a blazer here?

It may seem strange that the idea for *Hunger*, a film about a person who refuses food because of a disgust for digestive processes, arose from her impression of seeing an alcoholic who was all the more ordinary because he was a musician. On one hand, though, the quanta of the creative imagination need not give account to the logic of Newton's forces, on the other hand, there was some sort of logic here after all. Kolya kicked everybody out of the dressing room and drank nearly another half of a half-liter bottle while they talked, though he didn't became noticeably more drunk, other than, toward the end, persistently proceeding to invite Masha to continue, with an itinerary of bar and hotel. It goes without saying that Masha refused and *my child's at home* was true but it was also an excuse (and *I'm still nursing* was a total lie): she could have called the sitter, promising her fabulous compensation, and maybe Masha would have done that (if only because Kolya, even Kolya-the-alcoholic, was still a looker) but the problem was that by pressing Masha to "come to my room," Kolya was only executing an autopilot program when in reality he didn't need this at all. Looking into his eyes as he asked her *and how are you?* and talked about himself again and again (bands, albums, tours, *I have to figure out how to get out of here, too*), Masha saw a completely other essence where Kolya should have been. That essence was alcohol and it, like any living essence, wanted only to reunite with itself.

The main character in *Hunger*—a film that's allegorical to a greater degree than all Masha's previous films—explains his refusal of food in a similar way: *I suddenly realized that I've been feeding some sort of creature inside me all my life* (his daughter is sitting beside him at the time and intensely mourning with facial expressions; Masha knew how to make actors play lies: *I need real mourning here, do you understand?*). This, however, is only one of his explanations: another time he describes, in detail, what happens to food when it gets inside a person's system, and that detailed, fairly dry explanation alone made sensitive viewers stop chewing, if only for a short time (*for it is impossible,* as one critic noted, *to go to a film with a title like that lacking a sandwich*).

The screenplay for *Hunger* (Masha decided she didn't care about Hamsun—his heirs didn't own copyright to the word anyway) was written, miraculously, in two weeks, as if it already existed somewhere and Masha just hastily wrote it down. She was working nights again: after coming home from the studio, she let the sitter go, went for a walk with Anya in the Tiergarten, played with her at home, put her to bed, and annihilated several cups of coffee along with a few hundred kilobytes of disc space as she sat, as was her habit, in the kitchen until the middle of the night. That regimen was far more difficult for her to take now than ten years ago and in the mornings she had to swill down several more cups of coffee to bring herself into working condition, so her stomach put her on notice very quickly, as if it were mocking her: a few months later, when the pain (which felt like an unnatural hunger) will already be intolerable, Masha will, whether she wants to or not, go to the doctor and find out that there's nothing mystical going on, she just has an ulcer.

For a story with firearms, it's generally typical for one weapon to be hung up but for another weapon entirely to be shot: the day of the agonizing gig is memorable for Masha not because of seeing Kolya and not even because that was the day the idea for the new film came about (actually, even as Masha was rushing home in a taxi, she forgot to think about Kolya, who'd been left to finish his whiskey and choose himself a schoolgirl for the night, and that idea would awaken only a few days later: the genesis of this little demon-in-the-box *ex machina* will not even be completely clear to Masha) but that it was on this particular day that Masha let the beautiful Moroccan woman go and put Anya to bed, and then Anya suddenly stood up in her little bed, took Masha by the hand, and, looking into her eyes, seriously and painstakingly uttered *gimme dwaw*. Masha went crazy because up until now all she'd heard from her daughter was "a" or "o" and so, at a loss, she asked *what?* and Anya, deciding her mother hadn't heard her distinctly, repeated it louder: *gimme dwaw! –Good Lord, of course, sweetheart, here, here let's draw right now.* Masha pulled Anya out of the bed, sat her down at the table, got out brushes, paper, and watercolors, poured water into a glass, and for an entire half-hour, sitting behind Anya's back, helped her rub squirrel hair on torchon paper. They were both happy but Anya didn't see her mother licking away the tears that ran down to the corners of her lips as she leaned over the paper with Anya: Masha was like a fully inflated balloon, bursting with love for this little person who was holding her breath with diligence.

There are six months and six packages of torchon paper for Masha and Anya to use up before the final cut of *Plague*. Once the draft of the *Hunger* screenplay is finished, Masha will sleep like a human being for two nights and then she'll sit down to work again, swigging coffee, now alternating it, in equal proportions, with mineral water, and she'll draw. On the first night, just as she's putting pencil to paper, she'll be panicked, afraid nothing will work out for her, but just a half-hour later, during which time nearly half her pencils will be devoured, Masha will be struck by a powerful hot wave and slowly—as if it's all from the rectangular paper abyss in front of her—there will begin to appear the wind-blown slope of a mountain overgrown with sparse, scorched grass strewn with sand and, behind it, below, a chunk of heavy, transparent sea that is imperceptibly transforming into the burning-hot enamel of sky in the haze. In a hundred or more drawings (significantly, more than for any of her other films), Masha will create, in effect, an autonomous world where a hot wind will dry palm leaves and the brown horizon, thick-necked lizards will move cautiously about the rocks, and branches with warm oranges will sway heavily in oases on a mountain ledge—it will turn out that this world is waiting for her to find it.

That proves not to be easy. Right after work finishes on *Plague*, Masha and Peter will fly to *ins Land wo die Zitronen blühen* and spend a week and a half going from Venice to Naples but won't find appropriate locations. *Königin, where else could they live, just look around, this is just* Gott verdammt noch mal! Peter loved that expression, which Masha translated for herself, rather freely, with something she'd heard at one time in Petersburg: "fuck my bald skull." Peter will fly off with her not only in his capacity as her friend (at hotels they'll have one room with two beds), not only as her driver (only he will drive the dark blue Alfa Romeo he insists on—Masha will be left just reading the map and looking all around), but also as the actor for whom Masha has finally written a leading role. Pulling over to the side of the road, they'll climb out of the car and take a look around; motioning with his hands in horizontal arcs at slopes overgrown with stone pine trees, Peter (who hasn't seen the drawings) will try to persuade Masha that her character would most certainly have bought himself a villa right here, Masha will bite her lips and shake her head, and then they'll drive further along the narrow, twisting roads. That it had to be Italy was not a topic for discussion: it was obvious that a film about the North ("Mankind can't help but experience a yearning for the time when the North wasn't the north of a city but the north of a continent" is one of the first sentences Masha will write for the screenplay, though it won't make it into the final draft) actually has to be filmed with scenery that's truly from the South, and of course that south can't be anywhere but Italy. Only when they've returned to Berlin, though, will Masha clearly formulate why they've come home with nothing: *you know, Peter, I don't need Bertolucci's Italy I need Pasolini's, though I don't like that fop, either.*

It goes without saying that the week-and-a-half trip wasn't just work but also, to a large extent, a vacation from the crazy Berlin life, a time-out between the draining editing of *Plague* and the whirl of negotiations and contract-signing for *Hunger*: the producers will hold their heads when they hear it's another film about Russians and Russia (obviously a palm branch would have soothed their throats but that's still a month away). The slow (so it's a little better to discern everything) and taciturn (Masha took the silence like medicine and even forbade Peter from turning on the music) drive with a left-hand view of the sea, which would now creep off to the side, and now spring out from behind a bend, was for Masha rather like reading the Catalogue of Ships, something a poet is compelled to undertake every now and then in order to feel at home in the world. Peter would propose stopping here and there for a day or two but it seemed that Masha feared stops and, beyond that, she always hurried him at lunch: *hey, not too much, you still have to play someone hungry.*

It's possible that even Masha wouldn't have admitted to herself that this trip was partly a rest from taking care of her child, but even so. That, despite the fact that the thought of Anya—from the plane there to the plane back—droned continuously on the periphery of her ear: Anya was staying in Berlin with her father.

Until now, Roma had been taking Anya for outings every other day, from early December until spring: Masha had agreed to that routine not simply for the reason that any arguments on the topic would have been abhorrent but because the big thing was that she

wanted Anya to have contact with her father; essentially the idea of
a broken home was no less an oddity than considering the possibility
of having only the left or right half of an orchestra. Roma told Masha
he'd rented an apartment close by and was living alone; it wasn't
that Masha specially took the decision to reconcile herself with that
lie, but things just worked out that way on their own, as if there
was some sort of unspoken social contract where the befuddled
public doesn't understand either what kind of hangover she must
have had to contrive to come to that agreement or how to appease
a monster that had been summoned into the world through the
social contract's alchemic formulas: between you and me, Hobbes
was a person with the imagination of a physical-education teacher.
Anya still couldn't really explain where she'd been or who she'd
done what with, and though Roma would have accused anybody
who pointed that out to him of being paranoid, he took advantage
of Anya's silence: *what did you do? –We went to the zoo then went to
my place, played, I bought this little mat*, however it was inevitable that
Roma gave things away (innocently, it must be said, as innocently as
could be), if only because it would have never occurred to him to
buy the child some kind of *this little mat* and that, thus, a strategic
female mind stood behind his entire course of action. It was clear
that up until the moment when Anya would be capable of saying
she'd been *at Papa's with Auntie Dasha*, Masha would have to resign
herself to Anya being shared between a two-parent family and her;
anything else would have even been unseemly.

And so in the end—like a society that one day discovers itself
with the fait accompli of a concluded agreement and is forced to
reconcile itself with each of Minos's new claims—it turned out to be
obvious that Anya would stay with Roma while Masha was in Italy:
she couldn't leave the child with a nanny for a week and a half. One
inevitability flowed into another and, beyond that one, there was
no other reason Anya should spend, all told, every other weekend
with Roma except perhaps that, *Regina, you have to work, go ahead*

*and work in peace, what more could you want.* The very construction of that phrase wasn't so much Roma's as Dasha's, however it was becoming ever more difficult for Masha to separate the Dasha installed in Roma from Roma himself, and from there it was worth considering that one might have reached the conclusion that it was about time to take care of one's sails which is, since we're already headed in that direction, Ariadne's message, too: there's no alternate route out of the labyrinth, even if you're thrice a hero, and Masha truly did desperately need to work.

Dasha had popped out from around a corner not long before the second trip to Italy: Masha had steered out on to Unter den Linden—she hadn't exactly arrived early, most likely she just wasn't late—and after she'd squinted at Foster's sparkling Egg, she saw Roma kissing Dasha and Anya waving to Dasha. Essentially this was a very touching picture: a little girl with her papa alongside her, crouching and waving to a woman who's first backing away, then decisively leaving, and so when Roma straightened up, turned around (continuing to hold Anya's hand, the happiest of smiles on his lips), and saw Masha, who was unintentionally keeping Dasha in focus, it was obvious that Roma hadn't even wiped the smile off his face, so what was left for Masha to do? Only to ask *has she been here long?* and hear as an answer a lie that was so inoffensive that, in the first place, it didn't even seriously aspire to look like the truth, and, in the second, only someone unequipped with either taste or a sense of proportion could have gone off on them. Masha sat Anya in the bike seat and as Masha pedaled the whole way along Friedrichstraße, Anya swung her little hands around, babbling something that Masha couldn't hear through the roaring in her ears. Anya tried to turn around to be sure Mama heard her and understood, the wind was tossing around her hair, the same indistinct color as her father's; her little nose hatching out of her cheeks; and Masha wanted more than anything to press Anya to herself, to press and press. *What is it sweetie, what? –I has to go pee!*

When Masha heads for Italy again at the end of April, she'll leave Anya with Roma and Dasha, not just Roma. This time, she won't just bring her lead actor, there will be a cameraman, too; they'll land in Rome, progressing further and further south, and Masha won't stop Peter until, finally, they're close to Tropea; she'll get out of the car and sit on the ground after walking away from the road a little: rocks, sand, dwarf pine, broom, and arbutus cling to rocks, it's the very same landscape Masha drew in detail during those nights a year ago, only now it turns out she'd been seeing a mirror image since in reality the hill's slope will be rightward, not leftward, and its ledge faces in the opposite direction, too, and this, it goes without saying, will be truer. Peter will sit down next to her a few minutes later, turning his face away from the prickly sand. *Here*, Masha will say, *here it is. Do you understand now?* Peter will nod: *bingo, Königin, only here do I understand what kind of person this is.* Masha will stand, to show the cameraman which angles need to be shot. They'll spend four nights in Tropea, going out to the spot each day and walking around on the slope until they're exhausted. The cameraman (Erik, a taciturn Swede—it was important to Masha that a northerner do the filming), who's used up around a hundred rolls of film, will grasp that what he's been told about Regina—*even if she knows for certain that you only have three hours to live, she'll still force you to film and even keep you an extra half-hour, she's not human*—seems to be true, but it's already too late: Masha will manage to genuinely infect him with her future film, and so the future *Hunger*'s expanse, which is both dead and idyllic, will come through in the photos he'll hang on the studio walls in Berlin.

Masha won't see those photos until her return from Cannes. She'll walk quickly through the hallways so she can nod to the congratulators as little as possible, close the door to the room, pull a rolling chair into the middle, and, based on Masha's facial expression, Erik, who will be sorting through the photographs that haven't been pasted up, will think she's walked here all the way from France itself. As they look through the shots, Masha's face will relax, her fingers will come to life and tighten, and a stubborn, rapacious fire will ignite in her eyes: it's at this moment that it becomes clear to her that the film will happen, because she and Erik saw the same thing. And this is exactly why, when he asks her almost a half-hour later—*so how was it in Cannes? Everything okay?*—Masha won't tell him to kiss her ass right then and there, she'll just say: *they found out I devoured my own mother, screwed my father, and destroyed a sphinx, and I'd really been hoping to hide all that, but, like I say, whatta bummer, Traurigkeiten.*

Anya stayed with Dasha while Masha and Roma were in Cannes, and Roma had told Masha that as if it were something resolved and natural: *they're friendly, Dasha knows everything she has to, she actually loves Anya very much. Right, you little bedbug, you're friendly with Auntie Dasha, aren't you? –We're fwiends. –See?* At that moment, Masha grasped that she wouldn't be able to explain—not just to Roma but also to the child herself, which would be far more complicated—why she didn't want Anya to stay with Dasha yet again so, instead of making a scene (this, as she would grasp later, was her last opportunity to make a scene) she simply asked Roma not to call Anya a bedbug. They were sitting in an outdoor café in Mitte and Roma was helping Anya eat ice cream; the café was called Anna and Roma thought it was amusing to sit there.

After rumors popped up and began spreading during the festival that things weren't right with Regina's head—on the one hand, it was obvious that if another picture received the palm branch there would have been significantly less talk about the press conference and it might be forgotten completely, but on the other hand, Masha's antics truly did look strange and even the most benevolent publications wrote things like *if Regina had wanted to somehow acknowledge the rumors creeping through the general public, it would be difficult to find a more effective method than slamming a door in the middle of a press conference*—from that moment on, everything that might have been said about her was already being said in the conversational playing field of "truth or not truth," and it's obvious that if the question had arisen on its own, it was, more than likely, not truth. That's how people explained the refusals with which Masha now responded to all interview requests. That's what serious-minded analysts hinted at when recalling both how Regina had spoken to journalists previously and what she had said. If one wished, that's the conclusion that could have been reached from the interviews given (because of Masha's silence) by everybody who'd ever had the slightest thing to do with her over the last ten years. It turned out that this was a very convenient recurring theme for a critique written in the tone of "now, finally, everything's clear," and who doesn't want to write an article like that, anyway?

From here on out, no matter what Masha did, everything that ended up in the conversational playing field grew to resemble the actions of an insane person. When it emerged that a luxurious villa would be built (a gorgeous palace, according to one version) in Calabria to film the next picture, people began talking about gigantomania, *which is characteristic of unbalanced natures; beyond that, the question arises of whether reality is being distorted here, and is it true that the gigantic estate is being built to shoot the film and not just for the director, whose mother, as is well-known, is in an exceedingly sorrowful position in Russia?* At the Berlin premiere of *Plague*, two weeks after returning from Cannes, Masha dumped a glass of champagne on the shaved head of a creep who was sitting on a small sofa with his back to Masha and excitedly telling his small circle his opinion, *this isn't an accusation, but it's a medical fact, after all, that these illness are always hereditary, beyond that, they're most often in the female line*: the listeners on the other side of the little sofa were signaling to the shaved-headed man but he was so busy admiring his shoes that he decided they were just very subtly summoning a waiter with a tray and initially he didn't even understand what had happened, *Scheisse, couldn't you be more careful?!*, since he thought the waiter had stumbled. Someone managed to film the scene on a phone, and the clip had at least a half-million views within two weeks of going online: it looked on the screen as if people had been sitting and calmly conversing and then suddenly, out of nowhere… and it was obvious that only a crazed person could act that way.

By the middle of August—the crew was already packing suitcases and preparing to leave for Italy—Masha's ulcer was so much worse that she had to go to the doctor. After a humiliating procedure (lying on her side, Masha thought about how, maybe, there's no harm in reminding a person about his ontological kinship to the first worm) they prescribed pills and so right until her departure she went out to the drug store once a week for several multi-colored packages. An article where a pert female journalist retold, in approximate terms, her dialogue with the drug store's pharmacist (*does the young red-headed woman who comes to you buy antidepressants? –Why are you asking? –Do you sell psychotropic medications? –Yes, so what? –Does that woman come here for those? –Excuse me, I have no right…*) came out when Masha was already in Tropea. The assistant to the director who found it on the Internet showed the screen to Peter, and Peter forbade talking with Masha about the article: *let's not, otherwise her stomach will go bad again.* Masha and Erik were standing a little way off at the time, and Erik was quietly muttering something to Masha, pointing at the light meter.

Masha had no contact with any journalists until the actual press conference at Kino Arsenal (she agreed to the press conference itself not least of all as a concession to the producer, whose blood was boiling over her refusals), though this wasn't just because she thought journalists were disgusting: in reality, Masha was generally just having less contact with people. Once a week, on Friday evenings, she got on a plane in Lamezia Terme and after she landed in Berlin, she spent the weekend interacting only with Anya, nobody else. The rest of the time she worked, and when she worked, she was as self-possessed and energetic as always. Even at the times there was no work, when the crew was having lunch, waiting for the sun, or relaxing at the hotel in the evenings (they even dragged Masha to the beach a couple times), anyone who attempted to enter into contact with her came away with the impression that they'd torn Masha away from her work. It would be an understatement to say this was an organized strategy, that Masha surrounded herself with a membrane that nothing should penetrate—other than organizing shots, which filters were needed, what and how to act, and things of that sort—but if you were to dig all the way down, to what's not obvious, it must be said that the actors, artists, costumiers, and other amiable people who guiltily walked away from her (*Maria, come swimming with us! Maria, we have an excellent pizza here, want some? Ms. Regina, the international trade union of alcoholics invites you to a scholarly conference devoted to perceptions of free time within the context of the phenomenon of three bottles of Chianti; papers will be presented…* and however else actors crack jokes) were absolutely correct: Masha truly was working, in any case what was going on inside her could fully be called internal work, and it was as if some gas centrifuge within her was producing the pure material of loneliness, isotope by isotope, and although, by formulating the result of that work, we risk creating the impression that Masha was already somehow conceptualizing her feeling—what wasn't there just wasn't there, that's a little later—still, we must take a risk and state that (spit it out, would you!) what tortured Masha was that anyone who wants to remain one-on-one with the world must renounce not only family and not only one's native country but also love.

The last person Masha could make small talk with was Peter. It's obvious why it was Peter: he was the one who'd placed himself in the objectively funny position of *an ex who'd become a friend*—yes, words from the menu of female wisdom. But that's not all there was to it: Peter, who had also been in Masha's *Minus One*, was the only person remaining after A.A.'s death and after Roma left that knew how to interact with the gloomy Masha, and she was always gloomy now. Peter would stop by her room, take a seat with her in the breaks during shooting, or have dinner with her in the evening at the family restaurant, and he knew better than anyone that this Masha shouldn't be provoked into any conversation other than conversation about fresh seafood, cloud formations, or the local peasants' manner of dress. Peter was genuinely surprised only when Masha began rubbing her face with her hands in answer to these conversations, too, muttering *Lord, what is this crap you're talking, what is this crap?*

Of course Peter—there are certain privileges for exes—couldn't help but see that the current Masha wasn't the same Masha who'd gone so readily up to his room at the Radisson in Munich, and not even the Masha who'd shown him *Amber* at the rented house in Golden Küste when she was nine months pregnant. In the beginning, he explained this to himself as being caused by the break with her husband, then by regular separations from Anya, complex work on the picture, an ailing stomach, or journalists' toxic hounding. Then he finally plucked up his courage and got a hazy conversation going, in a roundabout way, vocalizing for the finale and almost unexpectedly for himself, what had been last to come to mind, that *a psychoanalyst is not at all the same as a psychiatrist, and going to one, I'd like to point out (*so what was there to point out? the *frutti di mare?), is not at all disgraceful.*

And since even Peter—a person who, unlike the reader, it is hard to suspect of inattention (if only because we basically know nothing at all about the latter, unlike the former, though, Lord forgive me, relative ontological status is problematic for both)—spoke about medical intervention, that means this is the perfect time to say a certain something. What, from the outside, might have seemed like an advancing transformation of Masha's psyche was, in reality, a deliberate internal path. In the end, the question must be asked—Did Masha understand what was happening or, put differently, Could Masha herself have written the novel *Masha*

*Regina*?—and the answer is that yes, of course, why not, she could have. This is why, after hearing from Peter about psychoanalysts, Masha merrily, more merrily than the situation demanded (Japanese tourists even turned around), began laughing and just said: *are you aware that Althusser, he was this philosopher, went through analysis with Lacan and later bumped off his own wife?*

It was there, in Tropea, that Masha saw for the first time, with a horrendous penetrating clarity, that the only person who would have fully understood what she had in mind was A.A. And that in another life, one that had come together more properly, she couldn't have wished for anything better than to be with him and love him because he was not, really, completely separate from her and had, most likely, been tragically removed beyond the boundaries of her being by her own "external understander". And when Peter—who was, over all, an ideal man—in answer to what was escaping from her in a drunken state (it was a hot night, it was insufferable in the hotel, they didn't feel like sleeping so were sitting on rocks by the shore)—*you know what just came into my head? That, in the end, a person faces the choice: to be alive or to be smart; and so the smart person, in horror, is forced into the second choice*—and so when Peter started, in roundabout ways, telling her how much everybody needed her, Masha thought about how A.A. would have calmed her just by saying that, *yes, Masha, honey, but the comfort is in knowing you never have to make that choice right now*. Peter kept muttering, reassuring Masha, and pressing her to his shoulder. In the end, she began pitying his clueless confusion: the cast-iron German needed simple, regular, singular *Grund*, on which to, ahem, install a pedestal for his composure (a drunken person, a real one, anyway, is in no shape for scorning pretty words). *Want me to tell you a little something?*—this was when they were already parting in the half-dark hallway of the quiet, nocturnal hotel—*the article, about how I ditched my mother and all that… –What? –I know whose handiwork that was. Hers, Roma's little bitch. –Why do you think that? –There's no "why," I'm absolutely certain.*

(There really was a *why* in the obvious logic with which Dasha was diligently, step by step, claiming territory from Roma's life; essentially, only one single, final thing remained for Dasha to definitively demarcate the border between Masha and what Dasha already called *my family*, though this was something that couldn't occur to Masha yet, even in a scary dream, however things will reach that point but, well, you can't just explain all that when you're drunk in a hotel hallway.)

And so it worked out that by the time the HFF student discovered *Pursuit* in a heap of archived discs in early autumn, Masha hadn't been in contact with the general public for more than three years, not counting the false start in Cannes. And, of course by secretly hoping that this game of keeping one's mouth quiet would finally force everybody to shut up and forget about her, Masha had bet on the wrong card. It was the exact opposite: the quiet murmuring of *Regina-nuthouse-mother-if-everything-they-say-is-true-nuthouse-this-happens-with-talented-people-now-we-have-to-call-it-bipolar* didn't stop, not even for a week, and when a thirty-minute film with some kind of mystical scurrying around and mischievous editing popped up on the Internet, the cineworld exploded like a package of popcorn. Initially, everybody who expressed a competent opinion about whether it was fake or not fake was paid for that opinion; then, in a chain reaction, it was everybody who, on the contrary, paid to have his opinion unveiled; then, finally, basically everybody simply had opinions for free. Of course it was the producer's idea to arrange a loud press conference for the occasion: even so, Masha didn't send him to do that four-letter thing to himself, though she could have limited herself to writing three lines in a message addressed to some movie-buff site or other, and it would have been no big deal. Masha agreed, though, and that's because it got harder each time to refuse the producer on things like this, and also because *they want a press conference, the bitches? They'll get their press conference, they'll all go bald, the clowns.*

Peter, who was, formally, the target of this monologue, sighed. *Sorry, I don't mean you.*

After leaving Erik and the crew to finish up shooting all manner of small things, Masha flew off to Berlin in very early October. She had to head straight to Kino Arsenal from Tegel Airport—not very much time was left before the start, just a little over two hours—but instead of hanging out on Potsdamer Platz for the extra hour, Masha decided to kill the time in a café away from the center, so she settled in, got breakfast, and politely shook her head at the waiter heading toward her with a pile of newspapers and magazines. After he'd already turned away from her, though, waving the pile, Masha caught a certain something, apart from the smell of the printing inks: her own photograph on the front page and a photo of Roma with Anya on his lap. For the entire remaining hour, Masha read and reread the interview, in which there was basically nothing criminal—the truth, only the truth, although not the *whole* truth—and in which a *talented young actress who brings happiness to the well-known cameraman* popped up twice on the periphery, and one of the photographs attested to her trustworthiness: a sweet woman in a pantsuit, legs crossed, palms out at her sides as if she's showing she's as transparent as a window on a sunny Berlin morning—and Roma told, with concealed regret, about how *Masha simply doesn't have time, she works so much, Anya lives most of the year with us and she and Dasha get along so well, we're like a genuine family,* and the interviewer added for her own part that, *here Roma, of course, is excessively modest because if what I saw isn't a genuine family, then I don't know what is.* Any unbiased reader would have to come to the conclusion that Regina (whose mother Roma flat-out refused to discuss) had gotten rid of the child because she was keeping Masha from shooting a new film and thank God the child had found such a healthy family and such a kind woman to replace her mother. Shaking with rage, Masha got in a taxi and dialed Roma. *Regina, don't go insane, it's just an interview, what did you see in that? I didn't really even say anything about you, you're paranoid! What're you saying? I can't hear you, there's some kind of noise on your end,* though it also turned out he and Dasha *wanted to talk about something anyway, when would work for you?* and so Masha should call them right after the press conference, *we'll make a plan then, how and what, the main thing is don't worry.* It goes without saying that there's no better way to make someone go berserk than to say not to worry, even if Roma didn't know that.

In the back of her mind, Masha was glad the day started the way it had started: the rage that was seething in her hands, chest, and belly had left her head cold, and she couldn't have thought up a better state for showing up at Kino Arsenal. The auditorium was full: the producer, who'd flown in five days beforehand to prepare the press conference, knew his trade. He was beaming when he greeted Masha outside, at the entrance: *you flew in, thank God! –What, were there other options? –Oh, you know, I wouldn't put anything past you.* Maybe he wasn't hinting at anything but Masha had already learned to see hints in everything and, after looking somewhere into the distance, she said she needed some warm green tea.

The press conference—links to a full transcript could be found by evening on any lousy little film blog—was, as one film critic expressed things, *a three-hour session mocking the entire journalistic community*; when Masha read that, she was certain her ploy had worked. *After briefly confirming that* Pursuit *truly is a work from her youth, Regina said she would speak frankly with the public for the first time in her life, that she wouldn't joke and wouldn't mess with anyone's head.*

In and of itself, of course, all that was nothing but an all-encompassing scam: Masha didn't answer one question from the audience during those three hours, and toward the end she even explained why: *in setting the goal of speaking seriously, one cannot have in mind a single one of those questions that arise on their own.* As she listened carefully to each person who took the microphone, Masha would nod her head and say things that had nothing to do with the matter at hand. The journalists grew bolder each time: *excuse me but you still haven't answered the question about your relationship with your ex-husband –I've ended up in a position where I have to imitate something akin to* Urbi et Orbi, *but I'm not to blame for that, though of course I'm aware that if you make films about something that's not completely obvious, even to you yourself, it's hard to expect the public to ask the same things you ask yourself, and it's good if you find two or three of those people, and if there aren't any of them right here and now, nobody's to blame, it's not even that the situation isn't amenable, it's just that the very system of* hic et nunc *is such that there's practically no chance that four sixes will fall in a row: things like that always happen to friends of friends, but not to you.*

The journalists were exchanging glances, the producer was hiding his face in his hands, and people were getting up and leaving the auditorium, but those who sat to the end needed to write something, and the most popular passage from Masha's speech for the next day's publications would be the one where she answered a question regarding what her new film would be about: *that's yet another question that can't be answered without saying something stupid. Questions like this are asked so there's something to write later in a press release: relevant problems in contemporary life, the loneliness of a person in the contemporary world, answers to challenges that contemporary life places before us, but these are all things that reek like toilets in Russian train stations. It's not things that interest me but their seeds. In order to talk about the seeds of things, you have to destroy the things themselves and, in doing so, you have to risk destroying yourself,* and so half the next day's newspapers came out with headlines like "Maria Regina Admits to Journalists That She's Contemplating Suicide." *A psychiatrist's commentary: it's complicated to confirm anything for certain but an inclination toward suicide is on the same level as megalomania—it's one of the symptoms of bipolar disorder...*

Let us bow to the authority of science: indeed, there is nothing more complicated than confirming something for certain, but in any case, of everyone who wrote about the press conference, it appears that only one person understood anything, a young film critic from Russia (he'd once surprised Masha with *The Power of an Exploding Wave* but of course she didn't remember his surname) who silently sat through the entire three hours at Kino Arsenal and then addressed Masha rhetorically in his Sunday article on a cultural site: *Frau Regina, what's up with the kindergarten behavior?* An hour after the producer's constrained voice thanked *all those in attendance for giving us your time*, Masha was lying in her bed on Friedrichstraße and quietly, intermittently, groaning from shame. She felt like at least sleeping a little before calling Roma but it was impossible to sleep: consciousness of her own idiocy agonized her as if she'd actually laughed at children for not being able to go potty, *so, Regina, are you satisfied? You're the smartest, right? You proved to everybody that you're a fucking awesome little bitch!* Masha shook her head and convinced herself to calm down, and she was angry that she couldn't and angry that she was angry; after an hour of furious tossing on the bed (the duvet came out of its cover and it was as if it crept away sneakily to save itself; it was obviously doing that on purpose), Masha bellowed, balled up the duvet and chucked it in the corner, and staggered off to the bathroom.

Only near the doors of the restaurant where they'd scheduled *the conversation, it'll just be the two of us, Anya will be with a sitter*, did Masha grasp that it was a Chinese restaurant: either Roma hadn't told her that on the phone or Masha hadn't completely come out of a drowsy confusion where the main theme was pangs of conscience (these things draw each other from memory's deep dark waters—they're like phonetic associations, and that's about the extent of it) and she takes the words *Chinese restaurant* as her own personal monster, torn loose from its chains, otherwise, it goes without saying, Masha would have insisted on meeting somewhere else. But it was too late: a guy dressed in some kind of Chinese garb was already opening the doors of the scary amusement-park ride in front of her.

It was too late and that's an opportune refrain for the ending of a book because what else can you say about a main character when the ending's already flickering through the remaining dozen pages? Other than, perhaps, that the character might think there are still some other options or that the author might think it's possible to say something else. In reality, it appears that we overlooked the point when it became entirely too late for everything: the train's wheels have already gone off the rails and we need to manage to finish speaking about what goes without saying, on its own accord, before the crash resounds.

It was too late for Masha to make herself out to be in charge of the situation and not just because she was horrendously frazzled by the flight, press conference, conscience, and failed sleep, but also because, really, she wasn't in charge of the situation any longer: Roma and Dasha were sitting on the banquette at a table, leaving only the chair across from them for Masha, and they looked as confident as a couple who'd come to the bank to pay off their mortgage. Today's a special day for us, my dear. I would not think of hiding it. Pages of an endless menu flashed, *like I said, we need to have a serious conversation with you*; faces leaned out of the darkness, squinting and smiling, *it's about Anya*, little dishes with a cloying scent, *I think you've already guessed*, chopsticks falling out of a fabric sock that's folded like an accordion, *she's already a big girl and she calls Dasha Mama*. Telephone. The ring of ceramic chopsticks. *Please bring a fork. No, I don't need it. You can see her on the weekends, just like now.* There was no karaoke, just some kind of Chinese pop instead and that, as it happens, infuriated Masha because it was as if the director of all this moronicness had been too lazy to use such an obviously winning plot rhyme. Roma was talking, looking at his hands, and Dasha was shifting her glance from him, to Masha, and back. *It's a far healthier atmosphere for the child, be honest with yourself, you don't have time for her. Excuse me, please, I'm the manager of this restaurant, may I ask for your autograph for our wall of fame?* Masha

was floating in a milky fog—it seemed like she came to the surface
at times—and then she saw the half-empty restaurant and a table
set with this effing food, heard the distant ring of dishes from the
kitchen, and the noise of an automatic coffee machine, and it was
as if she was seeing herself from the outside: a woman on the verge
of mortal exhaustion, holding her temples, capillaries probably
bursting, and, right now, now, I could go to sleep. The degrading
situation of a person to whom an obvious though objectively unjust
truth is being explained. *Good, where do I sign?* What could she say
to them? What do people generally say in these situations? Masha
said something anyway but then her tongue went still, it was hard
to move, and on top of that, Masha was afraid she'd be sick. Roma
went silent and Dasha impatiently crossed her legs. *Mashenka, it
will only be worse for you. You understand that first off, they'll send you
for a psychiatric evaluation and it's not important what the doctor there
says: for the court, the very fact that the evaluation was needed…* Fingers
wave, like soaring ash. *They could even remove custody, but this way
you'll still see Anechka all the time.* She called her Anechka, fuck this.

Like a person whose fingers lost their grip despite everything
and whose cry for help most likely gives way to a cry of horror, so
Masha realized—after sitting motionless on a rickety wooden chair,
swimming in a reddish-yellow haze, spinning in a whirlpool of the
smells of sweet meat—in one sinking instant that it was already
too late to fight for Anya, that she'd lost, and that had happened
*already*: Anya's estrangement had become unavoidable, and in order
for Masha to save herself, she'd have to fight, stand up for herself,
sue, and get into life, give it all she's got, but Masha was already
estranged from life. As she stood, Masha overturned the table
toward the banquette: sauces, pieces of orange meat, loose rice,
chopsticks, ethereal little cups, chopstick rests, napkins, salt, pepper,
vinegar, and dark-red splashes went flying—Dasha's hateful look and
Roma's unhappy gaze, waiters frozen in a stupor, diners gawking
in the corner—and all that was in soundlessness because all Masha

heard was her own spiteful moan—because she was moaning to make it look like she wasn't sobbing at full volume and she hadn't sobbed like this when her father died, when A.A. died, or when her father beat her mother one time, who-the-hell-knows-when, back in Masha's childhood.

In the apartment on Friedrichstraße (which is so repulsive she should—how had this not occurred to her before?—flood it with water, not on purpose but by accident), just after sitting down on a chair in the kitchen (because she has to think, has to think, to think through what to do), Masha limply, weak-willed, just rolls off into an incongruously delightful sleep at the count of three.

Masha's back on location in Calabria, broom stretches along the slope, juniper bushes glow in the sun, crowns of stone pines drown in the amber haze where the horizon breaks up, a salamander with red feet strides by feather grass roots, pale thick-fleshed flowers make their way out of crevices in the cliffs: it seems like they'll scamper back if you frighten them. A supple wind strokes the cheeks, a brief bleating is heard, and, up high, a falcon rises with a stream of hot air. They call to Masha, she turns, waves, and goes to film. Rails have been installed, reflectors have been placed, and the actors' makeup has been applied: everything's ready, it's time to begin.

# DISCOVERING AMERICA

Masha's life, like life in general, didn't change much.

Nobody will know anything at all, right up until the point when Masha will put a hole in the supreme public servant's portrait that hangs at the Russian embassy in Berlin (quite an amusing story, here's hoping there's enough time to tell it). Peter guessed that something was amiss, something imperceptible: Masha's work style had changed, with scrupulousness having been added to tirelessness and obstinacy, so now instead of shooting for ten hours straight and managing to do three scenes during that time, Masha shot for those same ten hours but only managed one scene, time and again forcing makeup artists to redraw faces, lighting engineers to reset fixtures, and actors to do five or six takes. It was as if she was always dissatisfied with something or that suddenly it occurred to her in the middle of working on a shot that it could be done better, and then it had to be started from the beginning; all that, though, isn't a problem in and of itself, not, at any rate, for a director with a name, so every time Peter attempted to start a conversation about it, things boiled down to *Königin, are you sure everything's okay? –Yes, why?*

In fact, it looked like Masha had simply lost her sense of time and the filming process had become for her something akin to an expanse whose length and breadth must be walked. This looked even more like the truth because a sense of that expanse had really become a key element for Masha during her work on *Hunger*: in shooting a film about Russia in Italy, she ran into the necessity of constantly retaining both those wide-open spaces in the work-related portion of her consciousness. At times, this looked like hallucinations, as if a gray and green central-Russian plain with a smoky color around the edges was ready to burst out from behind a withering Calabrian hill, spill its fog on a sunny slope with a view of the sea, and shower it with crumbly snow, and that an inaudible, metaphysical note of majestic despondence should burst into song at any minute, for that is exactly what differentiates Russian despondence from any other: it is inseparable from majesty.

The air that Masha was breathing was the very same air that people were breathing simultaneously in Pskov and in Tver, the sun she squinted at along with the Swedish cameraman was the very same sun that was now peering out from behind clouds and tinting the banks of the Volkhov and Volga Rivers with the gentlest raspberry sheen, and the earth along which she was running her crew ragged was the very same tectonic plate on which her great grandmother was lying (this was the first year of the war) when she cast out a little purplish blob that would, twenty years later, need to be delivered of a child, and, in birthing Masha's grandmother, she also birthed Masha's mother here, and Masha, and Masha's daughter: the shout of all expectant mothers merged into one triumphant wail of humanity that found itself on Earth.

This was the very same earth along which Masha's grandfather had driven his locomotives, a cigarette in his teeth, and the very same earth along which the rattling truck had once carried Masha's grandmother—she was young, with a smile that secretly acknowledged her absolute power—home to Masha's grandfather's sullen parents, and the land on which, just before the war, her grandfather had used deft hands sooty up to the elbow to make his tiny home, though it seemed huge to the ankle-biters crawling on its floor.

And it was exactly here, nowhere else but right here, where Masha leapt up from the director's chair to make the actors stop emoting, that her grandmother accepted an agonizing, hungry life *like people have*, buried her son and husband, lived through a metamorphosis that turned her strong, sexual body into a deformed receptacle for a waning consciousness, and she was basically (this is what makes the blood freeze in the veins) happy. It was in this same expanse that Masha's mother mastered the world of her own life using expanding circles: school, field at the collective farm, kitchen garden, dances at the community center, electric sparks on her spine when Masha's father stroked her back with his hand and clumsily kissed her on the lips, and, at some elusive point, the circles began narrowing, finally leaving her alone with her ghosts. All that—her mother feeds the neighbor's dog when she's fourteen; her father goes out on the first truck haul of his life at twenty-one; Masha's grandmother dies, holding Masha's hand in her own; and there's a thousand thousand more events that are concrete and filled with powerful emotions, like a mass of water cascading into an abyss—and all that happened, perhaps not now, but it was here. Where Masha jostled on the train to Petersburg and where she lost her innocence with a man who, essentially, touched her emotions and was her teacher, and where she rented her first apartment, and where she landed for the first time in Munich with completely bitten-up lips, loved the nervous cameraman for her films, and gave birth to his plump daughter: three and a half kilos is nothing to sneeze at.

This universal sensation chilled Masha with horror, not just for the same reason that a person who hasn't seen the sea in a long time straightens his back when he ends up at the shore, but also because at times the sea—just as if the edge of a lenticular lens were suddenly slipping to the side—turned into a metaphor, the meaning of which is that (unlike language, which can't keep up with thought) everything that's happened with people who've lived on the same earth as Masha happened not only right here but also right now.

As if whatever occurred with Masha didn't occur with her but with some metahuman essence containing all these stories: there was one and the same story; it wasn't repeating time after time, there was, literally, just one.

It's clear that the key metaphor of *Hunger* relays a similar sense. The main character refuses food precisely because he's been plunged into horror: his body's internal processes are independent of him, of himself. (Since discussion has turned in this direction: the fact that Peter managed to convey this made the role a genuinely major piece of work and it was certainly foremost among Peter's roles.) This wasn't just about food, though. Once he'd pondered the strange mechanism whose workings had placed his independence in doubt, the character found a similar effect everywhere. Everything he was accustomed to considering his property revealed attributes of an essence whose will exceeded his will. The aversion he experienced toward his relatives and partners was rooted not in disdain for their supposedly low moral qualities: on the contrary, they were all sweet people and he sharply put his daughter in her place when she lamented that, here they were, everybody'd torn over like they were on the way to a fire, though if it weren't for the money, they would have been neither seen nor heard, but no, the problem, as it seemed to him, lay elsewhere: *the money*, he says in another scene, *started rumbling around, like tremors before an earthquake, that's a lot like the feeling of hunger*. On top of that, everything that formed the foundation of human existence in him—a feeling of gratitude toward friends, a kindred feeling, and, finally, love for his daughter—all that unfolded like programs functioning independently of his will, too, otherwise why could he categorically not remain one-on-one with death, which had already crossed the threshold; *you can all just kiss my butt*, the character shouts at the crowd that's packed his bedroom, then he leans back against a pillow with an apologetic grimace on his face. The crowd exchanges understanding glances.

Basically, the comic effect of *Hunger*—the main character just can't manage to be left alone, no matter how much he lets the world know he doesn't need it, and the world responds by displaying its full understanding through the sympathetic smiles of his daughter, doctor, and friend: it's better to just be near a person in this sort of condition rather than disturbing him—is also a variation on the main theme of the impossibility of establishing the boundaries of one's own existence. "Arguments about Russia" work in a similar way in *Hunger*: *if someone starts saying in my presence that the blood-stained tyrant Stalin destroyed millions of people, I immediately understand that person didn't read Tolstoy in school*, says one of the characters; *I don't like Stalin, I basically don't like short people, especially with mustaches*, the daughter interjects in passing, the doctor mechanically runs his fingers along his upper lip, and Peter's character, who hangs on until the bitter end, finally finds himself mixed up in an argument from which there is not and cannot be any way out, an argument that fascinates him nevertheless, all the more because the cautious-kindly glances all around cheer him up, all as they're exchanging gazes as if they're saying "come on, come on" to one other, and in the end the main character becomes so disgusted that he again breaks into amusing hysteria for the others. There's additional irony to all this since the main character, who just can't stand cynicism, immediately blows up every time his cigarette-brandishing partner—a cynic par excellence who loves to flaunt his cynicism—states something in the spirit of *we only have two departments in the business: the department for exploiting staff and the department for staffing exploitation*. After hearing out a brief, breathless homily, his unruffled partner answers, extinguishing his cigarette: *you're the one telling me we have to think about people? Are you thinking about us?*

No, Masha hadn't set herself the task of making a statement about Russia and, strictly speaking, *Hunger* partially substantiates the impossibility of making a statement like that; just so nobody's left with the temptation of reading some sort of historiosophical meaning into the film, at the very end, that same cynic/partner summarizes the results of discussion with the doctor about how the "political power-society" system functions in Russia: *everybody's already getting fucked up the ass in this country, but giving a blow job would be shameful,* and then right after that line there's a shot of a nanny goat looking in the living room window, so a genuine Russian theme is included in the picture, not on the level of a statement but rather through the range of color in the shot, the sound of the wind, and unexpected rainfall. *All the world is Russia* says the daughter and that's her only sincere line in nearly two full hours, and so the film and the narration close the loop by returning to Masha's key sense, which doesn't lend itself to verbalization at all.

What's unsaid in *Hunger* remains more important than what's said: that's true not only in terms of the words the characters utter but also in general, in terms of the sense and mood of the film, and the unheard note the characters seem to hear without realizing it. After watching the edited film—this will be in Berlin, and Masha will kick everybody out of the viewing room except Peter—Peter will say: *well, you are a strategist, Königin.* Masha will make a surprised face and he'll have to explain: he has in mind the atmosphere that took shape in Calabria, where the crew was nervous that everything was going so slowly, that scene after scene was reshot, that *it's like she's shooting some twenty-hour epic in her own head,* and, in the end, that was all reflected on the screen like the vague anxiety that eats away at the characters as if there's a despondent monotonous melody sounding from far away on a sated sunny day. *No,* Masha will say, *I didn't do anything like that specially.*

Maybe Masha didn't but Peter had to—not just in his capacity as a performer in a main role but also as the most established actor in the group, the person who regularly answered questions like *so what was it like being filmed by so-and-so?* And *how was it shooting a picture with thus-and-so?*—by serving as something between lightning rod, entertainer, and staff psychologist. And though his schedule allowed him to be away from shooting, he never once left during the entire five months; he talked, admonished, calmed, listened, and distracted instead. Being the life and soul of the party (*come on, come on, an actor preparing others*, as Masha once joked back, in passing) is difficult work and others are paid money for that, but Peter accepted it completely consciously because it was important to him that the film be *ausgezeichnet* not only in the sense of being released but be *ausgezeichnet* in the sense of coming out winningly, too, plus Peter understood the role he was playing, and not just out of his professional fondness for Masha, but also because he simply wanted to be closer to Masha. There was little rationality in that wish—what's rational about unrequited love?—but even so, when Peter asked himself what was going on, he formulated it for himself this way: *I may end up necessary to her*—and the sense that Masha wasn't herself, that she was dragging something scary behind her, never left. What Peter didn't formulate—meaning he retained the opportunity not to take it into consideration—is that, in reality, the hope *she'll be mine again* was tied, *in spe*, to his being necessary to her.

And it goes without saying that nothing could have been further from the truth.

Setting aside everything that's already been said about Masha's inner state (what kind of state could a person be in after it's been explained that her own daughter doesn't belong to her?) as well as Masha's fate (the orbit of which was rapidly distancing itself from life in general, in the sense that's implied when someone asks "how's life?") this must be stated simply: Masha was in no shape for a relationship with Peter. As before, she left shooting in Calabria every Friday to fly to Berlin, where Roma gave her Anya for two days, they took walks, drew, ate ice cream, and went to the zoo –*Mama, a wolf! –Where, Anyuta? Oh, I see, shall we go over? –No, I'm afraid. –You're afraid? –I'm afraid of wolf! –You should say "I'm afraid of the wolf." –I'm afraid of the wolf*, and Masha gathered her strength: it now seemed more and more like the ill-fated incident at the Chinese restaurant was nothing more than a bad dream, that nothing irreparable had happened, and that when she returns to Berlin, to the studio, they'll simply give Anya back, just as things should be, and Masha will let Anya go see Papa on the weekends.

That, incidentally, is how a vulgar Freudian differs from a genuine one: where one will swallow the narrator's bait in the form of classical analysis, the other will take notice of the language's inertia; set formulations had woven a comfortable nest in Masha's vocabulary, describing a normal course of events and thus whatever actually happened couldn't command the status of reality. When Masha returned to Berlin after five exhausting months in Calabria, Roma's telephone didn't answer, the apartment in Schöneberg was locked when she came by the next morning, and the landlady Masha found after turning half the house upside down sleepily announced that the residents had moved out two days ago: *they paid up and moved out, I have no complaints.*

Masha went to the studio, to work. That wasn't a display of special courage or extreme indifference, though, but simply a case of "what else could she do?" Anyone at all—the landlady, the policeman the landlady had offered to summon, the attorney Masha had already fleetingly wondered how to find, if need be, after a shiver of aversion—would have said exactly the same thing; on top of that, Peter had told her the same thing after a tense meeting where they'd scheduled the upcoming studio work with deadlines, and the crew, feeling for some reason that it was best not to trouble Masha, agreed to all her inordinate demands, just in case. Peter then came over to her alone and demandingly asked, *Königin, you don't look like yourself, what,* lieber Gott, *happened?* and when she whispered to him that *they moved the fuck out, they stole Anya,* he went ashen and said, *well, hold on, don't worry yet, wait a day, they'll call you yet, they couldn't just up and go like that.* What could she do? Except maybe call the embassy during a break and make an appointment to see the ambassador, *tomorrow; the day after tomorrow then.* Because it was clear as day that they not only could but had flown off to Russia; otherwise there wouldn't have been any point in an escape.

When Masha finally got through to him the next morning, Roma came up with a thousand reasons: *Dasha's got these problems, we had to, plus they offered me a small job there, it's not for long, you can come visit, I tried to call you but...* Masha didn't want to explode, that would have been strategically unwise, but when he said that about calling, she doubled over and hurled the phone at the wall. *What does "call" mean? You couldn't just take Anya away, you don't have to call to find that out!* Did she yell like that in reality? In any case, the phone was smashed, and Roma didn't hear her. Back at the studio, after putting her SIM card in a new phone, Masha got several texts, cynical ones, to be sure, because in suggesting Masha fly to Petersburg (*we won't hide Anya from you* along with an exclamation mark that seemed to wink deceitfully), Roma knew perfectly well that she had to work.

And so Masha began editing, her mouth filled with blood—she'd been biting at her cheek the whole way to the studio—and surmounting horrendous pain in her head. When the cheery Cutter (a very tall, lanky guy whose Cheshire-cat smile switches to tenacious focus and back at the snap of a finger) is told two weeks later, in a whisper, about what everybody else already knows, but *Regina will kill you if it gets out,* meaning about what's going on, Cutter will whistle: he'd never seen a pace like this, such precision, attentiveness, and instant reaction; *oh, so that's what's going on,* yes, it is, and what did you want?

An inhuman capacity for work was the only indicator that someone—had there been a someone—might have used to assess the despair on whose brink Masha was attempting to restrain herself. After she'd let the crew go on a break, Masha would stay to edit, replaying mountains of material until she was dazed, and her assistant—a girl who seemed a little in love with Masha and whom Peter had warned that *if Masha's ulcer acts up again, you'll be to blame, you'll be taken to court for vandalism*—tried with all her might to convince Masha to eat: *they brought pizza, I ordered it with bacon. –Leave it on the table, please, and, hold on, make some more coffee. –What about the pizza?...* Other than that, nobody would have said there was anything amiss with Masha. The ambassador on Unter den Linden greeted her downstairs, escorted her upstairs, and spent a half-hour telling her that, yes, there needs to be *Einverständniserklärung* to take a child out of the country and so if the child left, that means they had the paper, and was Masha certain she'd never signed a paper like that, and that *to put together a court case, well, yes, that's possible, but it would take years* and *wouldn't it be simpler to fly to Russia and straighten everything out there, well, particularly because, really, you don't necessarily have to enter the legal arena to do that, what could be simpler than, as they say, resolving it within the family, you're not divorced, right?* Masha was silent more than she spoke and it couldn't have occurred to the ambassador that she wanted more than anything to grab him by the throat: Masha didn't doubt for a minute that this *striped dick* had personally forged a signature or, in any case, would have done so without even thinking.

It goes without saying that Masha wasn't suffering from paranoia, that she understood that the unfortunate *Herr Botschafter* most likely couldn't have taken part in her daughter's abduction, even if you assume he might have wanted to; that he hadn't witnessed the signature on the *Einverständniserklärung*; that he hadn't convinced Anya that *Mama will come see us later*; and he hadn't soothed Roma's conscience (*work's more important to her than the child anyway*), but even so, the *striped dick* had ended up (wrong place, wrong time, thank you, Uncle Sam) as a signifier in the top of Saussure's hamburger, which signified to Masha the whole toxic and tenacious (like burdock) *life* that had stolen her daughter. That's exactly why what happened two weeks later was nothing more than a fact in Masha's biography, and it's exactly in that capacity—as an idiotic anecdote—that what happened must be regarded.

And this is what took place. Once again, Masha made an appointment, the ambassador met her downstairs like the previous time and escorted her upstairs, where he began trying to persuade her in a confiding voice *not to blow an unnecessary scandal out of proportion, Maria Pavlovna, you must understand*, and after he'd uttered her name and patronymic a fifth time (Masha was counting), Masha took a Glock from her purse—prop managers are magical people, especially if they don't ask questions—and aimed it at his striped jacket. Essentially, she wasn't planning to shoot at all, it was just important for her to see something human in the eyes of the system, something that was like her, an autonomous person with her own sufferings, her own hopes, and her own sense of justice—fear, pain, or horror, since neither empathy, nor hope as she understood it, nor a kindred feeling of justice had been revealed on the exterior—and when she saw them (this all went on no longer than a half a minute: dilated pupils, facial skin turned chalky, tension in the whole body), she deflected the barrel to the side and all the same, so as not to arouse suspicion that this was all some clumsy bluff (although what else, Lord forgive us, could all this be?), shot, moreover she hit without aiming. If this had been her own screenplay, she would have deleted that spot, sending the bullet into the wall or, at the very least, a window, because this was just too head-on: into the portrait of supreme power that was hanging on the wall, symbolizing, for Russia at any rate, the blunt, impersonal strength that had destroyed Masha's life: the strength of necessity. The journalist from *Allgemeine* who will unearth this story will buy off the embassy cleaning woman and she'll tell him about the hole in the portrait but he'll decide not to include that in the article: nobody would believe it anyway, besides it was tasteless, not to mention that the impressionable cleaning woman had made up the hole, as sure as certain.

There was security, there was a search, there was appropriating the prop, and the ambassador, applying himself to a glass of whiskey, muttered *fucking hell, director, needs treatment*, and Masha spent several hours in a small room with a metal door: it might not have been a holding cell but the door was locked and they only let her go to the bathroom after long arrangements and under guard, then *Botschafter* finally came to her: *I want you to know that the issue was resolved in Moscow and, taking your status into account*, the matter was hushed up, *they'll return your things to you downstairs and, needless to say, you are prohibited from entering the embassy from this day forward*. Needless to say, the matter was hushed up not so much *taking her status into account* as because a story of this sort—*the hell do we need this, don't raise a fuss, you know that*—could have disrupted negotiations about some kind of agreements regarding parental kidnappings. Masha's shot plopped into cold standing water, not one effing frog in that swamp so much as croaked. Masha went outside to an Unter den Linden that was flooded with evening sun and smiling people were pointing: *look, it's our embassy, cool!* It seemed to Masha that they were jabbing their fingers at her.

Everything hidden will be disclosed—hello to children from the Land of Soviets who learned this in a tale!—and the story (*have you heard about Regina?*) spread unhurriedly but, ever gaining in reliability, got all the more reliable (*good Lord, yes, everybody knows!*) and two weeks later it was already the property of the filmmaking community of the entire Old World. Several yellow newspapers with available space wrote about *information from reliable sources*. But a crime is nothing without a motive: only after a Petersburg actress (who truly was a scandalmonger and party girl but you don't write that sort of ultra-short line on your CV: people write "actress" in situations like this) wrote on her blog *have you no shame, dear people, going through someone else's dirty laundry, huh? Saying she's nuts, sick in the head... I'd like to have a look at any other mom in her position...* only after that did the story come out of the yellow ghetto and become public property, not least thanks to social services workers who'd caught upon it. An embassy official denied *conjecture spread by the mass media*, Masha told all journalists to go far, far away, but even so, dozens of journalists wrote in five languages about *the shot that allegedly was fired* as an excuse to talk in some publications about *an important, as-yet-unresolved problem* while others wrote about *Regina's all-too-long silence*. Opinions multiply by dividing, like protozoa, and if one critic wrote about how *Regina, despite all the respect for her talent, could stand to finally undergo proper evaluation with specialists*, then another expert cautiously asked himself *is this part of the advertising campaign for* Hunger, *which, according to rumor, would only confirm the fact that Regina has run out of steam as a director? These days it seems like it's common to camouflage creative failures using aggressive viral advertising.*

Whenever someone emboldened at the studio would shyly hint to her: *Maria, didn't you read? They're writing things that would make your hair stand on end*, Masha would answer, invariably good-naturedly, *let's talk about that after work, okay?* However even if the emboldened person was still at the studio after work, he wouldn't be up for conversations, and would merely crawl off home. The producer fended off the journalists: press releases, calls, *sweetheart, have you totally lost your conscience, you couldn't've warned me you'd run material like this?*, denials and promises, refusals, *were you born yesterday? I'll give you an item, here's a news flash for you: director Regina hasn't been giving interviews for three years, to anyone.* At the beginning of the summer, a big interview with Peter came out in *Empire* where he spoke about *Hunger*, which was tentatively set to premiere in August: *I think*, he said, *that shooting that picture was the most important event in my life, certainly in my professional life, at any rate. I assure you that work on that level of spiritual tension is good fortune, a dream, and the ultimate test for any artist.* And also: *what I saw in the editing room surpasses all Regina's previous work.* Despite the fact that Peter would, undoubtedly, have said all that anyway, the producer called him in advance nevertheless: *just give them the what for, they've all gotten pretty cocky, they have no fear.* A few times he himself spoke for a switched-on Dictaphone and once, when there was a very cute young journalist and he'd relaxed, he said: *she's seemed to be covered in some sort of patina as of late, she's grown a shell*. This was, in the most comical way, the direct opposite of how things stood in reality.

Because in reality, something completely different had happened to Masha: twenty-four hours a day, even in her sleep—she didn't sleep much, jerking awake almost constantly, surfacing out from under a tight film of penetratingly despondent sleep—she was living in a membrane that had thinned to an unheard-of permeability. This is precisely why, if you think about it (because: how could it be otherwise?), she had, purely mechanically, limited contact with her environment. It wasn't even that her environment was hostile—what was hostile about the sweet kids at the studio?—it was simply that if a monad doesn't have windows, then it's obviously under threat of disappearing if it were to become a window. Meanwhile, that's exactly how Masha felt: as if she were a large window of squeaky-clean glass, taking up an entire wall. She felt this most acutely at the control panel, where she worked as if she'd dissolved within the film's frame, meaning it was, literally, as if she *were the frame*; this had happened before at her best moments, it's just that that state needed to be sorcered up specially, sometimes for a long time, both in the studio and outside. Masha still rode her bicycle (now, though, she wore an impenetrable motorcycle helmet: it looked stupid but nobody recognized her) and it felt to her like the life that was fattening up around her was imperceptibly digesting her, like a carnivorous flower's fragrant calyx. The branch that came under her whirring front wheel and broke in two with a triumphant sound of marvelous beauty; a panicked mouse hiding under a bush broke her heart with the perfection of the place it had found; Masha couldn't refrain from stopping to pick up a stupid red-and-black caterpillar, and the caterpillar blindly rushed around on the palm of her hand until Masha let it go, regretful; at the Tiergarten exit, the sun was blinking back and forth on house windows, with a hundred clearly distinct shadings; a paunchy old man was stopping to catch his breath as if he himself was the end goal of creation; rebellious young people sitting in a circle on the pavement sang "Knockin' on Heaven's Door," out of tune, and she wanted painfully, unbearably, to give someone the bicycle and sit down with them and *become one of them*; Masha sniffed the smell of rolls and coffee like a maniac; telephones thrummed like a sublime chorus; and a well-groomed mom calmed her crying child, whose sorrow was irrevocable, on a level with God, and all-destructive; and so every other day, Masha came to the studio in tears.

Did it get better in the evening? No. Even in shadows, the world was still filled with flowers, forms, smells, sounds, and voices: lights on signs, shop windows, and street lamps came together, in harmonious inflorescence as if intentionally; shadows of trees traced the contours of magical maps on the sidewalks; the smells of beer and hemp inebriated with an accumulated joy; the din of crowds on city squares and at the thresholds of dance clubs grew, exploded and subsided like a Wagner overture: all this sank into Masha, filling her, and it propagated, propagating within her as elation and despondence, as if it were a cancerous tumor of the soul. Masha would arrive at Friedrichstraße—this was how the cruiser Steregushchiy descended to the bottom when its own sailors opened the Kingston valves separating them from the dense salt water and frightened fish—toss her helmet by the door, sit for about ten minutes in quiet and darkness (relative quiet and relative darkness: the house spoke to her in a hundred voices; pipes quietly droned; a male voice shouted upstairs, muffled, in Turkish; cats echoed each others' songs outside; and the wall in front of her changed tone in rhythm with the television that was on across the way) after which she would summon her courage and call Petersburg. They'd immediately give the phone to Anya (who would just be getting ready for bed) and Masha would listen to Anya's prattling, which became ever harder and harder for her to figure out. Genuine horror, however, awaited Masha toward the middle of summer, when Anya ever more frequently began giving her father the phone after a minute or two of conversation: *fine, Mama, bye! –Anya, hold on, listen… –Hi, yes, she's watching a cartoon right now.* After that, Masha, frenzied, would fall on her paper and only then would life crawl off into its lair, growling every now and again.

Masha wrote two screenplays during post-production of *Hunger*: one was nearly autobiographical, about a girl from the provinces who goes to a high school for the arts (in the end, the heroine goes through a romance—it may be totally-real-life or it may be fantasy—with a good-looking teacher) and the other was sort of a wild variation on the Karenina theme, where everybody around Anna behaves as if they've already read the book, though they can't change anything: that wasn't enough for Masha, though. Beyond all that, Masha sketched on enough paper to fill two portfolio cases— there will be faces, animals, little urban scenes, and some kind of seemingly alien landscapes in these drawings—and she painted two pictures, too, after buying oil paints and stretching canvas on frame. "Pictures" overstates things: Masha's brushes weren't very obedient and the oil daubed out awkwardly unexpected blobs, so her attempts to recreate (of course, really, to restrain) Berlin's colorful mischief—daytime in one case and nighttime in the other—failed; Peter will later find them rolled up in the corner of the kitchen, and he will convulse when he unrolls them.

During that whole period, Peter invited himself over several times but Masha only allowed him in once: *Königin, I'm right nearby, I'm so smashed I just can't make it home*, and though, to be honest, he wasn't really as drunk as he wanted to sound over the phone, Masha didn't kick him out: *just don't bother me, damned alcoholic, I'm working. –Working? Chief, it's night around here, what kind of work are you talking about? –Shall I call you a taxi? –I'm quiet, I'm quiet.* Masha sat in the kitchen with her laptop as Peter wandered the hallway and rooms muttering *Gott verdammt*: he remembered this apartment differently. In front of him, in piles, there lay t-shirts, socks, and jeans; sheets of paper with sketches were scattered on the floor; clumps of dust trembled in the corners from drafts; torn, crumpled and folded plastic bags lay around; pencil shavings; books and albums, their pages pressed open by a coffee jar, another book, a statuette, whatever was handy; cups with yellow and black depths sat on the table; discs and cases were in a heap, all mixed up; shoes lay in the hallway, their soles facing up, as did a fallen and abandoned scarf; and in the kitchen a mountain of dishes swelled from the sink, bristling in all directions with knife and fork handles, like a military fortification: *Königin, did your housekeeper ask for political asylum in Switzerland? Do you want me to find you a new one? –Hint taken, thanks. –No, really.* Masha slammed the laptop shut and whirled around on her chair: *okay, we'll count that as I've worked.*

For about another hour, they sat with whiskey (Masha sniffed more than she drank), Peter gossiped, and he even managed to make Masha laugh a couple times and talk her into giving him a role: *anything at all, boss, you know that. –Would a corruptor of an underage girl work? –Only if she's more underage than you. –Well almost,* and then Masha went off to bed, *you coming? Sorry, really, I only have one bed now.* She gave him a second blanket and Peter crawled right out from under it, toward her. The hand that stole its way under her t-shirt met no resistance, instead, Masha said, distinctly, at full voice, *Peter, aren't you tired of screwing? –Huh? –I'm saying you're a grown man, you've probably been screwing for about thirty-five years, you ought to be tired of it.* Peter took his hand out from under her t-shirt and embraced Masha over the shirt. *I'm sorry, Peter, I didn't mean to offend you.* They woke up just as they'd fallen asleep: embracing.

Masha will not find a housekeeper but Peter will only learn that when he returns to Berlin after the premiere of *Hunger*. One move remained for Masha on the playing field of her life (within the confines of this text, at any rate; all other moves, if they will, indeed, exist, will need to be accomplished outside the margins of the text). Because the premiere of *Hunger* will be set for Köln.

Why Köln? Because Masha vaguely wanted this premiere to strike a rhyme with her first festival triumph? (*And the Oscar goes to,* jokes the emcee, then there's a fanfare and shots from *Huguenots* as she makes her way forward, and this will carry from the speakers: *Russland, Akademie der Teatralischen Künste, Petersburg, HFF.*) Because it was important for her to take a walk in silence along the embankment, where Roma had once frozen still for half a minute, looking at her, surprised, as if he were glimpsing her for the first time, yes, as if within the expanse of Masha's memory—Mnemosyne's values are not subject to inflation—he'd remained standing with an extended hand, lean on me? She hadn't been to Köln since those days. But if that's how things were, it wasn't, at any rate, the main thing. It was important on principle to neutralize the horror of the premiere as much as possible—crowd, champagne, smiles, camera flashes, questions, congratulations—and Masha felt like she'd fall apart and not be able to withstand the Berlin level of inherent pointlessness for any similar event; in Köln it was possible to get by without shedding much blood and even, perhaps, sit things out somewhere in a corner. The producer played hard to get, for appearances, but quickly agreed, deciding it would be even better: asociality was a commodity for public relations, too, though the asociality has to be of superior quality, without any coyness. The press release (thank God Masha didn't see it) advertised *the premiere of a new picture from the most enigmatic director of our day, intentionally removed from the confines of festival bustle and the capitol as well.*

Skipping ahead, inasmuch as that's possible, it must be said that the premiere came off beyond Masha's wildest dreams: no bustle at all, no smiles at all, deathly silence, whispered conversations, the rising thunder of applause after the final shot, pubs full of critics and journalists who rapidly ran off (the refreshment tables remained untouched). A considerable number of reviews came out in the next several days, and the majority were, as they say, friendly—*Regina proved; brings to a new level; there's no doubt it's a masterpiece*—however they all drowned in the same information tsunami that had already begun rising that evening and then swamped all the news feeds the next day: *the premiere of Maria Regina's new film took place in the director's absence.*

Things were like this. After flying to Köln and settling in at the hotel (it wasn't the same one, no, her room faced one of the cathedral's rose windows, but that didn't matter: a glass set aside, a t-shirt pulled off, and an instant of indecision all still made Masha chew at her cheeks), Masha went out to buy something that would help her feel more independent that evening and bought a skirt as red as an overripe raspberry, and then when she got back to her room she realized that now she'd have to shave her legs, too. She lounged around naked for a while, drank two fingers of whiskey, had a look at the colorful sea of tourists below; when her phone thrummed as its battery ran down Masha didn't hear it, but she felt the taste of blood in her mouth and started licking at her cheeks with her tongue and she wanted to somehow answer her own despondence—she felt ill at ease—she needed to sit down and draw but there wasn't time, and after sitting on the bed with another swallow of whiskey she fell into a long trance, thinking about what it would have been like if she were here along with Anya and brought her to the cathedral and then bought her something and then they ate ice cream together, then she jumped up, she had to hurry, she pulled out the razor, and went into the bathroom. Masha slipped in the bathroom as she blindly reached for the shampoo and as she was attempting to grasp anything at all, her left wrist slid on the razor that was waiting on the bathtub edge, after which she fell anyway, hit her head on the enamel edge, and passed out. It would be an understatement to say this wasn't a suicide attempt: that wouldn't have been like her at all, not in the slightest, and who would slit their veins with a safety razor, with the shower on besides, but nevertheless the impressionable hotel manager, whom the producer shouted at over the phone, *in the bathroom? Get her out of the bathroom!* was absolutely convinced of an attempt so after a brief shriek *—What? What kind of crap is going on there?* she began prattling on: *Lord, Lord, she took her life.*

Ideas possess a will of their own and a craving for life: since the thought of suicide had popped into the sentimental manager's head, it instantly captured the producer (*I just knew it! I really felt it!*) as well as two ambulance squads (it was the producer who called for the second one, to be on the safe side), and roughly an hour later you couldn't elbow your way through the hotel lobby because of the journalists, photographers, maids, waiters, and distrustful and curious hotel guests: *Regina? Hold on, that's somehow familiar.* Masha came to easily—smelling salts, pain in the back of her head—and attempted to brush aside all the people bent over her as she sat in a chair, but in answer to her *you're all paranoid, I just fell by accident, bandage my arm, and that'll do it,* she heard, *I understand, Frau Regina, but even so, allow us to help you, at least for our own peace of mind, I promise there won't be any medicines,* and she grasped (particularly based on the collective glance that darted around like billiard balls) that the more she spoke, the worse things would be. So she kept quiet.

Masha submerged freely into silence, as if she'd long been ready for it. As if the social conventions that had been forcing her to answer questions and keep up her end of pointless conversations had been cast aside and a formal excuse had appeared, finally, to not respond to call signals from without. Peter saw her off to the hospital and he spoke with her for an hour after the doctors gave in and agreed to leave them alone: *you didn't do that, I asked the maid, the water was on, you have a bump on the back of your head, the razor, well? I'll get you out of here, I'll raise such a racket that they'll simply be forced to let you out, tomorrow;* Gott verdammt, *it's the twenty-first century, a free country, they're keeping a person in the loony bin, and they'll be on their knees yet begging you not to say anything bad about them; but I can't do this alone, you have to help, too, you have to at least agree, please, Königin,* and Masha was lying with her eyes closed, fluttering her eyelids only occasionally, when he screamed particularly loudly; as Peter was riding into downtown Köln that night, he was far from certain that Masha didn't need at least a little psychological help. The next morning he spoke far more amicably with the doctors (*two, maybe three weeks, then it will be possible to form an opinion with certainty…*), and then he began efforts to get her transferred to another clinic. After calling Peter and the doctors every day, the producer flew to Berlin (*Hunger* required special attention: *this is especially important under the circumstances that have developed, this is, essentially, a war and we need to win it*; two assistants nod their heads) and only Peter remained in Köln, and so he called, inquired, talked, consulted, and transferred money: a week later, Masha was in a spacious automobile with tinted windows, leaving the Köln hospital for a quiet clinic a couple hundred kilometers south in the shadow of the mountains, where a day's stay cost what Peter earned in a day on the set. After speaking with Peter for almost two hours, the doctor—calm and attentive face, puffy little lips fighting their way through an even lawn of mustache and beard, *you're saying she draws?*—advised bringing Masha's tools and paper, *pencils, paints, pastels, what does she draw with?* and so Peter flew to Berlin after saying goodbye to Masha, *I'll be gone two days, there and back, what shall I bring for you?* and holding cold but gradually warming keys to the apartment on Friedrichstraße in his jacket pocket.

There, on Friedrichstraße, Peter sorted through her drawings and shreds of paper with Russian written on them; washed dishes; swept the floor, doing everything himself and not wanting to allow anyone in; gathered books; folded clothes; sat on the bed holding his face in his hands, and it would have been easier if he'd cried but he just couldn't; he slept restlessly, in a sweat; packed all the pencils and paints he could find in a bag; *Gott verdammt, Gott verdammt*—and in those same minutes, a doctor brought Masha outside and invited her to have a seat on a bench: a larch smell, the smell of skin warming in the sun, a squirrel starting to bolt across the path but getting frightened and jumping back on a tree trunk—it's like a shadow. *Frau Regina. Shall I be honest? I haven't followed your artistic work that closely, film isn't my biggest passion, I saw* Minus One *at some point, of course, but in recent days I've watched everything, that's natural, it's also a big honor and responsibility to help you. I'm absolutely sure you won't be staying with us for long but I hope very much that you and I will become friends. I like your work a lot, though it's uneven, as is probably the case with any artist, particularly a major one. I'm a dilettante in this, don't get me wrong, but since I've been granted the chance to speak about my impressions with the director, it would be a sin not to take advantage of that. Essentially, all your pictures are about one thing: what tortures you is the theme of a person growing up, clashing with the world, and departing, or something like that, into some sort of airless expanse, if by air you imply everything that's as natural as breathing. Maybe I'm not explaining myself very well here, I'm sorry. This is in your very first picture, in* Huguenots: *as they're acting, the children themselves don't notice that they've become adults and now everything's very serious and it's time to die.* Minus One *didn't make that big an impression on me, even back then, it's too linear or something, I think you'd agree with me about that now, right? The connections, abstractions, and pitfalls in life that keep hold of a person so he can't escape them, and anyway, who doesn't dream about chucking everything and flying off to Cuba, right?* Save *is basically about the same thing, about those pitfalls you can't avoid, you still fall in, and if it's not one thing, it's another. You don't mind that this is turning into kind of a cinema seminar here? You stop me if this is unpleasant for you.* Amber, *of course, is your best work, at least in my view. Sure, I haven't seen* Hunger *yet, but it hasn't been released yet, has it? In* Amber *there's some kind of enigma, some kind of impenetrable depth where the gaze gets lost. Well, maybe that's something kind of impish. It's bad when you can easily explain a film, but you can't explain* Amber. *Beyond that, I don't know, but they do call you a comedic director, am I right? But you obviously don't think so. Now* Plague *is funny, very funny. I don't want to say it's not deep—there are kids again, like in* Huguenots*—but* Amber *is obviously more serious and so I think you somehow felt freer with it. I haven't seen* Hunger *yet, but judging by what they're writing, I should like it. You know, I really urge you to see your stay here as simply a rest. You're essentially at a sanatorium. No medicines at all, no procedures at all, so swim, take walks, eat to your heart's content, read, draw, or just hang around doing nothing. You don't really have very much free time, do you? So there you go, consider this a vacation. Has it been a long time since you've taken a vacation? Believe me, you need that more than you might think. Compose yourself, gather your strength, and when you fly back to Berlin again you'll see everything will start to go a little differently. Work will be in full swing but everything will be in hand, you'll stop getting tired, and I anticipate the pleasure I'll get from watching your pictures for many years to come. I don't think I'm mistaken if I say you have a heap of plans? Now, hold on, I'll remember it, it was in the same interview where you said the only true discoveries are geographical, any others aren't worth anything. Hold on, hold on...*

I'd like to make a film about Columbus, about how he secures his expedition, leaves no stone unturned, implores, threatens, persuades, compels, then he assembles his ships, looks into the sailors' faces, chases the loaders, draws his fingers along tarred crevices, commands setting sail, his hungry gaze, harsh hands, hot wind, sails slap, wood creaks, and dense water splashes below, the sides heel, and dissatisfied simple men's voices shout, the ship's priests sing ever more forebodingly each day, supplies near their end, there are no maps whatsoever so there's nowhere the crew can point a finger, topsails and yardarms knock, the water changes its color and wrinkled faces pale looking at it, the quiet oppresses and they flog several sailors as edification for the others, you can't be parted from your sword and feet cling to the deck ever more spitefully, the sky darkens and lightning approaches stealthily and ever closer, the crew must be shouted at with full force, but there is no map, no, no, no, then shark fins circle between the ships, cutting the water like razors, a contemptuous gaze down into the water and the same gaze for a delegation representing the whole crew that asks to turn back, flog them, flog them, and there is a salty, wicked desert as far as the eye can see, all around, and, other than the stars and a compass, nothing connects these three little slivers of wood to the world, and they are slowly making their way forward, on only the will of Columbus, where to, nobody knows where to, and birds land on the masts and the sea grows gentler and the wind carries unfamiliar smells and a skinny little sailor shouts, frightened, from somewhere above: *land! Land!*

# ACKNOWLEDGMENTS

VADIM LEVENTAL

Thank you to Irina, who put up with chapter after chapter for five years, as well as the other first readers of the novel. To Alexander Mikhailovich Terekhov, for his support in the form of invaluable comments not all of which, unfortunately, could be applied to a text that was already beginning to cool; to Elena Danilovna Shubina for a proposal that would be flattering for any author, not just a beginner; to Julia Goumen for her first-class work; to Viktor Leonidovich Toporov for being straightforward; to Leonid Abramovich Yuzefovich for his advice and support; to Pavel Vasilyevich Krusanov for voluntarily taking on the enormous work of editing the text; to Boris Valentinovich Averin, the most attentive reader on earth, for his kind words about the novel; and to Natalia Kurchatova for her unanimity.

LISA C. HAYDEN

A novel as complex as *Masha Regina* inspires many, many thanks to friends and colleagues. Vadim Levental was unfailingly patient, quick, and humorous in explaining quirky imagery and numerous literary and cultural references in the book. He was also tactful, even reminding me that Masha couldn't identify all the references he's woven into the novel. I'm also grateful to Vadim for reading the entire manuscript and pointing out some spots that needed correction. Among other things, he noted a geographical error I'd made: with its gridded street patterns, white nights, and the eternal presences of Gogol and Dostoevsky, St. Petersburg plays a big role in *Masha Regina*. It's a luxury to work with an author who's willing to be involved in a translation in so many constructive ways and I appreciate his understanding that some elements of a book need to adapted slightly for non-Russian readers.

It's also a luxury to work with Oneworld: I'm grateful for Juliet Mabey's interest in contemporary Russian literature as well as her edits to and comments about my manuscript. It felt like a gift to be able to work with copy-editor Will Atkins on a second book. Will's suggestions and probing but tactful questions went a long, long way in developing my manuscript into a much more readable book. It was also a great pleasure to work again with production manager Paul Nash, whose deadlines, instructions, and schedules always make it easy to know what needs to be done and when.

A number of translators helped with *Masha Regina*, too. Liza Prudovskaya read a whole draft, checked it against the original, and provided detailed answer to my questions, often cluing me in on specialized vocabulary. I borrowed a few lines from Alan Shaw's translation of Alexander Pushkin's *Feast During the Plague*, which Masha adapts for the screen; I also quoted one line from Marian Schwartz's translation of Leo Tolstoy's *Anna Karenina*. Katherine Young, a poet and translator, gave me a much-needed refresher, by email, on meter.

Vadim thanks his wife, Irina, for putting up with *Masha Regina* for five years, so I suppose my husband, Park, is lucky that he only had to put up with *Masha* (and probably a few too many grilled-cheese sandwiches) for less than a year.

# MORE WORLD FICTION FROM ONEWORLD

*The Unit* by Ninni Holmqvist (Swedish)
Translated by Marlaine Delargy

*Twice Born* by Margaret Mazzantini (Italian)
Translated by Ann Gagliardi

*Things We Left Unsaid* by Zoya Pirzad (Persian)
Translated by Franklin Lewis

*Revolution Street* by Amir Cheheltan (Arabic)
Translated by Paul Sprachman

*The Space Between Us* by Zoya Pirzad (Persian)
Translated by Amy Motlagh

*The Hen Who Dreamed She Could Fly* Sun-mi Hwang
(Korean) Translated by Chi-Young Kim

*The Hilltop* by Assaf Gavron (Hebrew)
Translated by Steven Cohen

*Morning Sea* by Margaret Mazzantini (Italian)
Translated by Ann Gagliardi

*A Perfect Crime* by A Yi (Chinese)
Translated by Anna Holmwood

*The Meursault Investigation* by Kamel Daoud (French)
Translated by John Cullen

*Minus Me* by Ingelin Røssland (YA) (Norwegian)
Translated by Deborah Dawkin

*Laurus* by Eugene Vodolazkin (Russian)
Translated by Lisa C. Hayden

*Masha Regina* by Vadim Levental (Russian)
Translated by Lisa C. Hayden